Just Causes

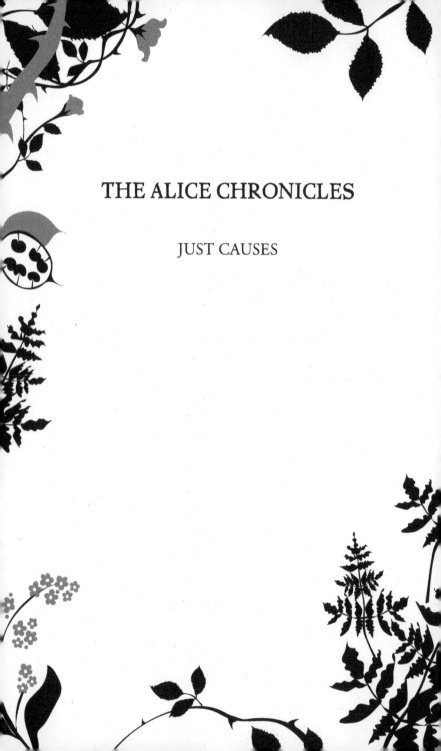

THE ALICE CHRONICLES

JUST CAUSES

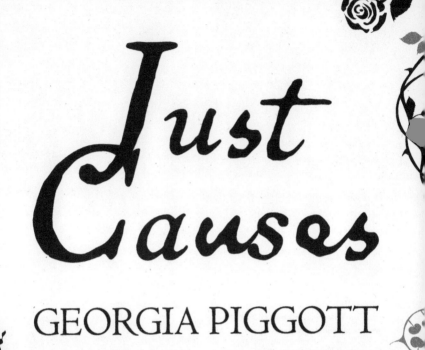

Just Causes

GEORGIA PIGGOTT

Crumps Barn Studio

Crumps Barn Studio
No.2 The Waterloo, Cirencester GL7 2PZ
www.crumpsbarnstudio.co.uk

Cover design by Lorna Gray

Printed in the UK by Severn, Gloucester on responsibly sourced paper

ISBN 978-1-915067-16-6

To all those tutors and fellow writers and critics who had the courage and the honesty to tell me the truth, my heartfelt thanks.

PROLOGUE

NOVEMBER, YEAR OF OUR LORD 1618

In the clearing surrounded by coppiced stumps, Grover Price stood regarding the woodsman's hut, and wished himself anywhere but here.

The woodsman's tools, the woodsman's small food supply lay scattered and spoiling on the ground. Grover had not meant it to come to this. It was as well Harman's Copse was isolated, for what he and Aled were doing here rubbed the shreds of Grover's conscience like grit in the shoe.

Not that intrusions were likely. Buried in the dark heart of the woods, few souls ever ventured as far as Harman's Copse. Master Cazanove, the new owner of the woods and thus, as he let it be known, of the woodsman also, took a poor view of any who strayed from the time-worn track.

In fact, his suspicion demanded that Grover made periodic sweeps to flush out intruders, and his influence ensured the law's reprisal against the discovered. Whippings, brandings, nailings by the ear to the standing stocks ...

The previous woodsman had lived here for three decades, since the days of the Spanish invasion, latterly supplying logs for Master Cazanove's halls and chambers, charcoal for his kitchens. He had led a solitary existence, unvisited and unvisiting, except at last by the pestilence, which had taken him in the summer just gone. Then less than a month ago John Kelsey had moved into the hut in the centre of Harman's Copse.

There were few men Grover Price liked, but this new young woodsman he did not object to – and one of the first things Grover learned was that John smelled a hard winter coming. Time would tell, but Grover had taken the warning and pilfered a sizeable hoard of fuel, just in case. So when he heard John Kelsey was struck down by a coughing sickness, Grover experienced an unaccustomed pang of sympathy.

The feeling did not extend to Kelsey's wife. Rarely venturing far from the hut, self-sufficient and practically unknown in the village, she earned Grover's approval when she came down to the big house to let Aled the steward know her husband was laid low. Only for a day or two, she insisted, just a winter cough, and she herself would cart logs and charcoal while he was sick. There would be no interruption to the supply of fuel.

And quite right too, Grover thought. What was a wife for, but to fetch and carry?

But what she did not reveal was that she had brought her toddler away from the infected hut. She had hidden him in the hayloft above the stables. A sickly child, unattractive and needy, the boy immediately started to grizzle when Grover discovered him and demanded to know what he was doing there. Instead of being silenced by his growl, the whine increased to a wail. Irritated, Grover had nothing but scorn for this weakling. He turned away and went straight to Aled.

Once he had told the steward, Grover felt easy. It was somebody else's responsibility and Aled was more than capable of dealing with the woodsman's wife.

But Aled had smiled and gone in turn to Master Cazanove.

Among the trees, Grover sighed and paused to draw a splinter from his palm. Too late now to wish he were not a Cazanove man. He had nearly finished boarding up the woodsman's hut, and at least John Kelsey had given them no trouble. Alone inside and woken from uneasy sleep, he merely nodded at Grover's account of why they were here, and sank back on his sickbed, engulfed by a wet bubbling cough. Not yet aware of his master's paper-thin liberality, Kelsey clearly saw nothing amiss with the story that repairs were being undertaken on Master Cazanove's orders. He even asked Grover to thank the master.

Grover took the opportunity of the brief pause in his work to ease his back and look about him. All around the clearing, clusters of hazels sliced off at knee-height stuck their angled points upwards like tapers in a pot. Nearby, bundles of cut saplings, each around two ells in length, lay stacked neatly to season. Next year Kelsey would fire them into charcoal as the old collyer used to. Meanwhile, Grover had a job to do, and with Aled as his taskmaster, Grover had developed the habit of appearing to be busy. He pretended to inspect his hammer, turning it this way and that, while twenty paces off Aled slouched, arms folded, against a tree trunk.

Thinking about the woodsman's civility, his skill in reading the seasons, Grover reflected that there were probably many things Kelsey knew that Grover would find useful. He took a deep breath, holding up a board. 'Did the parish constable order this, then?' If it were indeed the pestilence, the parish constable should have been told immediately.

Aled scoffed.

After a moment, and another deep breath, Grover pushed on. 'It's not pestilence, is it? I've seen plague and it doesn't look like—'

5

Aled turned that unblinking gaze on him. The very air seemed to chill.

'Grover Price,' Aled murmured, approaching at a saunter. Grover tried not to cringe as the steward leaned and dug thick fingers into his shoulder. This close, Aled's breath betrayed a hearty breakfast. Ham, fresh from the smoking loft, and strong March beer. Grover's stomach grumbled. His own meal was hard bread, harder cheese, and a pot of watery small-ale.

Aled breathed, 'Hear me plainly. If Master Cazanove says it's plague, what is it?'

Grover groaned. 'All right.'

'What—is it?'

'Plague.'

'Plague—what?'

'Plague, Master Steward.'

'Good man.' Aled released his grip and clapped Grover's shoulder in friendly fashion – except that from Aled, nothing was friendly.

Grover ventured, 'What if he gets better, boarded up in there? Who will help him?'

Aled paused as he walked away. 'You may nurse him if you wish,' he said over his shoulder. 'Inside.'

Panic froze Grover's blood. 'No, I didn't mean—'

Aled laughed, so Grover, heart thumping, laughed too.

Then of course it happened, just what he feared. Pounding feet, twigs trampled, dry bracken brushed aside. Kelsey's wife burst into the clearing.

She came to a halt, stumbling on her hem. The round-eyed toddler at her hip tightened thin arms round her neck. Hoisting her little one close, she stared at the half-boarded hut, the planks, the two men. For a few seconds she stood there, face and neck flushed, breathing fast under her bodice, her long skirts festooned with dried leaves and twigs brushed past in her headlong rush. Wisps of hair that had escaped from under her cap stuck wetly to her forehead and cheeks. She looked, Grover thought, as though she had run all the way from the house up that steep hill, and carrying an infant too.

Then, 'What's this, Master Steward?' she asked.

When Aled did not reply she rounded on Grover, who felt a sudden need to busy himself with boards and tools. 'Grover Price? What are you doing?'

Grover nearly looked up, but no, Aled could deal with this.

Still panting for breath, the woman's voice rose wavering. 'I demand to know what's going on!'

Demand? Grover quietly whistled. That'd sit sweetly. He cast a cautious glance at the steward, who with arms folded high across his chest and feet planted wide, had fixed his flint-coloured eyes on the woman. He wore this smile. Neither widening nor fading, just there. The infant fidgeted, the wan little face creased and his mouth stretched wide in a howl.

'Grover!' the woman begged over the child's cries. 'Grover, tell me!'

Time for Grover to turn away. If she'd only come later, they'd have been finished and she could have quietly set about levering all the boards off again – her punishment neatly delivered. He grabbed a saw and attacked a plank as he asked himself fiercely, Hasn't a few weeks here been enough to tell her that Master Cazanove never forgives?

Especially mothers with sickly little monsters like that one, all eyes and clinging hands.

Behind him came scuffling sounds and the woman's disbelieving objections.

And the child was in full-voiced wail again.

Grover sneaked a look. She was pinching and scratching at Aled's hands, trying to squirm out of his grip on her shoulders. Aled loosed one hand briefly to slap her. It was a short-lived, unequal tussle, as he forced her inexorably backwards. Grover wondered how much harder she would fight if she weren't hampered by her boy. She had a determined set to her mouth. Just as well she did, she was going to need strong resolve to stand by and watch while Grover finished boarding her man up in the hut.

But Grover's jaw dropped as Aled shoved her into the hut and slammed the door. Not the woman too? The child? The hammer felt heavy in his hand as he realised Aled had prepared for this. He had known all along that the woman was going to come running. Knew, because the Master must have planned this whole train of events. And Grover, all unknowing, had helped them.

That was why the woman had run full tilt up the hill. From Cazanove to Aled to the hut. She'd been sent here.

Aled, his foot jamming the door, bawled at Grover. 'You gapeseed, get a board fixed across before the whole family breaks out and we all catch the plague!'

Aled repeated, 'The plague!' loud and clear for the sake of the woman inside.

He almost drowned out her pounding, her screaming, 'It's a lie! You know it! There is no plague here!'

For a few seconds Grover's thoughts swirled and he rummaged aimlessly in the nail box while the woman hammered and kicked at the door. 'Let us out! Let us out!'

He hated it, the noise, the brat's bawling, the impotence. All the relief of passing on his discovery melted away. Into its place flowed fear and anguish. It wasn't his fault. All this

– it wasn't his fault. In the torment of his thoughts, Grover's resentment of her spilled over.

It was *her* fault. She started it, bringing her brat down to the mansion to sleep in the hayloft. How dare she? Keeping him clear of her man's fever? Huh! Spreading it to all and sundry, more like. Serve her right, serve them all right. Grover clattered lengths of timber, partly to show Aled he was doing something, more to shut out her cracking voice begging from within.

'Grover, please – help us!'

It was only for a day or two, he told himself while the woman continued to plead.

'Take my little boy. Save him, I beg you!'

And he could always say after, it was an honest mistake. Not that anyone would ask. You didn't question the master's orders if you knew what was—

'Grover, you midden-rat!' Aled roared from the door. 'I will squeeze your balls till your eyes bleed if you don't stir your idle arse!'

He would, too. Grover schooled his face and hurried over with wood. With unaccustomed energy, he hammered planks across the door, desperate to silence the child's terrified screams that jolted his breathing, sending pains through his chest. Shut up, you insect! For Christ's sake, shut up!

The woman's begging had faded to quiet sobs of 'Please, oh, please!', and that was worse.

Shut up! Shut up! Shut up! he shouted in his head. He gritted his teeth against all the noises that threatened to burst his skull. It's not my fault, I'm only carrying out orders.

At the window, the little boy's fingers were struggling for purchase. With vicious satisfaction, Grover shoved the final board against the gap. There was a yelp. He took a nail and battered it into the wood. Took more. Bash, bash, bash. Job done.

Job done. He backed away from the gagged and blindfolded hut. The three were held, but in Grover's head all thought was blocked out by a terrible rushing noise. Stories of old hauntings pressed into his skull like Aled's crushing fingers and all around him misty shapes gathered among the coppiced trees. He threw his tools together and snatched up the unused boards. Aled had already left, striding away through the trees without a backward glance. But for Grover, something lingered unfettered. Even after he'd left the place far behind in the woodland, he found himself constantly swinging round as the woman's stricken face seemed to shadow him.

It went on for four days. Ever and again that flicker at the edge of his vision, that sense of something reaching for him.

At last, Cazanove gave the order to unboard the hut.

For the rest of his life, waking and sleeping, Grover's thoughts would be stained with the sight of the bodies, the stink of death.

1

OCTOBER 1625

Alice knows she shouldn't be here.

She has been careful, watchful, deceitful even, to get to this point. Throughout, she has never wavered in her intention. But now the time has come, her heart is pounding with the enormity of her plan.

She really shouldn't be here. Her parents would be appalled if they knew. Would accuse her of shameful, unwomanly behaviour. She has waited patiently – or rather, impatiently these past weeks until finally her father started to cut their small copse with that great billhook.

She hates the thing. Her stomach churns just to look at its gleaming blade like a predator's beak. But the billhook is the key to her plan, the cuts it inflicts on his hands are her excuse for being here. Here, with her fingers none too steadily lifting the latch to the apothecary's shop, pushing open the door.

She steps out of the drizzle and watches her breath float upwards to mingle with the bunches of air-dried herbs hung about the shop's rafters. Some of them have been hung there by her hands – but those on the higher hooks are Frederick's. He can reach up easily to the crossbeam as he has done so many times over the two years since he started practising his trade, replacing the old apothecary. The gently rustling

13

bunches waft the scents of a distant summer.

What on earth does she think she is doing? She can hear the accusation as though it has already been made. Abandoning modesty, risking censure, getting herself talked about. If it came from her mother, Alice would feel she had let her mother down. If from her father, she would feel she had let herself down. Somehow it is so much more difficult to be reprimanded by him. She tells herself, always keep the door to Father open. Even though it is her mother, in disappointed lament, who can reduce Alice to private tears.

Well, she's here now. She closes the door. From the still room at the back comes the scrape of a drawer, the clink of spoon against glass.

A sign, that's all she wants. Something to give her hope, a reason to resist the alternative. Her mother has laid siege to her for months now, mainly because at the age of eight, Alice made the biggest error of her life. The neighbours' young son cut a sapling, whittled it into a bow and strung it while Alice chased chickens, grabbing tail feathers at his bidding. He presented her with the result and Alice shot flabbily at various targets. The sheep continued grazing, the cows rolled their eyes, even the rabbits didn't run far.

'Gerald Cooper makes good bows and arrows,' she informed her mother and his. 'I'm going to marry him.' The women smiled, and looked at each other, and a plan was born.

But now Alice has her own plan.

The door from the still room opens and Frederick Marchant, apothecary, pokes his head out. He wears a white linen shirt, sleeveless jerkin, straight hose, black stockings, black shoes with bone buckles, and his sleeves are rolled up for working. Straw-coloured hair flops over his forehead and he pushes it back.

'Mistress Edwards, a pleasure to see you.' But he says much the same to all his customers. 'How's your mother?'

'Give you good day, Master Marchant. Mother is well – it's Father. He keeps cutting himself doing the coppicing, so I've come for some self-heal salve. Your receipt brings him comfort.' She is aware she is gabbling but this is her story; the only reason she could contrive for coming here.

'I thought I wrote it out for you. Am I mistaken?'

She is prepared for that. She smiles, spreading her hands. 'I cannot remember where I put it.'

'There now,' he says, and adds after a few seconds, 'I hope other things may be remembered and bring comfort.' He is giving her a look she cannot quite fathom. Is he too remembering their pleasant hours together when she helped him in the summer? Or is he just being polite? Usually she engages with the swordplay of words, but today she is all to pieces.

Helplessly, she murmurs, 'I forget.'

'I'm sorry to hear that,' he says, face closing. He turns away to scan the shelf. 'No, the salve isn't here, but there's a fresh batch in the still room I can dispense.' His voice has become brisk, practical. 'How much do you need?' She tells him, and he disappears once more.

Left standing in the middle of the shop, she berates herself for not thinking beyond this moment. For naively assuming the conversation would slip effortlessly towards its inevitable sunlit end. Now, he will come back, she will pay for the salve and he will pull open the door and wave goodbye. Goodbye Alice, goodbye to your hopes, your future, your silly little plan. What on earth made you think such a man would want a young woman like you, short, plain, with unruly kinked curls? Out you go into the drizzle. In fact, to crown it all, it's

15

no longer drizzle, the rain is now sheeting down. In a sudden gust it hurls itself like tossed gravel against the window, drips and runs from the eaves. The houses across the road are blurring in the downpour.

Then she sees the figure, coming into Hillbury from the Woodley direction. He has a strange, rolling walk, made comical by the faults in the window glass. He holds his arms out from his sides as he picks his way through the puddled ruts made by the many creaking carts that use this road. He is heading for the shop, in no apparent haste to escape the rain, but rather as though in dogged determination to reach his goal. He stares at the little shop as he approaches, muffled to the eyes with a scarf wrapped round head, face and neck. Its ends hang limp over a dog-eared kersey jacket as dark with wet as his breeches.

Alice has moved away from the window by the time he pushes open the door and steps in. Below the holed stockings, blistered toes stick out of his boots which are held on by strips of knotted cloth. He drips from scarf and jacket and sleeve, not that it matters on the packed-earth floor of the shop. He doesn't seem to notice anyway, nor that he has left the door open. Alice moves past him to close it, and before she can stop herself her hand flies to cover nose and mouth. He stinks.

He reaches the shelves and bumps against them. A jar teeters and settles. The mottled sores on his hand are a new sort of rash to Alice but she knows Frederick can offer the right treatment, if only because he stands alone in tending these vagrant poor. She admires and fears for the apothecary in equal measure.

From the stranger's hands she glances up at the muffled head. Through the slit, his eyes look out at her. His eyelids are crusted with wart-like pustules. In the silence, footsteps sound from the still room, a stopper squeaks, paper rustles.

The stranger reaches for the scarf ends. As he unwinds the soggy folds at his throat, Alice gapes. Around black, slug-like swellings on his neck, smaller eruptions crowd, black, purple, orange, like gangrenous ulcers. With a weary sigh, he loosens the last fold of the muffler. From brow to collar, his flesh gives the impression of having blistered in a fire. His arms drop, his knees give under him, and he is suddenly boneless, a sodden bundle of rags sliding down the shelves, bringing pots and bottles crashing. He lies on the floor staring, as liquid splashes and leaf dust floats and settles on his unblinking eyes. Rot-stench fills the air.

Even as she stands rooted, she hears Frederick's 'God save us!' and feels his swift grasp round her waist. Unthinking, she tries to prise away such familiarity, but already her feet are off the ground, he has her in his hold and in two strides they are in the still room. He puts her down, backs off, looking away. 'My apologies,' he murmurs. His hands were warm, smooth.

For a second, her mind runs wild. She can hardly give a polite 'No matter, sir,' at a moment like this. She is still facing the doorway and, perversely, what steadies her is the sight of the corpse. She's never seen a case but she doesn't have to ask its name. Nose buried in his kerchief, Frederick passes her and kneels down by the body, carefully lifting cloth and inspecting.

'So that's what it looks like, then?' she says. *Altra mors,* the terrible death, the black death.

'Late stage,' he says. He rises, backs off.

'Is there nothing that could have been done for him?'

'If he'd lanced the first buboes days ago, here, or here,' indicating his own armpits and groin, 'he might have had a chance.' So that was why the stranger had that wide-legged gait, she realises, the swellings must have been agony.

Now the urgent words and Frederick's hand at her back as he drops a pot and a twist of paper in her basket. Drawing her away from the corpse sprawled in the shop, steering her to the side door. Her objections, her offers of help, all overridden. Finally she takes a stand, refuses to move. In the narrow space, she fancies she can sense his body warmth through her clothes. Standing there, too close for acquaintances, too far for — looking up into his face, while he looks anywhere but into hers. His breathing comes faster as words spill from him.

'— need a pest-house … should isolate the sick to protect the well … must make up more of that vinegar mixture.' His mind is already working, totting up the stock of protectives, the volumes he will need, rue, wormwood, sage … 'Mistress Edwards, take care, stay at home, avoid the village for now. Promise me?'

And she argues back, 'I visit every week. They need the food I bring. Are you going to promise me to avoid the village too?'

'It's different for me—'

'How, different?'

'I can help them, heal some at least.'

'While I can only feed them.'

He runs an exasperated hand through his hair. It promptly flops down again. 'Then at least be sure not to step over any threshold where sickness is. The miasma carries—'

'I know all that. Did I not help you during the summer?'

'It is my duty to care for the sick.'

'If I am to take care, then you too must agree—'

And so on, each trying to extract the impossible promise from the other. Finally, Marchant-the-Bracing-Apothecary. 'Don't worry about me, I shall be the safest one around. I'm the one who makes up the mithridate, remember. Enough to dose the whole—'

'Don't.' Without thinking, she puts her fingers to his lips. And he reaches for a little curl of kinked red-brown hair that has escaped from under her cap, and coils it round his finger, while her heart thunders so loudly – surely he must hear it?

Whether or no, he steps back, recollecting himself, hands falling to his sides, and for a few seconds they just stand there.

When she can endure it no longer, 'I must go,' she whispers, vision blurring. Hood pulled up, she tugs at the latch and steps into the teeming gloom between the houses.

But before her hurrying steps bring her to the mouth of the passageway, a touch on her shoulder, she turns, and somehow his head is bent to hers, her face cupped in his hands while her arms go round him, and body fuses to body. In the shadow of death Alice Edwards and Frederick Marchant have found their life.

She says *Yes my dearest love, yes* to Frederick, but as she makes her way home, she is already thinking, Mother will never countenance this.

2

'How can you ask me to break a promise, Father?' Alice heaves her overladen basket and settles it among the logs on the cart. She knows he is impatient to leave – doesn't want her with him.

In this slippery wet it takes fifteen, maybe twenty minutes to get the loaded cart safely down the hill to the village. Then there is the unloading before the return journey, and her father has enough to occupy him without this extra work. And Alice has her own reason to go into Hillbury, apart from taking the food. To forestall him while she argues, she pretends the basket is insecure and needs wedging. She pushes at the handle and fiddles with a couple of logs underneath it.

'People are expecting this,' she tells him. 'You know they depend on it.'

Every Monday either she or her mother does the round to those in need. These days, with her mother's indifferent health, it is more often Alice.

Around them, the fog which earlier wrapped the trees is clearing, but the air is raw and the rain is back, drifting past the house like lengths of fine lawn. Beyond, the thatched ricks stand like squat sentinels, impervious to wind and weather. Already, a million tiny droplets cling to her cloak and face, and her father, working his chilled fingers, scowls at her. 'Leave the basket alone, the logs will hold it. And it's not breaking a promise if I deliver instead of you.'

'It would be if you deliver to the wrong places.' She's careful not to add *like last time.*

James Edwards crams on his wide-brimmed hat and pulls his greatcoat close. 'I don't want you anywhere near the village at present. It is a risk you do not have to take.'

But Alice has too often heard him describe her as *my wilful daughter* when he thinks she is out of earshot. There is no small pride in his voice when he says it.

She points at the logs. 'What of your own risk, Father? You're taking these.'

The street bonfires, fed with local timber and dusted with sulphur, constantly spread their cleansing reek through the village. But despite this, the plague is picking off one here, one there, and people are starting to leave.

Alice places a booted foot on the wheel hub and pulls herself up onto the cart. Her father gives her a look, which Alice studiously ignores by frowning at a smear of white chalk-mud on her cloak where the hem has brushed against the spokes. 'Father, I promise not to go into any houses where there's the smallest chance of plague.'

No chance of plague in Frederick's house – as he told her, he is the one with the mithridate.

'Not into any houses at all.' But he has not ordered her off the cart, and so the balance is tipped.

'Very well, Father, I promise.' She can stand at Frederick's door instead.

He clicks the mare into a walk and Alice pulls her cloak close, tucking her hands into its folds as the cart jolts forward.

'It's a blessing for us, living up here,' James says. 'We're removed from the village.'

I know it too well, Alice thinks, and Frederick on his rounds is down there in the thick of it. I wish he would wear that mask he brought back from Venice, the one with a sort of horn on the front that you stuff with cleansing herbs to breathe through. But Frederick flatly refused. Said he was not about to cast terror into his patients' hearts by walking around looking like a skull with a drippy nose. Alice didn't laugh. And now, only two days ago, the sexton died, and he wasn't even near any patients, not until they were in their winding sheets.

'I can always get some snatchers' vinegar if you want it for protection,' she tells her father. A glance at his open-mouthed look makes her laugh. 'You're shocked!'

'Is that the sort of language Marchant taught you in the summer?'

'Snatcher's vinegar is just a name. Apothecary Marchant recommends that particular mix of herbs. It's not only the body thieves who need it.'

He shakes his head. 'I don't know who's worse – the snatchers, or those who cut up these stolen bodies. I tell you, Alice, it's an offence to God. One day they will answer for it.'

The cart rocks and rumbles on as a silence falls between them. The mare Athena trudges half-asleep down the familiar sloping track towards the village. Alice always used to take her father's view but those brief summer months helping out overworked Apothecary Marchant have opened a gap between duty and conviction. It is unlikely her father will ever accept that it might be God's will for the knowledge locked within the dead to be used for the benefit of the living. In this country there are precious few who think so – it is abroad in Florence and such faraway places where they are quite open about it. She knows this because Frederick Marchant told her, he has been there.

She struggles to find a safer subject. 'Who will do the

22

burying, now that Sexton Whitehead is dead?'

'I was going to ask the vicar that,' he says, 'but I just missed him. I saw him this morning heading up the Sherborne road. That means he's for Bristol, to ask the Bishop for help through this pestilence.'

With the combined souls of Hillbury, Westover and Woodley to minister to, the vicar has been asking for a curate since the last plague seven years ago.

'Poor man,' she says. 'It's the worst time of year to make a journey.' On either side of them, the rain that has been falling for days collects in every hollow. Meadows are sinking, ditches gurgle and puddles have formed everywhere, slippery with rotting leaves and overflowing in chalky rivulets, washing loose stones down the track.

Her father nods. 'With only himself and Marchant to visit the sick, they'll never cope if the plague truly gets a hold. They're both stretched to the limit already, ministering to all three parishes.' He sighs. 'The Bunting brothers will probably help with the burying, they have that cart.'

She says tartly, 'If a certain lady of the mansion put some effort into helping the poor and sick, we might all be a little less stretched.'

'Mistress Cazanove, you mean?'

'Mistress Starch.'

'That's not kind, Alice. Especially about someone you've never met.'

'It's what everyone calls her. Mother says she goes about thick-bodiced and high-buttoned.'

'Unlike you,' her father retorts, 'who drive your mother distracted by leaving off cap, partlet and anything else you think you can get away with. And incidentally, despite Mistress Cazanove's vexatious conduct, your mother treats her kindly, a discipline you would do well to observe.' There is only so much licence James Edwards will allow his wilful daughter.

But Alice is her father's daughter. 'Would that be the same way that you speak kindly about Master Cazanove, Father?'

'All right, Alice, well parried. But think about it, Cazanove's not part of our local circle.'

'Or rather, you're all courtesy to his face and avoid him whenever possible. I had noticed.'

'Steady, Athena, steady there.' James draws on the rein as the horse slides in the mud. He admits ruefully, 'I cannot like the man.'

Alice leans back to check that the basket is not shifting. She understands her father's point. 'He might have saved those three in Harman's Copse back in 'eighteen.' Alice remembers this because she was sent for safety to live with her grandparents in the summer of 1618, returning only when the infection was over. Then this tragedy had struck. 'If they had lanced the buboes early, they might all three have survived—'

'*Lanced the buboes?*' James looks at her in mock surprise. 'That's an exacting phrase for a young lady. More of Master Apothecary's wisdom?'

Alice's heart is in her mouth, but she moves on, 'I'm told Master Cazanove never even consulted the old apothecary.'

The basket is secure. Alice straightens and looks across the valley to where the skeleton trees stand in progressively fading greys up the rise. The top of the hill is shrouded, invisible. In there, far from the track, out of sight, lies Harman's Copse.

It is not only the rain dripping down her neck that makes Alice shiver. Some say the copse is haunted. Three figures. She has never been there. 'There's such a shortage of woodsmen,

24

charcoal-makers,' she goes on. 'Look at you, flaying your hands cutting our coppice.'

Her father says, 'There are those who say that the loss of his woodsman was a judgement of the Lord on Cazanove's blatant display of wealth.'

'Judgement?' she fires up. 'It wasn't God who killed the woodsman, it was Cazanove doing nothing when he must have known the family had the plague! These self-satisfied, know-it-all bigots—'

'Alice!' Her father chuckles. 'How you find fault today.'

Alice bites her lip. *Why won't people listen to Frederick? He doesn't try to blame it all on God.* 'I believe Frederick is closer to the mark,' she counters. 'He suggests it's the malignant miasma that carries the plague. Why else do we keep the sulphur fires going?'

A silence follows and Alice looks to see if her father is laughing at her again. Far from it, he is giving her a considering look. A very considering look. *'Frederick,* eh?'

Trust her father. One slip and he pounces. 'Master Marchant, I mean.' Despite the chill, suddenly her face feels aflame. Now the fat is well and truly in the fire.

'Sits the wind in that quarter, Alice?'

It's blowing a gale in that quarter. She recalls a dried sprig of tiny blue flowers she discovered in her basket after she visited his shop that day. He had wrapped it in a twist of paper. Some hold the plant to be good for coughs, but she didn't go there for cough remedy. The Latin name is *myosotis*. Most call it forget-me-not. It is under her pillow now.

'Has he said anything?' her father demands.

That kiss. Simply thinking about it now causes her heart to thud against her ribs. When they finally parted, they laughed at Frederick's straw-coloured hair plastered dark to his face,

25

the water dripping from nose and chin onto his sodden shirt.

'Alice!' her father insists, and she is back on the cart swaying and bumping along the track, the village coming into view.

'He says he will not risk visiting you while the plague is with us.' Forget-me-not. *Forget you, Frederick? How would I do that?*

'So you've been meeting.' It is both a question, and not a question, and instinct warns her to keep silent. 'I should never have allowed you to help him out in the summer.'

'Nothing happened in the summer, Father.'

'When, then?'

This is not the way she intended to broach the subject but it is too late now. She might conceal, but she will not lie. 'About three weeks ago.' Actually two weeks, five days and four hours to be exact.

'So how did he contrive a meeting? Or was it you who contrived it, miss?' He has never used such a severe tone with her.

'I went to get some self-heal lotion for your cut hands. You remember?'

'We have self-heal growing in abundance. No need to buy it from him!'

'Oh, *Father.*' Treading a rocky path between suppression and revelation. 'I needed to know.'

'Do you not think that if he wanted to ask for your hand, he would have come to see me long since?'

'He had no reason to hope. Mother told him months ago that I am to marry Gerald Cooper.' Did Mother suspect, even then, and did she speak out in order to nip in the bud any presumption on the apothecary's part? The cart rocks into a deep rut, sending a great splash of muddy water into the

26

hedge, and Alice grabs her seat to stop herself falling.

'So what makes him think I will welcome him?' her father asks.

'Nothing at all.' This is worse than she ever imagined. Alice knows that in her mother's view, Frederick is a nice enough man *for an apothecary*.

'Why did you not mention this at the time, Alice?'

'It was the day that poor man died of plague in the shop. I could hardly bring up the subject then, could I?'

He does not answer that. Instead, another harsh question. 'How often have you been meeting since then?'

'Only once, last Monday by chance. Outside the inn.'

'The inn!'

'Don't paint it in those terms. Dick Winter was slouching outside so I stopped to ask him how the ulcer on his leg was – the one I treated a few times in the summer, you remember? Master Marchant came by as I was walking on.'

'Tell me you didn't stand passing the time of day in full view of the entire village and all the gaping louts in the taproom?'

Under her cloak, Alice angrily crosses her arms. Her father is deliberately making it sound awful. 'He barely gave more than a nod in passing, but he said that he will come and see you as soon as it is possible.'

'Which you also forgot to mention?'

Alice burns. Suppresses the fierce thoughts that threaten to break into words. *You know Mother is adamant I shall take Gerald to husband. Why are we wasting words on finer points?*

'Do you not hold that honesty is something you owe us, Alice? We have these other hopes for you, as you know.'

'They are not *my* hopes.' How can her father not realise that a childhood friendship is not enough for a lifetime's submission to someone like Gerald?

'It's a long-standing arrangement,' he adds.

'Mother believes love for Gerald will come after marriage. I keep trying to tell her it won't.'

'He's respectable, he's a neighbour.'

As though that's enough. 'I need more than—'

'The Coopers have been in Hillbury for generations. That's more than you can say of Marchant.'

'Oh. That's your argument?' She plumps her elbows on her knees, her head in her hands. 'I feel nothing for Gerald.'

'He's your age.' Displeasure has sharpened his voice. 'For heaven's sake – anyone would think we're asking you to marry an ancient.'

'Father, I ...' Gerald fumbling for her hand while she tries to smile and extricate herself at the same time. 'I can't help shrinking away when he is near me.'

'God-a-mercy, child! That's just your innocence.' Her father is not listening, any more than her mother does. What use to tell him that when Frederick touched her hair, her whole spirit soared. 'Know this, Alice,' he says, 'as soon as you're married, all that changes. The companionship will help you get used to it.'

That willingness to accept even the possibility of a loveless marriage is what does it. Alice jerks upright, rounds on her father. 'Then know this, too, Father! You'll have to hold Gerald's new flintlock at my back to force me to marry him! Am I to promise to obey him? You talk of my honesty. How low do you rate its worth, that you would have me perjure myself before Vicar Rutland, simply to keep a longstanding arrangement that is none of my making?'

She stares into his eyes, holding his gaze, defying him to look away. Yet when he does, it feels like an empty victory, as if he has left her behind, as if it is she who has failed to hold him. So that's that. He will follow the course her mother wants, probably bring it forward now that he has stumbled across this secret. Pressure will be brought to bear. It will start as of now. But at the very least she owes Frederick a note, some explanation, to prevent him coming to Hill House and being sent away with disdain. *A nice enough man – for an apothecary.* Today might be her only opportunity. Alice begins to plan how to contrive a message, how to deliver it.

Her father draws on one rein to start the turn from the track into the village. He says, 'There is to be no more calling on the apothecary, no messages via the village children, no lingering to catch words with him, nothing, do you understand?'

She hangs her head to conceal the look she cannot conceal, aware that her face is set in mulish lines.

'Do you understand, Alice? I will have no whispering about my daughter.'

Reluctantly she nods, she will not disobey her father in any mean, furtive way.

'In return I shall talk with your mother.' And as she stares speechless, he goes on, 'I promise nothing. Your mother will be extremely vexed, to say naught of Emeline Cooper.' But he has not said that *he* is vexed. Nevertheless, the bar between her and Frederick has been set, albeit not in the overwhelming way she imagined. There is a small rent in the shroud of the marriage plan. Small, but she can work on this.

When her father adds, 'I hope Marchant knows what he's taking on when he comes asking me for your hand,' her heart takes flight and her gasp nearly chokes her. She wants to throw her arms round him, but she is mistress enough of herself to know that would spoil everything. She folds her hands in her lap and says simply, 'Thank you, Father.'

After a moment, James says, 'The Coopers are not as plump in the pocket as they would have us all believe. They count on your portion and it would be a blow, even more so now they've had a bad year. Especially Emeline. Likes her touches of distinction, does Emeline.' It is the closest he has ever come to stating his opinion of Gerald's mother, Mistress Cooper. Alice, revelling in hope, hardly listens as her father muses on an attorney he has been considering for a marriage contract, there is some fellow he met when he was up in London last Spring for the old king's funeral. '... told me of an introduction he could give me,' James says.

'To a London attorney?' she asks. 'Why not the attorney in Woodley, Attorney Handley?'

'Him?' He shakes his head as he pulls Athena to a halt outside the forge. 'He'll do as he's told if someone makes it worth his while. When you marry Alice, I want an honest attorney, not one that people like the Coopers can pay to slip words into the contract to favour them.'

3

'Have you heard the one about Cazanove's buttocks?' says the local wit. 'They're the only generous thing about him.'

The sniggers ripple quietly in corners. It's a small revenge for the powerless, whispered behind hands so that the 'butt' of the joke has no idea it is doing the rounds.

At this moment Rupert Cazanove's copious hind quarters are exercising him in a different way. He eases himself on the inn's best backstool and struggles to stay awake. But no matter which way he moves he can find no comfort. The voices all around him come as though from inside a box, blurred, echoing. He tries to blink away the mist hazing his view of landlord Patten talking with a customer. Cazanove can see his lips moving, but the words are vague fragments without sense. It is inconceivable to him why Patten is not grovelling here in front of him.

He should be, Cazanove reasons, I've just raised his rent enough to make the angels cack. That'll teach him for not sending a barrel up to the mansion. Not ready to be tapped – huh! Cazanove pictures landlord Patten falling into debt and despair, and gives a series of snorts that could be taken for a laugh. A few heads turn in his direction, but at his glare they hurriedly look away again.

He wishes now he had not come. The headache only gets worse with all the noise in here. He tries to raise his head to order them to shut up, but the only movement is the wax-chandler's hand on his shoulder, the man's concerned face swimming into his vision. He shakes off Alaric's arm but slides sideways on his cushion, feels the worm Grover Price on his other side push him upright again.

Sniggers break out here and there. Curse them all, these tittle-tattlers with their clay mugs, their cheap brews. His rich October ale sits there on the table before him, the first time the inn has served him his drink in pewter. Not before time. Polished and gleaming. The ale tastes the better for it. Let them watch with envious eyes as he tips it to his lips and takes his time finishing his drink. His arm wavers out and he reaches for the handle. Jesu, such an effort!

'Gimme—' he mumbles and lurches forward.

Someone steadies the wobbling table and moves the tankard out of harm's way.

He slumps back. What was it he was thinking just then? He cannot recall. Why don't they bring his meal? They brought food readily enough two days ago when Ralph Cooper came in to see him.

Cooper's face! Ha! Cazanove snorts again. It took two repetitions before the little man realised their deal was off. Too late Cooper realised the trap he had walked into. Soon he will beg Cazanove to buy his fleece at any price. Only a fool would try to hide that sort of quantity from the Guild's scrutiny. Cazanove is, of course, different. He's big enough to carry it off.

At last, someone puts food in front of him. He eyes it, sees a creamish-white heap, some sauce or other slopped over, and suspects it's hiding a brace of stringy birds. He's surrounded by whey-faced women making whey-faced dishes. Do they think that's good enough for a red-blooded man? With a supreme effort, he lifts his arm and sweeps the dish aside. His satisfaction is complete as he watches it clatter to the flags and slither across the taproom, spattering thick-stockinged calves and mud-caked boots. One of the birds fetches up under a table. In the stunned silence as eyes turn on Cazanove, he observes a drinker furtively grasp the bird and stuff it, sauce and all, into the slit in his breeches. In a long-abandoned chamber of his mind, Cazanove registers a time years ago when he would have counted himself fortunate to do the same.

The commotion has brought the landlord running. At last, Patten is grovelling, but it is spoiled by his brawny woman shouting about the insult to her reputation. Then Patten again, promising him beef, beaten, seasoned, baked and plenty of it! Beaten. A maggot of excitement writhes in Cazanove's belly. Beat.

An age passes. The starched edges of the ruff around his neck dig in and scratch; his body servant has shrunk his neckband, the heedless cur. And his legs are so cold. To make matters worse, the street bonfires larded with sulphur against the pestilence give off an eternal yellow stink that lingers in his nostrils and creeps into his clothes. This thumping in his head, this heat and tightness in his face. All he wants is his bed.

'Get my ...' he starts. He cannot recall the word. It has four legs and he sits astride, in the ... what? He glowers at his body servant. 'You. Help me up.' His tongue feels deadened, it is an effort to form words. The man continues talking with the other two at the table. Cazanove repeats it louder but the man ignores him. It is as though Cazanove has not spoken.

His whole mouth feels strangely numb as he tries again, 'Do as I say, damn you!'

He knows the words he wants to form, but no one heeds him. Every last small-ale sot is slighting him! Him! Rupert Cazanove. Even the worm Grover Price takes no notice. Rage takes hold of Cazanove. 'You dare to make a mockery of me?'

But his bellowing is locked in his head. No roar fills the room, no answering hush checks the clamour of inn-talk. Not since his youth, when he sold "miraculous cures" made with flour and water and dyed with butchered dogs' blood, has he been so shunned. Once more he is nothing, and the remembrance jabs fear deep in his bowels.

'Help me,' he whimpers, rocking his body back and forth. 'Help me.'

They look up as the table wobbles again. One of them draws out a kerchief and leans towards him. He feels dribble being wiped from his chin as though he is a witless dotard. He wants to bang on the table, restore the balance of dread. Why won't his arm obey? What is this torpor? And when he struggles to get up, his legs are no longer there.

What is happening … to me …

to … me …

4

The cart shakes as James Edwards jumps down. He lifts Alice's basket to the ground and turns to greet Daniel Bunting just poking his head round the door of the smithy.

James says to him, 'I didn't see you or your brother this morning, so I stacked the logs over there. I hope that suits?'

He walks past Daniel's door, pointing behind the smithy. Alice steps down and nods to Daniel, who gives her a smile and a wave.

'I'll be back at home in about an hour, Father,' she calls. James puts up a hand in acknowledgement, already rounding the corner of the building, Daniel following.

The rain persists, washing out colours of wall and thatch to shades of grey. Behind the houses opposite, the dripping black boughs of leafless trees dim into progressive murk up the hill. Even the wispy smoke struggling from chimneys sinks down the roofs as though defeated.

Wagons have churned parts of the road into a quagmire. Except for a knot of children gathered under the jutting first floor of a house at the other end, the way through the village is empty of people. The bonfires here and there down the road give off heat-haze but little flame, and the smoke is more grey than yellow. She must remember to ask her father about sulphur; he got hold of some recently when Frederick's supply ran out.

Part-way down the street, the bonfire outside Nick Patten's

tavern is still hot, and beyond it, she sees the inn door open. Out comes a huddled group, three men staggering as they prop up a fourth. Rupert Cazanove is a large man, of the combined girth of two of his supporters. His flushed face droops and he is hatless. His legs move as though stuffed with straw like a scarecrow's, bending as his weight presses on them. He wears a warm doublet of padded green damask. Canion-hose of a like material bulge over hip and thigh, closing around the knee in a deep band above the stout, stockinged calf. One of the lacing points holding doublet and hose together has come loose. A stain darkens the cloth. Has he spilled his drink? Or worse, is he so far gone he has peed himself?

It is a shock to Alice to think Rupert Cazanove can get himself into this condition, the man who terrifies his workers with his bullyings and beatings – the man who is always the master.

Further up the street, shorter but equally amply fleshed Abel Nutley, representative of the Justices, emerges from a house and struts towards the inn, frowning at the sight of the lurching group. Alice can almost hear the disapproving tuts from his puckered mouth. Landlord Nick Patten is still holding open the inn door, watching his customers' departure. Alice feels a moment's pity for him, about to be faced with the self-important littleness of Hillbury's parish constable.

One of Rupert Cazanove's lolling arms is around the shoulders of Grover Price, labourer for whoever will employ him, but generally known as a Cazanove man. On the other side is Alaric Ford, the wax-chandler. The third she does not know, he walks behind, supporting as best he can and pushing Cazanove's legs forward with each step of his own. In one hand he carries a large, wide-brimmed hat the same green as Cazanove's attire. Presumably this is Cazanove's body servant.

They weave towards the little alley at the side of the inn that leads to the stables. As they round the corner, Cazanove falls against Alaric who collapses under the weight and the two subside into a heap in the mud. Grover Price simply lets go and saves himself.

Halfway between laughter and disgust, Alice watches the spectacle. By the time Alaric and the body servant have heaved Cazanove upright, Grover has fetched a big, showy chestnut stallion from the stables at the back of the inn. Alaric Ford catches sight of Alice. He grins and rolls his eyes. Chalky mud clings to Cazanove's stockings, and more is smeared on his doublet and hose. Alice hopes for the manservant's sake that he is adept at brushing his master's clothes.

Rupert Cazanove rouses long enough to mumble inarticulate sounds but not long enough to help the men who pull and push and eventually heave his inert form over the saddle. There he dangles, a fat-bellied sausage, legs down one side, head and arms the other. Having at last disposed of their burden they stand for a moment catching their breath, before Alaric returns to the inn. He makes apologetic signs to Alice – *I would pass the time of day, but see, I am all over mud.*

The other two walk either side of the horse, holding their sagging load in place, and with Grover's hand on the rein they proceed up the alley towards the hill. At the top they will pass through a deep belt of trees crowning the ridge and then down the other side to where Cazanove's great mansion stands, a bare mile from the village.

Alice follows a little way up the alley for that is her way also. From there, a track leads to the cottages of Baker's Row – although they are hardly to be called cottages even, they are so poor. Each winter reveals a little more of the disintegrating wattle walls beneath the plaster, a little more of the rotting windows where glass is unknown. To Alice's recollection only minor repairs have been made over the years. Those who live here are the least regarded, some so close to starvation that the next stop for them is the oblivion of the Poor House. Consequently, Alice sees new faces all the time on her visits. Joshua the baker used to own the cottages. Perhaps he tired of making empty promises about repairs; she has heard a rumour he sold them recently.

She watches a small boy relieve himself against the wall of the first hovel. Another new face. His out-at-elbows jerkin and coarse linen breeches do not look as if they will keep out the cold when winter bites. He pushes open the door with grubby hands. In the gloom of the interior is the usual beaten earth floor, a table, one stool. No smoke issues from the chimney. The door drifts closed and the latch clicks.

In the fifth cottage along is the miller's widow. Alice always looks forward to her visits here. Old Goody Hamlyn retains an astonishing cheerfulness amidst her stark reduction in comforts. Usually, she will invite Alice to sit by her meagre fire where they exchange news, but in these days of plague she accepts the unwisdom of inviting another into her home. She is profuse in her thanks for what Alice leaves at her door.

Alice makes a handful of other visits at this end of the village. Some she calls on are fretful and anxious, taking it as a personal affront that she will not venture into their houses. Most are glad of what she brings. Existing hand to mouth, they are always the first to suffer when times are hard. Alice recalls Rupert Cazanove's rich, warm worsted clothing, and regards the thin, frayed kersey in which these people huddle. Many of them, she knows, work at Cazanove's dye-works upstream from Hillbury. It is a situation that Cazanove takes advantage of; if they complain of their wages, he soon replaces them with others who will do the work.

Alice's last visit nearly an hour later is further afield, a little way from the village at a house on its own in the lee of a belt of trees. She does not need to call here, but she is curious, so her excuse is that she still has a few late apples left in her basket. As she knocks on the door, she hopes they will not feel patronised by her calling. There is no saying with Grover Price these days. The door opens a crack and a small, slight woman peers through the gap. Her eyes just a shade too close together in a thin face give her the appearance of a hungry mouse on the lookout for tit-bits. 'Yes?'

'I called to ask after Master Cazanove, Mistress Price. I saw Grover helping him earlier. He appears to have been taken unwell.'

'Disordered humours, I suppose. Grover got him home,' the woman says, as though Alice is accusing her husband of abandoning the man.

'I feel sure Master Cazanove was glad of the assistance. Is he well now?'

'It's not the plague, if that's what you think.'

No, Alice thinks, more like a thumping headache and a furred tongue in the morning.

Grover appears behind his wife. The door is still open a mere crack and all Alice can see is his face, flesh the colour of uncooked pastry, and small eyes like shiny currants. Ever a taciturn man, he has become over the past several years nervous and suspicious. 'What's it to you? Spreading gossip?'

She ignores the slur. 'These days, Grover, we all fear on behalf of our neighbours.'

'It's like she says.' He jerks his head in his wife's direction. 'Not the plague.' Grover's eyes narrow as he adds fiercely, 'And you needn't go round telling everyone he was drunk, neither.

Didn't even finish his pot.'

'It was a sudden illness, then, was it?'

Grover's eyes narrow. 'Look. He'd been quiet for a while, we saw he was nodding, we got him out and home. That's all,' he says. 'An ague, see?'

Oh Grover, she almost protests, do you think me a dullard? How could it be an ague when the man was not shivering? Aloud, she says, 'I may call there to see if Mistress Cazanove needs anything.' And immediately regrets her inquisitiveness. She doesn't know Rupert Cazanove to speak to, has never met his wife.

'He's got Wat there, can get anything he needs, and she's got a woman for her wants, apart from the army of menials. Folk don't need to poke their noses in.'

'Wat. Was that his man I saw with you and Alaric?'

'Wat's there to attend the master,' Grover says, and adds as though explaining to a child, 'It's what a body servant's for.'

'Well, I shall trouble you no further, Grover, except that I have a few apples still in my basket. I should be glad for you and your goodwife to have them if you wish.' She draws back the cloth to show them. Grover's wife looks hopeful, but he answers for them both. 'We've plenty of our own so we don't need yours. We're not looking for charity.' The door closes with a snap.

Alice sighs. She will have to go up to the Cazanove mansion now, if only to prove to herself that Grover Price is not going to tell her what to do.

5

By the time Alice stands within the wide stone-arched porch and lets fall the door knocker at the great three-storey mansion, she is fervently cursing her own nosiness and wondering what excuse she can give for being here. After all, what can she do for a man whose riches probably outstrip the combined wealth of Hillbury, Woodley and Westover? Offer the last of the Hill House apples? Look at the size of this place. Alice wonders, when he built it did Rupert Cazanove intend to flaunt his rise to affluence as a self-made man, or his fecundity through the sheer number of bedchambers? If the latter, he must be disappointed now, because there has been no issue from his union with the baron's daughter he married some six or seven years ago.

Alice has a fleeting hope that her knock has not been heard in the recesses of the vast house and she can leave unseen. Seconds drag out and her hopes rise. She takes a few steps back from the nail-studded oak, drawing a sigh of relief.

A bolt is drawn back and the great door eases open a few inches on well-greased hinges to reveal a simply dressed woman. A waiting woman, judging by the plain cap and narrow lace. Her expression has not the hostile defensiveness of Grover Price's wife, but she has a determined set to her chin, and her stance defending the space between door and jamb offers no welcome.

Alice introduces herself. 'I am the daughter of Mistress

41

Edwards.'

There is no response; the door stays only a few inches open. Perhaps the woman has never heard of Mistress Edwards – Alice's mother – who makes poor-visits while Mistress Cazanove does not. Perhaps, Alice realises, the waiting woman merely thinks her uncouth for calling at the main door without previous acquaintance.

'From Hill House on the other side of Hillbury,' Alice adds. Still no response. She ploughs on, 'I saw Master Cazanove was unwell in the village and I came to enquire of your mistress if there was any way in which I can help.'

'He is back here now,' the woman says. Her quiet voice is not cracked nor her face lined, but the grey hair tells its own story. Her subdued manner lends an air of uncertainty. 'He is back here,' she repeats.

Alice struggles on. 'If it is the apothecary you need, I am going back past the village and could send a message to him.'

Or go myself? No, I promised.

The woman seems even more confused by the offer of help. She hesitates. Then, 'Wait there. No, come in, I shall fetch my mistress.'

She pulls open the door as she speaks and departs down the shadowy screens passage towards the nether regions of the house. Alice steps over the threshold, concluding that the women of Cazanove's household are as terrified as everyone says. She rubs her hands together and a shiver shakes her frame. Although the rain has eased now, the draught through the open door draws past her towards the great hall from where she can hear the multiple crackles of a huge hearth. She reaches behind her and pushes the door to. Having got this far, she is curious to catch her first glimpse of Cazanove's lady, who rarely comes into the village, and never attends the local gatherings such as May Day, harvest celebrations and the like.

Footsteps sound on the marble flags and from the other end of the screens passage a tall, thin figure approaches, walking slowly, followed by the waiting woman. At first, Alice can see only her face, wax-pale against the sombre gown buttoned to the jaw. The face appears almost spectre-like, floating, as she emerges from the shadows of the passage. Rumour in the village holds that she was considered too old to be marriageable before Rupert Cazanove offered, eager for a baron's daughter – so Alice was expecting someone in her mid-thirties. But seeing this wan, drained-looking creature Alice reckons she must be well on the wrong side of forty, though her carriage is upright and no stoop of age shows in her gait. She has thin lips and bruise-dark shadows under her eyes that give her the appearance of exhaustion. She holds her linked white hands at waist level, almost covered by deep, unadorned cuffs.

'Mistress Edwards.' The voice, barely above a whisper, obliges Alice to lean forward. The woman perhaps notices the movement, for her head comes up and she squares her shoulders. 'Mistress Edwards,' she repeats in a clearer voice, 'you happen upon us by surprise.' It is not an accusation, more a mannerly regret. 'I would offer you refreshment, but my husband' – her gaze slides away along with her voice – 'my husband needs me.'

But Alice has not come to sit in comfortable conversation with the woman who neglects her obligations to the poor. 'Thank you, Mistress Cazanove, I did not expect refreshment. I saw your husband unwell in the village and I came to see if there was anything you need, anything I can do.'

'Oh. I see.' The woman takes some seconds to consider Alice's offer. 'No, that is, I thank you but there is nothing

43

we need.' Her voice takes on polite formality, 'It was most kind of you to call.' She steps past Alice and pulls the door wide. The message is clear, and Alice feels like a shouldering market-wife. *I should have called at the kitchen door. A place like this, what was I thinking?*

'Can I send for Apothecary Marchant?' she offers, clinging to the wisps of her dignity. 'I shall be going back past the village and could have a message taken to him?'

'Apothecary Marchant?'

Alice goes on, 'He will be the best person to prescribe a simple for your husband's malady. May I send him a message?'

'Send for him? No, indeed no, mistress. In truth, he was here but a short while ago.'

'Master Marchant was here?'

'We saw him passing,' she indicates the way to Westover, 'and bade him come in. He has seen my husband—'

Her voice breaks down at that moment; she puts a hand over her mouth and turns away. The waiting woman intervenes.

'Mistress Edwards, you should leave this house. Apothecary has told us that Master Cazanove has contracted the plague.'

6

Now it is too late. She promised her father, gave her solemn word not to cross any threshold, and then through sheer idle curiosity stepped in. Now she has breathed the miasma of that doomed house. An hour later, still cursing her carelessness, Alice stands at the door to the winter parlour at Hill House wondering how she is going to tell her parents they must shun her until they know if she has the infection.

A sharp knock at the front door gives Alice a breathing space, and an unwelcome caller. She opens the door, calling to the two women servants to save them the trouble. Standing with his back to the door, hand on hip, foot tapping, is Abel Nutley. She last saw the parish constable entering the inn as Rupert Cazanove and his little retinue staggered out. The self-appointed chastiser of the erring turns; he is armed with an official-looking sheet of close writing and stamps his feet in the chill. 'Your father is within, Miss?'

'Yes, indeed Master Nutley, you wish to talk with him?'

'I'm here to say there is a quarantine set for the next thirty days. You will tell him.' It is a command, Abel Nutley never makes requests, at least, not to those he considers inferiors – labourers, women, apprentices, vagabonds. 'By order of the Justices. None may enter or leave Hillbury. And you are to stay in your own home. It's on account of the pestilence o' course.'

He says it, Alice thinks, as though he himself has ordered

45

the quarantine for a judgement on the village. He waves the paper in her face, pulling it sharply back when she reaches for it.

'Thirty days?'

'Ay, from today, now.'

'There will be overseers?'

'In the village only. I don't have enough to traipse up here.' Thank God for that at least, Alice thinks. Abel Nutley's vision of overseeing the quarantined will likely be concerned more with ensuring their obedience to the rules than with offering them comfort in extremity. She still holds out her hand.

'I should like to read the quarantine Order, Master Nutley, to be sure we understand what is required of us.'

He thrusts his head towards her, face tight, fist clenched around the paper. 'I know what's in the Order and I'm telling you—'

'Bit of a draught,' her father says, coming out into the hall. Ann Edwards follows in the wake of her husband. 'Oh, is that you, Nutley?' he adds with polite neutrality. 'What can we do for you?'

The parish constable bows and smirks. 'Indeed it is, Master Edwards. I was explaining the quarantine but women don't understand these things.' Alice grits her teeth. Abel Nutley hands over the crumpled paper to James' outstretched hand, and goes on, 'It carries greater authority than the apothecary's little plans. Not that I would speak ill of—'

'About time too,' James cuts across him, scanning the sheet. 'From what I see here, it comes a very poor second to Frederick Marchant's plans, which my daughter helped to put together when she was assisting him in the summer. Perhaps you did not know?' James steps to Alice's side, resting an arm round her shoulder.

46

'But he—' Abel Nutley starts to say.

'— Of course, he based his ideas on the measures prescribed in Florence and Padua,' James sweeps on. 'Where they know about this sort of thing. Thirty days, is it? Who is affected?' He returns the paper.

'It applies to Woodley as well, Master Edwards,' Nutley says, bowing again, 'but not Westover, they have no plague there.'

'And you will be in charge of the overseers?' Alice asks.

Abel Nutley draws himself up; he is almost her height. 'Of course.' He bows again to James and sends Alice a narrow look. As he turns to leave, he adds over his shoulder, 'I shall apply the Orders to the letter on boarding up infected households!'

'I bet you will,' Alice says softly as she closes the door.

7

It's the miasma. You stand in the infected air, you breathe it in. You die. Except it is not Alice who is dying.

Ann Edwards, never in good health, sickens within minutes of Alice arriving home, lingers two days before succumbing. Then the two maidservants, Mary and Henrietta, yield within a day of each other. Ian, the only other man around the farm since the summer labourers left after harvest, has disappeared, as has their shepherd, so there is a chance they have escaped it by leaving the village.

When Daniel Bunting and his brother David from the smithy arrive with their cart Alice is overwhelmingly relieved to see that it is empty. They must have come direct from the graveyard just down the hill by the church. She does not know how she could have faced the sight of neighbours she knows lying lifeless on its boards. Now they are asking the terrible question and she tells them about Mary and Henrietta.

The brothers have muffled their faces in vinegar-soaked scarves, and Alice leads them through the hall. But all three watch in horror as her father stumbles down the last three stairs and collapses sweating against the newel-post. Alice runs to support him.

Daniel is immediately there too. She stoops to lift, looking up. 'Help me get him to his bed.'

He scoops up James in his great blacksmith's arms, and Alice leads the way to the chamber over the front door.

David climbs the stairs behind them, panting a little with the exertion, and helps remove James's boots. Alice watches the two exchange a considering glance; almost she can see them agreeing to return in five days for yet another body.

Not my father, not while I can prevent it.

'Master Bunting,' she says, drawing the coverlet over her father and smoothing the damp hair off his forehead. 'When you are back in the village, will you ask Master Marchant to send some more mithridate? I'm nearly out, but if he can get some to me quickly, there's always the chance it will bring down the fever.'

Daniel says nothing, stares at her across the curtained bed.

'Some call it the Treacle,' she explains. 'Ask him for the London Treacle.'

Daniel bites his lip and glances at David. David is looking down at his feet and she feels a chill creep around her heart. 'What? What is it?'

At last, Daniel says, 'Mistress, have you not heard? 'pothecary's dead.'

8

In the fog of sleep, Alice comes bolt upright in a single movement, the coverlet falling away as she strains to hear the sound again. She might have dreamed it. A wailing, yearning call, as though at a great distance, falling away in despair. And yet close by. After all, it has woken her.

The faint glow of the frosted night creeps around the shutter pulled across the window. In its weak radiance the curtain stands at the head of her bed like a dark pillar against the wall. She never pulls her bed-curtains, hating the stifling sense of being enclosed. Her mother long ago gave up warning her of the evils of night airs. Alice turns her head to where the dark shape of the door stands slightly ajar, where the sound came from.

She draws her legs from under the covers and slides out of bed, her feet scarcely registering the chill of the floorboards. Briefly she considers dipping a cloth in the vinegar decoction and tying it over nose and mouth. To what end? The house is virtually empty now; the house that not ten days ago resonated to the voices of six people. Now, the only other occupant is her father.

James Edwards lies sick and weak. Both he and his daughter are well aware that he has travelled far along his allotted days since the swellings first appeared. She lanced, but the buboes reappeared. There is no more medicine, no more hope. He keeps apologising that he did not take them all to a place of safety. She reminds him over and over of what her mother said before she died, that it is in God's hands. She has not yet found the courage to confess that her blithe entry into the cursed house of Cazanove is to blame.

Despite the night, she has no need of flint and tinderbox, not in her own home. A wrap pulled hastily round her shoulders, she pads through the dark house to the main chamber, feels for the latch, pushes open the door. The window, close-shuttered, offers no aid, she must feel her way, but the bulk of the bed, the furniture ranged around, is a map in her mind. She stands for a few seconds by the door, straining her ears for the sound of his breathing.

'Father?' she whispers, unwilling to wake him if he has found the mercy of sleep once more. Silence. She tries again. Holds her breath, listening. Still no sound. Not even a shallow breath. More urgently now, she calls, 'Father!' and the word trails a strange echo in the dark. Fingers searching, she feels her way along the wall past chest, past chair. She reaches to pull back the bed-curtain. Not there? It's always there! Has she missed her direction in the dark? Not possible, here is the night table, solid under her palm. She stretches out to locate pillow, coverlet. Her hands touch only wood panel, and the criss-cross of ropes that once carried a feather mattress.

Alice sinks down onto the bare wood of the bed frame, overcome by the weariness of realisation. How many nights now has she made this futile journey, so utterly convinced each time that she has heard a call, that her father, the last, is still alive? She drops her head on her arms and sinks into a tearless void. They would all still be alive but for her.

'I promise,' she said to her father, and within an hour broke her promise. Now they are dead and it is all her fault. And to complete the divine punishment, her dearest Frederick too. Alice Edwards the executioner.

9

She has found yet another utterly pointless task to fill the time. Days she has spent, she has forgotten how many, scrubbing every corner and crevice of the house, desperate to rid it of its charnel-house stench. She burns linen, bedding, mattresses until the stink of scorched feathers makes her retch. She boils bed-hangings to destruction, reducing the delicate crewelwork border so lovingly stitched by her mother to a crabbed and shrunken stream of muddied colour-runs. Driven by the need to cleanse everything, she has chosen this morning to wash the set of pewter plates, the wooden trenchers and all the glazed mugs and bowls.

The effort of hauling buckets of water from the well in the courtyard, fetching brands for the fire, heating pot after pot, barely dulls the edge of her remorse.

She is busy at the task when behind her, the latch quietly lifts and the door creaks.

Someone pushes it slowly open. The tread of a stout working boot, certainly no woman's, crunches onto the stone flag. Little by little a hat brim, a close-muffled face appears round the door, tousled hair, an eye.

'You!' she cries.

Daniel Bunting freezes in equal astonishment, and they both stare. She is the first to recover. 'Forgive me,' she says, 'I did not expect to see anyone.'

He is much bigger than his wiry brother, heavier in face and body unlike David's sinewy frame. David the wheelwright. Daniel the smith.

'I'm sorry I made you jump,' he says. 'I thought I'd come to—' He stops.

You thought you'd come to pick up my body, a seeping black-spotted corpse.

She watches the fingers of his massive gauntlet wrap round the door. For a fleeting second she thinks he is going to drag it shut and bolt for his life.

'It's all right,' she says quickly. 'There's no plague here now.' Nothing but silence and frost and the endless days.

'I wasn't thinking of plague.' Perhaps he means it, but he has not yet crossed the threshold.

She rises, wiping her hands on her apron as she moves towards the barrel of small ale. At last, a living person, someone to talk to. 'Will you take a pot of ale?' Seeing his hesitation, she adds, 'It's been many days since you buried Father and no signs, you see?' She points to her face and neck, shows him her palms. 'Will you come in? Please?'

She takes down a mug and the act seems to decide him. He steps in and pushes the door to. 'No signs on me, either. And thankye, I'll be glad of a pot.'

He draws off his hat and gauntlets and unwinds the scarf covering nose and mouth. These he places on the table, but his greatcoat he keeps on. He shuffles across the flags towards the fire, sits down and hunches over, elbows on knees. The stiff folds of the greatcoat give his form the appearance of a massive rock planted there on the settle.

She turns to the barrel and pulls out the stopper. Ale gurgles into the mug as she asks, 'What news, Master Bunting? I see no smoke rising from the valley these past days. Has everyone left the village now? How are you faring, you and your brother?'

'I guess you might want me to take a look at your two mares. They must be wanting their exercise.'

Horses? What have the horses got to do with it? They're the easy part of her day, though he's right, she hasn't exercised them. She plugs the barrel, looks afresh at him. Poor man, so bowed down from his usual self. Slumped on the settle, gazing unblinking into the fire. She passes him his ale and he nods his thanks. Takes a pull and dabs his mouth on the back of his hand, puts the mug down. The silence stretches.

Finally she asks, 'What's happened?'

He looks round at her.

'In the village?' she adds.

His mouth opens and closes but no words came out.

'I've had no news at all up here,' she says. 'I do not even know when the days of quarantine will be up.'

He leans back against the boards of the high settle. 'No more do I know, missus, but it don't matter, you don't need to stay in your own house now.'

'I don't?'

'They're all gone.'

'Gone? Where?'

'Everybody in the village, all the little babies and the old ones and the young maids and lads and—' His eyes fill and he bites his lip.

Very carefully, she asks, 'What do you mean – gone?'

He shuffles one boot against the other. 'I buried the last of them today.'

'Dead? Everyone?'

'So many,' he says. 'I never seen so many.'

'It's not possible. You don't mean everyone?'

'Right down to the last. I came up here 'cos I thought

54

you …'

You thought I would be another duty on your grim list of cares. But my broken word has condemned me to life.

'Quite a few packed up and left,' Daniel continues, 'even after the quarantine order. But then Abel Nutley went round putting the fear of God and the Justices into the rest and they stayed.' He adds, 'And then Nutley deserted anyway, the bastard.'

'And left you and David the job of collecting and burying?'

He nods. He and David, she thinks. Incredible that they have survived. And without these two, where would this village be? What would it be? An open grave. That stranger's rotting corpse multiplied beyond imagination, if it were not for Daniel and David. *David?*

'Is David with you? Ask him in for a drink.'

'He's not here.'

'Surely he is not sick?'

'No, he's not sick.' He shakes his head, staring into the flames. 'I shouldn't have let him do the heavy work. I should have made sure he didn't do the digging.'

'Daniel?' That hint of breathlessness she heard on the stairs that barely registered because her father was sick. *Please no, please.*

'It was too much for him.'

'Was? Daniel, where is he? Where's David?'

'He were lucky, I suppose,' Daniel says. 'He never got the pestilence. He had a seizure and he was gone.'

She stares at him. Something she has heard somewhere, *Put out the light, and then put out the light.*

'It were so quick,' Daniel is saying. 'I didn't know till I looked round.' He shrugs. 'I miss him.'

The silence draws out while all she can think is how tiny

55

the word 'miss' is, for the weight it carries.

She casts around in her mind, rejects the impulse to voice the nothingness of a comfortable eulogy and sits down beside him, resting her hand on his arm. 'Losing David, you didn't deserve that, not after all you two did.'

He moves to put his own hand to cover hers. 'No more you your parents, missus.'

There is nothing Alice can say to that. What would he think if he knew that she has to live with the responsibility for her parents' deaths, and that of the two maidservants, and that she cries Frederick's name into her pillow every night.

They sit thus for some minutes, staring into the fire. At last Daniel stirs, withdraws his hand and reaches once again for the mug of ale. If she doesn't do something, she realises, he will drain his drink and leave. She cannot face the thought of being on her own again.

'Daniel,' she says, 'I hazard you've not yet had breakfast. If I rouse this fire, will you eat with me?' She picks up the poker. The action recalls a day some weeks ago, bringing a brief smile to her face.

'Do you remember the last time you were up here?' she asks. 'You and David were helping my father with the coppicing and the three of you came in to breakfast.'

'I do. David called your father a clumsy collyer.'

'He was always cutting himself on the billhook or the sharp ends of hazel.'

'And you were stood right here with your pot of self-heal in one hand and that poker in the other, I remember, and we weren't sure which you meant to use! Here, let me have that.' Gently he takes the poker from her and riddles the fire, clears the ash, adds sticks and a brand. A small kindness that she does not deserve.

While he goes outside to uncouple his cart and stable his horse Rowan, she busies herself cutting bread, ham, cheese, adding a few spoonfuls of preserved fruit from her store, re-filling his mug. She pours another for herself and by the time he is back she is putting the little meal down on the settle between them. He cuts a hunk of the hard winter cheese and folds thick slices of bread round it. In his great hand it looks not much, but it is more than she would need in a day. He eats steadily while she sips at her ale and breaks off little bits of cheese to nibble, waiting beside him. Usually he smells of smoke and horse, sometimes a hint of hot iron. Today he brings only the whiff of frosty air.

They eat in silence. He bites off great mouthfuls and his fingers, blue when he first stripped off his gloves, flush red as the warmth of the fire reaches him. His face turns a ruddy hue. Before he is finished, he is unbuttoning his greatcoat and pulling off the woollen kerchief tied at his throat, stuffing it in his pocket. Finally, he stretches out his legs towards the fire now burning brightly, and sits with the cleared trencher in his hand. 'That were good, thank ye, missus.'

Alice takes the wooden plate, carries it across to the table and returns to sit beside him once again. 'Now tell me again, please,' she says. 'Tell me what has happened in the village.'

'Tis as I said,' he replies. 'There ain't nobody left.'

'No one at all?'

He shakes his head. 'It took all of them, old and young, good and evil.'

'But some got out, you say?'

'Nick and Margery Patten down at the inn – they cleared out that day we were all quarantined. And quite a few others. Your ma's friends the Mistress Cushings. And I think your lad, Ian. He must have gone, we never found him or his girl.

57

But most just stayed.'

'We all thought it would be like it was in 'eighteen – if we kept a sensible distance from each other, it wouldn't spread. Though my parents sent me away then, even so.'

'More would have left, even to go and live in the woods, hauntings or no. But then Abel Nutley cried his threats up the street and they didn't dare.'

He falls silent for some seconds staring into nothing. 'I never seen anything like it – whole families we'd find when we broke down the door. David and me, we took them away and gave them a decent burial but our words weren't up to much without Parson Rutland.'

'But he only went to Bristol to ask assistance. Isn't he back?'

'I've not seen him from that day.'

'He should have been back within a week. Poor man, don't say he sickened on the way.'

'David, he wrote down the names and kept all right and proper.'

'And of course Sexton Whitehead was one of the first to go, so he couldn't stand in for the vicar.'

'Like David said, the three men most needed, 'pothecary, parson, sexton. Seemed like God didn't want to help the living or the dead. In the end we had to dig a big grave, put 'em all in together.' He stops and turns away to brush the heel of his hand across his eyes. 'Sorry,' he whispers.

She is silent, the enormity of his words forestalling her enquiries after particular individuals. After a few seconds, he turns to look at her again. 'I was glad to be able to join your da with your ma.'

'I am more grateful than you know,' she says. 'And for looking after Mary and Henrietta.'

Errant Henrietta, no more creeping back to work after secret meetings with lads from the village. Mary, older, wiser, such a support to Alice after Ann Edwards handed over more of the household duties to her daughter some years ago.

Daniel runs a great hand over his face, takes a long breath. He is looking away from Alice now, heaving deep shuddering gasps, struggling with himself. She can think of nothing useful to say. If this were Henrietta in trouble she would put her arm about her, draw down her head and let her weep on her shoulder. But this is a man. And not even a man of her household.

After a bit, he breathes more evenly and a thought occurs to her. 'Daniel, perhaps more left than you realise. Perhaps they will be back in a few weeks when the danger is over.'

'Ah,' he says, 'maybe you're right.' But his tone says the opposite. He puts his hands on his knees and pushes himself to his feet, starts to fasten his coat. 'Well, I said I would take the mares out and I will do that now missus, if you're willing.'

'They are very restive,' she agrees. 'I've not given them the exercise they need.' She follows him to the door, hands him his hat, his gauntlets. 'What will you do when you have taken them out?' She feels she should have done more, that he has done all the giving and is now going away.

'Something else you've a need to be done?'

'I meant, where will you go?'

'Oh.' He shrugs. 'Back to the smithy, I suppose. Nowhere else to go.'

She nods and he lifts the latch. She watches his back as he heads for the stable. One man, who has served all his neighbours so well, going to exercise her horses, then return to the loneliness of the smithy where the very walls will declare his brother's memory.

'Daniel!' she calls and steps across the yard.

'Missus?'

'Don't go back to the smithy.'

'Why not?'

'There's no one there. In the village, I mean. It can't be good to be on your own. Why don't you come back here for a bit?'

'For a bit?'

'Just while there's no one in the village.'

Daniel hesitates and thinks a moment. 'You have jobs for me to do?'

Well, I didn't mean—' She is embarrassed. She didn't mean to treat him like a manservant, working for his keep, but he goes on,

'There must be jobs a-plenty need doing. I could help you with them.'

'Could you?'

'Surely. You'll want the sheep seen to up over the hill. Your shepherd left at the first hint of plague, I heard.'

She sighs. 'He did. I try to keep an eye on them. They'll need moving to fresh foraging before long, but it takes me forever.'

'I could stay for a bit and do things like that for you.'

'Will you? You will find it easier if you stay a few days perhaps,' she says, and adds, 'if you've nothing special to do at the smithy, that is.'

'Stay here?' Suddenly he looks shocked. 'You mean, sleep here? I don't know as that's the right thing for me to be doing.'

She realises what she has unwittingly said. 'But perhaps you would rather go home.'

'Not that, missus. I don't know as I want to go back home at all. But I'm not sure I should stay here. What will folk think?'

She gives a short laugh. 'What folk would that be? Anyway, I don't much care what they think. I can feed you better than you'll feed yourself, and you can help me with the heavier work. Where is the wrong in that?'

She looks up at him, head and shoulders taller than herself. 'To tell the truth, I should be grateful for your company. Plenty of stable room for Rowan alongside Cassie and Athena.'

There is a little silence before he says, 'I could maybe stay a day or two, missus, and see if you still need me after that?'

She brightens. 'That is, if you still wish to be here. And please, don't call me missus. You're doing me a kindness.'

He shuffles his feet in their great boots on the hard-packed earth. 'I'll take the horses out now. Thank ye for the meal, Ali-er, … thanks.' He turns and steps quickly into the stables.

Afterwards, she offers him a chamber in the house – the one Ian used to use – but he is firm in his refusal, declares he will be quite happy in the hayloft at the top of the barn, and so they agree on this. It is also a bonus for her; the horses are invaluable to her, and after the disruption of plague, she knows the countryside will hold scattered bands of rootless marauders, people who have been forced to leave their home villages. With scant means of earning a livelihood, even the soberest might come to feel that the value of a horse makes it worth the stealing, even at the risk of hanging for it.

10

Within a day she knows she must go into Hillbury to see the devastation for herself. If anyone has returned, they might be in distress and needing help. If they see the broken doors and empty houses it will be a terrible shock. There is also the question that Daniel raised about the vicar. If he comes back, he will need to know all that has happened in his absence. He might return at any time, might already be back, and it is right she lets him know. She tells herself that while she is going in that direction it is only natural to continue on into Hillbury. And no, she won't mention it to Daniel, at least not beforehand – he will only worry. She will tell him this evening – perhaps.

From the kitchen window she watches Daniel shrug into his greatcoat and fetch his horse from the stable. She waits while he mounts up and kicks Rowan into a walk, heading down towards the saw-pit, to pick up the track round the hill to the sheep. On the way he said, her father's billhook and some sacks in hand, he will cut holly from the copse as well – sheep like that as a change and it will help to conserve what grazing there is.

Once Daniel is out of sight, she hurries up to her room and sorts through her chest of clothes. She dons a fresh chemise, warm wool skirt, padded waistcoat, and ties her hair up under an embroidered cap. Her kinked curls will surely escape its confines, but at least she will start out fit to be seen.

She is glad of the fur lining to her cloak as she sets off; her breath briefly mists the air and carries away on the breeze. The vicar's house by the church lies on the way from Hill House towards Hillbury. She rounds the barn to join the track. This is the opposite direction from the way she and her father drove in the cart that day such a short while ago, such a lifetime ago. This route goes down a long slope curving past the church and leading on to the centre of the village. See the village first, she thinks, then find out if Vicar Rutland is back.

Alice walks into the deserted street that was Hillbury, and stops to look around. An escaped lock of hair drifts against her cheek. For a few moments it is though she has arrived in the early morning before anyone is up. Almost she expects to see wisps of smoke rising from the bakery chimney, hands opening the shutters to start the day's cleaning. But no fires burn and the windows are not shuttered, they are boarded.

She walks slowly past the houses, not too close. Along the road at intervals are the remains of the sulphur fires, testament to the failed attempts to hold back the pestilence. Twin ashy furrows lead for short stretches out of each dead bonfire, showing where the death-cart was driven through. All along the street, not only were windows boarded, but doors as well, to prevent escape.

The stories Alice has heard over the years, of healthy people succumbing alongside ailing family members, have been repeated here. Constable Abel Nutley has, in his own words, followed the letter of the law. The fact that the Plague Orders are half a century old, that people have been calling for change for years, is clearly of no interest to him. He openly despised Frederick's proposal to isolate the sick in a specially designated pest house, to be cared for by paid nurses. He said as much that day he called at Hill House. It is hard not to

63

blame Nutley for the destruction of a community. But she cannot escape the reflection that if he is guilty of doing as he was told, how much more guilty is she, who broke her promise and brought destruction to those she loved?

Through gaps in the rough boarding of the weavers' cottages, the tallow-merchant's house, the tailor's rooms, is the evidence of life interrupted. Here and there, rotting grey-green food slumps on tables, seeping a faint smell of decaying vegetation and worse. Views of life interrupted made visible by David and Daniel when they broke into houses to collect their grim cargo.

Despite the time of year, a few flies buzz around her head and land on her face. Disgusted she flicks at them and hurries on. The same faint scent of mouldering death is everywhere. Her admiration for Daniel and his brother grows with every house she passes. The idea that they actually entered these tombs causes her to wonder anew at their courage.

At one open door the thought creeps through her mind that some skeletal thing could still be there inside, propped up and staring out with dead eyes.

She turns quickly away, trying to brush the haunting thoughts from her mind by hastening across the road to walk down the other side. A breeze teases more strands of kinked curls from under her cap to waft in her face. The only sound is her footsteps on the frozen ground. In her thoughts, the dead still inhabit the houses behind her; perhaps even now they are moving unseen to watch her through gaps in the boarding. The breeze hints at sighing spectres lurking round every corner. All the woodcuts of gaping skeletons she has ever seen conjure ideas of crouching phantasms. Black eye-sockets watch in silence from the bonfire ashes, while bony grins flicker behind distorted panes and floating bloodless hands grope at her back, ruffling her cloak. Every now and then she feels compelled to glance behind.

A creak directly overhead has her scurrying with a cry into the middle of the way, only to laugh shakily at herself as she looks up.

On the top floor, a casement swings to and fro, caught in a gust. This building stands out from most with its jettied floors. It was under these overhangs that the little group of children were sheltering that day when Alice and her father came down with the cart. The double-fronted house belongs to a prosperous merchant. She has often seen him at church taking surreptitious naps within the relative privacy of his family pew. A wife and three children, also his mother, live in that house. Lived? She wonders if they are all now sleeping that endless sleep.

Inevitably drawn, she turns and walks away from the huddle of buildings to the last dwelling. Just there at the edge of the village, she stops outside the only house she would willingly enter. She puts her hand to the door and can feel it is only on the latch, not barred inside. Frederick Marchant's apothecary's shop. Peering through the little window, she looks with dismay at the bare shelves, stripped of their contents, probably within hours of his death, when people would have tried any remedy to ward off the dread disease. Almost overwhelming in its appeal is the temptation to walk into Frederick's house, to stand in the doorway to the still room and see the little table where he made up his simples, to feel again his comforting nearness, see his smile, touch his dear face …

But Frederick is under one of those mounds in the row of new graves by the church. A whole life funnelled into two letters scratched on a wooden cross.

The day her father died, she broke quarantine and took the little dried sprig of forget-me-not from under her pillow to find where Frederick was laid to rest. She buried it there in the mound over his heart.

Forget you, Frederick? How would I do that?

With an effort, she takes her hand from the door. Frederick is not here, not any more. She sets her face towards the village again.

11

The inn is a different scene. She peers into the taproom through a gap in the shutters. It is completely clean and tidy. No food moulders as evidence of disturbed meals, no broken boards over the windows to spoil the ordered stillness. The door is barred on the inside, as she would expect, but walking up the alley where she saw Rupert Cazanove collapse that day, she can see across the yard that the door to the kitchen passage is slightly ajar.

Alice walks over to close it. It is not like the landlord's wife to leave doors unsecured, and Margery will not like it if strangers enter the inn while she is absent. At the door, however, curiosity steals over Alice. She cautiously edges in.

Within is a clean, fresh smell that is a relief to breathe. She looks both ways, almost expecting Margery to stride out of the kitchen to scold her. This end of the inn Alice knows well from regular visits with her mother to discuss village needs with Margery. Today, opportunity beckons the other way.

She tiptoes down this less familiar passage. Mock herself as she might, she cannot feel quite comfortable in this male place. Surely Nick will emerge amazed from the taproom and ask her what she thinks she's doing. Only a certain sort of woman is seen in taverns, and even her tolerant father would baulk at this.

The taproom is dim from the secured shutters, but enough daylight enters between the slats to reveal the room. No litter of dirty mugs or used plates. The hearth is swept and laid, and by the door from the passage the barrels rest on their trestles, closely bunged with not a drip on the floor below. Nick and Margery must have roped in the children that afternoon when quarantine was declared, to sweep and polish the place before they left the same day. She walks across the stone-flagged floor past a handsome sideboard with smooth waxed surface. Dark wainscoting runs along the adjacent wall and in its centre, the door to the street is barred.

An oak cupboard stands in the corner. She pulls it open and peers inside. Rushlights and holders, and a set of bright pewter tankards. They remind her of some she once glimpsed in Frederick's parlour, and with an effort she drags her thoughts away.

A few tables furnish the taproom, a variety of three and four-legged stools and two settles by the hearth. A tobacco jar stands on a high shelf, some dice alongside, pipes crammed into small recesses in the brickwork of the fireplace, ready for smokers. Glazed mugs hang from a rafter near the barrels. The paraphernalia of men at ease.

The aroma within the taproom seems to emanate from the very walls, from decades of soot, old tobacco and the familiar yeasty whiff of ale, warm and comfortable.

She wanders back down the passage and out into the yard, securing the door behind her and pausing for a moment to look. One of the little window panes in the brew house is broken. Shards litter the top of some barrels stacked within. Outside, more barrels, probably empties waiting for Nick Patten's next brewing session.

When she hears the sound, her stomach lurches. She backs against the kitchen door, preparing to slip inside. She can bar the door from within. There it is again. Her heart hammers as she strains to catch its direction. It seems to be in the yard but is faint and barely recognisable.

'Who's there?' she calls, and hates how her voice wavers.

It comes a third time and her breath escapes in a long sigh of relief. This is no spectre. This is a real cry of distress.

'Where are you?'

Silence.

Alice calls again, 'If you can hear me, call out. Where are you?'

The response comes, sadly sobbing, 'Mammy said to stay here.' Now she has it placed, a storeroom at the far end of the yard. It is a simple structure, wood and plaster with a rough thatched roof, no window. Alice hurries towards it, lifts the latch and pushes at the door, but something behind resists her efforts. 'My dear,' she calls, 'can you open the door and let me in?'

But the wail only grows louder. 'You can't come in. Mammy said to stay here.'

How to persuade this child? She opts for simplicity. 'My name is Alice and I live in a house on the hill. Where do you live?'

'With my mammy.' The voice is so young, the child may not even know where. Alice tries again. 'Would you like to show me?' No response. She goes on. 'Don't you think your mother wants you to go home?'

'He took my mammy away,' says the little voice from the other side of the door.

No child should have to bear that. 'He took my mammy too,' she says.

Where was this child when Daniel collected his mother? How long has he been here? She decides on another approach. 'Are you hungry? Would you like something to eat?'

There is no answer but Alice can hear rustling followed by a fumbling on the other side of the door. There is the scraping sound of a box being dragged, then another, and Alice gently pushes at the door. Blinking in the sudden light, the child stands thin, dishevelled and filthy, clutching a cracked dark yellow piece of cheese in a grubby hand. He cannot be more than four years old. Alice's first impulse is to take him in her arms, but this buckles in the waft of stench from within.

Margery Patten uses this outhouse for hanging freshly killed poultry and game, and something unmentionable has rotted from its hook and fallen on the floor. It has been eaten by rats. On a sort of platform in the roof pitch, hay is stored for the inn's stables. It is clear that the child has slept up there, burrowing a nest for warmth. He must have lived here for several days, she reckons. Along with rotting bird, the place stinks of piss and worse.

She squats down so that they are on a level. 'Tell me your name, what are you called?'

'Samson.' The child reaches out a grubby hand with dirt-caked fingernails to trace a silken tendril on her embroidered waistcoat.

She resists the urge to pull away. 'Well, Samson, that's a good strong name for a strong little boy. Do they call you Sam?' He nods. 'Then I shall too. Do you want to come and eat with me?'

'I'm thirsty.' He puts his hand in her outstretched one. She stands up and leads him out.

'I shall give you something to drink at my house.' She is terrified of letting him drink or eat anything down here in this place of death.

'When's my Mammy coming?' he asks, and Alice thinks, I cannot tell him this here, now, poor child.

Time enough later to try to trace the fate of his family. She will ask Daniel if he knows who Sam is. He will likely know, living in the village.

'She's not here at the moment,' she says. 'We'll go up to Hill House. That's where I live, on the hill. You can have something to drink and eat. I can give you a wash and find you some fresh clothes maybe. I expect those are a bit scratchy for you.' The child says nothing. 'Your Mammy would like you to be clean, wouldn't she?' He regards her in blank incomprehension. Alice eyes what looks suspiciously like lice amongst his sticking-up hair, and her scalp itches. 'Come along, then.' Together they pass the kitchen, the empty stables and out into the alley.

'We live there.' Sam points past the bakery and turns his steps that way. Alice allows him to lead her round behind the bakery's large jutting chimney. Some yards back from the road is the track to the row of small hovels, thatched and low, that have been there since before the bakery was built. Several have a red cross roughly daubed on the door and some have been boarded up.

'My mammy's there,' Sam says, pointing at the first house of the row. She has a vision of a small boy, poorly dressed, peeing against the wall and then pushing open the door. Surely the rest of his family are not still in there? She cannot possibly take the child in there if bodies are inside.

She pushes at a disintegrating board across the window, working it to and fro with her fingers until it moves enough for her to peer through the slit she has made. No one downstairs at least, but several flies buzz out.

'Sam' she kneels down to his level, 'I shall go in and I want you to be very good and wait here for me. Will you do that?'

She dreads entering the place, there is that awful smell of

rotted meat again. Who can say if it is animal or human? Her stomach heaves in protest.

'I want to come with you.' His face is crumpling as he looks at her. He is not going to stay outside, she realises. He is probably terrified she will disappear and he will be left alone again. Alice smiles to reassure.

'Then you shall. This is what we'll do. Do you hold my hand and I shall go in first. We'll stay together. Yes?'

He nods. Cautiously she pushes at the door. It creaks open. The smell of putrefaction is every bit as bad as the other houses. A few flies buzz sluggishly. Both of them recoil, batting the air. Handkerchief to her face, Alice turns and looks into the ground-floor room. Fireplace against the wall, ash on the floor and a cooking pot suspended over it on a tripod. The floor is earth, hard packed by generations of feet. This is nothing like the clean orderliness of the inn – to the left of the fireplace is a table with a single stool by it. On shelves set in the wall, beside a chipped pot, part of a loaf is spotted with furry circles of green and grey.

The smell seems to be coming out of the cooking pot hanging over the cold ashes and as she leans over, she realises the meat in there – probably rabbit – is heaving with maggots. Bile rises into her mouth. She gags, hauling Sam away to the doorway, where she takes several breaths of the air outside.

'Sam, no one lives here any more,' she says gently.

'She's in bed,' Sam insists. He is getting agitated now, trying to pull her back across the room.

'But no one has cooked a meal for days, Sam. The meat is rotted in the pot.'

'I want to see,' he wails.

It is understandable that he wants to see for himself the place where he last saw his family, she reasons, so perhaps the least harm will be to let him see upstairs for himself, if it's fit to be seen.

'Sam, don't cry.' She draws him to her. Tears are making streaks through the dirt on his face. 'I will go up and you can wait below where you can see me, and when I'm ready, you can come up. Will you do that?'

'Yes,' with a sniff, wiping his nose on his sleeve.

Like all these hovels, the way to the upstairs room is a ladder fixed in the corner leading up through a square cut out of the ceiling. She settles Sam by the wall and climbs the half-dozen rungs, talking to him all the while. Reassuring him, she hopes.

As soon as she is high enough, she steels herself to look into the room. The raw breeze blows freely through the rotted window, no shutter to withstand it. Against the wall a plain wooden bedstead stands on the rough floorboards. The mattress is of straw, its plaited ends have unravelled and stick out under the sacking that covers it. Over this is laid a rough brown blanket slubbed with black and grey flecks. There is just one bed, but that is not uncommon in a hovel like this. There could have been any number of people living here. She is only aware she has stopped talking when she feels Sam beside her. He has climbed to a level with the floor. 'She's gone away,' he says.

'Yes, Sam, she's gone away.' She feels stupid and inadequate. She cannot lie to him that his mother will come back. What to say, that such a very young child will understand? But it is Sam himself who supplies the answer. 'Is she with God?' he asks.

'Yes, she's with God and He is looking after her.'

Then, hesitantly, 'How many of you were living here, Sam?'

'My mammy and my sister. Is she here?'

Alice shakes her head. 'Your sister has gone away too.'

'Can I see them?' he asks.

'One day, Sam, yes, you will see them again.' And she silently hopes for his sake that this is true. He seems satisfied and goes back down the rungs. They leave the house, shutting the red-daubed door behind them. Alice leads him through the village, past the boarded-up houses. He looks and looks but says nothing, and soon they head up the hill towards Hill House. Part-way up, as she has been expecting, he flags and wants to sit down. But his thin little frame is already shivering in the chill air. She puts on a cheerful voice, as though they are playing a game.

'Sam,' she says, 'would you like to ride piggy-back? It will give you a nice high view to see things.'

She takes off her cloak and lays it across the branch of a fallen tree. 'Look, step up on the trunk here.'

She puts her back to him and he wraps his arms round her neck. 'Up you come,' she says and hoists him. Under her woollen skirt she is wearing the stuffed roll around her hips that gives the cloth a wider fall at sides and back – his little legs rest there. Resolutely she closes her mind to what might crawl out of his clothes and into hers. Needs must.

She picks up her cloak and throws it around the two of them. The boy laughs briefly as the hood falls forward covering his face, he pushes it back and Alice ties the strings in front. Putting her arms under his knees she starts off up the hill.

It is only much later that she realises she has forgotten to find out if the vicar is back.

12

Sam is tired and fretful by the time they arrive at Hill House, and Alice is sagging. Although small, Sam's weight has added to her uphill walk. She is glad to be relieved of her burden in the kitchen.

She adds wood to the still warm fire and settles him by it. As she stands back she takes her first real look at him. His thin arms protrude from frayed sleeves, his skinny neck and bony legs make his body look like sticks fitted together. He is filthy from head to toe, hair sticking out, neck grimy, clothes soiled and worn past saving. His fingers he holds out to the glow are grey, the dirt collected in dark crescents under his nails. His knees are scraped in common with most small boy's knees, but the blood is dark, old, the dirt ingrained. What she can see through the holes in his footwear, hardly to be called shoes, is yet more grime. Her instinct is to prepare a bath and put him in, clothes and all, but for this scrawny urchin it is more pressing that he eats. She breaks a piece of bread from that morning's loaf, pulls the leg from a joint of chicken and taps a little small ale into a mug. It will stave off his immediate needs.

While he slurps his ale and tears with his teeth at the food, she takes off her waistcoat and cap, dons an apron and draws up the sleeves of her chemise. There is a bucket of water that Daniel drew this morning, and she carries it over to the hearth. Into it she pours hot water from the cooking pot sitting ever

75

ready by the fire. Sam stares in evident puzzlement while she fetches towels and a blanket from a coffer in the hall. She is talking to him all the while, explaining how he will feel clean and comfortable, how she will find him warm clothes – she has not yet worked out where these will come from – and how he can sleep in a bed with real feathers. But when she gently removes his rag of a shirt, he starts to wriggle in her hold. As she wrings out a towel in the bucket and starts to scrub his neck the trouble really starts.

'Don't!' he yells. He struggles and wriggles, howling at what is clearly for him the unaccustomed shock of water on his skin.

'Sam, you will feel so much better when you are clean,' she tries to explain.

'Ow! Ow!'

'Sam, I would let you soak it off in a bath, but I haven't the time to warm it for you. Come now, this won't take long.'

'It's wet!'

She laughs. 'Of course it's wet, it's water. It's the only way you'll be clean.'

'I don't want clean!' Fury reddens the little boy's face. He tries to pull out of her hold. 'My mammy doesn't do this!'

No, she thinks, clearly not. 'This won't take very long, Sam.' It is his hands and feet that are the worst, they are layered with dirt. She rubs first at one then the other, frequently rinsing and wringing out the towel. The water has taken on a sullen brown tinge and a stale reek hangs in the air.

'I'll run away!' He bends to the bucket and before she can stop him sweeps a wave of muddy water straight at her where she kneels on the flags. It splashes her face and arms and spatters her apron and the floor around.

'Go ahead.' Alice pushes sopping hair from her face

while her sleeve drips muddy water. 'Are you going to hide somewhere in the house perhaps?'

'Yes!' He stamps a small foot.

'Then be sure to take the bucket with you, so that you may make splashes everywhere you go.' She pulls him onto her lap and bends him all unwilling over the bucket, dousing his hair time and again with the towel.

'I hate you!' Sam shouts, his voice muffled from between his knees.

'Go to, go to, Sam, this isn't so bad. It's nearly finished. What about something more to eat?' She drops the mired cloth in the water and he stands upright, his face a study of mutiny vying with uncertainty, while she reaches for the dry towel. 'You're still hungry aren't you?'

'No!' he says, then, 'Yes.' The tears gather and he stands thin-shouldered and drooping, while she rubs him dry and wraps the blanket round him.

'I want my Mammy,' he sobs.

'Oh Sam, dear.' She picks him up and sits him on her lap. She puts her face to his, kissing his forehead and wrapping her arms round him. 'I know, sweeting.'

As he cries into her shoulder she sees the disgusting crawling creatures that still cling in his spiky wet hair. One by one, she picks them out and flicks them into the fire. The movement distracts Sam, and he laughs at the wet fizzing, then the popping sound as they explode.

'Now, what do you say to some warm ale?' She thrusts the poker into the heat and crosses to the barrel. Half a mugful will suffice. Weak as small-ale is, in his frail state she is aware he could quickly become drunk.

She brings it back to the settle, and steering clear of Sam's reaching hands draws the poker black-red from the fire and dips it in the ale just long enough to warm it.

While he sips, she takes a brick from a small stack by the hearth and settles it amongst the hot embers. His clothes she pushes to one side. Later she will burn them. As for his little shoes, disintegrating though they are, he'll have to wear them out of doors for now. When things start to return to normal she will get to a shoemaker, it will be eight pence well spent. But for now a proper meal, and to distract him while she prepares it, she asks, 'Do you have any brothers, Sam?'

'No.' His fingers wrapped around the warm mug, Sam peers into the depths of his ale. He has tucked up his legs under him and is curled in the corner of the settle.

'What about your father? Where is he?'

'He went to get a bloody drink.'

'Is that what he said? He went to the inn?'

Sam shrugs.

'And when he came back, what did he do then?'

'I don't know.' Sam yawns.

'Didn't he come back?' Alice asks.

'I went to look for him but they wouldn't let me in.'

'What did your Mammy say?'

'She said he's a toss-pot and they'd carry him home but they didn't. Why did they paint red on our door?'

'Because your Mammy was not well, Sam. Tell me why you were in the haystore.'

'Mammy had black spots on her face. She was cross with me, she kept saying, *Go away, go away.*'

'She wasn't cross with you Sam, she just didn't want you to get black spots as well.'

Sam takes a few mouthfuls of the warm ale. 'I brought her a rabbit.' he says.

She looks at him thoughtfully. So that's where the one in

the pot came from. He must have stolen it from someone's meat store.

'She wanted my sister to eat it, but she had big black spots. Then my Mammy got spots. She said, *Go away and don't come back,* but I did.'

'You went back home?'

'I was hungry.'

'And what happened?'

'She was asleep, and my sister was asleep and they wouldn't wake up, I shook them.'

Heavens, he was in the house only a few days ago, touched them. Will he start the fever soon? Whether or no, it's too late now.

'The man took them away. I saw.'

In disjointed fragments, Sam tells her the story of his stay in Nick Patten's haystore. He went to look for his father again at the inn, where he found no one at all. The horses were gone from the stable and the whole place was empty, just as she herself found it. Sam used a nail and got into the back of the inn. You can do it with a strong twig, he tells her when she wonders at his unexpected skills, but his father said a nail is better because it doesn't break. He goes on to explain that you can only do this on empty buildings, because ones with people in are barred on the inside. As it was, he was able to walk around with no one to stop him. He found the cheese there.

After a while he went out and kicked stones around the yard, trying to aim them through the door of the stable, or at a stack of empty barrels. When he tired of that he picked up pebbles and threw them, and one went through the window of the brewhouse. In Sam's experience, when things break, a big angry man comes storming out. Sam fled into the inn and hid.

That was when he heard a cart trundling down the road. He went into the taproom at the front and climbed on a stool to peer between the slats of the shutter. The cart was being driven by a man muffled to the ears, his hat rammed down on his head. In the cart Sam could see arms lolling, clothes flapping in the light wind, and here and there a foot, shod or bare. As the cart came alongside, he saw his sister's little form lying straight and still, in the shift she had been wearing the last time he saw her. Sam cried out but the cart kept going. He wanted to run outside and ask the man where they were all going, but something held him back. His sister lay alongside a figure who seemed to have no interest in her, for the arms did not enfold her but lay straight, palms upwards, face turned away. And that was strange, for the lank hair, coarse linen skirt and tarnished wedding ring Sam knew well.

13

Telling his story has taken away Sam's appetite. Sitting curled against her on the settle, face flushed from heat and tears, he stares into the flames. Gradually he falls silent and his eyelids droop. While he dozes on the settle, she wraps a towel round the brick now grown hot from the embers and takes it upstairs. She pushes it between the sheets of her own bed. Back in the kitchen she wraps the blanket close round him and carries him upstairs, settling him into the feathered softness and moving the wrapped brick to rest against his feet. He barely wakes, eyelids fluttering, and she sits with him until the long lashes rest quietly on his cheeks and she can hear his measured breathing.

It is much later when the clouded sky is hastening the onset of evening that she leaves the chamber for the third time, satisfied that Sam is sleeping soundly. She enters the kitchen as Daniel pushes open the door from the yard. 'I took both mares out,' he says, shrugging off the greatcoat and hanging it over the back of the settle. He sits down before the fire and stretches out his legs, grunting slightly as he rests his heels on the hearth. 'Gave them a good run again.'

'I imagine they were ripe for it.' She brings him a piece of pie.

'Ah, they were that.' He bites gratefully into the meat. 'I've put Rowan in next to Athena today, they seem to rub along well together. What's this?' picking up a small shoe.

81

'There's a child. I found a child in the village.'

He stops chewing and stares at her. 'You went into the village?'

'Only to look around.'

'I thought you were going to Parson Rutland's.'

'I needed to see for myself. It's difficult to imagine it when you haven't seen it.'

'But there could have bin vagrants there, masterless men. Times like this they'll be wandering the country. You shouldn't have gone on your own.'

'I never thought of that. Anyway, there were none, only a little boy.'

'Lord's sakes, how did I come to miss one? I thought I'd found all the bodies, where is he? I'd better go and deal with him afore it's dark.'

'Not a body, a living child, Daniel. He's alive and well. At least, he is well at present. He has no tokens of pestilence on him. I've put him upstairs to sleep.'

'Who is he?'

'I don't know. I was going to ask you. His name's Samson. Sam. Do you know a Sam?'

'Sam?' He shakes his head. 'Where did you find him?'

'In Nick Patten's haystore. I heard him crying and went to see.' She bends to pick up the little jerkin and breeches.

'How old is he, then?'

'I suppose about four. He was terrified.' She holds the ragged remains at arm's length. 'These are infested. I'll have to make him some fresh.' She drops them on the fire where they take flame immediately. 'He says they were in the bakery cottages.'

'Who were?'

'His family. They must have rented it recently.'

'How did he get in the haystore?'

'There's no lock on the door. Sam's mother told him to get out of the house, she had the plague herself.'

'Where's his mother now then?'

'She's dead, and Sam's sister. You collected them, apparently.'

He sighs. 'Poor little fellow. I should've checked the inn, but you see I knew they'd all packed up and gone from there the afternoon quarantine started. Nick came and told us they were all going off Honiton-way to Margery's kin till all this is over. I never thought to check in there, I knew it were empty.'

'Don't blame yourself, Daniel. I think Sam would have come out once his cheese ran out,' Alice says. 'But there is something I need to ask you. He says he saw his mother and sister in your cart. They were in the end cottage of Bakery Row. The end nearest the inn.'

'Cazanove's cottages?'

'Is that who owns it now? I didn't know. Do you recall collecting them?'

'Yes, she was upstairs with the little girl in bed by her side. She was one of the last. Two days ago? Yes, the day before yesterday. So he was there in the haystore two days!'

'At least that. I think he had been in and out, going back home for food, but the last time he went his mother was dead. He thought she was asleep, so he went back to the haystore to wait until she said he could come out.'

'Thank the Lord you went down there.'

'I only hope he doesn't have the fever on him already.'

'If he does, I've still some of the vinegar mixture at home, Alice. I'll bring it up tomorrow.' It is the first time he has used her name. He does not seem to have noticed and she almost missed it herself. She is glad of it, of the companionable

83

feeling it gives her.

As he sits finishing his ale, she says, 'I suppose his father went away before the family became sick. Sam says he tried to find him in Nick Patten's but got turned away of course. So that was before quarantine was imposed.'

Daniel makes a face. 'And his Da's been away that long? He'll not be back then, will he?'

'I imagine not. Master Cazanove must have rented it to them. Is he dead, do you know?'

'We buried him in the woods this side of the mansion.'

'I don't know how else we can find Sam's family.' She pushes herself to her feet, 'Come and see him, Daniel. He looked so peaceful when I left him.'

She lights a taper. She does not need it for herself but he is unfamiliar with this house and could stumble on the dark stairs. They tiptoe up and cross the boards into the room where Sam lies now on his back in the big, uncurtained bed, one arm on the coverlet, the other crooked on the pillow. His long lashes lie on his cheeks, and his breathing, barely audible, is smooth and even. Daniel steps over to the bed the better to see the sleeping child, and very gently bends down and smooths a damp lock of hair off Sam's forehead. As he straightens and turns back towards her, he smiles.

It is the first smile she has seen in the lifetime that has passed since his brother was well, her parents were alive and the village bustled with people.

14

Later, sopping up meat juices with the last of his bread, Daniel gets up. 'I'll take the lantern and check the horses are settled,' he says. 'The young lad seems to be sleeping on.'

'A merciful thing if he sleeps through the night, I think,' Alice replies. She starts to gather plates. 'I shall go and sit with him for the rest of this evening. It will comfort him if he wakes in this strange place.'

It does not take her long to clear the meal and wipe the plates clean. As she goes around the kitchen putting things away, she glances out of the window. Shadows swing to and fro as Daniel moves around in the stables. The sight reminds her of Ian doing the same job, an age ago it seems. At that moment Daniel comes out of the stables, stands the lantern on the ground and shakes a small pan of grain in his hand, calling to the chickens, tempting them inside. She thinks of how much she owes him for all these unasked kindnesses. From the shelf above the fire she takes a little wooden box, prising off its lid to check inside. Satisfied, she closes it and sets it on the table. She lifts the heavy door latch and goes out into the frosted darkness, crossing the yard to help steer the last of the hens into the stable.

He empties the grain inside and pushes the door to. 'Cold out here for you Alice, you're not wrapped against it.'

'I wanted to say, you are welcome to make yourself comfortable in the kitchen,' she says. 'The fire will be warm for some time yet, and there is still some tobacco in my father's jar if you fancy a smoke. I've put it on the table. I'll be upstairs with Sam now.'

'Thank ye Alice, tis kind of you.'

'It's wrapped in cabbage leaves so it's still moist.'

He follows her back into the kitchen. 'There are two or three pipes up there.' Alice points. 'Choose which you will.'

'Never worry, I have my own.' He picks up the tobacco jar, looks inside, sniffs, murmurs an appreciative, 'Ah.'

'And, Daniel?' He turns to her. 'Thank you for being here,' Alice says. 'I feel much safer.'

He looks down, slightly nodding, shuffling his feet in their patched boots. 'I'll call up when I'm going out to the barn, so's you can put the bar across the door,' he says.

Alice walks back through the kitchen to the hall and climbs the creaking stairs as quietly as she can, slipping into the chamber. Sam is on his side, half out of the bed, still fast asleep and she gently eases him back. The child stretches and takes a deep breath in his sleep and settles down again.

15

The scream of fright and dismay tears into Alice's sleep and jerks her awake in an instant.

'He's taking my mammy! Don't take my mammy!' he cries. 'Mammy, Mammy!'

Alice is up and talking, reassuring, calmly talking. 'It's all right, Sam, I'm here.'

'Don't take my mammy!'

'All right, sweeting, it's all right.' Talking all the while, she gently possesses herself of the child's flailing arms. 'I'm here, Sam. All's well.'

Not that anything can be well, with his mother and sister dead, his father gone. But she continues to reassure, gradually pushing aside the shreds of his nightmare, reaching the comfort of her presence into Sam's terror. She cannot hold him and at the same time get to the tinderbox to light a taper, but a faint radiance from the night sky shows her Sam's staring eyes and distressed frown. His little mouth is half open, the lips working, every now and then he heaves a gasping sob. His mind's eye can see what Alice can only imagine. He is no longer struggling against her but he remains in his other world.

'I'm here Sam, this is Alice here. I'm going to stay with you, Sam. It's all right my dear.'

'Taking her away, taking her away,' wails the child, and Alice rocks him in her embrace. Eventually he will emerge from the nightmare's grasp but she recognises that he might carry this shocking memory for some while yet, until the stability and routine of life at Hill House pushes it to a distance where he can look at it and not be afraid. In the meanwhile Sam stares straight ahead in the frost glow and even when she puts her face down to his, his look passes through her as though through a ghost. His child's lips form the words 'Mammy, Mammy,' but no sound comes out. Alice holds him close until his stiff little shoulders relax and the stare recedes from his eyes. Still holding him, still murmuring soft words of comfort, she lies down with him, pulling the coverlet over the two of them. Gradually Sam's breathing slows and he sleeps.

Much later Alice lies wakeful in the dark listening to his even breathing. She lightly strokes his palm. The child turns towards her in his sleep and reaches out, one hand on her neck, the other clasping her hand. At some point not long after, Alice falls asleep, holding him lightly in her arms.

When she wakes in the dim dawn, Sam's eyes are already open, looking at her from the other end of the bolster that pillows their heads.

'When's my mammy coming?' he asks.

16

For the next several days, Alice devotes her time to Sam. The child is clearly in need of comfort and reassurance, though reassurance on the question of his parents is impossible without sliding around the truth. She will not lie to him, but death he does not yet understand.

'Your mammy had to go away, Sam,' Alice says, 'but I found you and I will look after you as long as you need me.' The child looks at her with wide grey eyes.

'She was asleep and he took her away in a cart.'

'She was very ill, Sam,' Alice explains. 'Sometimes people are so ill they can't stay at home any more.' She is not sure how much he has grasped, but Sam seems satisfied for the present and Alice starts to relax.

17

Daniel and Sam compete to roll themselves from the top of the slope behind the stables, down to the bulrushes around the little duck-pond; a dozen yards, bouncing over crackling frosted tussocks until they come to rest amongst the marshy grasses, gazing panting at each other in slightly dazed surprise.

Until Sam jumps up and cries, 'Again, Daniel! Again!' Then Daniel rises to his knees in mock weariness and struggles to his feet, before shouting, 'First to the top!' and up they go, Daniel just allowing Sam to win at the last, and Sam dancing in triumph at his victory against such a mighty adversary. Alice laughs as she has not done for too long, and Sam squeals and shouts, giggles and dances and jumps, skipping with glee and windmilling arms and legs in sheer excess of energy.

Alice watches them start the long laughing roll again. She stands at the top of the slope, secretly wishing she could join them, applauding them both when they manage not to roll into the water, and cheering Sam in his race back up the slope.

She is hard put not to laugh at her own handiwork in fashioning new breeches and a jerkin for Sam from garments that used to be her father's. Baggy, uneven, and with her big stitches showing all too plainly, Sam's garb falls far outside any pretence of fit. But Sam does not seem to notice, and Daniel, apart from a single astonished start at first sight of Sam in his new clothes, says nothing.

That night, searching out one of her father's shirts for more alterations in the chill of the empty main chamber, Alice goes to the foot of the bed where the coffer stands. She heaves up its lid and the hinges creak as she opens it back onto the bed ropes. It needs her taper held close to see what she is doing. She pulls with her free hand at sheets, bolster cases, a coverlet, peering under each for the linen she seeks. But the taper is hampering her and she puts it down to pull two-handed at a coverlet, which comes away suddenly. Underneath, metal clangs against metal. She had forgotten the collection of pewter platters, items from her mother's family. She stops dead, waiting for Sam to cry out or wake with another nightmare – he has had them every night. Seconds pass. She stands holding her breath, straining her ears for the sound of a whimper or cry. As she cocks her head to listen, she sees the reflections of her taper in two of the windowpanes. They are tiny, just pinprick echoes. They twinkle like stars on a frosty night.

Twinkle?

She turns her head to look at the real flame rising oval and still.

18

'Daniel! There's someone out there; I've just seen them!'
        'Outside?'

'More than one. I saw lights! Two lanterns. Come and see.'

Daniel rises from his chair in the kitchen and goes straight for the stout wooden plank by the back door, swiftly slotting it into place to bar against the outside. She looks at him, puzzled, before realising.

'Not directly outside,' she says. 'I mean, down in the village. I saw them from the bedroom window.' He takes up the taper and follows her. As she leads the way up the stairs, she explains, 'They seem to be coming down into the village from Westover, or from the south maybe, I couldn't tell for sure.'

She is already at the top of the stairs and turns, waiting in impatience for him to catch up, anxious that the lights could disappear before he gets to see them. In silence they steal into the large chamber above the front door. She stands by the window looking out as he sits the candle on the night table by the bare bed and comes to her side. They scan the dark.

'There, see? That light there, and another to the left of it.' She points them out but the trees are getting in the way, the lights come and go as they flicker past the bare branches. Even so, in the dark they are clearly visible, the only points of light. 'They're much nearer than they were,' she says. 'They must be almost in the village now. Who would it be, do you think?'

'I see them. And a third there behind. It can't be travellers, not at this time of night.'

With a surge of joy, she says, 'Then it's people coming back home. They'll have to return sometime.'

'No, I think we're still in quarantine.'

'But some left before quarantine, so they wouldn't know that.'

'True. They wouldn't.' Daniel pauses, then, 'Mayhap I should go and find out.'

The nature of his tone forestalls her pleasure. What she has seen as a blessing he views as a threat. 'You think these are not villagers?' she asks.

'Villagers would return by day; no point in wasting lantern light stumbling around at night.'

'Who, then?'

He avoids answering her question. 'Whoever they are, they'll find shelter a-plenty amongst all the empty houses.'

A new thought strikes her and she turns her head to look at his shadowy bulk. 'Daniel, remember what you said when I told you I had been into the village. You said that there could be masterless men on the road. What if these are such? They will have seen this light, as surely as we see theirs. It must be the only one for miles. What if they come up here?'

Against the glow of the taper behind him she sees him shake his head. 'They won't come up tonight. As soon as we take the light back downstairs there'll be nothing to guide them. I'll go down to the village in the morning. I can leave at first light. I must find out who they are. Vagabonds or villagers, we need to know.'

'Take Cassie, she's swift. If they're vagrants you can escape them.'

He laughs softly in the dark. 'I'd sooner take Rowan. I can imagine poor Cassie's legs buckling under my weight!'

19

Daniel draws Rowan to a halt and quietly dismounts well back from the road through the village. On the hard ground, the horse's hooves could betray his approach, so he will walk the rest of the way. He loops the rein over a bough and takes a firm grip on the piece of branch he picked up on the way down. His plan is to make it to the smithy, deal with any violent vagrant there and arm himself properly with an iron bar. Then he can flush out others who might be hiding in the empty houses.

The smithy is quiet and as he approaches he sees the bar is still across the door. Nobody in there then. It is the work of a moment to lift it away, pull open the door and collect a long poker. In the silence he pauses, remembering. All his life he has lived in this village, was apprenticed at the age of eight to the blacksmith here. David had been next door with old Dick wheelwright a year or so by then. He was already an expert in Daniel's young view, the things he knew about felloes and shafts and lathe work. Just looking at the smithy, he sees David. He sighs.

Having closed up again, he steps quietly across the yard and, standing behind a tree trunk, peers cautiously down the village street. What he sees causes him a quiet chuckle at his own precautions. He props the poker against the tree and strides across to the inn, hailing Nick Patten who has just gone inside. The landlord leans out and a smile stretches across his genial round face. 'Dan! Come in, come in. We just got back last night. Come and have a drink.'

20

It is some while later that Daniel is preparing to rise from the settle in the taproom. Margery has joined them by the fire for his news. The landlord's wife is a comely woman of rounded form. It is said that the customers come to the inn as much for sight of her – and her cooking – as for any greeting of the landlord. Of a comfortable middle age, she retains a bustling youthfulness that serves her well in her role as wife, poultrywoman, mother of five and cook to the inn's patrons. Both she and her husband have been sobered by discovering the number of deaths, grateful for their own survival and that of all five children.

'We were with my brother in Honiton all the while,' Margery says, 'but we had to get back.'

'With Christmas coming, you see,' Nick says, 'we had to think of business.'

'Christmas?' In his mind Daniel struggles to deal with the idea of Christmas. Their bustling practicality sits awkwardly with all that he has seen these last weeks.

'Quarantine's over in a couple of days, you see,' Margery adds. 'No need to stay away any longer.'

'There's one or two others already back, I see,' Nick tells him. 'Nat Abbott, Silas and his old lady.' He drains his mug, pressing a hand to his belly straining against the jerkin. The belch rises and gurgles, even so.

'And there's more coming,' his wife says. 'We overtook

a few on foot yesterday who'll most likely arrive sometime today.'

'Jem Thorne we saw too, poor lad, he lost his sister and her girl. But you'd know that, I suppose.' Nick looks closely at Daniel. 'Have you not seen anybody?'

Daniel realises he has given the village little thought, up there at Hill House with Alice and Sam. Sam. 'That reminds me,' he says. 'Alice found a boy in your hayloft.'

'Oh, "Alice", is it?' Margery says. 'How nice.' Daniel wishes she wouldn't put it like that.

'Vagrant I suppose,' Nick says, apparently oblivious. 'Left it in a stinking mess.'

'No, a young boy, not more'n four or five. Half starved, his mother dead. He needed somewhere to hide. He was in your store a few days before she found him.'

'That's who it was! Is the young lad all right?' Margery's motherly instincts leap to the fore.

'He's up at Hill House. Name of Sam. Do you know him?'

The two look at each other, shake their heads.

'Lived in Baker's Row.'

Margery scoffs. 'There you are, then. Fly-by-nights.'

Daniel ploughs on. 'His father came in for a drink, mayhap a couple of days before you left.'

Nick says, 'I remember a melancholy young fellow coming in for small ale. Stranger. He had a few pots and left. Not one for talking. Sat on his own near the door. Next thing, I turned round and he was gone. Never saw him again.'

'Like I said,' Margery says. 'Here today, gone tomorrow.'

Nick turns to her. 'You said you thought you knew him from somewhere.'

'I remembered him, yes,' Margery agrees. 'I'd know that face again. I've seen him around somewhere.'

'Well if you see him again, either of you, let one of us know, will you?'

'Have a word with Parson Rutland,' Nick suggests. 'I see he's back.'

'Is he?' Daniel asks in surprise. 'I didn't know.'

'You've not been down that end of the village at all, Dan?' Nick asks in surprise.

Daniel feels a twinge of sheepish guilt. 'No, I've been helping on the farm at Hill House.'

'Oh, I see. We knew their man Ian was planning to leave,' Nick says. 'Master Edwards must be grateful for your help. No business for you here, I suppose?'

Daniel cannot now avoid telling them of Mistress Edwards' lone state. To his relief, neither asks where he is sleeping and he volunteers nothing. He doesn't want more barbed comments from Margery. 'I'm going back there now.'

'On her own, eh?' Margery says. 'Well, you'll need breakfast before you go. Just give me a few minutes and I'll have something ready.'

'I thank ye, Margery,' he says, 'but Alice is doing breakfast there for me.'

'Breakfast at Hill House, eh? And her on her own.' She glances at Nick and says no more, but in her look, another "How nice" threatens.

'Dan!' Nick breaks in. 'Just thought of something. Margery's brother in Honiton. Owns as sweet a set of fire irons as you could wish for. If I describe them, can you make some for me?'

21

'Well?' she says, bursting from the house as he leads the horse into the stables. 'You're all right. They didn't hurt you."

He laughs and turns to her. 'No, they didn't hurt me. Gave me a mug of ale actually, and Margery offered me breakfast if I'd wait, but I said I had breakfast waiting me here.'

She draws a sigh of relief. He realises her eyes are watering, hears the unsteady laugh at her own night-fears. 'So the Pattens are back at the inn? Already?'

'And all the family. Twas their lights we saw.'

'They are well, and the children?'

'All five hale and hearty and not a trace of fever throughout.'

'Thank goodness! So ... no masterless men?'

'Not unless you count Bart Johnson. I saw him at the far end of the village.' Bart is well known locally for an idle fellow. 'Don't worry, Alice. No vagabonds, no vagrants. Sam is safe. Where is he, by the way?'

'In the winter parlour. I lit the fire and he's playing with those wooden figures you whittled for him. Will you come and have breakfast?'

'Gladly, soon as I've seen to Rowan,' he says and heaves off the saddle to rest it on the bench by the stall. 'And Margery says quarantine finishes day after tomorrow, she kept count.' He takes a wisp of straw and begins to work over Rowan's flank.

'Where will you be today?'

'I must go back to the smithy. I'm fashioning Nick a set of fire irons. I'll be back this evening. What of yourself?'

'I must collect the windfalls and preserve them today. I've left it overlong as it is. And the medlars and quinces still on the tree. But do give Margery my best, and all the family, and I will call on her as soon as I can. And to save her the trouble, tell her I will do some extra bread and go and see if there are any in need.'

'You'll need water for your preserving. I'll draw you a bucket or two afore I go. Oh, and another piece of news,' he adds. 'Parson Rutland is returned, got back yesterday he tells me. I've just seen him on my way up. He sends his greetings.'

'Is he well? What happened to delay him?'

'He's well enough. They had the pestilence in Bristol and he was quarantined when he arrived. They're hot about the Orders there. Had a bad time of it years ago, he says, and learned the lesson.'

'How did he take the Hillbury news?'

'He's a very unhappy man, Alice. Found it hard to believe we've lost so many, and he not here the whiles. He's going to bless the graves we made, and he wants to go up to Woodley, and see for himself how they are at Westover. He asks you to bear with him and he'll call by in the next day or two.'

A guilty look passes over her face. 'I never thought to ask about Woodley. How did they fare?'

'Quite bad at first but then it went away, from what I heard, so in the end their losses were much less than here. Westover came off best, I think.'

'Abel Nutley told me they weren't even being quarantined.'

'That's right. So we couldn't go over there to see how they fared. We'd have heard for sure if they'd had the plague.'

'Poor Vicar Rutland; he went to get help and came back to all this.'

'He would tell you that the Lord giveth and the Lord taketh away, Alice.'

He is surprised by the unaccustomed tartness in her reply. 'The Lord seems to have taken away rather more than his fair share from Hillbury!'

22

Later that afternoon, Daniel catches sight of the Pattens' eldest boy rolling a small-ale barrel into the taproom. 'Ah, John. Your Da back there, is he?

'He went out, Dan,' the lad says and hoists the barrel into position lying on its side on a trestle. He nudges it until the bung on the end plate is at its lowest point, ready to dispense. 'Ma's in, I'll get her.'

'No, don't do that—' But John is already calling for Margery.

Reluctantly, Daniel goes over to the fireplace to wait, and stands warming his back. Nick always keeps a good blaze, even with nobody in the taproom. It helps warm the whole place, he says.

A quick footstep in the passage and a smiling Margery hastens into the taproom.

'Dan! Give ye good day again.' She stands on tiptoe and kisses his cheek as always when not in company. Daniel shuffles and gives her a brief smile. She goes over to the corner cupboard and takes out a fine pewter mug.

'Nick's gone over to Woodley to see the maltster there,' she says, turning to the barrels. 'He's going to ask him to deal with the grain until we have someone to malt it in place of Josh Baker. He was a good neighbour, was Josh, we shall miss him. Don't know who'll bake for the village when they all return.'

She comes back to Daniel and hands him the full tankard. 'Nick's best, that. No, no, nothing to pay, Dan,' as Daniel reaches into his pocket. 'Sit you down; take that cushion there. Fanny's watching the kitchen the whiles, so we can be comfortable for a bit.'

She steps onto the hearthstone, steadying herself with one hand on his shoulder, while she reaches up to the shelf above and brings down a jar.

'There, make yourself a pipe. Nick won't be long.'

'Thankye, Margery, but I'll not start a pipe right now.' Daniel holds up the tankard. 'This'll be fine.' He frowns and looks closer at the pewter. 'Have I seen this before? Fine workmanship.'

'No, you won't have done, it's a new set.' She stretches over him to put back the tobacco jar. 'We got them a short while ago. They're for our special customers.'

Her voice is warm, caressing. He holds up the new-forged poker between them. 'I came to bring this,' he says.

'That was quick. Let's see it, then.' As she takes the poker from him, her fingers lightly brush his hand.

'It's what Nick ordered. I've added a hook at the top there to hang it. Oh, and' – reaching into his pocket again – 'a nail to hang it on.'

Margery sits down beside him, turning the implement over in her hands. ''Tis rarely handsome, Dan. You've made a fine job of it,' she says, 'as you do all things.'

As she turns towards him her knee touches his thigh. Daniel leans away into the corner of the settle. 'Well, I should be—' he starts to say.

'Nick will be mighty pleased.' Margery continues to commend it, tilting it this way and that. 'I'd say 'tis much finer than my brother's.'

'If he approves it, I'll make up the ash scraper and the log roller likewise. That was all I came in for,' Daniel says. 'So I'll be on my way.' He rises.

Margery lays a hand on his sleeve. 'Oh, you've not finished your drink, Dan. Do not run away afore your mug's empty. I wanted to talk to you anyway.'

Daniel sits down again and Margery jumps up, leans across him to reach for a log. Lightly he puts a staying hand on her shoulder and she twists her head round, her face inches from his. Margery's eyes are bright under enquiring brows, a smile plays at the corner of her mouth.

'Sit ye, Margery,' Daniel says. 'I will put a log on, if that's what you want.' He selects a split piece of branch and drops it on the flames. 'So what was it you wanted to talk about?' Sparks crackle up the chimney.

'Talk about?'

Daniel leans back in the settle and folds his arms, waiting.

Margery thinks a moment, then, 'Ah, yes. Do you think John our eldest would make a baker in Josh's place?'

'John? I really know not, Margery. Why do you ask me?'

'I thought he might have talked with you, respecting you as he does.'

'I only saw him for a few … Does he?'

'We all do, Dan. Surely you know that?'

'I did not, but thankye, Margery.'

'So, has he said anything?'

'Your John?'

'Yes.'

'No.'

'No?'

'Not to me. I always thought he would do the brewing or have his own malting floor, mayhap. But I did not think he showed any great interest in baking. You'd have to apprentice him, of course. Why not ask him?'

She briefly squeezes his arm. 'That's a very good idea. How clever you are, Dan. I shall do so. 'Twould be a blessing for all if he would take it on for the nonce.'

'Well, Margery,' Daniel drains his tankard. 'I believe I really must go back now.'

'Why not stay till Nick gets back? There's nothing else doing and you could have your supper here, Dan?' She looks up at him through her lashes. ''Tis jacket of brawn and a spiced custard to follow. What say you?'

'That's kind, Margery, and tempting too, but Mistress Edwards cooks supper for me at Hill House, you see.' He has taken to calling Alice this, since this morning. He stands up.

'At Hill House? So you have your suppers at Hill House now as well? 'Tis a longish walk, only to come back after.'

'I don't come back.'

'Don't you sleep at the smithy?'

'Not at present, Margery. You see, I'm helping Mistress Edwards on the farm. I told you, she's on her own now. She has a snug hayloft there, so it saves me the walk to and fro each day. Oh, and she sends her best and says she will call on you as soon as she can. And I'm to say she's doing extra bread.'

'Kind in her, I'm sure,' she says. 'There now, you'd have thought she'd have found the time to come and see old friends while there can't be much doing up there. You've made the time.'

'I wasn't sure who was in the village when I came down earlier, Margery. Could have been anybody. Anyway, I think she's got preserving of all sorts to do today.'

'Has she? Of course she had Mary and Henrietta to do her fetching and carrying before. So she's roped you in for the donkeywork, has she?'

'It's only what her father and Ian did before. It's a lot for one man, let alone one woman.'

'Well then, she'll have to find a man or two to take your place, won't she? And a maidservant as a companion to keep things proper.'

'I suppose so. I'd not thought much about it,' Daniel says. 'And not many labouring folk around at present.'

'Now they're returning, she must let them know she is in need,' Margery says, in practical vein. 'The likes of Dick Winter will do. John said he saw him earlier.'

'I wouldn't wish Dick Winter on anybody,' Daniel says with feeling. 'An idle shirker, if ever there was.'

Margery purses her lips. 'She'll have to take what she can get,' she declares. 'Too many others have been lost. You'll be needed here in the village, Dan. She can't hang on your coat forever.'

23

'Samuel is looking for Zachariah,' Sam informs Alice as she puts her head round the door to the winter parlour.

He holds up the two figures Daniel has whittled for him out of pieces of wood. They have names already. 'Samuel is riding on his horse' – a bent faggot taken from the wood-basket – 'and he's looking for Zachariah in the forest.' He places one of the figures somewhat precariously astride the faggot and puts both under the chair. 'When's Daniel coming back?'

'He'll be at the forge for the rest of the day,' Alice tells him. 'He doesn't expect to be back until it's dark.'

'I want to show him Samuel on his horse,' Sam says. He sounds aggrieved, and she thinks, it would be different if there were other children, you would be running around outside with them.

'I need to pick the windfall quinces,' she replies.

Sam gets up and trots after her. 'Can we roll down the hill?'

Alice smiles, remembering her own frustrated wish as she watched Daniel and Sam. 'I'd look very strange rolling down the hill.'

'Why?'

'My skirt would fly up over my head!'

Sam dances about in his four-year-old's glee. 'You'd look

really funny, Alice.'

I can think of another word for it, she thinks. 'I know a fine game,' she says. 'But I must pick the quinces first.'

He follows her out to the quince tree outside the winter parlour on the sunny side of the house. Most of its fruit is now windfall and some has already been pecked by birds seeking winter nourishment. Even at this late end of the year, the hard, knobbly yellow fruit has a slight perfume that rises to fill the air as they collect. It takes them a matter of minutes to garner each basketful of usable fruit, which she takes into the kitchen. There she empties them into the wooden tub, a cut-down barrel, which she has already lugged out ready for use. Sam's enthusiasm to get the collecting done deprives his pickings of any discrimination, but she can easily weed out the rotten and the slug-eaten as she goes along. Sam hangs around for a while, watching her rinse the first batch of fruit, and plays hopscotch on the floor flags while she cuts the fruit into chunks and drops them into the large pot of water over the fire for the slow simmering that will follow. Every now and then he asks if they are going to play a game. Eventually she swings the pot on its chimney hook to hang above the flame, wipes the table clear and adds brands to the fire. 'We can leave the quinces now, they'll take a long time to soften,' she says, holding out her hand to him. 'Now, come into the barn with me.'

Sam follows her out of the kitchen. The barn stands facing the stables on the opposite side of the yard. She pulls open one of the doors and in the dimness shows Sam a large stack of straw piled all along one side against the long wall, several feet deep and stretching half-way across the barn. The crisp, dry smell is strong in the enclosed space. Above the straw is an open hayloft set in the roof space of the barn. Its floor is a couple of feet above head height. A wooden ladder leans against its edge and hay is stored thick under the pitched roof. That is where Daniel has chosen his bed in the grass-scented warmth.

Alice points to the stack of straw at their level. 'See, Sam? We can run from here and jump into the straw.'

Sam's face holds the sceptical look of one being offered short commons.

'Like this,' Alice says and runs across the barn floor, launching herself at the pile. She lands, sinking into it and sliding down to rest at the bottom of the stack. Straw glides through the air and spreads around the barn floor. 'See?'

She gets up, bits hanging from her chemise and sticking to the thick, felted fabric of her working skirt. A few are caught in the wisps of hair that always escape from under her cap. As she pauses to pick slivers of straw from her sleeve, Sam powers his small body forwards and flies head first into the rustling mass, sending out a shower of gold. His legs kick and he emerges, shaking his head clear of straw and laughing at the pleasurable sensation. 'Again!' he cries, and races back to the barn door for his next run. Alice runs with him and they land together, rolling over and giggling at each other's straw-covered clothes. Over and over they dive and retreat, shaking off the chill of the day in the vigour of the game.

Then Sam has an idea. 'I know,' he cries, 'let's go up the ladder and jump from there. I climbed the ladder with Daniel,' he adds, when Alice hesitates. Surely no harm in it, she thinks, it's only a few feet above the straw pile. As long as they jump on that side of the barn, they will have a soft landing. She did it many a time herself as a child. She guides him ahead of her up the ladder and stands for a moment, looking at the flattened hay in the corner, considering what it must be like for Daniel coming here to sleep each night. Hay is warm, of course, and he has his blankets. And he was right, he cannot sleep in the house.

While she is thinking this, Sam has rushed ahead. He is laughing delightedly, 'Look, Alice!'

She turns, he is right on the edge, knees bent ready, and she calls out in quick alarm, 'Sam, wait—'

But he has launched himself over the edge, arms and legs all haywire. There is a rustling thump. That is all. An age seems to pass while she stands rooted. Time and to spare for guilt, dread, remorse to rise up in the silence. Alice steps quickly to the edge and looks down. Sam is lying stock-still on his back in the straw. He grins up at her. 'Fooled you, fooled you!' and kicks and laughs in triumph. 'You thought I was dead!'

Momentary unreasoning anger. She wants to shout at him, tell him how close he came to that state he now laughs about so easily. But it is merely a childish conceit, he has no thought of what he is saying. Her ghosts are her own and must stay that way.

'What a rascal you are!' she says. 'You gave me such a fright. Now, move aside, I'm coming down.' She launches herself off the edge and lands up to her knees in straw. Well, they are here now, an afternoon's merrymaking and a feast of laughing such as usually only Christmas celebrations allow.

Round and round they race, up and jumping and landing and climbing back up again, egging each other on and making longer and wilder jumps. Legs flashing, Sam's oversized shirt ballooning, Alice's skirts flying, time and again they land in shrieking disorderly heaps on the straw now filling the air with yellow chaff, the wisps floating to rest in an ever-widening spread across the floor.

As far as the door, suddenly jerked open, from where a

cold enquiry slices through their pleasure.

'Is this the way callers are greeted in this household?'

Sam stands up, straw-bedecked and staring. Alice has just slid off the straw heap to floor level, skirt round her thighs, kinked hair loosely matted over her face, linen coif long since discarded. Annoyed with herself for feeling flustered, she too stands up, pushes back her hair, shakes out the straw.

Standing in the doorway is a man, arms crossed, a heavy travelling cloak draped on one shoulder. Even without the high-crowned hat he is tall.

'I hate to disrupt these frolics but perhaps when you have the inclination you might fetch Master Edwards.' His contempt stings as much as her own discomfiture.

Walking towards him, she asks, 'Who wishes to speak with him?'

Against the winter light outside, his face is obscured.

'Jerrard, of High Stoke by Guildford,' he announces. The name, the place, recall nothing to her, and she regards him, wondering if she should know.

He stands head and shoulders taller than her, like Daniel, and is probably only a year or so younger than Daniel as well, but there the similarity between the two men ends. From fine lawn collar to waist, pearl buttons glimmer down the front of his doublet. Plain hose of fine wool skim narrow hips, finishing mid-calf. His boots and the hem of his cloak show the muddy signs of travel.

As she stops in front of him, he says, 'And you might hasten yourself, girl! It's a chill day to keep a caller waiting.' He leans against the doorframe, crosses one long leg lightly over the other. 'The master?'

'Indeed, you shall not see the master any sooner, no matter how I hasten,' she says. Close up now, she sees a frown of irritation gather, narrowing his eyes. She goes on, 'You may speak with me instead, sir.'

He looks her up and down. 'In that seam-rent rug-gown?'

'I crave pardon. Perhaps you expected wired hair and strings of pearls?'

'I expected civility and deference, not this bottle of hay I see before me.'

Alice's resentment smoulders. 'My name, if you care to hear me, sir, is—'

'I care nothing for your name. It is your master I wish to see. Since he is evidently from home I shall return tomorrow. Meantime I've no interest in one who apes her mistress' ways.' He strides towards his elegant grey mount standing quietly at the corner of the barn.

'Nor I in a swaggering nupson – neither well-spleened nor well-spoken!'

He turns, rein in hand.

She knows she has overstepped the bounds, but the idea that she would 'ape' anyone has roused a devil in her. '*Dux femina facti!*' she calls after him. 'And in case your Latin is as rusty as your manners – *sir* – that means a woman leads the endeavour you see here. You *were* talking with Alice Edwards, daughter of James and Ann, lately dead. Do not trouble yourself to call tomorrow, I have no business with one of your address. Come, Sam.'

In the silence as he stares dropped-jaw, she swings away and stalks to the house. Casting wary glances behind him, Sam dashes after her across the yard and into the kitchen. She shuts the door with a snap and stands for some seconds clenching and unclenching her fists, before a little explosion of mirth, as quickly stifled. *Oh goodness, Alice Edwards, the first visitor in weeks and you forget yourself in spectacular fashion!*

'What's funny, Alice?' Sam stands guardedly a few paces away. Her heart still hammering from the encounter, Alice sees the worried frown, the anxious eyes. Another bubble of laugher escapes and she goes over to him. 'Dear Sam.' Kneeling on the flags she puts her arms round him. How to explain the fierce spark of malicious pleasure at having silenced the man? All those hours of laboured conjugation coming to her aid with that timely phrase of Virgil.

'I hate him,' says Sam in a succinct blend of loyalty to Alice and apprehension of the stranger.

'What excellent taste you have.' She kisses him and stands. 'So let us forget him and go back to the quinces.' The spoon rests on a plate on the table where she left it. As she picks it up, the door opens and Jerrard stands there.

'Mistress Edwards,' he says, and holds up his hands as she turns on him in hostile displeasure. 'I am sorry, I thought you were a servant.'

Sam places himself four-square in front of her, the top of his head almost reaching her waist. 'You were nasty to Alice.'

'Hush, Sam,' Alice rests her hand gently on his shoulder and in a cold voice she answers Jerrard, 'Sir, if you think you have licence to address a servant in such fashion, you certainly have no business here.'

'What I meant—'

She turns her back on him and draws the spoon through the bubbling quinces.

'I met your father in London.'

She stops stirring.

'I should have realised his daughter would be one of like mind. I can offer no excuse for acting like a lobcock.'

Reluctantly, she turns round. 'If I accept your apology, we are back where we started. Do you tell me your business and you will be free to leave the sooner.' She watches the icy east wind stir the hem of his cloak. Even here by the fire its chill swirls around her ankles. It will do him no harm to stand there a little longer.

'My business, as you call it, originated with your father and was but a courtesy call in passing through. I am much grieved you say both he and your mother are dead.' He thought for a few seconds. 'It cannot be more than, what, eight or nine months ago that I met your father.'

'I should tell you, Master Jerrard, we have lately been visited by the pestilence, in case that has some bearing on your wish to visit."

"Oh. I'm sorry," he says, clearly at a loss.

"And the whole village is no more than a shell. We do not know how many lost their lives but it's well nigh all who did not escape in time. Apart from a few who have since returned, the houses have only ghosts for inhabitants.'

His face registers shock, as she intended. It is rare, from all she has heard, that a plague takes a whole village. Then, 'We heard that some of the northern cities had suffered, and London had it in the summer of course, Oxford also to some degree, after His Majesty moved the Court up there. But I was not aware it had come this far west. They don't have it in Sturminster, where I lay last night.'

'We believe it was brought here by a lone traveller,' she says, remembering the poor disfigured corpse, 'and affected only us here in Hillbury, and Woodley to the north.'

'I was passing this way on my own affairs,' he goes on. 'I planned to stay a night locally and renew my acquaintance.' He considers for a moment. 'The plague was here *lately* you said. Are you still quarantined?'

She shakes her head. 'By rights we are still in quarantine

another two days,' she explains, 'but there have been no new cases for over a week.' She cannot keep the bitterness from her voice as she adds, 'There have been no people to become infected.'

He nods his understanding and that seems to be the end of the conversation. He pulls his cloak closer round his shoulders as he says, 'Mistress Edwards, I greatly regret having intruded upon you. If you will kindly direct me to a good inn, or an alehouse with bedchambers, I will be on my way.'

She looks at him afresh. This is a man who is simply cold and irritable after a long while in the saddle. He has ridden out of his way to pay his respects to her father. It is likely he knocked in vain at the front door and then came round to the back to find, as he thought, servants cavorting. Perhaps he can be forgiven his sharpness, his incivility.

She weighs and summarily dispatches considerations of single women and unknown male company. Not so unknown if he knew her father. 'You'd better come in, sir. It's not often we have visitors from outside this area.' Nor is she ready to sacrifice the added pleasure of having news to tell Daniel when he returns from the forge. 'I can direct you to an inn,' she goes on, 'but first let me offer you refreshment. Do you take your horse into the stable. You will find blankets and hay there for his comfort, and water in the trough.'

He looks grateful but hesitant and she goes on, 'I should like to talk with someone who knew my father, though it was only a short acquaintance.' She shivers. 'And it's a raw day and we shall all of us expire of the draught if you stand in the doorway much longer.'

The grey horse by the barn is every bit as graceful as she would expect of this elegant traveller. While he tends his mount, she uses the time to grab a fresh coif, pulling it hurriedly over her obstinate curls. By the time he returns, she is checking the quinces simmering lightly over the fire, pressing them with the back of the wooden spoon. They are still quite hard; it will be a while yet before they are soft enough to be mashed into a pulp and sieved of their pips and skins.

Jerrard steps into the kitchen, closing the door behind him.

'Tell me,' she says, 'how did you meet my father?' She shakes the droplets off the spoon and rests it back on the plate.

'I was in London with company and your father came to our aid when we needed rooms.'

'He went up for King James's funeral,' she recalls. 'That was – let me think – May?' She indicates that he should take the settle by the fire and lifts two ale mugs from the shelf. 'He told us he had shared his room with others.'

She recalls her father returning in high humour, his talk of the 'interesting company' he had fallen in with on his London visit. She bends to the barrel.

Jerrard undoes the ties of his cloak and tosses it over the back of the settle, adding his gauntlets on top, before sitting down and stretching grateful hands to the flames. He keeps his hat on, she would hardly expect a gentleman to do otherwise. Bringing back the full tankard, she reaches for the poker resting in the hot coals and plunges it for a few seconds into the liquid, which hisses and bubbles, and spatters droplets onto the hearth. As soon as she hands him the warm mug he wraps his fingers round it, and she feels a pang of shame for her hostile treatment of him. His face is kinder than she had thought. The weariness of long journeying shows in the shadows under his eyes, the lines around his mouth. He takes a long draught.

'An excellent brew,' he says, savouring it. 'Was it your mother who had the fine hand with the malt?'

'No, sir. In late years I have run the household, including our still room. My mother ever preferred her frame and needle.' Alice, filling herself the smaller mug, heats the ale likewise. She beckons to Sam who all the while has stood silent by the table, moving only to keep it between himself and the stranger. Sam approaches and takes a few sips, then whispers in Alice's ear. She nods and he leaves the kitchen to go back to the whittled Samuel on his faggot horse, seeking Zachariah lost in the forest. She sits down at the table and regards her guest stretching out his long legs in front of the blaze. What a long time it has been since this house has seen a visitor under its roof. In former times, of course, it would have been her father bringing a guest. She would simply have served them ale, occasionally venturing into the conversation if her father was in mellow humour. But this guest is now hers. She feels a sense of pride in her ability to offer hospitality. Her earlier anger quite forgotten, she settles down to enjoy the company of this man.

'Tell me of my father in London,' she asks him. 'He always found the place very noisy and crowded and he hated the stink of it. He said you cannot get away from it, no matter where you go.'

Jerrard smiles. 'Yes, that's something you get used to after a few days; then you hardly notice it.'

'I made him a pomander, but I think he did not like to carry it in company when other men do not use them. Apparently, they're no longer the fashion in London, but he was glad of it by his pillow to help him sleep.'

'I suppose we were not long enough there for your father

to accustom himself. Egerton visits often and is used to it, but Tillotson shared your father's disgust – Egerton and Tillotson were my companions,' he explains. 'We met your father by pure chance. London was bursting with people, all there to see the great sight of King James' funeral. We had taken rooms but the scaly landlord let them to another party who I swear offered him a bribe. We came back from a visit around the sights to find our boxes in the inn-yard and Tillotson's man all in a fluster. While we were remonstrating with the landlord, your father came out of the inn and suggested we share his room, because it was the largest in the house.

'That would be my father,' says Alice, amused. 'He hated poky rooms. He liked light and space as he was used to here.'

'Then I fear in the end he had the worst of the deal.' Jerrard smiles. 'With four of us in the room we were climbing over each other to get to our mattresses. But it was mighty civil of him and saved us a wasted journey and much disappointment.'

'Perhaps he felt that by increasing the landlord's income for the room, he was less likely to find himself also ejected.'

'There was much of the same at many of the inns, we found out afterwards.' Jerrard takes a pull of his ale. 'Those two days were excellent business for all of London. And a fine sight we were rewarded with. I have never seen the like of such a procession.' His eyes glow, remembering. 'Not often we get to see such a display, such finery as you would hardly see at a coronation. Such colour and pomp, and the great bier all decorated and hung with rich silks. I was a mere boy when I went to Queen Bess's funeral, and I swear that was never as fine as this.'

'And a king's ransom to pay for it all. For one man.'

Jerrard looks at her but says nothing.

'I enjoy a great sight as much as the next person,' she goes on, 'but with a coronation coming anyway, surely it were better not to spend such a sum on a funeral. Fifty thousand pounds – that's what they say, did you know that? Such a sum would surely have paid a year's wages for every working man, woman and child in London.'

'It's true that His Majesty was more open-handed within his own circle.'

'While the poor of this country have multiplied marvellously in my lifetime. Look, we have the Poor House at Westover that we all have to pay for. And there are so many in need, there's talk now of another at Woodley. I think my father went to the funeral as much to thank God for James's departure as to see the sight!'

Jerrard gives a shout of laughter. 'I had little enough time for James Stuart too. I drink to his son's better tenure of the throne.' Raising his tankard and taking another draught. 'A good thing I am not a justice though, mistress. Do you always air your beliefs so freely?' He leans back, smiling at her.

She had better be careful. He might be the sort of man who would privately approve of Abel Nutley's aptitude for fault-finding. More, he might inform on her. She lowers her eyes and folds her hands in her lap. 'Forgive me, sir, if I forgot for a moment my parents' guiding principles of modesty.'

What arrant nonsense I'm speaking!

'Your parents were of the puritan persuasion, were they, madam?' He sounds disappointed.

'Heavens, no!' Alice says, startled out of her brief pretence at piety.

'Thank the Lord for that!' he says. 'Come, tell me more of James Stuart and his perfidious ways. That will be a deal more pleasurable than a lecture on gravity and sobriety. This young

Charles, I don't know how he will make out. I cannot help feeling, had his elder brother lived he would have been more enthusiastic for the throne.'

'We must give him time; it's not yet a year. But I dearly hope he will do something for the very poor. And it's high time the Plague Orders were reviewed. They are inhumane, the way they lock up sick and well together.'

'You feel strongly on the subject,' he says.

She almost says, Oh, you noticed? but checks herself. Strangers as they are, mockery has so far caused only friction and high words. 'Sir, I am one of three survivors from a whole village. Not half a mile from here are row upon row of new graves. We do not know yet how many of those who took flight will return. And that is just one village. Our vicar went to beg help of the Bishop at Bristol, and by mischance they too had the plague. Instead of being here where his calling dictates, he was quarantined there, a virtual prisoner throughout.'

'No minister at the burials?' He makes a silent whistle.

'Not even a sexton. When I think of the show of a King's funeral while ordinary folk like us had to say our farewells privately because a Plague Order kept us all locked up in our homes, I can't ...' She stops.

Jerrard says nothing. She adds in a quieter tone, 'Good people, most of them, Master Jerrard, only asking to live ordinary lives. And that is their reward. People died here in droves. You cannot imagine—'

For a few seconds words will not come. *You cannot imagine the absence, the silence, the fury.*

'And where was the money that would have helped our apothecary here?' she demands. The rage that has built silently inside her, the long-stifled resentments, are suddenly gushing out in a flood of words to this man she doesn't even know.

121

'He wanted to build a pest-house, as they have in Padua, to separate sick from hale. We know where that money went, don't we?'

She plants the flat of her hand on the table. 'One man, fifty thousand pounds! What a mighty king he must have been, Master Jerrard, to be worth all those deaths!' Alice sits back, recalling herself.

'I am sorry,' she adds. 'Sometimes my tongue truly does run away with me.'

'On the contrary,' he answers. 'It was refreshing to hear.' In the silence that ensues, he looks around and indicates out of the window. 'So, you direct this place alone? Your brother is lucky to have a sister so devoted to his property.'

'My brother, sir?'

'The young lad. Is he not your brother? Does he not inherit?'

'Oh, Sam!' She shakes her head. 'Sam is an orphan. I found him starving in the village when everyone had left. His parents were poor people who rented a cottage here shortly before the plague came. His mother died and we do not know what became of his father.'

'Not amongst the dead?'

'No, or at least not here. He might come back, perhaps.'

'If his father does not return, you will put the boy in the Poor House.'

'Never!' At the suggestion of an instruction Alice is more strident than she means to be. Immediately, she relents. 'I mean, I could not do that. Life there is such unending punishment and it's not his fault he is an orphan.'

'Well, what about the landlord who rented out the hovel?'

'He's dead. Of the plague.'

'Then you have a nameless orphan on your hands, mistress.

If he's not to go to the Poor House, you'll have to beg him, you know.'

'Beg him?'

'Appeal to a justice to make him your ward – what else do you intend but adoption?' He drains his tankard and sets it down. 'I wish you success, mistress. I think I have kept you long enough and pray you will excuse me now, I need to find an inn for the night. Where would you suggest I try?' He reaches for his cloak as he speaks and swings it round his shoulders.

'Go into the village, sir,' Alice advises. 'Your shortest route is the track that leads down past the barn and that belt of trees.'

She points the direction through the window. 'Master Patten the innkeeper has just returned. I'm sure he will be able to accommodate you. It's warm, it's clean, and there's no plague. And Mistress Patten's cooking is a local legend. If not there, perhaps the sign of the Swan at Westover, they were never quarantined, I hear.' She follows him to the door as he ties the strings of his cloak.

'Perhaps we shall meet again,' he says, 'when I return this way in due course.'

She hears only polite vagueness in his words and answers in kind as she reaches for the latch to open the door. 'Perhaps so, sir.'

He sweeps her a brief bow before turning to go. With long strides, he reaches the stable and a few seconds later emerges leading the grey to a stand. Lightly he vaults into the saddle and looks round, his hand half-raised for a parting wave, then sees the closed door.

Standing well back in the gloom of the kitchen she watches through the window as he checks his sword in its sheath, buckled close under his pack, and turns the horse's head towards the track beyond the barn.

Dick Winter crouches on the doorstone, knees drawn up, and picks aimlessly at the scab on his shin. Ever since Alice Edwards dressed it for him back in the summer he has repeatedly watched the ulcer scab over and is unable to resist the temptation to pick away at its edges. Time and again it bleeds afresh and forms a new scab, which comes yet again under his scrutiny. Now once more the edge is loose and keeps catching on his probing fingertip, but the rest is not yet ready to come off. Still, it's annoying, having that hard bit loose, neither on nor off. He brings up his other hand and tries to squeeze a bit at the edge between dirty fingernails.

'What I say is,' he says to his three companions, 'where's the outdoor relief?'

'What outdoor relief?' Oswald Thatcher, newcomer to the group, leans against the house wall on Baker's Row. 'Why would they pay us outdoor relief?'

Jem Thorne, younger by a couple of years than the others, strokes his chin where his beard might be, had it yet grown more than a few pale wisps. He has seen his friend Bart do this. Secretly, he admires Bart. He props himself against the wall three paces away and looks hopefully at Dick. 'Are we getting outdoor relief then?'

'We should be.' Still worrying at his scab, Dick does not look up. 'We gave our all. Tisn't right.'

'Gave your all?' Oswald frowns in puzzlement.

'You weren't there to see it, my son.' Bart Johnson, the fourth member of the group, kicks stones along the gritty track. 'It was us kept the street fires going. Watched night and day we did.' He passes a stone from one foot to the other and back. Bart fancies his talents, thinks he would make a good tumbler. 'Wore ourselves out in the service of our neighbours.'

'And kept warm and watered while you did it, as I heard,' Oswald mutters to himself.

'Wassat, Oz?' Dick asks.

'Nothing.'

''Tis as Bart says. We did all that till we were forced to flee for our lives. And what thanks did we get? A big round nothing!'

'It were surely nice and warm round the fires,' says Jem, remembering.

'Small reward for all our vigi … vigi … hard work,' Dick says glumly. 'Fetching and heaving and running to and fro to keep an eye—'

'You didn't do nothing, Dick Winter,' Bart retorts, hooking out a pebble from where it has lodged under the doorstone, and dribbling it from foot to foot along the track. 'Any running to be done, I did it,' he calls over his shoulder.

'Didn't say you didn't.'

Bart returns with the pebble and Jem puts his foot out to tackle. He misses and Bart laughs. 'And Jem here, he did all the fetching of logs, and all the heaving onto the fires.'

Dick looks up grinning. 'Yeah, *all* the fetching and *all* the heaving.' Dick and Bart look at Jem and laugh.

Jem adds, 'And I went and got the sulphur and put that on the fires too, didn't I, Bart?'

'That's right, Jem.' And the two laugh again.

Oswald brings them back to the point. 'So what about

this outdoor relief then, Dick?'

Dick's grin vanishes. 'I dunno. I've been asking Nutley. He acts for the justices, he should know.'

Bart makes a face. 'He won't tell you a thing. Tighter than a bee's arse is Abe Nutley.'

'He says there's no money to hand out.'

'So why don't you just forget it?' Oswald says.

'But it stands to reason,' Dick insists. 'Damn!' he adds, as a small chip of scab comes off without the rest. 'It stands to reason. After we went away there was nobody here to give outdoor relief to, so there must be pots of it saved up, so why can't we have it?'

'Outdoor relief's for the homeless Dick! People who live out of doors,' Oswald says.

'Exactly. We were out of doors for days on end, looking after the fires and they didn't give us anything for all that out-of-doors time.'

'It's true, what he says,' Bart assures Oswald.

'More than a week,' Dick goes on.

'Eight days.' Jem says. 'My Ma said we did eight days on the fires. All the days except two in the middle when Nick Patten's boys pushed in first.'

'There you are then. Eight days is more'n a week, and then there's the two days when we were avail ... avail ... ready to work if needed.'

'Yes,' agrees Jem. 'We waited in Nick Patten's place in case we were needed.'

'So eight and two is' – Dick stops picking at his scab to hold up his fingers – 'ten. That's two weeks, near enough, so please you, Master High and Mighty Nutley! Two weeks at fourpence ha'penny a week is ... is ... two lots of fourpence ha'penny,' he finishes. 'Each!'

Oswald scoffs. 'That's not much anyway.'

'It's a deal of drinking money,' Bart muses. He sits down at the other end of the doorstone from Dick. 'Where are we going to get it then?' The two look at each other.

Dick grins. 'Can't ask Rosemary Miller now.' He sniggers.

'Or Goody Hamlyn,' adds Bart. They each put their palms together, gazing heavenwards, and guffaw.

Jem brightens. 'Margery Patten helps the poor. Why don't we ask her?'

Dick rolls his eyes. Oswald shakes his head and smiles. Bart turns to Jem. 'You ask her, then, Jem. How about it?'

'Me!' Jem's eyes dart between his friends. 'Well no, I don't – I mean – it's just – she terrifies me!'

Bart turns back to Dick. 'I do hear the widow Cazanove may be open to help a poor man in need.'

'Mistress Starch?' Dick pooh-poohs. 'Who says?'

'Word is.' Bart is not giving away his sources.

'She's never helped any in Hillbury afore. She don't even live in Hillbury, she's Westover.'

'Uh, uh. Cazanove's place is, strictly speaking, in Hillbury. So Mistress Cazanove is a resident of this parish and therefore …' He pauses, looking significantly at Dick.

'… obliged to pay poor relief for Hillbury.' Dick's eyes glow. Then he frowns. 'But it's like I say, she's never helped us before.'

'Her old man was alive then. Rich as Solomon and mean as he could hang together.'

'Think we can go and touch her for it, do you?'

'Got to be worth a try. Soon as she's back.'

'But,' Dick reasons, 'if she's never helped before, stands to reason she's as mean as him.'

'Not if she's atoning.'

'What's that?' Jem asks.

'What?'

'What's a "Toning"?'

The others ignore him.

'Atoning for what?' Dick asks.

'For him being dead. You know, sudden death, wrath of the Lord and all that.'

'I heard it was plague like all the rest.'

'Ah, yes. But what if we were to suggest that a bit more atonement on her part,' Bart rubs a thumb and fingers together, 'might help the wheels of the Lord's bread-cart run a little smoother?'

'Cart?' Jem gasps. 'You're not going to run her over?'

'Shut up!' Dick and Bart say together.

'What d'you think then, Dick?'

Dick claps his friend on the shoulder. 'Bart, my old friend, I think we should pay Mistress Cazanove a visit. After all,' and he takes hold of the loosened end of scab, grits his teeth and pulls sharply. 'I am a poor man with an open wound, in need of succ … succ … '

'Help – yeah, right,' says Bart.

25

Alice walks back from Vicar Rutland's house deep in thought. She has asked his advice and he has given it, honestly and openly as is his way. Unfortunately it is not what she hoped for, but what did she hope for?

And she has seen David Bunting's list of Hillbury's dead. The Vicar has added the names to the parish register. He has finished off with more names from Daniel's recollections, Daniel having no writing skills. Ever since Daniel told her of the numbers of dead, she has wanted to know the truth of how many – to see it written down. She asked the vicar if he would mind if she looked at the register. She has known him all her life, he taught her to read and write, the casting of figures and a modicum of Latin, tutoring that was only hers because she had no brother. Now she almost wishes she hadn't asked.

The way back home rounds the belt of trees shielding the north end of the farm buildings and behind it is the barn and beyond that the roof of Hill House. Sam briefly runs into view, disappearing behind the barn. Sam's mother and sister were listed as 'unknown woman and girl-child'. Sam re-appears, looking down the track. The next moment he is running and shouting, 'Alice! Alice!'

She kneels down, holding out her arms and he cannons into her, knocking her off balance and drawing a joyous laugh from her at his fervent greeting. Sam's father, Vicar Rutland thinks, might not have deserted his family; perhaps he has gone off to seek work. But admits he never met the man, so how would he know?

'So, young man, what have you been doing this morning while I was out?'

'We picked the medlars,' Sam says. 'Daniel went up the tree and he let the basket down to me and I put them in the box. Come and see.' She gets up and Sam slips his hand in hers. It has become a familiar gesture already. She wanted the vicar to agree with her that Sam's father, after all this time, has made his escape. But Vicar Rutland says no, he thinks the man is smart, that he simply housed his family in order to move more easily and find work. When he returns, what grief awaits the poor fellow.

Catching sight of Daniel in the barn Alice pauses. 'I hear you've brought in the medlar crop?' She isn't planning to tell Daniel she has seen his brother's list. Daniel hardly needs telling, he was there by his side every time David added a name. And for her, the second name down hit her like a judgment. The memory of what might have been is still raw. Thoughts of him frequently haunt her sleep. Forget-me-not.

'You said the medlars should have been picked long since,' Daniel is saying, 'so we made ourselves useful. They're in the kitchen.'

Alice smiles her thanks. 'Gramercy, Daniel, we'll have some in a spiced tart this evening.'

Sam pulls her by the hand into the kitchen and proudly points to the box on the table.

'You've been busy,' she says, eyeing the heaped fruits. Sam starts pointing out the biggest ones. Vicar Rutland suggests that Sam's father deliberately chose remote Hillbury because it was cheaper than Sherborne or Dorchester, and probably all he could afford. For her part she wonders if he placed his family where they couldn't easily raise a hue and cry at his disappearance.

'Come, Sam,' she says, 'let me show you the way to eat a medlar.' She sorts through to find a few of the largest, ripest fruits. Sam makes a face at these soft round objects like large rosehips. For him, the task ended with putting the fruit in the box. Sam has clearly never tasted medlars.

'I don't like it, Alice, it's brown.'

'You wait. Royal princes fight for the first taste of these.' She isn't sure how true this is, but certainly the medlar is popular, being one of the few late-cropping fruits of the year. Leaving your family, the vicar says, is not the same as deserting. She works the soft flesh through a coarse sieve to separate it from the skins and pips, all the while wishing she could not see the sense of the Vicar's words. To the pulp she adds sugar grated from the loaf in the still room and mixes it into a paste. Tasting it first herself, she holds out a spoonful to Sam. After an initial hesitation, he takes a small amount on his finger to test and she watches his dawning pleasure in the gritty sweetness. Vicar Rutland has faith that Sam's father will be back to claim him. What other pleasures in his young life will Sam never know?

Sam is engaged in piling medlars on the table into a tower that soon topples and several fall to the floor. Some are already so ripe they burst where they fall.

She wonders about his father, the man who announced his intention of 'going to get a bloody drink'. Is he a violent man, or simply cast down by yet another ill turn of fortune? She revolves the questions in her mind as she works. If Sam's father does appear she will note very carefully how Sam responds. If he gives his father the sort of greeting he gave her, then she will let Sam go, if not with a glad heart, at least with her heartfelt blessing.

A small hand depositing the squashed medlars in her apron pocket rather dampens that noble thought.

She pulls the boy to her and ruffles his hair and his eyes are bright with mischief as he smiles up at her.

26

'Tell me, did Mistress Cazanove die in the plague?'

Daniel is caught unawares by Alice's question. He has kept out of the way all day since Alice arrived back from the vicar's looking mulish. But she has cooked a satisfying supper as she always does, and the medlar tart thing was very good. Now he settles by the kitchen fire and props his booted feet on the hearth while he fiddles with tobacco and tinder box. She is looking more content and he has been thinking she will tell him what the vicar said. Instead, without warning, this question about Mistress Cazanove.

'No, I think not,' he says, to give himself time to think. 'No. She must have left. We went round to the house a few days after we buried her man and it was all shut up.'

'You don't have to hide it from me that they were all dead in there.' Alice sounds quite sharp.

'That's not what I said,' he says, 'or meant.' He wishes she would let him tell this at his own rate. 'I said it was shut up, as in gone away, like the inn when Nick and Margery left. I suppose Cazanove had other houses. Why do you ask about Mistress Cazanove?'

'When she comes back, if she comes back, I must go and ask her if she knows anything of Sam's family. Would you like a top-up?' She points to his empty ale mug.

'Don't mind if I do.' He holds it out. 'But she never visited the poor.'

'No, but she might know who her husband rented to. He must have kept records. The vicar thought it was worth asking.'

He watches her face as she pours from the barrel, recounting what the vicar said. What has been said about Sam? he wonders. Alice is not looking at me like usual, and every now and then she glances away and up as though to see the lad through the ceiling, up there in his bed.

He says, 'It's right the lad should be with his own. His Da'll want to come and find him when he feels it's safe. I'd be in a frenzy if it were one of my own, not knowing, and that.'

'What you say,' Alice replies, clearly with reluctance. 'I feel in my heart it's the right thing.' She trails off as she hands him his drink.

'You've got mighty fond of him, Alice, as you would. But a father feels too, especially for his only surviving kin. When he finds out he's lost wife and babby, he'll be thanking the Lord for Sam's deliverance.'

'Of course, I know you're right,' she concedes. 'The best thing will be seeing Sam run to embrace his father when he comes.' She picks up the poker and knocks aimlessly at a disintegrating brand. Sparks fly upwards. She adds with a sigh, 'At least then I shall know he will be happy.'

He leans back in the settle and pulls on his pipe. *So that's what it's about. She wants to keep Sam.*

'I wonder if I might persuade his father to work here on the farm,' she muses. 'In that way, I can see that Sam is properly fed, and I can provide better accommodation than that awful hovel in Baker's Row. What do you think?"

Daniel finds the subject of others coming to work at Hill House Farm strangely unwelcome. While Alice adds a log to the fire, he casts around for something to divert her thoughts.

He takes the pipe from his mouth. 'I recall Cazanove's death. He went the same day quarantine was brought in. His wife sent his man Wat to find Parson Rutland, but the vicar had left by then, so Wat fetched up at the smithy when he heard we were doing the burying. Just as well he did, we'd have missed calling at the mansion, it being rather outlying on that side of the woods.'

'She was very distracted when I was there that day. She had just been told that it was the plague. I suppose she thought they would avoid it, being so far out.'

'The Coopers are outlying too, but they left, even so.'

'Master Cooper had sent his wife and Gerald away to his sister's long before,' she says, throwing the poker down and getting to her feet. 'Like they knew something the rest of us didn't.'

'True, Master Cooper was the last,' Daniel agrees. 'He was hanging on for a spot of business. It didn't work out … he left that same day.'

'Are they back yet, Daniel, the Coopers?' At the table she starts piling dishes.

'Haven't seen them.'

'And Mistress Cazanove? She's still away?'

'Don't know. I've not been up there recently.'

'So Master Cazanove died very quickly then, like my mother, but different indications.'

'Ah well – that was just it.'

She pauses in clearing the table. 'What was just it?'

He gives a couple of puffs at his pipe before he answers. 'Wat had already started digging the grave afore we got up there to make Cazanove ready. And tis not as if he had the plague, anyway.'

'Who?'

'Cazanove.'

'What are you saying?' she asks.

'Davy and I talked about it. Between us we lived through a few plagues and you get to know. But Cazanove had none of the usual signs. No plague I ever saw looked like that.'

'Like what?'

'There's sometimes two types when it comes, sometimes three. There's the sudden death, not common, when they just collapse and die for no reason. Then there's the strangling cough, and there's the five-day fever with death-tokens. Like your father, God rest his soul. Then there was Cazanove.'

'What about him?'

'His man Wat told us Cazanove only fell ill that day, and for sure there were no swellings. He didn't cough or spit blood. There was no fever, nor yet he didn't fall down without warning.'

She leans her hands on the table, looking across at him. 'I saw him being supported out of Nick Patten's. He looked weak, no strength in his limbs. Coming from the inn I thought he was drunk but it puzzled me that Rupert Cazanove would do that, get drunk in public.'

'When we collected him, his face was all purply red, sort of swollen. Just didn't seem like plague to me. Davy didn't think so neither.'

'Did you say anything to anyone?'

'With everything else going on we just buried him where Wat showed us and moved on. Wasn't till later we talked about it, not much point dragging it up then.'

'Apothecary Marchant told her it was the plague.'

'Oh well, I guess he knew.'

'You don't sound convinced, Daniel. What else would it be?'

'I don't know what it was. All I know is, Davy and me, we were at Nick's that day when Cazanove came in. He was in a high temper, worse than usual. Worked himself into a frenzy, seemed to be out to do down everyone he could. Davy and me, we weren't going to sit through another scene, so we left.'

She has started to wipe the bowls they used, but at this, she stops. 'Another scene?'

Daniel takes the pipe from his mouth. 'A couple of nights before, he had a set-to with Master Cooper, some deal they'd set up between them that had kept Master Cooper here long after he'd sent his family to his sister's for safety. Wool and dyes, something of that sort. The two of them at the corner table at Nick's. I remember because Ralph Cooper's rarely allowed off the rein by his lady. No common alehouses for her man.'

'What was going on?'

Daniel considers. No harm in saying it now. The thing died with Cazanove. 'Cazanove got him to set aside part of his wool clip and not declare it – at least that's what your father thought; I remember talking with him when he brought the logs down. To get it spun and woven on the quiet without involving the guilds, and split the profits on the sale. And you know that's illegal. Your father reckoned Cazanove was trying to ruin Cooper. Judging by the way Ralph Cooper got up and left after high words with Cazanove, I suspect your father was right.'

She says, as though quoting, *The Coopers are not as plump in the pocket as they would have us all believe.* He'll be in straits, what with that and the bad harvest this year.'

'Cooper's tarred his own hand by keeping back his fleece. Now he can't do anything with it. Doesn't have a leg to stand on. Your father said to us Cooper was leaving for his sister's on that Monday. And that,' Daniel goes on pointedly, 'was the day Cazanove died. Makes you think.'

Alice looks thoughtful. 'Master Cooper must have been angry if he'd been negotiating for all those months since the sheep were sheared. Losing part of his wool clip in a lean year can't make things easy, especially with Emeline Cooper so anxious to maintain appearances.'

'He was surely mad that day. Then Cazanove turns on Nick. As I said, that day, the day you saw him, Davy and I were taking our midday meal at Nick's and Cazanove struts in. Shouts from the door that he's upping the rent on the inn, with immediate effect.'

Alice gasps. 'What?'

'Nick's a bit of a rogue,' Daniel half laughs. 'We all know that, but you don't treat any man in that public way.'

'Master Cazanove seems to have made himself popular that day.'

'I've never seen Nick button his lip so tight. Then when the meal comes, Cazanove tips his plate on the floor and says to Nick it's not fit for pigs. So Margery storms in looking fit to burst at the insult to her cooking, and Nick has to manhandle her out and tell her to prepare something else. That's when Davy and I left. We reckoned Cazanove was out to pick a fight and we weren't going to oblige him.'

'My father never invited him here. A man who made his money by grinding every last ounce from his dyeworkers was not welcome at Hill House.'

'Few would mourn Cazanove. I reckon somebody helped things along.'

Alice, putting away dishes, half-laughs. 'Daniel, as if anyone would.'

'I don't say as I'm right, Alice, just that the thought crossed our minds.'

'Either way, you think an apothecary's opinion was wrong?'

'Can't ask him now. I speak as I find, Alice.'

'Come now. You're saying someone murdered him. Who would wish to do that?'

Daniel grunts. 'It'd be easier to say who would not.'

'But Master Marchant would hardly have diagnosed the pestilence if he thought otherwise. He always took such pains.'

'Anybody can be mistaken.' Daniel puzzles at the battle of thoughts in her expression.

'But Alaric Ford and Grover Price are dead too,' she says, and he realises she saw his brother's plague roll when she went to the Vicar.

'— and for all we know, his man Wat also,' she adds. It seems to Daniel that she is saying it as proof that Cazanove had the plague, that he passed it on to those others.

'Most of the village are dead, Alice.' He watches her eyes move, a frown come and go.

'Daniel, when Master Cazanove went into Nick's on that Monday, did he look drunk to you? Was he reeling, unsteady?'

'The way he always walked, planting his legs apart like he did, he could have been slightly drunk and you wouldn't know. But that day, no, I don't think so; he was swaggering, not reeling. And piggy-eyed. That's what told us he was looking for another fight.'

Alice picks up some sewing and joins Daniel on the settle. It is a shirt of her father's that she is altering to fit Sam. Daniel can see the neck is far too big, like Sam's other new clothes, but it is good linen and if the lad does not care, what matter?

'If he was well when he walked into the inn and ill when

he walked out, what happened in the inn?' she asks.

'Well, apart from Ralph Cooper and Nick, his man Wat Meredith surely weren't stricken with grief.'

'What did he say?'

Daniel bites his lip. Wat only came to work for Cazanove earlier this year. David saw Wat as an outsider, but Daniel likes Wat, despite knowing very little about him. Daniel didn't mean to mention the suspicions he and David exchanged, but somehow it is so easy to tell Alice things. 'Wat said something like – Cazanove was dead and small loss it was.'

Alice eyes him closely. 'Or he said, *"The old bastard's snuffed it at last, thank God".*'

Daniel's eyebrows shoot up. 'Ah, well, near enough, yes.'

'But you cannot believe he is guilty, merely for saying something like that.'

'I don't.' Daniel hesitates, then adds, 'There was something else.'

'What?'

'I was out back later on that day, piling the logs your father brought down, when Wat arrived. As I walked in, he and Davy were talking and I heard him say, "I should have done it months ago."'

'Did he? And what did David say in reply?'

'Nothing much, he just shrugged. Said something like "Well, he's gone now." It wasn't till days later Davy and I talked of it again.'

'Yes?'

'Davy said it wasn't plague. That was the first I knew he had suspicions too. It was me who mentioned Wat.'

He wishes he had not started this. He can see Alice is thinking hard. She asks, 'Were the two of you thinking to do anything about it?'

'We had other things on our minds at that time.'

'Yes. Of course. I'm sorry.'

There is a silence and Alice inspects her sewing. Clearly she is not happy with it. As he watches she sighs and starts to pull out stitches.

Daniel goes on, 'Anyway, can you see us going to Abel Nutley, and him looking down his nose and calling Davy "my good man"? Davy didn't really care about Cazanove, Alice. No more'n me. I wouldn't worry about him – he's gone.'

'But if it was murder, there must be a holding to account.'

'Nobody regrets him.'

'Perhaps not, but—' She threads her needle once more. 'Tell me, when you overheard Wat talking to Davy,' she says, 'were those his exact words? "I should have done it months ago"?'

'Near as dammit. Why?'

'I mean, did he say "I should have done it *months* ago" or "*I* should have done it months ago"?'

Daniel pushes out his lip and shrugs. 'He just said it.'

'You see, it means something completely different, the way the emphasis is put on different words. Do you recall?'

'He just said it,' Daniel repeats, and adds sightly mocking, 'What a wily mind you have, Alice!' But she has already moved on.

'Who put him in his grave clothes, do you know?'

'We did. When Davy and I went there he was still dressed. The women hadn't been able to change him into his shift. He was too heavy for them.'

'And?'

He shrugs. 'And nothing. We took him away and buried him.'

'But you saw his body. Did he have any marks that should

142

not have been there?'

'Marks?'

'Injuries, I mean. You said he was bloated in the face.'

'I never said that.'

'Piggy-eyed. Purple and swollen. Bloated. Same thing. So you would have seen if there were marks of strangling around his neck for instance.'

'No nothing like that. His ruff was tight but only because of his double chin.'

'And you said there were no plague tokens, so you must have seen his armpits, his groin, all of him in fact. Were there any marks, scratches, anything unusual?'

His face warms with unease at her close questions about a man's body. 'Nothing out of the ordinary. We weren't looking for any, of course.'

'What about his head? Had he been hit, were there any bruises?'

'No, I'm sure of that. That thick hair of his was matted, so the women got me a comb and I went all over. I'd have seen if there were any swellings or cuts.' He looks over at her. 'I did notice mud on his doublet and down his hose – all down his right side it was, and his hand.'

'That was where he fell over when they were getting him to his horse. Tell me, had he been sick? When I saw him, the front of his doublet and his canion hose had some sort of stain.'

'We'd have smelled it. Perhaps he fell in a puddle as well as the mud.'

Alice shakes her head. 'His hose were wet when he came out of the inn.'

'Perhaps it was when he threw Margery's cullis on the floor.'

'Cullis? No, the cream in it would have smeared white. He was in dark green, it would have showed.'

'Ah. Mayhap he upset his ale.'

'That's possible, I suppose.' He waits, watching her think, and she goes on, 'If you are right, and it was not drunkenness and not the plague either, what was it?' She seems to be asking herself as much as him. 'I think I shall go over there anyway. If his widow is back she may appreciate some company.'

'Mistress Starch. Huh! She's never unbent enough to seek a neighbour's friendship before. I wish you joy of her company.'

'How will I know if she is returned?'

'Nick at the inn will know, soon as she is.' Daniel pulls a face. 'Or she'll send one of her minions to find out why the rent hasn't been paid.'

'I confess I've never had a good opinion of her either,' Alice says, 'but the case is altered now she is a widow; she may be glad of a caller. She may wish to speak of her loss.'

Daniel gives her a sideways look. 'Oh yes?'

'That's not why I'm going there.'

Daniel draws on his pipe. 'Course not,' he says.

She breaks off the thread and regards her work. 'But it would be quite natural for her to talk of her husband.'

Daniel looks at her, raises ironic eyebrows. 'Not that you're curious about him, of course.'

She points at the hearth. 'The fire's dying down, can you see to it?'

'Alice, you—'

'Will this do?' she asks, holding out the shirt with its strangely amputated sleeves.

'Fine. Alice, you can't—'

'I only want to ask what she knows of Sam's father! What

144

if I say I shall restrict the conversation to that?'
   'I'd say pigs might fly,' says Daniel.

27

In the end, it is a few days before Alice visits the Cazanove mansion. In the great courtyard behind the house she calls to a young maidservant who is beating a rug slung on a rope between two poles.

'If your mistress is at home, I should be glad of a few minutes of her time.'

The girl stares at this stranger standing in the kitchen court. She bobs a curtsey and makes for the nearest doorway.

'My name is—' But the girl has disappeared inside. Alice catches sight of her peeping out through the kitchen window, then she is gone.

Alice looks around while she waits. The well-set cobbles are bounded on all sides by kitchens, wash-houses, storehouses, granary, stables, workshops, a coach-house. The corner archway through which she has just entered is open to the track she has walked from Hillbury village. The house itself is vast – the kitchen court extends no more than a third of the way along the west-facing back wall. The remainder, she guesses, will look out onto pleasure grounds, a knot garden or some other suitable view for the many reception rooms.

She has not long to wait. The waiting woman who answered Alice's knock on that previous visit comes to the kitchen doorway. Her grey hair sits strangely with her more youthful complexion. Perhaps, Alice muses, she is one of those fortunate women who never fully age in the face. The woman's look shows her recognition.

'Mistress Edwards,' she says.

'Give you good day,' Alice greets her. 'I heard in the village that your mistress has returned.'

'Indeed, she has. Was there no reply at the front?'

'I didn't come to the front, I shall not disturb her if she would prefer not. I wished to offer my sympathies on the loss of your master.' In truth, Alice has no wish to re-live that last disastrous visit to the front door of this house. She still catches herself regretting. She is always thinking, *if only I hadn't.*

The woman seems to find nothing amiss in what Alice says. She steps back, inviting her in. 'My mistress is in weeds of course, with the master taken. But I believe she will see you.' She leads Alice into a long passage at the back of the house.

They pass still rooms and storerooms and enter the main part of the house. Alice follows her guide across the rear of the screens passage that leads from the front door. She can see herself standing there that drear afternoon, the two women grey-faced with horror '... *the apothecary has seen my husband ... leave this house..... the plague.*'

'The master was dying at the moment you called,' the waiting woman tells her, as if reliving similar memories herself. 'My mistress was in a frenzy to remove everyone.'

'From the miasma. Yes I understand.'

'In truth, I know we flouted the quarantine, but I do not think wild horses would have kept the household here, once they knew.'

'I promise you I am not here as Constable Nutley's spy,' Alice assures her. 'It must have been a hard decision to come back.'

'Not if you knew the house in Wells. That place is

sackcloth and ashes, even in the height of summer. Grey, cold, inhospitable.'

'I meant, hard to return to the place of such recent loss.'

The woman is silent and Alice curses her own thoughtlessness. The Cazanove servants must all be anticipating the future with a degree of dread. Rupert Cazanove was by no means a popular master, but while he lived it meant stability for them.

They come to a door, the woman knocks and murmurs Alice's name, and stands back for her to enter. The room, though small for the size of house, is as large as the hall at Hill house, and no effort has been spared to dazzle the eye.

Moulded plaster strapwork criss-crosses the ceiling with motifs of flowers in the lozenge-shaped spaces between, all picked out in an extravagance of gold leaf. A rich rug covers a table against one wall and on it sit two fine pewter candlesticks and a dish piled with oranges.

Next to the table is a polished chest with drawers and on the opposite wall stands a carved stone fireplace with a fire brightly blazing against a solid iron fireback. One entire wall of the room is covered by a tapestry of hunting and hawking, while intricately worked linen-fold panelling runs floor-to-ceiling around the other three, except where the large window brings in the light between its delicate stone mullions.

But it is the woman on the window seat fixing the needle in her canvas who takes all Alice's attention.

For a few moments as the maidservant announces her, Alice stands stock still. It takes that time to recognise the figure rising from her seat in acknowledgement. Dressed all in black save for wide falls of cream needle-lace at neck and cuff, most women would have looked wan. She is unsmiling, that is hardly surprising, but here is a face of warm colour.

The gaunt shadows are gone, the gaze is straight and clear.

Is this how Mistress Cazanove the baron's daughter looked before her husband's closing life came to age her prematurely?

The gown is not high-buttoned as it was on Alice's first visit, but falls away slightly where the lace parts to reveal strings of gleaming pearls against the skin at the base of her throat. The sleeves do not cover her hands but finish at the slight wrists. Her fingers are long and delicate and Alice unwillingly recognises the similarity to her own mother's, the needlewoman's hands. Whatever excuses Mistress Cazanove affects for her idleness when it comes to visiting the poor, the embroidery frame is no pretence.

Alice makes her curtsey to the woman standing before her, which is accepted with a well-bred incline of the head. She offers her condolences, but perhaps her status is held too low for this high-born lady to respond directly.

Instead, the widow says, 'It is kind in you to call, Mistress Edwards. You will take refreshment? A glass of wine?' Her voice is measured and calm, her manner civil but not open.

'I thank you, no. I am come to ask a question of you,' Alice responds.

'I see. Then please take a seat. Thank you, Esther,' to the hovering maidservant.

'I hope I do not intrude on you,' Alice says quickly as the door closes.

'If that were the case, Mistress Edwards, my maidservant would have denied you entry.' She walks over to the well-banked fire and sits.

At her gesture, Alice takes a cushioned chair opposite. 'Now that we are free to move around once more, I have come to you at the earliest opportunity.'

'We returned but two nights ago,' Mistress Cazanove says.

'I understand there has been much loss in Hillbury. I heard you suffered the loss of both your parents.'

Alice has not prepared herself for this. Even as the widow expresses a correct level of sorrow for the loss of two people she hardly knew, Alice is tempted to retort to Mistress Cazanove that had *she* not shirked her responsibilities to the poor and sick, Alice might not have needed to make so many visits into Hillbury, and her parents might still be alive. But that will not cancel out the blame Alice knows she alone carries.

'You too have had a grievous loss, Mistress Cazanove.'

The widow shows no more inclination than Alice to speak of her loss. 'I recall your mother used to visit some of my husband's tenants.'

Alice looks down at her hands lying in her lap and concentrates on not clasping them into fists. She would like to observe that her husband kept his tenants more like slaves, given the conditions they lived and worked under.

Mistress Cazanove, perhaps spurred by Alice's silence, continues, 'Your mother was very good to them when I was unable to visit them. And you too, I understand?'

Alice says carefully, 'We felt our visits were welcomed when other help was scarce.'

'As a wife,' comes the reply, 'I was bound to follow my husband's wishes. He insisted on a separation between the household and the working folk.'

It is almost an apology, but Alice remembers how Emeline Cooper would use the same trick on Mother. Yet another version of "My husband insists" – *'Oh, well, I would help you, with all my heart, my dear Ann, but you know how stubborn Ralph can be about these things.'*

And soft-hearted Mother always fell for it, took it all on herself.

Mistress Cazanove is speaking again. 'I am so sorry I am not able now to thank your mother in person, but you are to know that I heard of it and was grateful for her charity.'

How can this woman sit here and say these things when it's all too late? There is a pause between them. Alice takes a deep breath and reins in her nature, reminding herself what she is here for. 'You may or may not be able to help me, Mistress Cazanove, but Vicar Rutland suggested I ask you. It is about those cottages at the back of the bakery.'

'The ones they call Bakery Row? Baker's Row?'

'Josh Baker sold them a while ago and it's said your husband was the purchaser.'

'My husband certainly had dealings with Joshua, he came up to the house a couple of times, I recall. Not that long ago. What is your interest in Baker's Row?'

'I have a young boy in my care,' Alice says. 'His father may have rented one of the cottages very recently, probably around the time the pestilence started. There was a wife and young Sam and a girl-child, a baby. Sam's father seems to have gone away in search of work, and the mother and sister died.' She is putting the best gloss on the father's intentions she can. She fears that if she talks of their extreme poverty, the widow might be the next person to suggest that the Poor House is the best solution for the boy.

'And Sam is the child in your care? Can't he tell you where his father has gone?'

'Sam is only about four years old. I have cobbled his story together from what he has been able to tell, but it is incomplete at best.'

'And you wish me to fill in the blanks?'

Alice nods. 'It is only fair his father should know what has happened.'

'Yes.' The widow gets up and crosses to a dark, polished chest to pull open one of its drawers. 'I was thinking back as you were speaking.' She draws out a sheaf of stiff papers, scans them and discards. 'No. No, not that one. No. It will be in here somewhere, I feel sure.' She puts aside the sheaf and delves further into the drawer, bringing out more papers. Once again she sifts through, finally taking one by its corner and shaking it free of the rest. 'Here's a find. This is the deed of purchase for Bakery Row. See? Dated earlier this year. Now, let me see if I can find who lived there.'

She pushes the papers back and pulls open another drawer, then a third, all the while sorting through folios of thick crackling parchment and thin, torn sheets, dog-eared bills and greyed notices, legal papers, letters, lists. 'He did not always keep things tidily, and he allowed no one else to see.' She draws a sheet from the bundle in her hand. 'This sort of thing would do as a starting point.'

She passes it across to Alice, who sees that it is a note about Goody Hamlyn, the miller's widow who occupied a cottage in the Row and used to welcome Alice's visits. It is doubtful whether the old lady could even read it, but she had been obliged to make her mark. Cazanove making sure he got his pound of flesh.

While the rich widow continues her search, Alice glances at the rent payable and nearly gasps. No wonder the little goodwife needed all the help she could get from neighbours. A wave of anger rises to Alice's throat at the gilded and padded luxury around her, cushioned seats, gleaming pewter, waxed wood. All this comfort paid for by elderly millers' widows, poverty-stricken dye workers, desperate, out-of-work young fathers. She could happily strangle Mistress Cazanove with one of her own silk skeins. She finds she has stood up.

'How can you——?' she starts, and stops herself. *How can you pretend to be so blind to it.*

'Yes?' Mistress Cazanove turns from her search.

'I mean ...' Alice thinks fast. 'How can you know if your husband had one of these for Sam's father? You do not know what name you are looking for.'

'Oh, I shall know,' Cazanove's widow says, turning back to her search. She seems not to have noticed Alice's shift in tone. 'There was a man. He called to see my husband. I didn't see him, but I heard him shouting. It was a few days before that day you called. He was saying something about 'paying in blood.' She pauses, catching her lip in her teeth. 'Poor man, a wife and family to provide for.'

She returns to her hunt, peering and stretching into the back of the drawer. 'It was late in the day, very chill – I recall this because I had come in from the kitchen court and was warming myself by the bread oven when I heard him. He shouted that if it was blood my husband wanted, he would sign in his own. Later, I found a spot of blood on the floor in the hall, and the quill stained red. That was where they were, in the hall. So I imagine he pricked his finger and made his mark in red.' She reaches the bottom of the drawer in her search, then closes it and gets up.

'I cannot find it at present, Mistress Edwards. If you will be patient, I will have a further look elsewhere in the house and when I find it I will send Esther to you.' Mistress Cazanove returns to her seat.

'I shall be glad to know anything you find that may show who he is,' Alice says, and remembers the other matter she had in mind. 'Did your husband's body servant take any illness?'

'Do you know Wat, then?' The widow looks puzzled by this new direction.

'No, but I saw him helping your husband from the inn.'

'Ah. No, Wat took no hurt,' she says. 'Apart from my husband, and Grover Price and his wife, the entire household is well, God be praised. We were fortunate indeed.'

'Alaric Ford fell victim.' The widow looks blank. 'The candlemaker,' Alice explains. 'He was the third man who helped your husband when he fell ill at Nick Patten's.'

'The candlemaker? Doesn't he have a family?'

'A wife and several children, the youngest hardly out of swathing and the next well on the way. We think they must have left after Alaric was buried. If they survived, they are going to need much help when they return, to stay out of the Poor House.'

'I shall make sure I am told when she returns. If she is in need of a roof, the cottage you speak of in Bakery Row might suit, now that it is empty.'

That'll help keep those nice fat rents coming in, buy you another rug to cover some unused table in some forgotten room. Again she recalls herself.

'Daniel and his brother were in the inn that day,' she says, 'when your husband took ill.'

'The Bunting brothers?'

'They saw your husband in converse with Nick Patten. Daniel said it was quite heated. I hope that did not contribute to your husband's collapse.'

The widow makes a wry face. 'My husband was not so feeble. He would joust with any man and take pleasure in it.'

In Alice's view, it would have been pleasurable to him only as long as he had the last word. She replies, 'Nick Patten was greatly dismayed when your husband told him he was raising the rent on the inn.'

Mistress Cazanove is startled out of her impassivity. She

shakes her head. 'He had no reason to raise it. He used to say it was one of the most profitable things he ever did, buying the inn.'

Alice shrugs. 'Apparently he said it to Nick in front of everyone. Then when his meal was served he tipped it on the floor.'

The fire in the hearth flares red, mirrored by the sudden confusion in the widow's face.

So she does have a weak spot, Alice thinks, and pushes further. 'A shame to waste food, especially when Margery Patten is such a good cook.'

'I trust there was no breakage.'

Of dishes, Alice wonders, *or of heads? And would you care either way?*

'I am sure Margery Patten cooked as good a meal for my husband as ever she did,' the widow says. And then, unexpectedly, she seems to be offering an explanation. 'He was in high choler when he left here. Esther and I spent all morning preparing the midday meal, and we were most careful over it.'

'A wife would always be careful over what she cooks for her family.' Alice says, piously inquisitive, wondering why Rupert Cazanove chose to go the inn instead of dining at home.

'This was special. It was something he did every year, to celebrate the recovery of his business after the last plague. Esther and I always prepare it. This time I sat down with him and Esther attended us.'

'Didn't you usually sit down with your husband?' For Alice the turn of phrase is so strange, she blurts out the question without thinking. To soften the discourtesy, she adds, 'We always dined together when my parents were alive.

I miss that.'

It seems to draw fellow-feeling from Mistress Cazanove. A fleeting smile passes over her face as she recalls. 'I too dined with my parents when I was a girl. But my husband preferred to dine alone and I attended him. It was only for this meal that he liked me to dine with him.'

'We used to exchange the day's news over a meal,' Alice tells her. 'My father would talk about the farm, my mother about her visits to—' she stops herself in time from saying *the poor*, and changes it to, 'friends in the village. And I would show off to my parents or our maidservants the latest Latin I had learned with Vicar Rutland! How shameless I was!' She adds, remembering, 'What noise and laughter there was round the table!'

The widow has listened to Alice with a wistful look on her face. In this softer humour she appears almost likeable. 'Perhaps it was as well you were not at our table that day,' she responds. 'Before the first course of dishes was over my husband declared that my talking made his head ache. I am inclined to think it was because he had had nothing to drink. All he ate was a variety of roast meats, and you know that will always make a man thirsty.'

'Was Master Cazanove not a drinking man?'

'It was my fault. I meant to send Wat for a barrel from Nick, but in all the preparations I forgot, so we were down to small ale only. My husband never took small ale. He declared what we had prepared to be revolting and the food at the inn vastly superior. He would say things like that, it was just his way. What man does not occasionally upbraid his wife so?'

Never in my life did my father tell me or my mother that the food we served him was not good enough.

'When my husband stalked out of the house I begged Wat

156

to go with him,' Mistress Cazanove goes on. 'I did not know what he might do; he was in such a taking.'

There is something in Mistress Cazanove's voice which makes Alice suspect she often took the precaution of sending a man after him when he went out in a rage.

I had no idea how hateful he was, thinks Alice.

Shocked, she says, 'Forgive me saying this, but if your husband already had the pestilence on him, mayhap he was suffering disordered humours that made him behave a little wildly?'

'No doubt you are right, mistress.' She sounds politely hostile in the face of Alice's sympathy. The brief confidence has faded.

Alice persists. 'It is known that some plague victims suffer wild behaviour.'

'Indeed?'

'Since Apothecary Marchant recognised it for the plague, no doubt he had seen similar cases.'

'I understand Apothecary Marchant was among the dead, poor man.'

'He paid a high price, trying to save others.'

But Alice's pointed remark is wasted on Mistress Cazanove, whose thoughts have already drifted back to her own griefs. 'Well, my husband has paid the last price, and may he sleep the sleep he deserves.'

Amen to that, thinks Alice. 'And will you stay here?'

'The attorneys are looking for his brother. They say he is a seafarer. I never met him. Bernard Cazanove will inherit everything. Much younger than my husband, a child of a second marriage I believe.'

'But what about you?'

'You need not concern yourself, Mistress Edwards, I have

enough to live in a modest way.'

Alice wonders what 'modest' means to this woman who lives surrounded by silk and tapestries, rugs and cushions, carved wood and gilded plaster. Goody Hamlyn the miller's widow on Baker's Row would have called her own situation 'modest', yet she relied on the unpredictable goodwill of her neighbours, had an earthen floor in her cottage, and no glass in her windows.

Clearly it is time to leave. Alice rises and takes a deep breath. The widow might take offence at what she is about to say, but she feels duty bound to make the effort. 'I shall be going back through the village,' she says. 'Would you like me to call on Master Patten and give him your assurances that there will be no rent increase? They will be glad to have such news before Christmas.'

To her gratified surprise, the widow assents, and at that moment there is a knock on the door. The maidservant steps in, slightly breathless. She hesitates a moment, glancing at Alice, then says, 'It's Constable Nutley to see you, mistress, on an urgent matter, he says.'

The maidservant's awe of the parish constable is not shared by her mistress. 'Of course, ask him to step in, Esther.'

The door closes and she says to Alice, 'I suppose this is about my removal to the Wells house after my husband's illness. You remember the Plague Order; it will be a kindness in you if you will stay a moment.' The widow is shrewd in her assumption. Abel Nutley is well known for dotting each 'i' and crossing every last 't' in his search for misdemeanour.'

'There could be a simpler explanation,' Alice says. 'He might be checking on your church attendance. He loves to catch someone lapsing.'

'We attended regularly at the cathedral while we were

in Wells.'

'Oh dear, how disappointed he will be.'

But either the widow does not choose to share the irony with one of Alice's stamp, or she has more pressing thoughts. 'Perhaps he knows there was no true service when we buried my husband in the grounds here.'

'If you are concerned about that, I can tell you that Abel Nutley is in a weak position to challenge you.' Alice drops her voice as she hears footsteps approaching. 'Ask him how long after the start of quarantine he packed up and left.'

Esther re-enters the room at that moment, the well-fleshed parish constable shouldering past her and nodding to the lady of the house. Abel Nutley is by trade a scribe, much happier sitting with quill and paper than walking the countryside. But since much of his work involves visiting the offices of attorneys, bailiffs and stewards around various parishes, he has not unwillingly taken on the task of keeping an eye on the doings of the parishioners. Although it obliges him to exert himself more than he enjoys, he prides himself on his knowledge of the law and finds satisfaction in discovering and reporting the smallest transgressions.

When he has had time to cast an approving eye round the showy furnishings, he waves a dismissive hand at Alice and jerks his head to Esther. 'You may go.'

Alice stands her ground; Esther pauses, eyes on her mistress. Abel Nutley has already plumped himself down, legs spread wide, in the chair by the fire that Alice has just vacated. He licks a fleshy finger and flicks through the sheaf of papers he carries. Alice glances at Mistress Cazanove who stands regarding the man before her.

He starts to read aloud. 'Now, it says here you are Ursula Philippa … Mary … Caza—' His voice trails off as his eyes travel up the figure before him. The baron's daughter raises her eyebrows a minute fraction. Clutching at his sliding papers, Abel Nutley stands up. 'Mistress Caza—'

Ursula Cazanove looks over his head to the maidservant. 'Thank you, Esther.'

'I shall be directly outside if you need me, mistress.'

The door closes and Abel Nutley jerks his head at Alice. 'She can go too.'

Mistress Cazanove turns to Alice, who is busily keeping the grin from spreading across her face. 'Mistress Edwards, I apologise for detaining you but I trust it will not be for long.' She sits and indicates the seat next to her. 'Pray make yourself comfortable. Now, Constable Nutley, you already know who I am so let us dispense with trifles. Please be seated. How may I serve you?'

Abel Nutley throws Alice a narrow look and his mouth opens in protest but he thinks better of it. He retrieves his fallen sheets and sits down again. Now he has two bright spots of red on his cheeks that are nothing to do with the heat of the fire or the extent of his exertions in walking here. Within his bulging doublet, his stomach settles on his thighs like an oversize pudding. 'Ahem, I understand, m'lady, your late husband was buried here in his grounds?'

'That is so. The vicar was not here to—'

'Have you visited his grave since that time?' Armed with his rustling paper authority Abel Nutley is already re-asserting himself.

'No, I have not. You see, we have been away in—'

'And have any of your household visited the grave?'

'I do not believe so. There would be no reason.'

'So nobody has been there since he was buried?'

Ursula Cazanove pauses to gather her thoughts before

speaking. 'Master Nutley, amongst the stacks of statutes, is there now some misdemeanour involved in not visiting a grave?'

Abel Nutley scowls. 'This is a serious matter, madam.'

'And I am indeed serious. What is the purpose of your questions, sir?'

'You shall find out in due course, madam. The grave is in Harman's Copse, is it not?'

'Indeed.'

Abel Nutley puffs out his chest and tilts back his head so that he can look down his nose at the tall woman opposite him. 'So you are not aware that your husband's body is no longer there?'

'No longer there? What do you mean, no longer there?'

'I mean, madam, that the snatchers came and took away the corpse!'

All colour is washed in a second from her face. She stares wordless at the little man. A hand goes up to her mouth.

'My people had information,' Constable Nutley declares. This, Alice can see, he is hugely enjoying, the opportunity to vaunt his alliance with the wider hierarchy of law enforcement.

'My people,' he repeats, 'informed me that two men were heard by one of our listeners in a tavern in Dorchester. They were talking of Harman's Copse. Now, our listener happens to know of Harman's Copse so he was able to pass on the tidings to the right quarter.'

The "right quarter" smirks and draws himself up another inch. 'They talked of a most interesting body that had been snatched. They said—'

'Master Nutley!' Alice interrupts. What is the man thinking of? 'You cannot say this to Master Cazanove's widow!'

The constable closes his eyes and puts up an admonishing

hand. 'Wait, miss, you have not yet heard all.' Alice bites her lip. Unthinking, she reaches out a supportive hand to Ursula Cazanove. She is alarmed by the fluttering, fast and irregular, that she can feel in her companion's wrist.

'We have them in gaol now,' the constable says. 'The undeniable evidence that links them directly with the crime was the blood on their hose and shoes.'

He seems oblivious to the widow's rapid breathing. He wriggles himself a half-inch higher, ignoring her soft mew of distress, his head waggling from side to side as he prepares for the climax. Alice, running a supportive arm round Ursula's waist, feels the trembling of her frame.

A smile threatens to break across Nutley's face. 'For they were boasting of the body being so fresh that when they attended the opening of the head, they all jumped back, for at that moment …' he pauses in readiness.

Ursula's hand has come away from her mouth and she is panting hard, a look of panic in her face. 'I can't breathe!'

Drops of perspiration stand out on her forehead. Alice watches helplessly as Ursula clutches her chest and cries, 'Call Esther! I can't breathe! Esther!' She thrusts Alice away and stumbles to the window, tugs open the casement and leans gasping across the sill as Esther bursts into the room.

'… a vast quantity of blood flowed out!' Nutley finishes with a flourish. No one is listening.

28

Alice stands in the screens passage as Esther and Wat Meredith descend the last few stairs. 'I shall stay with her now, Mistress Edwards,' Esther says. 'She will be well, but I have never known her troubled with a panic like this. And I've been her maidservant nearly all her married life.'

'May I ask, mistress, what happened in there?' Wat says. Like the others, he has a wary look, as though habit has inured him to being slapped down for presumption. 'Is she in trouble with the justices? If I ask the constable, he'll not tell the likes of me.'

'No, she is not in trouble, Wat,' Alice tells him. 'I am sorry to say it, but the body-snatchers have been to your late master's grave. The details are very bloody and Master Nutley took much pleasure in relating them to your mistress.'

'One day,' says Wat between clenched teeth, 'I'll put that man through a wall. First those louts from the village wanting to harass her, now him.'

'Which louts?' Alice asks, though she has a pretty good idea.

He says, 'We'd no sooner arrived back yesterday than Oz Thatcher and Dick Winter came looking to touch the mistress for money.'

'Money for what?' Alice asks.

'Dick Winter tried to tell me he'd burnt his leg helping with the plague fires,' Esther explains. So I said, what a pity I didn't have any decoction of elm bark. I had another treatment for the likes of him.'

'Elm bark?' Alice repeats. 'I didn't think that was much used anyway, except by charcoal-burners.'

Esther looks away. 'Perhaps not.'

Alice fears she has embarrassed her by querying her homemade cure, but before she can explain herself, Wat says, 'That was no burn, he'd scraped his leg or something, to make the blood come. Told us it wouldn't heal.'

Alice scoffs. 'The only reason it won't heal is he won't leave it alone. I poulticed that for him in the summer and I've repeatedly told him not to pick at it.'

'In the end I used a comfrey salve, only I added lemon juice.' They both grin at Alice's wince. 'It was to staunch the blood, of course!'

'And the lemon stung him like anything,' Wat adds, 'and he was hopping around in agony.'

Alice is enjoying this. 'Poor Dick,' she says. The story of work-shy Dick Winter meeting his comeuppance is the more welcome after the tight combativeness of her visit to the mistress of the mansion. She feels herself begin to relax.

At the same time, Alice sees a different lady of the mansion, inspiring a level of loyalty in these two, of protectiveness from Esther, and fierce chivalry in Wat – one who is not directly her servant, but has stayed on, or been kept on, despite his role of body-servant no longer existing. She asks him, 'What will you do now, Wat? Will you stay here, or move on in due course?'

He does not look directly at her, but away, as though some other thought is occupying his mind. 'She says she wants me to stay,' he answers. 'But I'm not sure what will happen to me.'

As Esther excuses herself to return to her mistress, he

seems to rouse himself, remember his role of servant. 'Shall I fetch your mount, mistress?'

'Thank you, Wat, but I walked here through the woods over the hill. I shall go back that way.' She is already heading along the kitchen passage.

'Then I shall accompany you,' he says firmly. 'Too many doubtful characters around for a lady to be on her own.' He takes a jerkin from a hook and shrugs it over his wide shoulders, ushering her out by the kitchen and through the court.

They round the end of the house and head up the long slope crowned by trees, in which Harman's Copse, the site of the plundered grave, lies hidden.

'I am obliged to you for your company, Wat, though I don't really believe Dick would do anything malicious. Oz Thatcher I don't know so well.'

'Oh, Oz is all right. He may come and work here, take Grover Price's house. You know Grover and his wife died in the plague?' She nods, she saw David's list at the vicar's house. 'While Dick was cutting a caper for Esther's benefit, Oz asked me about work. He used to be stable-lad to Sir Thomas Harcourt at Woodley. A fellow like Oz could do worse than work for the mistress. But we'll have to wait and see. She tells us there's a brother of Cazanove's will inherit.'

Wat looks less than enthusiastic about the idea. Alice says, 'If you don't wish to work for him, Wat, I feel sure there will be a wide choice of work now in the village, with so many lost.'

He does not reply directly but continues his previous thought. 'As I said, I don't think Oz is any harm. No, it was who we met in the woods when I was seeing them off the land.'

'Who was that?' Alice asks.

'Bart Johnson.' He casts her a sidelong look to see if she has understood. 'Yes. A nasty piece of work that one. I'd not trust him near any womenfolk of mine.'

'What was he doing in the woods?'

'Apparently they cooked up this idea between them to come and beg. Bart persuaded them into it, then sat down when they got that far and told them to go on ahead. He said if three arrived it would look like "hordes of poor". My guess is he knew we'd take one look at him and chase off all three without a groat. Dick told me all this as we went back because he was mad at Bart and had decided he wouldn't give him a share of anything they got anyway.'

'Have they tried this before?'

'With the master here? Never! They knew better.'

Alice, probing, says, 'I must confess I did not know your master very well. My father never sought his company.'

'No, your father wouldn't. Decent men took a wide berth round him.' Wat does not mince words. 'He was well hated by most.'

'And by his wife?'

'The mistress? No, she didn't hate him.'

With these brief words Wat withdraws into himself. They continue along the track through the woods, while Alice ponders. After several minutes, he suddenly bursts out, 'Really tried to please him! Made him a wonderful meal that day, she and Esther did. I saw it all laid out ready on the hall table. Neat's tongue, partridges, mutton stew, roast meats, spinach tart and everything. All so dainty with parsley sprinkled over. And whitepot and custards and all manner of sweetmeats. They saw me looking in the hall door and described what it all was for me. I never saw such a spread, a picture to look on.

And what did he do? Threw it all on the floor!'

As Alice pricks up her ears to this news, Wat's indignation spills over. 'Well, that served him right, some of it went in his lap! I saw it wet down his front when we caught up with him.'

'Was he drunk?'

'Not that day, I'd have smelled it on him. He always took wine with his breakfast, but that was hours before. No, he was in one of his foul humours.'

'So the meal was wasted?'

'I heard the crashing from up in his chamber and legged it for the stairs. I just got down when Esther came running to tell me the mistress wanted me to follow him. I went into the hall, thinking the mistress might be hurt. There was food and silver everywhere. He'd gone round and swept just about every dish off the board. Only things left were some fruit and her plate with half-eaten meats. And their gowns all over greasy and spattered where he'd thrown stuff at them in his black humour.'

'Didn't the kitchen servants come to help? They must have heard, surely.'

'They know better than to show their faces. Shut the door and pretend it never happened, that's what they do.'

Alice feels that she sees the widow with new eyes. For all her affluent ease, Mistress Cazanove was no more protected from her husband's nature than the poor tenants in his cottages.

By now they have topped the rise and are on the downward slope. Hillbury village has come into view. Wat says, 'I saw Grover coming out of the barn and grabbed him, we caught up with the master ambling along, muttering about nothing to drink. All that ungoverned choler because Nick Patten hadn't sent a barrel up to the house.'

Wat slows and says to her, 'Anyway, here you are mistress – I believe you are safe now, and if you will forgive me, there is much for me to do. I should get back.'

Watching his retreating back, Alice wonders about the man who hated his master but would not leave him; who is so fiercely loyal to his mistress, but does not seem to know whether he will stay with her, or serve the brother, or what he will do.

29

Apart from her foray on the day she found Sam, Alice's only knowledge of the inn is the kitchen and storerooms. On many occasions in the past, carrying messages from Mother and discussing Hillbury villagers' needs, she has sat with Margery Patten in her kitchen. This is the landlady's stronghold. Here Margery reigns supreme, keeping baker, butcher, carter, the occasional poacher and even the landlord in firm and absolute order. Her five children also fall into this category, though young Nick, the second boy, bodes fair at age nine to outwit both his parents at every turn. Half the village knows that he steals food when his mother's back is turned, or filches ale from the best barrel for a dare, replacing it with a mixture of small ale and mead until the customers accuse the landlord of watering-down. A beating from Margery he dreads more than one from his father, and so it falls out that he is more often discovered in a drunken stupor than groaning from a surfeit of sweetmeats.

Today, however, Margery is not in the kitchen; only young Nick is there, riskily absorbed in the delights of a coffin pie when Alice puts her head round the door.

He jumps, and guilty crumbs fall from his mouth before he realises this is not his mother.

Alice cannot hide her smile. 'I'm hoping to speak with your father. Is he here?'

He nods. As he leaves to fetch his father, he stuffs the last of the pie into his bulging cheeks, chewing and swallowing as he goes.

Alice hears the father's, 'What's she want then?', and young Nick's, 'I dunno, do I?' before the two come into the kitchen from the taproom passage.

'Miss Alice, give ye good day!' Nick senior calls. He adds in a lower tone as he comes up to her, 'Most grieved to hear of your parents.' His voice returns to normal as he continues without pause, 'How can I serve you?'

'Thank you, Nick.' Alice is relieved not to have to discuss her parents for the second time that day. 'I have been visiting Mistress Cazanove who is just back. You know she is now widowed?'

'Oh, yes,' Nick says. 'But tell me, Missus, who's to inherit? Did she hint? I may be landlord here, but I've my own landlord to worry about as ye might say.' Young Nick, with a nine-year-old's curiosity about adult conversations, hangs around quietly behind his father.

'They say there's a brother,' Alice says. 'The attorneys are looking for him. All I can say is that Mistress Cazanove looks very much mistress of the manor for the time being. Did you ever meet his brother?'

'Never, but I hope they find him soon. Tis not right for a woman to inherit such riches.'

'Well, I can't answer for that, Nick, but I am bidden to pass on her assurance that there is no intention of making any changes to your lease at this time.' Alice tries to keep the words bland. She is aware that to Nick Patten it will be anathema to discover that Alice knows of the threat to increase his rent – and worse that his reprieve is being delivered by a woman.

'Ah, is that so? Well, tis neighbourly of her for the time

being until things are properly taken over by this brother.'

'Mistress Cazanove also wished to let you know she is sorry that her husband in his illness overturned the meal you served him that day. She hopes there was no breakage.'

'Course there was no breakage!' Nick swings round as Margery strides in from the yard, carrying three chickens by their legs in one large hand, necks swinging, eyes greyly blank. 'How could there be breakage? We always served him on pewter dishes here, no common earthenware for him. And he had one of the new pewter tankards for his drink. We know how to look after men of his station. What does she think we are?'

'I feel sure she meant no offence, Margery—'

'And the cullis was the stoutest he could have had outside the king's court.' She waves the dead fowl in her hand. 'Made from my own chickens and good Rhenish wine. None of your die-away leafy mutton stews here.' She leans towards Alice, a belligerent gleam in her eye. 'She doesn't know how to feed a man, which is why he came to us!'

Margery is justifiably proud of the inn's reputation for food.

'I heard that he left a good dinner behind there. Seems odd that he should overturn your dish too.' Alice keeps her expression bland.

'Trying it on, he was,' Margery says. She swings the chickens onto the table and proceeds to tear off feathers. 'Just because Fanny made it 'stead of me. Nothing wrong with that cullis!' So that, Alice realises, was further reason why Margery was ready to do battle at the time. Protecting her daughter, who was cook that day.

'So Fanny is now in the kitchen alongside you, Margery? She grows up fast,' Alice says.

'She's eleven, old enough to be doing her bit, and she's a good cook.'

'And Ma had only just got back from her poor-visiting,' adds young Nick, finding an entry at last into this adult exchange.

Margery bristles. 'Who said we wanted to hear from you? You should be helping John in the brew house.'

'Fanny can't cook anyway!' young Nick retorts. 'She forgot to salt Cazanove's cullis!' Dodging his father's reach, he speeds down the passage and disappears into the taproom.

'She did not! That was a good cullis!' Margery shouts after him. They hear the door to the street open and slam. 'I'll wash his mouth out when I get hold of him!' she fumes. '"Cazanove" indeed! Where's respect in the young these days?' She turns on her husband. 'Has he been at the barrel again?'

'Go to, woman, go to, tis just high spirits,' Nick says tolerantly.

Alice grasps her opportunity before the wrangle becomes a row. 'I saw Master Cazanove as he left here that day,' she says. 'Grover and Alaric were helping Wat to support him.'

'I couldn't work it out,' Nick says. 'You'd have thought he was a green'un, but it was only some autumn ale he had. I tapped the barrel that day for the first time and it's the best I've ever made, but it wasn't so strong as all that, and he only had the one pot.' He winks at his wife. 'I meant to tell you, he wanted some up at the mansion but there wasn't that much of it so I was hanging out for a better price like you always say. Then we left home all of a sudden, so that's a barrel saved. Make much more by the pot down here than what he was willing to pay.'

Margery adds, 'As stingy and sneering as he could hang together, that one. He hadn't even finished his pot before he

172

started throwing his weight about. In the end Nick had to tell Wat to get him out.'

'My guess,' Nick says, 'my guess is he had a few before he came down here.'

'I heard not,' says Alice.

'Probably needed fortifying,' Margery says, ignoring her, 'having to look at that milk-and-water creature moping around the house all day with her long face. Enough to drive any man out of his wits.'

'There was another matter I wanted to mention,' Alice says. 'When you came back from Honiton, you will have found your haystore at the far end had been occupied.'

'Daniel told us,' Nick says. 'The little boy you've got up there.'

'I'm still looking for his father,' she says, 'The family were in one of Josh Baker's cottages but mother and baby died and the father had already left, we don't know where. If you hear of him, you'll let me know, or Vicar Rutland, won't you?'

'Dan asked us to as well,' Nick tells her. 'Nothing yet.'

'Master Cazanove's cottages now, not Josh Baker's,' Margery says. 'Why don't you ask her up the mansion?'

'That's why I went there, Margery. Mistress Cazanove doesn't know, but is looking for any records her husband may have left.'

Nick turns to Margery. 'You said you thought you knew that young fellow who came in for a drink.'

'I remember the one,' Margery agrees. 'And I'd know that face again. I've seen him around somewhere, I'm sure of it.'

'I'll let parson know if we hear anything,' Nick says.

'Or tell Daniel,' Margery adds. 'He comes down to the smithy every now and then.'

She is looking down, plucking feathers at random from

one of the chickens. There is a little silence and she looks up at her husband. 'It'll be quicker for me to step along to the smithy than you to go up the hill, Nick.' She shrugs. 'No matter, suit yourself, if you want to walk all the way up there to parson's place.'

Embarrassed without really knowing why, Alice steps in. 'Nick, I feel you are owed some recompense for the ruined hay where Sam took refuge.'

'No need, no need,' Nick says. 'The place is cleaned out long since, and there's little enough harm, since the boy didn't have the pestilence.'

'If I ask Daniel to bring a bottle of hay when he next comes, will that suffice?'

'How long's Daniel to be up at your place, then?' Margery asks. An innocent enough question, but for the narrowed eyes.

'While there is so little business at the smithy, he's helping with the work Father and Ian would have done,' Alice tells her, and adds truthfully but also for Nick's benefit, 'I am grateful for a man's help, I could not manage else.'

'Sleeps up there, too, I hear?' Margery says. Nick shoots her a quick look but says nothing.

'He says he is very comfortable in the hayloft,' Alice replies, holding Margery's gaze.

'It's not unknown for night wanderers to make their way into houses where there are women alone.'

'Vagrants, you mean, Margery?'

'Whatever you like to call them, Alice.'

'Which is why Daniel insists on my putting the bar on the door at night.'

'While he goes out to his comfortable hayloft.'

'Exactly so.'

At last, 'Well,' Nick says with forced brightness, 'there we are.' He looks from his wife to Alice and back again, and nervously rubs his hands together. 'That's good then!'

30

'That officious simpleton Nutley!' Alice explodes, pacing to and fro across the kitchen. 'He has to tell his bloodcurdling stories without let or hindrance! And to the widow as well, to lay out the gory details of Cazanove's snatching. He should be pilloried! That would dent his inflated self-regard!'

She casts a wild glance at Daniel as he sits on the settle by the kitchen fire. 'She couldn't breathe. She was gasping and he just ignored her and carried on! Thank goodness Esther was right outside. She just pushed Nutley aside and went to her by the window. I had no idea what to do, but Esther took Ursula's hands and sat on the window seat with her and talked quietly to her until her breathing slowed and her panic passed, and she could be taken upstairs.' And Nutley sat there waving a paper at me, like this!' She makes a flapping motion in Daniel's face. 'He wanted a signature, for goodness sake!'

She curls her fingers back round her mug of posset as she paces again. 'What an idiot!'

The smell of spices wafts from the smooth sweet mixture. In the silence following her outburst, she comes to a halt in front of Daniel. 'What?'

'Your face, Alice. He certainly got under your feathers, didn't he?'

She gives a reluctant laugh and sits down at the other end of the settle. 'Even so, it was wonderful to see her put Abel

Nutley in his place when he arrived. He didn't know whether to sit or stand, and ended up calling her *My Lady*. I could have thrown my arms around her noble neck.'

'Wish I'd been a fly on the wall,' Daniel says.

'He wasn't punctured for long, but the remembrance will be bitter for him. Not only were three women watching, but two of us he had just tried to dismiss.'

Her thoughts revert to her other news. She says, 'I hope it's a very long time before the maidservant is sent with news of Sam's father.'

Daniel gives her a sideways look. 'Ware, Alice, don't get too fond of him. His Da could be back any day.'

'I can't help it. You're fond of him too, admit it.'

Elbows on his knees, staring into the fire, Daniel smiles. Then, 'So what else did you find out about Master Cazanove?'

'I confess I did encourage her to talk about it. I think you were right.'

'Right about what?'

'There was something strange about his death, though I don't know what it means. Apparently there was an argument about his midday meal at home. They had prepared a special meal at his behest, but he barely touched the first dishes before he threw the whole lot on the floor. That was how his breeches became soaked, by the way.'

'What'd he do that for?'

'Said it was disgusting or something.'

'Mayhap his Missus put poison in the pudding.' There is a twinkle in Daniel's eye.

'I may not like the woman, but I don't think it is fair to suspect her of that. Withal, she can't have done,' Alice says. 'She and Esther prepared it together.'

'Then this Esther must have slipped something in, while

milady wasn't looking.'

'Stop laughing at me, Daniel!' Alice says, half laughing herself. 'Mistress Cazanove was eating with him. Had what he had. She'd have been taken ill, too. Do you know,' Alice turns to him, 'in the normal way, he made her attend on him at meals. What a man! We always ate all six together here, and we weren't alone in that. Even Ralph Cooper would never make his lady wait on him.'

'Can you see Ralph Cooper making his lady do anything? He's more likely to have to wait on her.'

Alice laughs again. 'True. Anyway, Cazanove arrived at the inn muttering about leafy stew or something and that was what prompted the rich cullis. Nick said he only served him the one pot of autumn ale – Nick thought he was already drunk when he arrived.'

Daniel looks doubtful. 'His words weren't slurring when he told Nick about putting up the rent, leastways, not so's I noticed.'

'Mistress Cazanove says he didn't have a drink with the meal because they were down to small ale, and that wasn't good enough for Milord. And Wat says he didn't smell any drink on Cazanove's breath.'

'Ah, so you met Wat?'

'He walked me back through Harman's Copse because he said Bart Johnson was there yesterday and might still be hanging around. Called him a nasty piece of work.'

'He's right there,' Daniel says with feeling. 'Piece of cowshard.'

'Anyway, as regards Cazanove, he probably wasn't drunk.'

'No.'

'If we agree he didn't succumb to the plague, what's left? *Was* he poisoned?' Alice pauses, thinking. 'If he was taken ill at the inn, I think we have to believe it could have been poison working. But who administered it, and when?'

'Margery might well say he was drunk, if it was her slipped something in his food.'

'Margery didn't prepare it. She was out doing her rounds. Fanny cooked it.'

'Oh, well, insult to her daughter's cooking, threatening her man. Quite the tiger is Margery when she's aroused.'

'Oh, no, surely you don't mean—?' She recovers herself. 'Daniel, you're laughing at me. Again!'

'Just a little. Still, if the man was murdered—'

'If?'

'— and the widow about to inherit?'

'No, the brother gets everything apparently. I must say, though, for a woman about to be dispossessed, she looks quite untroubled.'

'Got her family money tied up safe, I expect.'

'She cites a small settlement, though that's probably a small fortune to the rest of us. You know, Daniel, I have a strong feeling that her marriage brought her little joy. She looks much younger now, even allowing for the fact that she was aged with worry when I paid my first visit.'

'So, what did you think of Wat Meredith?'

'I couldn't make him out, but to her credit, Mistress Cazanove seems to have inspired great loyalty in him towards herself. Not only him. Esther as well, so protective of her mistress. If looks could kill, the one she gave Nutley as she took Ursula out of the room would have struck him dead on the spot.'

'So we're back where we started, with nobody and everybody to suspect. That's so?'

'All we know is that he threw his meal on the floor, left the mansion in a black choler, and at the inn they thought him drunk, though Wat didn't, and he apparently had nothing more than autumn ale. He went red in the face and looked as if he'd fallen asleep. At some point Nick told Wat to get him out. When I saw them in the street, I could tell he was nearly witless and they threw him over his saddle like a sack of parsnips to get him home. Master Marchant saw him up at the mansion and diagnosed plague, and Cazanove died soon after.'

'Within the hour. Wat came to us well before dark to say his master was dead.'

'And you buried him in Harman's Copse, and he was snatched fresh from his grave. So much blood had collected in his head that it poured out when they started to cut him up. Do you recall you noticed he was looking piggy-eyed? He would if his face was bloated.'

'You have a *herbal*, Alice; why don't you have a look in it?'

'Of course! I think of it as a book of salves and simples, but it shows the malignant plants too.' *And if I discover something, what then? What will I do with any knowledge I find? And what will I do if I find nothing?*

They are both silent with their thoughts. Daniel takes a mouthful of posset and rolls it appreciatively round his mouth before swallowing. 'Pretty little clearing that, in Harman's Copse.'

'Whereabouts, Daniel? It's not near the path.'

'No, much further in. There used to be a woodsman's hut. It made sense to bury Cazanove there, they never came to church at Hillbury and we couldn't bury him at Westover on account of they had no plague.'

'The only time I heard tell of Harman's Copse was when the new woodsman and his wife and child died in 'eighteen.

They'd only just arrived and they died of plague.'

Daniel makes a face. 'That's what Cazanove put about when they burned the place down after.'

'You're saying that's not what happened?'

'Grover Price knew something, he let slip one night years ago in his cups.'

'What did he say?'

'I don't know what he meant exactly, he was in a strange melancholy.' Daniel considers for a moment. 'Something about a trinity. Said he was talking to the spirit. He said, *"For earth thou art, till thou return to earth".*'

'I thought it was "dust".'

'Just so. Dust was what David said over all the graves we dug. But Grover insisted earth.'

'What did he mean, then?'

He shrugs. 'Curious fancies beset him that night.' There is a pause while they each think their own thoughts. Then Daniel asks, 'What's a 'leafy stew', anyway?'

'What?'

'You said Cazanove was muttering about a leafy stew.'

'A chamerchande. You know, mutton stew with parsley. Daniel, didn't you ask Grover what he meant by earth instead of dust?'

'Next day I did. He denied everything, said I was lop-headed.' He shrugs and sits back, glances at her. 'You know something, Alice,' he says in a wheedling tone, 'I wouldn't mind a chamerchande for supper one day. Can you get parsley this time of year?'

'You can if you dry it in the summer.'

'Of course, chicken cullis was a good choice for Cazanove, given that Margery's known for it hereabouts.' He raises his mug, a grin pulling at his mouth. 'But your sack posset beats 'em all, Alice.'

'Pooh! Honeyed words. Daniel, do you realise tomorrow is Midwinter's Day? It's nearly Christmas. That reminds me, Susan Cushing and her sister are returned. I met them as I was coming out of Nick's. As Susan was Mother's oldest friend, I have invited them with their maidservant to come the day after Christmas and stay through to Twelfth Night. No revels, of course, but I should so like to have company in the house. And with you here too, that will make six of us.'

'Alice, it's very kind of you but I'm just a blacksmith.'

'A blacksmith? Oh, now, that is bad. Still, I'm just a yeoman's daughter, and Susan and her sister are ladies in reduced circumstances, and Sam is from Baker's Row.'

'You forgot the maidservant.'

'Oh, haven't you heard? She's a princess in disguise. Any more objections?'

He spreads his hands.

'Good, that's settled, then.'

31

Alice leans back in her chair at the head of the table in the hall and regards the six others ranged around the board. Vicar Rutland on her right is already shaking out his sleeves in the throes of reluctant preparation to take his leave. She is fond of the vicar, having been tutored by him, and having enjoyed his kindness and understanding all her life. She is also aware that his presence at her table will help in publicly cementing her ownership of this land. He looks at the waxed board reflecting the candlelight in soft pools of yellow, the remains of the meal littering the pewter dishes, the cracked nut shells and orange peel scattered on the wood. He turns towards her. 'A memorable Christmas indeed, Alice.'

'I hope so, vicar. I am glad you found the time between services to sup with us.'

'Such a board as I have not enjoyed in years,' he says. 'You have done us proud.'

She smiles her thanks. 'In fairness, I should tell you,' she says, 'that the onion tarts and those marchpane sweetmeats were Susan's contribution. And her sister brought the oranges and figs.'

For the first time in weeks, the table in the hall is being used for a household meal. Alice has raided coffer and court cupboard for pewter and pudding bowls, set a wax candle in every holder she can lay her hands on, polished the knives to a gleam, and reverently brought out the Venetian goblets from the court cupboard in the winter parlour. This morning, Sam helped Daniel to gather evergreen boughs, and on their return, danced around in an ecstasy of excitement at the preparations, his eyes big at sights the like of which he has never seen. Alice watched him doing cartwheels through the hall and felt she could have joined in.

When the Cushing household arrived mid-morning, the sisters helped Sam build a makeshift crib, in which the faggot-horse became an ox for the day, and the two whittled figures, Samuel and Zachariah, took on the roles of Joseph and Mary. Charles Rutland arrived in time to express due admiration. They gathered, all seven, round the table, polished wood reflecting the gleam of glass, faces glowing in the candlelight. Alice and Susan, as heads of their respective households, have reversed their station in true Christmas tradition, and played maidservants to the rest.

'And I did not know your father had such fine wines,' the vicar adds, swirling the last of his around his glass.

'Truth to tell, he did not,' she admits, laughing. 'Daniel acquired that Spanish wine, but from what source I felt it wiser not to enquire.'

'Good food, wine, company. What more could anyone ask?'

'You have all of you helped to make it a happy day.'

'Tell me, what is young Sam doing down at the end there?' he asks.

'Ah, he appears to be instructing Susan in the correct way to eat a medlar. He had his first taste of them here.'

He laughs, then bends his elbow to the table and she leans the better to catch his words. 'Would I be right in assuming an attachment between Daniel and Susan's pretty little maidservant?'

Alice glances at the fair-haired beauty deep in converse with Susan's sister. 'I too noticed she looks under her lashes at him, but in truth vicar, I have seen no partiality on his side.'

'A pity. He is not one to thrive in the solitary life.'

'No, he enjoys company, and see how gentle he is with Sam. He will make a good father some day.'

'He is a warm-hearted man with, I imagine, a strong disposition to fondness for a caring woman?'

He is right, she thinks. What if Daniel were to take a fancy to Susan's maid, and marry her? 'I should rejoice for Daniel to find a wife,' she says, 'but not just yet, I still need his help here.' She laughs at her own jest.

'I believe, Alice, you should not expect him to remain satisfied with his current station at Hill House for long.'

She sighs. 'I know, and I must find his replacement. He will want to go back to the smithy in due course.'

'I wasn't thinking—'

Here Daniel gets up and comes round to lean an arm on the back of Alice's chair. He addresses the vicar. 'I believe, sir, Alice should stay well away from Margery Patten for a few months, for her own safety.'

Charles Rutland frowns in puzzlement. 'What's this, Daniel? What is the danger?'

'Why, sir, Mistress Patten might discover that Alice's hand in dressing a capon in claret and orange is finer than anything the inn can produce.'

'Daniel!' Alice's face grows warm at the compliment.

'I see exactly what you say,' Charles Rutland replies and nods sagely. 'We must protect Alice for her own good.'

'And ours.' Daniel adds.

32

Alice, returning from the village towards the turn of the year, looks up the track to see Hill House ahead beyond the belt of trees. Daniel is there, coming from the yard and stooping to pick something up. Holding it in his hand, he straightens and appears to be talking to another person out of Alice's sight. As he turns, he sees her and indicates to the unseen person. Ready for Sam to career round the corner and race towards her as he always does, she breaks into a smile and a run at the same moment.

A corpulent vision in shades of green steps into view, brightening at the spectacle of the girl running towards him. Alice's heart sinks as quickly as her pace, she curses under her breath. What is Gerald Cooper doing here? And hard behind that thought, where is his omnipresent mother?

His many-tucked hat sits at a desperately jaunty angle, sporting a large feather that dangles as though recently under feline attack. His doublet is the peascod sort – with an exaggerated belly like a strutting cockerel – except that his needs no stuffing to create its paunch. Sulphur-tinged satin bulges between the panes of his cabbage-hued breeches. His round face is flushed red from exertion, made worse by the way his stout neck is hemmed in by a ruff that sticks out beyond the line of his shoulders.

Gerald is the picture of discomfort. No one, Alice reflects despairing, no one wears such great cartwheels these days. She wonders briefly what has happened to Gerald's second chin. Corseted into submission by stuff and starch, no doubt.

The thing Daniel has picked up is a large kerchief with which Gerald now proceeds to mop his visage. Torn between the impulse to laugh and exasperation that now he will think she was running to greet him, she walks towards him, composing her face into friendly welcome. She dips a brief curtsey.

'Give you season's greetings, Gerald,' she says. 'I did not know you had returned. Is all well with you? Are your father and mother well?'

'Yes, I thank you, they are ... I am ... we are well.' He is always tongue-tied in her presence.

'No doubt you were assiduous to avoid all spotted fish while you were away, and other such hazardous sources of infection?'

'Indeed,' Gerald assures her. 'I was most careful to shun all dangers. They served charrfish one day and I would not even enter the room where it was. And I burned the letter I received without breaking the seal.'

'Very wise, Gerald. Every precaution should be taken to guard against pestilence. The dangers of inkblots cannot be overstated.' Behind Gerald, Daniel shoots her a look, she ignores him. 'And here is a new bravery,' she goes on, regarding the ells and ells of satin that sway around Gerald's calves as he moves. 'I declare I have never seen its like!'

That at least is true.

He strokes and pulls at the cloth, and looks pleased. 'It is the very latest from the Low Countries. Twelve shillings an ell! The tailor says it is called Pluderhosen, he vows it has a great deal of elegance.'

'It certainly has a great deal of fabric, does it not, Gerald?'

'The green here,' he fingers his verdant silk doublet, 'and the yellow, they complement one another, the tailor says. Do not you agree?'

'None can hold a candle to such array,' is the best she can manage.

'I am glad you like it. And I chose the points myself,' he adds, fingering multiple bows of brimstone-coloured laces threaded through the waist of his doublet holding the breeches in place.

'You are quite the fine gentleman. It must take you at least half an hour to dress.'

'Near an hour actually. My mother wished me to dress fine, but even she was becoming quite impatient.' Without warning, he has possessed himself of her hand in both of his and bends a wet kiss to her fingers. 'Alice, I am glad to see you well! I mean, that is, I am sorry for the loss of your parents and I feared for you. I feared very much and I wished ... except ... '

'Except you could not risk your own family's safety by coming here,' she finishes for him. 'You were quite right, Gerald, and we did not expect it.' She wriggles her hand free of his damp grasp and surreptitiously wipes it on her skirt.

'That is partly so,' he begins again, 'but also we left early, that is ... I wished my father had told yours about the Plague Orders ... but my mother said—' He is still fumbling for words when a strident voice calls from the house.

'Gerald! Are you to be forever with the servants in the yard?'

Gerald squirms in his finery as his eyes dart to the house, then back to Alice.

'Do you go into the house,' she tells him, 'and let your mother know you are delayed because you saw me returning.'

Obediently he directs his steps to the door, risking a slow garrotting as the holding cords on his cloak augment the strangling effect of the ruff around his throat.

She turns to Daniel. His face is impassive, she herself is struggling with the enormity of what Gerald has just hinted, but before she can say anything, 'I directed her to the winter parlour,' Daniel says. 'I offered her some of the brew we drink but she refused for both of them. I think her son would have been glad of it. Even though it's only for the "servants".'

'Daniel, I am sorry, but you know Dame Cooper. She is forever giving offence. But I shall take Gerald a mug of ale, for he is monstrously heated in that get-up. What has he been doing?'

Daniel grins. 'One of their horses cast a shoe, so Master Cooper is gone to the smithy thinking I'll be there to fix it, except I'm not going there till the morning. Meantime the dame bethinks herself she'll ride over to visit you, and drags that outsize frog along of her.'

'But they've only two horses!' exclaims Alice. 'You do not tell me she made him walk in those delicate boots?'

'She surely did. Likes her consequence does the dame.'

'Poor Gerald.' Alice tries not to laugh at the idea of Gerald and his mother making their stately progress, he walking alongside her horse like a bow-legged groom. 'I shall lend him Cassie for his journey home, and he can return her tomorrow when he is more suitably clad.'

'Poor Gerald should try being half a man and tell his mother he can make his own way in life,' Daniel says. Then, 'Do you wish I should saddle her up? Cassie, I mean.'

'Dear Daniel, I should be very grateful.' She looks around. 'And I think Sam likes to watch you do that. Is he around?'

'About somewhere,' Daniel says. 'He was in the still room

189

earlier. Do you want him?'

'Not at present. As long as he is within call.' She takes a deep breath. 'And now I must go and be polite to Mistress Cooper. And try to prevent her son from melting under my roof.'

'That was wicked of you about the inkblots, Alice.'

She feels her smile broaden. 'I know, but I couldn't resist it. He takes these satirical pamphlets so seriously. He really believes he will contract plague from anything with spots.'

33

'Mistress Cooper, it is kind in you to visit so soon after the pestilence.' She drops a curtsey. The woman on the cushioned seat by the winter parlour hearth inclines her head in unsmiling acknowledgement.

Emeline Cooper's lean face and long nose are complemented by a thin-lipped mouth that is generally tight shut when not airing a complaint or criticism. She dresses mostly in dark green or grey, neither of which hues enhance her sallow cheek. Her hat today, like her gown, is redolent of a conifer forest. It sits straight on the top of her head, high and tapered towards its flat crown, with an uncompromisingly straight brim. Her gown of fine wool, too lightweight to be English cloth, is whaleboned to her upper form with not a crease to be seen. She takes pride in her spare frame, and it is said the young Ralph Cooper fell not for the woman but for the waist. In keeping with this her shoulders are narrow and fleshless. As are her opinions.

'Gerald,' Alice goes on, approaching him on the other side of the hearth 'I feel sure you could do with a little refreshment. I believe your mother declined for herself?' She hands him the tankard, which he eyes with evident relief. Before his mother can gainsay him he takes several gulping mouthfuls and sits back with a satisfied sigh, almost succeeding in subduing the belch that gurgles in his throat. He is still wearing his cloak but Alice feels unequal to the task of helping him extract the ties from under his ruff. She takes a chair between the two.

'I hope you had a comfortable Christmas with your relations,' Alice says into the stiff silence.

'We did not,' Emeline Cooper says. 'We had a miserable time for the entire visit and were most uncomfortable.'

'I am sorry to hear that. Were you cramped for space?'

'On the contrary, Alice, there is no need of such a large house, even with three children. They have far too much space. It takes forever to get from one's chamber to the parlour. And they have furbished it with new things. New, new, new, everywhere you look. They have painted the panelling, I tell you!'

'I believe it is still quite fashionable to do so,' Alice comments.

'And they have upholstered backstools, just like any tradesman!'

'I thought you told Father you wanted some like—' Gerald begins.

'I was plagued by Ralph's sister all the while. It was "Emeline, do join us in this" and "Emeline, wouldn't you like to do that", simply so that she could show off all her expensive appointments. You know how it is, Alice, when a woman gets above herself.'

'You surprise me, madam. I met her last year, I recall, and she seemed so very pleasant.'

'Trying to rise above one's appointed station makes for a pathetic creature, my dear.'

This, Alice reflects, from the maltster's daughter, who within months of her marriage, changed the name of her husband's property from 'Coopers' to 'Cowper' in an attempt to conceal the trading origins of his forbears.

'And their travelling coach! So large and ostentatious, just the sort of thing I abhor!'

'I am sorry to hear you did not enjoy your visit,' Alice says. 'Was your husband equally glad to return?'

'He! Oh, no, he spent most of the time out hunting and hawking with the men! And Gerald here abandoned his mother in favour of his scrubby little cousins. I am a patient woman, Alice, but there is a limit to my endurance. I was polite to her of course, I always am. And so she believes we left on the best of terms.'

Alice pictures Ralph Cooper's sister seeing them all off with relief in her heart and a dry handkerchief to her eyes. 'You and Gerald went there before Master Cooper of course,' she says. 'So you had a longer time to bear your inconveniences. He only joined you later, I believe?'

'Yes, he stayed on to try to close the … to put all in good order at Cowper before he left.'

'Of course, he would want to do that,' Alice says, carefully sympathetic. 'He must have been glad he acted quickly in getting you away to safety.'

'As to that!' Emeline Cooper dismisses any possibility of her husband's prudence. 'He could have chosen better, given the weeks and weeks we were stuck in that place.'

'In a crisis, perhaps one does not think with so much foresight,' Alice suggests. 'And you must have been most anxious when you left, knowing Master Cooper was staying at great personal risk with the plague threatening.'

But Emeline Cooper is not to be so easily caught out. 'Had he received the Plague Orders, Alice, of course I would have been most anxious. 'But they came later.'

'And how was your journey back?'

Emeline Cooper reverts to her catalogue of misfortunes. 'We had to come home all three together in that pint-sized coach that my husband refuses to replace. I've told him time and again, especially when we visit Sir Thomas and Lady Harcourt, that it is so lowering to be seen in such a shabby, cramped contraption.'

'Father says that it is more than made up for by being invited to the Harcourts anyway,' Gerald says.

His mother ignores him. 'And then halfway home, the wretched wheel became stuck in mud and we had to spend the night at a most inferior inn, and I have been quite unwell since.'

'I see you have not had an easy time of it, Mistress Cooper.'

'And then on top of everything, Alice, we find on our return the galling news that your mother and father are dead.'

Alice cannot trust herself to speak.

Even Gerald whispers a warning, 'Mother!'

'I mean, of course, galling for you, my dear Alice. Although I too feel it greatly. I am a woman of deep, though private, feeling.' Emeline Cooper reverences her deep though private feeling by lowering her eyes and placing a hand on the cage around her bosom. 'A terrible thing to have happened and I knew that despite my illness I had to come here to commiserate with you, and to speak with you on the subject of your future.'

Alice wonders to herself for the hundredth time what her mother ever saw in Emeline Cooper. Alive, Ann Edwards was a prophet without honour on the subject of the Coopers. Dead, she commands Alice's restraint towards them. But Alice draws the line at betrothal to Gerald. In any event that conversation with her father still echoes in her mind. " ... she would surely get her hands on your portion ..." That, and Gerald's admission in the courtyard, that his father implemented the Plague Order long after it was actually issued.

Mistress Cooper comes straight to the point. 'Alice, 'you are alone in the world, and without that parental guidance which is so necessary to a maidenly female.'

'I am indeed alone, madam, but I have my memory of my parents and long years of their good influence over my life which I am not like to forget in a hurry.'

'A young woman on her own is liable to the evil temptations of life, and cannot be expected to fend for herself, Alice.'

Alice frowns in puzzlement. Evil temptations? 'But I appear to be fending quite adequately, Mistress Cooper. I have known this house and its routine all my life. Indeed, I have been running it since I was a girl.'

'I am talking of your moral and spiritual welfare, in which your parents, God save their memory, were woefully inadequate.'

'Madam, I protest!'

'Your parents were seen at church but once on Sundays, and it was the talk of the village.'

'Something my parents instilled in me, madam, was never to listen to village gossip,' Alice says tartly. 'I believe it was not a concern to the vicar, anyway, or he would have voiced his disquiet when he took his Christmas meal with us four days ago.' *Put that in your pipe and smoke it, dame.*

'I advise you not to bandy words with one who is your elder and better, child.'

Alice almost laughs at her transformation from maidenly female to infant.

'Is it not apparent to you, Alice, that the vicar came to your Christmas meal because of your past waywardness? He was of course trying to bring you back into the fold.'

'Mistress Cooper, I am confused. Please help me. Are you concerned at my inability to protect my virtue, or at my sparse attendance, as you see it, at church?'

The flicker of hesitation in the other woman's eyes is temporary respite for Alice. There is a pause, then Emeline Cooper smiles. Whenever Emeline Cooper smiles, Alice is tempted to look for sight of a swishing tail under the dark skirts.

'Alice, your soul is in danger of corruption. It is an evil world out there. There are temptations from all quarters which a woman on her own, weak as she is, must be hard put to resist.'

'You say so? What influences? Please be clear, madam? I am unaware of any such.'

'Ah, that is the very way in which such enticements will seduce the unwary.' She puts out a thin hand to grasp Alice's arm. 'I judge you are in need of protection, Alice, which I can give you, now in your time of need, you poor thing.'

So I am not even an infant now, Alice reflects, merely a *poor thing*. 'What aid is it you offer me, madam?'

'To care for you, to …' Clearly she cannot quite bring herself to say, *to love you*. She amends instead, '… to be as a mother to you.'

'And what does Gerald think about this?'

'Gerald does not wish anything other than what his mother wishes, do you Gerald?'

'Yes, that is, no, or, er …' Startled out of passivity, Gerald appears uncertain whether to give his accustomed Yes, or whether in this case Yes means No. He wriggles in embarrassment.

'You see? Gerald is in harmony with his mother.' She fires a quelling look in his direction and he dwindles once more. 'We wish you to come and spend the remaining days of Christmas at Cowper, Alice. We have come this morning precisely for this purpose.'

'That is most kind and I thank you, but you see, I have guests.'

'What guests?'

'The Cushing sisters and their maidservant.'

'A maidservant is not a guest Alice. And do you think me a dullard? I can see there are no guests here.'

'They have returned to the village for the day, to see that all is well at their house. They are back in the morning to stay until New Year's Day. I am but just returned from walking them down there.' In truth, Alice reflects, Susan is wary of overstaying her welcome and this is her way of giving Alice a break, a day to herself.

'Well-a-day, as it's only the Cushing sisters, they will not mind when they know it is Cowper you are visiting.'

'But I should mind very much to curtail an invitation and send my guests away. It would be most discourteous!' Alice gives the other woman a straight look. 'My parents taught me to keep to my word.'

Emeline Cooper regards Alice with narrowed eyes. 'You will learn, Alice, that it is not wise to call on your upbringing to support your wilfulness. You are without family in this house and it is not seemly for a respectable young woman to live so. I can offer you protection when you come to live at Cowper. It will be best for you, and I can keep an eye on you. On your welfare, that is.'

'It is most kind of you, but I am comfortable here, madam, and I have Daniel for my protection as you have seen.'

'And that's another thing. It is not fitting for an unmarried woman and a servant to be sharing the same household.'

'Daniel is not a servant. He is his own freeholder, as you know. He came here to help me while his work remains low at the smithy and I provide him with meals in return. In any event, Sarah Coppen had a manservant and everyone still liked and respected her.'

'Sarah Coppen was different – she was much older.'

Alice opens her eyes wide. 'As I understand it, madam,' she says, 'the temptations are much the same for old as for young?'

'Alice!'

Even Gerald sits up at this.

Then the door flies open and Sam hurtles in. 'Alice, Alice! I saw a rat, and it ran round and round and we trapped it in the corner and Daniel got a spade and he squashed it – squish! – like that and I want to pick it up but he won't let me—' He stops as he meets the stony stare of the woman in sombre garb. 'Who's that?'

Alice rises and goes over to him. 'Sam, come and meet Mistress Cooper and her son Master Gerald Cooper. They are our neighbours. Mistress Cooper, Gerald, this is Sam. He is presently under my care.'

Sam keeps close to Alice as she introduces him. Gerald looks genial, his mother forbidding.

'Would you like to see the rat?' Sam asks the frowning woman. 'It's all right, it's dead.'

'No, I do not, and Daniel Bunting should be finding you useful employment instead of sporting with rodents.'

Sam takes exception, not so much to this string of incomprehensible words as to the tone in which they are expressed. He fastens on the name he recognises. 'Daniel's my friend!'

Alice, foreseeing a disastrous encounter, says, 'Sam, I will come and see the rat soon but at the moment I am busy. Do you go to Daniel for a little while, and well done for catching it, I'm proud of you. Did you touch it at all?'

'No,' Sam says, wide-eyed.

'That's good. Daniel is right, you must not touch it. Now, off you go, and I will join you soon.' Sam trots out of the room, turning at the door to stick his tongue out at Mistress Cooper's back.

Alice returns to her seat and says, 'That is the other reason why I must remain here.'

'What child is this? He cannot be a relation?' The older woman is horrified.

'No, a casualty of the plague. His mother and sister died. They were living in Bakery Row but no one knows who he is. I found him in the village and brought him here.'

'Bakery Row? That explains the terrible clothes. Just a poor child, then?' The stress on *poor*.

'Yes. Poor, hungry, cold, and in need of care,' Alice says, keeping her voice even.

'The people who live in those cottages behind the bakery—'

'Lived, Mistress Cooper. The rest are all now dead.'

'You must learn not to interrupt, Alice. Those places are hovels. They don't look after them, nor make the necessary repairs. And their station in life is negligible. What in heaven's name did you think you were doing?'

'I thought I was caring for an orphan in need until we can trace his father.' Her hands are clasped so tightly in her lap that the nails of one are digging into the palm of the other.

'Worthy sentiments, my dear, but he is just a stray brat. Get rid of him. Send him to Westover.'

'The Poor House?'

'Abiding Place, Alice, there is no need to be crude. You cannot keep such a one.'

'I think he's a rather engaging little fellow,' Gerald volunteers.

'Much you know about it,' his mother snaps. She turns to Alice, 'How old is he?'

'About four, I believe.'

'Then he can go to Nick Patten as a pot boy, or he can scare the crows off the crops. Either will give him a living and he will be off your hands.'

'I believe he can do better than that by staying here,' Alice counters. 'I will teach him to read and write and he is already interested to see how Daniel looks after the horses, and in the work at the forge. He is eager to learn all sorts of—'

'Gerald, that reminds me, when we arrived, did you not send the blacksmith down to the forge to attend your father? It appears he has disregarded you, you had better go out and repeat the order.'

'Mother, I believe he has business here and is not—'

'Go and tell him, Gerald, do not argue with me!' Gerald stands up, but Alice interjects at this point. 'Mistress Cooper, many of those who own horses are not back after the pestilence and there is little business for Daniel at present, so he only spends half a day here and there at the forge. You will find him there tomorrow morning.' She turns to Gerald. 'Daniel is saddling Cassie for your journey home.' Alice also now rises, and Mistress Cooper has little choice but to unbend her frame and depart.

Out in the yard Daniel and Sam are nowhere to be seen. Cassie, duly saddled, stands nuzzling the Cooper's mare and Alice bears with Gerald's effusive thanks as he leads first his mother's horse and then the borrowed mare to the length of tree trunk by the stable door that acts as mounting block. While Gerald makes his goodbyes she focuses on holding the stirrup so that his saddle doesn't slip, and then steps back keeping her hands firmly clasped behind her. 'If you bring Cassie with your mare to the forge tomorrow, Gerald, I shall ask Daniel to be ready for you, and he will bring Cassie back here after.'

'I could bring back Cassie myself?' he offers.

'Thank you, Gerald, but Daniel will be coming back here anyway.'

Alice watches their departing backs, mulling over the information Gerald let slip. *"I wished my father to tell yours."* So Ralph Cooper deliberately delayed implementing the Plague Orders. He sent his own family away, probably when he first knew the Orders were to be issued, and that was weeks before Abel Nutley came waving his Plague Order. And Cooper had stayed to close the deal with Cazanove about the sale of his fleece. Side-stepping the guild must have been worth a great deal of money for him to risk so much. But to murder Cazanove when it failed? Ralph Cooper? Without his Lady Macbeth at his shoulder to push him into it? That did not ring true, somehow.

Daniel and Sam appear from the barn. While Sam jumps crab-like sideways imploring her to come and see the dead rat, Daniel says, 'Sorry he rushed in to join you like that, I tried to stop him but he was gone like a shot.'

'No matter, it was worth it to see her face when he offered to show her the rat!'

Daniel smiles a slow smile.

'Mistress Cooper thinks Sam should earn his own living,' Alice tells him.

'Does she, now?'

'She thinks you are being kept from your smithy by your work here.'

'I see.'

'And she thinks my parents' deaths "galling".'

'She *what?*'

'You see, Emeline Cooper shared a common wish with my mother that I should marry Gerald, and now that her ally is gone, it's going to be doubly difficult for her.'

Daniel grins broadly. 'Not her day, is it?'

34

Daniel has toyed in his mind with the idea of returning permanently to the forge. He has been into the village regularly since coming to Hill House. There is sometimes a farm horse which wants shoeing or the lynchpin to a cart wheel which needs making. But no more than a moment's work. It puts him in a melancholy, seeing the sparsely peopled street where once there was so much bustle. He wants to leave all that misery and death behind and get on with life again. He wants to feel normal, be busy, have things to plan for.

Everywhere he goes, his brother David is there; mending a spoke out front, fitting an axle, hacking a new shaft from a seasoned branch accurately and finely with the adze, then smoothing with the pole lathe, his foot treadling up and down and little curls of shavings flying from under his hands. Daniel has never managed to master that thing. That's the trouble. He cannot put David out of his thoughts while he is at the smithy. Everything brings back David. Up at Hill House thoughts of David still bother him at quiet moments but at least there is usually something else going on. Daniel welcomes the distractions. Sam for instance. Forever talking and asking questions and wanting to try things.

'What's that hanging on the hook?'

'That's called a bridle.' The boy's father clearly never owned a horse.

'What's it for?'

Athena stands patiently as Daniel and then Sam fits the bridle on her.

'There's ... three, four, five stalls and only three horses.' He has picked up simple counting so rapidly. 'Does it hurt when you put the horse's shoes on?'

'No, they like to feel the protection of iron.'

'What are these two sticks joined together?' Picking up one end of a flail and swinging it perilously close to Daniel's shins.

'Whoa, there, young Sam. Think I'd better have that.' Daniel possesses himself of the wooden staff with the short heavy stake swinging from it by a strip of leather. 'It's for threshing the grain out of the straw. You put the sheaves on the floor and you hold this end like this, and swing your arm round so the other end comes down hard and knocks the grain out.'

'Can I try?'

'Maybe when you're older, Sam. Tis not a plaything.'

'That frog man looked sad.'

Daniel thinks but does not say, *so would you with a mother like that.*

'Alice says we shouldn't squash the rats. She says that the old cat will get them anyway.'

And again Daniel keeps his thoughts to himself. We don't have to tell Alice everything, and I know for sure young Ian who used to work here would kill them. Many's the time we sat around outside the inn taking bets on how many we'd get. John Patten, Nick's eldest, was best, of course. He had the most rats, with all that malted grain around.

'Alice says funny things when she's asleep.'

'Oh, yes?' Daniel is half-listening, recalling rat contests.

'Yes, she says "Frederick" and sometimes she cries. But

she's asleep.'

Daniel feels as if the flail has been slammed against his ribs.

'Who's Frederick, Daniel?'

Only one Frederick I know. Knew.

'Daniel?'

'Mmm?'

'Who's Frederick?'

'Oh, I expect it was just a dream.'

There is a short silence, then, 'Does your father beat you?'

Only one way this child knows about beating. 'Well, young Sam, when I was little he did, but he soon stopped when I grew bigger than him!' He manages to grin at Sam, who laughs gaily.

'I want to be big and strong like you, Daniel.' The boy is flexing a minute forearm that Daniel could easily circle with thumb and forefinger.

'In that case, young man, you can help me shift this stuff in the corner here. Lord, but there's a mighty lot needs clearing out in this place. We'll do it now, before the ladies come back for the rest of Christmas.'

So the two of them set to work in the end stall of the stables, pulling and turning and inspecting all manner of dusty, cobwebbed debris; broken broom handles, a threadbare rug, old sacks, metal hoops, leather buckets, a two-handled saw, some apple baskets, a wooden candlestick, a rusty billhook, a stool with a split leg where the dowel was set too close to the edge, odd lengths of rough-cut wood, a wide spade for turning grain on the malting floor, a few old cracked leather bottles. Every now and then a spider runs for its life. The chaos gradually diminishes.

While Daniel sorts and discards, coughing as he disturbs

the dust of years, Sam appropriates one of the hoops and plays cherry-pit, throwing pebbles into it from a distance. And Daniel thinks, *how is it a woman I've known for years can so disturb my nights and give me thoughts I shouldn't be having, sweet and bitter at the same time?*

35

Daniel watches as Alice fishes a cloth-wrapped mutton pudding out of the pot suspended over the fire and drops it steaming into the bowl he holds. He puts it on the table and by making quick pulls at the wet knots his wary fingers unwrap it and he draws out the cloth. In the steam from the meat liquor he smells the spices Alice added in the cooking. He has come to look forward to this evening meal, and not only for the food. It is the time when they share the day's events.

'Are you still thinking you should get back to the forge?' she is asking him. In the few days since the Coopers' visit, she has come to face the fact that this arrangement with Daniel cannot last much longer. She cuts a chunk for him and a slice for herself.

He nods his thanks. 'Sooner or later.'

'In due course we shall all get back to a normal life, I suppose,' she says. 'I cannot continue expecting you to be here; you will want to return to the smithy, and I must find a man to manage the land and the livestock and possibly a girl to help in the house.'

'So you won't be sending Sam out to work, then?' he asks through a mouthful of meat. He enjoys watching her instantly fire up.

'That woman! Can she not even remember her own son at that age? Didn't her mother's heart ever stir at sight of him?'

'At Gerald? You're not serious, Alice?'

'Oh, poor Gerald. But how dare she treat Sam as an inferior? A pot-boy indeed!'

'I'll take it that's "No" then?'

She laughs in spite of herself. 'Assuredly that is "No", Daniel.'

'I knew Gerald at that age,' he remembers. 'I was not more'n eight or so myself. I'd just started at the smithy. David was already next door with old Dick wheelwright. One day Gerald came in with Master Cooper, sitting up in front of him on the horse, and they both got down; something needed with my master. I recall Gerald went straight over to David next door and stood there asking questions just like Sam does, and David told me later, young Gerald knew all the woods, ash and beech and all, one from another like, almost as well as David himself. Don't know what happened to that interest of his.'

'My mother saw a similar thing,' Alice recalls. 'She always said Gerald would have been happier as a wheelwright or making furniture. No possibility of that in his station.' She pushes the pudding round her plate, sopping the juices with a piece of bread. 'I had a look in my herbal.'

For a moment Daniel is puzzled; then, 'What did it say?'

'I know this sounds really strange, but Cazanove's symptoms fit with hemlock poisoning. Staggering, bloated face, headache. When I found it, it gave me such a jolt. I suppose I didn't really believe it until then, but this is so clear.'

'Hemlock,' he muses. 'How would you take that?'

'It would have to be disguised in a drink, I suppose. The herbal says it smells foetid. The ancient Greeks used it to execute people. Now what do I do?'

'Ask yourself this – when did Cazanove have a drink, and

who gave it to him?'

'He didn't have one at home because he didn't want small-ale, which was all they had. Nick confirmed that in a way – he told me he had held back from sending up one of his new autumn barrels that day. And Cazanove only had roast meats at home, no liquids, not even the mutton stew because we know he upturned that on himself. Wat said Cazanove had last had wine with his breakfast. And down at the inn both Nick and Margery told me he only had the one drink there.'

'The wine at breakfast, then?'

Alice shakes her head. 'Hemlock symptoms come on quickly. They would have shown long before midday. So who's lying?'

'Someone at the mansion or someone who works at the inn.'

'Of course, there is a third possibility.' Alice says.

'Which is?'

'Someone else got to his drink at Nick's.'

Daniel purses his lips. 'It's possible. It was a mite crowded in there when he came in.'

'Do you think Grover Price could have?'

Daniel shrugs. 'Who knows?'

'When I saw Grover later that day, he was so insistent that I should not go up to the house. Claimed it was an ague or some such. That was no ague, he would have known that.'

'He was a very strange man these past few years, Alice. You must have noticed.'

'Short-tempered and suspicious with everyone. I remember thinking so while I was offering them some of our apples.'

'Well, if that's who it was, that explains it.' Daniel sits back, ready to close the subject. 'Let the dead bury their dead and leave it be. No good can come of blackening Grover's name. They'll just call you names.'

Alice pushes back her stool and rises to clear the table, not as ready to forget the subject as her companion. 'When Wat said he should have done it long ago, mayhap he was only regretting that Grover got there first.' She falls to thinking.

'Alice,' Daniel breaks the short silence. 'I've been meaning to say, if it's all the same to you, I don't think I'll be hurrying back to the smithy.' He notes her pleased face as she turns to him. Don't think about it, he tells himself. She's just glad of your help. It's no more than that.

'All the same to me?' she says. 'Indeed, it's much more. I am so grateful for any time you are able to be here. But I thought you would want to pick up your real trade again.'

He shakes his head. 'Not enough now to keep me going,' he says. 'There's odd bits on the mornings I go down, but until people come and fill the place again I can't make a living. Come the spring I'll move on, I think. Find somewhere else to set myself up.'

Yes, he thinks, now I've said it, it feels right.

'Working the farm,' she says, 'it's not considered skilled, you know.'

He forces a laugh. 'Good thing your father didn't hear you say that. He always joked me that he was the more skilled because he had to turn his hand to all sorts.'

'True,' she admits, 'but the world sees it differently.' She wipes the table clear and throws the crumbs out of the door.

'I was brought up on my Da's bit of land, Alice, so I know well enough what's to do and when. I can see you through the tilling and sowing at least and give you time to look around for the right man to manage your summer labourers.'

A glowing smile sweeps over her face as she reaches out

to lay a hand briefly on his sleeve. 'I'm so glad you're here, Daniel. I hardly know how I would have coped without your help.'

He gets up heavily and says, 'Don't forget to put the bar across the door, now I'm going out to the barn.'

36

The warm-bread smell fills the kitchen at the moment Daniel, with Sam in tow, pushes open the door, back from their February walk round the fields. They are both wrapped close against the raw day and Sam is chattering out the knowledge he has picked up from Daniel on good care of the land in early Spring. But good husbandry is abandoned as Sam sniffs the air in the kitchen. 'Can I have some, Alice?' He reaches for the loaf she has just put down on the table.

'Careful, Sam, it's hot. I'll break off a piece for you soon. It looks nasty out there, Daniel?'

He takes off his felt greatcoat and shakes it. Droplets spatter the floor. 'It turned to sleet. Ice tonight, I reckon.'

'That nasty man's coming,' Sam says, and as an afterthought, 'Nice horse.' He shrugs off his mired jerkin with its thrice-turned-up sleeves, and hem that comes down to his ankles. The jerkin sags in a damp heap on the floor.

'What nasty man? Goodness, you're covered in mud, Sam!'

'That man we don't like,' Sam says. He passes on through into the house.

'So Gerald's coming again, is he?' Alice sighs. 'I suppose Mistress Cooper's with him too?' She puts the last loaf next to the others on the table to cool.

'No, not Gerald,' Daniel says. 'This must be your visitor from afore Christmas.'

'Jerrard?' Alice asks, whipping round to look. 'I thought we'd seen the last of him.' She feels her hair and tucks a couple of stray locks into place.

'Well, I'll be getting back to work,' Daniel says. He is looking at her, and she wonders why she feels flustered.

'Unless you'd like me to stay ... as a friend?' he asks.

'Yes ... No ... That is, you're welcome to stay, Daniel, you don't have to go away because I have a ... because someone comes.' She smooths her skirt and draws down the sleeves she rolled up for cooking.

'I'll just stay so he knows I'm around,' he suggests. 'Then I'll be going.'

'This will only be a courtesy call on his way through.'

'Looks like he's here now anyways,' Daniel adds from his viewpoint by the door. He stands aside for her to pass. Across the yard, Jerrard's eyes light as she emerges. This time he is neither travel-stained nor weary. He springs from the tall grey and treads quickly across.

Alice suppresses a smile. 'Your honesty is, er, dishonoured, sir.' He stops dead, stares at her nonplussed. She goes on, 'You picked a bunch of honesty. In dismounting you crushed it, did you not notice?' She indicates.

He glances back at the roll behind his saddle. Beside her, Daniel's silent laugh is a puff of vapour in the freezing air.

'Ah,' Jerrard says, and looks sheepish. He returns and retrieves the mass of moon-white papery ovals on their bent and brittle stalks. 'I did not know it was called honesty,' he says.

'Perhaps you call it the satin flower?'

'Truth to tell, I don't call it anything. It was the only thing I could find that wasn't grey or brown.' He sets one or two of the sprigs straight. 'Mistress Edwards, I lay my honesty, such

213

as it is, at your feet.' And he gravely presents the remains of the posy with a grand flourishing bow.

In spite of herself, Alice is amused. She allows herself to smile properly as she takes the bunch and drops a brief curtsey. 'I thank you, sir.'

The two men face each other, each head and shoulders taller than Alice between them. Daniel folds his arms across his chest.

'Sir,' Alice addresses Jerrard, 'this is Daniel Bunting, who has been a good friend to me since the pestilence. I have known him all my life. Daniel, this is ...' She hesitates, realising she does not know the man's first name.

'Henry Jerrard,' says Jerrard, smiling down at her. He nods to Daniel, 'Your servant, sir.'

'Likewise,' Daniel says, toneless. He continues to look unblinking at Jerrard. The three stand thus, each regarding the other, until Alice shivers. 'It's a mite chilly out here. Will you step into the house and take some refreshment, sir?'

'I'll be in the barn ... Alice,' Daniel says.

Alice nods. 'Supper will be a little late this evening. I shall have to wash Sam from head to toe. I cannot imagine what you two got up to out there. Master Jerrard, do you follow me.'

37

For a few minutes, Daniel works aimlessly in the barn, picking up implements and moving them around. Seeing Jerrard's grey still out in the yard, he leads the horse into the stable block, fetching water in one of the old leather buckets, and an armful of hay.

'What did that swaggering puckfist have to come back here for, then?' Daniel wonders aloud. He knees the bucket towards the animal's head and drops the hay in the manger. 'Nobody needs him. Sam don't like him.'

The grey bends an elegant neck and takes a mouthful. 'What does he want, eh?' The grey rolls an eye but keeps eating. 'Still, you're as fine a one as a man could hope to see anywhere,' he says, running an appreciative hand along the dappled neck. 'If nothing else, he knows how to pick his horseflesh.'

He grasps a broom and sweeps up the straw which has blown in little eddies around the stalls. 'Suppose he thinks he's being gentlemanly, staying in the kitchen where she can call me if she needs. All tricked out in his finch-egg finery, laughing in that "Oh, what a lob I am" way, to worm himself into her good graces. Making that silly twirling bow.'

In the dimness of the stables, Daniel sticks out a burly leg and flaps his hands in angry imitation. 'And all he's brought her is a bunch of squashed stalks! And she'll fall for it because she's soft-hearted and he's smiled at her.'

He makes his way past each of the horses, sweeping straw as he goes. He recalls with pain the time after Jerrard's last visit, when Alice spoke joyfully of how Jerrard had shared the details of his brief acquaintance with her father in London at the time of King James' funeral. It was no better when Daniel visited the forge soon afterwards and dropped into the inn on the way home. Nick was full of praise for the generosity of the man after he stayed the night and parted with several coins.

Daniel completes his round of the yard and leans moodily by the door to the stable. Earlier today he'd opened up one of the ricks and carted a load of grain still in straw back to the barn. There he had piled it on the hard-packed floor of the middlestead and opened the great double doors on either side. It had taken a hard hour's work with the flail to thresh out the grain. Now there is winnowing to be done to get rid of husks and chaff, but he finds he cannot drag his eyes from the kitchen window. He can see only the back of the settle from here. It is quiet in the kitchen.

He wonders if he is close enough to hear if Alice calls to him. It might be she needs him now and he hasn't heard, what with the horses rustling the straw. Shouldn't he go into the kitchen anyway?

Strange sort of behaviour, he thinks, for Jerrard to knowingly visit an unmarried woman on her own. He begins to picture Alice being progressively distracted, embarrassed and finally offended by this stranger taking full advantage of her lone state while he, Daniel, hovers around outside, timid as a nowt-head. Make a bold move and stop the stranger in his tracks? Or stay put because he can't decide what to do?

By degrees, Daniel begins to view the quiet from the kitchen in a more sinister light. Why is he staying so long, what is he doing? He must have finished whatever drink she's given him.

He decides he will cross the yard. After all, he tells himself, he needs to sweep the grain together ready for winnowing. He walks slowly and, as would be quite normal, of course, glances in at the kitchen window in passing. With a shock he sees Alice at the kitchen table. Jerrard is standing across from her, leaning an elbow on the settle, watching her prepare a meal. Good God, she's having to offer him a meal to keep him at a distance! Daniel is well aware that Alice will not have planned to feed Jerrard. The commotion when he arrives back at the inn, in the dark and not hungry, will set Margery Patten's tongue wagging worse than a terrier's tail on a rat-scent.

No, of course Alice doesn't want to give him a meal. Besieged and desperate, she is doing the only thing she knows to keep the man off her. Clearly, Jerrard does not care one whit for her reputation, and when he has gorged his fill, there will be nothing to stop him advancing on her. She, wanting to believe she can manage this on her own, will retreat and retreat until she has her back to the wall …

'Oh, I think not, my fine fellow; tis time for you to be gone!' Daniel is striding purposefully across the yard towards the kitchen door when it opens and Alice looks out.

'Ah, Daniel,' she says. 'I thought I glimpsed you in the yard. I'm preparing Sam's supper now. Master Jerrard is just leaving.'

38

As Jerrard rounds the corner of the barn and disappears from sight, Alice stands a moment or two in vague surprise at how quickly the time has passed. Henry Jerrard brought with him a fresh breath of the world beyond the limits of Hillbury, and in an instant, it seems, has taken that world away again. No wonder her father talked of the 'interesting company' he fell in with on that trip to London. Henry Jerrard is blessed with the gift of sharing stories as if he is used to providing a pleasurable half hour for friends. As she was walking with him to the stable, he said, 'So that is two orphans you have.'

'Two?'

He seemed to be concentrating on loosening the grey's rein. 'Is not Daniel also in your care? Why else is he not at his forge?'

'I suppose so, yes. They are my family for the time being.'

His voice was softer as he said, 'And who cares for orphan Alice, I wonder?'

The thought hit her, Frederick would have, but she answered instead, 'I am glad of their company. What more could I wish?'

Before she realised, he took her hand and dropped a light kiss on the fingers.

And now he is riding away, while she holds that hand cupped in the other.

This won't do. She shakes herself free of musings and returns to the house. The bath stands to one side of the fire where Jerrard placed it for her, ready for Sam. She sees him there again, putting down his tankard of spiced ale and leaning to help her.

He had asked, 'No news of Sam's father, then?'

'None. I visited Mistress Cazanove. She is the widow of the man who owned Sam's cottage, but she cannot find a record of his new tenant. The vicar and others have put the word around the village, but we have heard nothing.'

'If he returns, you will let Sam go?'

'I shall have to, though it will be difficult.'

'If his father is that poor, he will wish Sam to learn a trade as soon as may be.'

Alice was horrified. 'You too? Why is everyone wanting me to put a boy of four to work!'

'I am speaking about the father, Mistress Edwards, not you. The poorer they are, the earlier they start.'

The thought had never occurred to her. 'Then I hope Sam may go for a stableboy, he is very fond of horses. He admires your grey.'

'Ah, he has a good eye, then.' Jerrard's smile was catching. 'An exceptional beast. And exceptionally expensive too, but a joy to ride.'

He was keenly interested in Hill House Farm and the work she and Daniel are doing to keep it going. Listened to her explanation of the difficulty of finding men willing to work on the land. 'It's hard enough in winter anyway,' he agreed. 'They would all rather go for the better earnings of a trade. But after such a pestilence, they must be especially scarce.'

'I would need at least two, probably three, at present, to

replace Daniel and do the work that will be needed over the coming months,' she said thinking of the extent of the farm, the combination of grain, livestock and timber.

'A heavy responsibility, Mistress Edwards. And not all men would be willing to work for a woman.'

She thought of Mistress Cazanove and her dye-workers and wondered how she was faring as their new overlord. 'It's not something I can allow to defeat me, sir. At all events, from abbesses to alewives, I can think of women who are the heads of houses and have at least some men working to their direction. My small piece of England is a responsibility I am fortunate to have. Which reminds me, sir,' she said, rising, 'that I have another small responsibility who needs his supper. You will forgive me I hope, if I start on that now.'

'I must be on my way,' he said, immediately rising, but she felt a reluctance to let go his company so soon.

'Do you finish your ale at least, sir. 'Talk to me of your family, your home in Surrey.'

And he leaned against the settle, watching her while she worked between table and stillroom. He told her of the house where he grew up and still lived. He talked of journeys to London, the plays and masques staged there at the Swan, the Curtain, even the Globe before it burned down. Described visits to the old archery butts in St George's Fields, journeys up and down the river; and the hunting and hawking around the area where he lived. And of the gradual decline in demand for his wool, as all trade in the tough English wool was declining.

'You have brothers and sisters, Master Jerrard?'

'Neither. At least, none that survived to adulthood. For the most part I played as a child with the children of our tenants.'

'And you have children of your own now?'

'No wife, no children. Sometimes life without companionship seems bleak. But,' he added, brightening, 'I have a modest little manor. And with hospitality such as this to enjoy on my travels, I have nothing to complain of.' He drained his tankard and took up his cloak.

'Perhaps we shall see you here again, sir.' It sounded stiff and formal to her ears, the sort of thing her mother would have said, but he didn't seem to notice. He inclined his head towards the stalks of honesty lying on the table and said, 'If so, I shall bring you a better posy than that sorry sight there. Sweet violets, perhaps, to match your eyes.'

She glanced up at his face to see if he were in jest, but he was intent on drawing on his gloves. 'In the morning I shall be off home to see how my own household of responsibilities have been busying themselves in my absence.'

'Then your parents no longer live there?'

'I fear not. They died some years ago, within two months of each other.'

'That was hard for you,' she said with feeling.

His eyes met hers. 'As you yourself know, mistress.'

39

'Sam's a lucky lad then, eh Alice?' Daniel says, eyeing the tub full of warm water in front of the kitchen fire. Few are so lucky as to have water heated in such quantities for a bath. Some while has passed since Jerrard left. Sam is kicking his heels against the stretcher of the kitchen chair and gnawing ever smaller pieces off the last of his chicken leg.

She hooks back a stray strand of hair behind her ear. It is a gesture she repeats often. Daniel can't help noticing she is forever tucking back those twisty curls when they fall over her cheek. And they always fall down again.

Alice tells him, 'He says he slipped in that shallow bit of the stream where the ducks go in, but even so, how did he get mired both front and back?'

'The rain's made mud of it down there. He fell again as he came out.' Daniel and Sam share a grin at the recollection. She is relieved that Daniel seems to have recovered from his irritation when she opened the kitchen door, to see him, all swinging arms and grim determination, come to a sudden halt two paces from her. He mumbled something about doing some whittling for Sam, edged past, evading her eye, and shambled through to the winter parlour.

'Well, a full bath will be something new for him, and it's so cold outside now, it will warm him before he goes to bed. So, Sam, if you have finished your supper, you are about to have a treat. A real bath to soak in, fit for a gentleman, with

222

beautiful warm water.'

Sam jumps off the chair and goes to stand by the tub. He runs his fingers to and fro, trying out the warm water, smiling at her as he splashes it. Alice says, 'you can put Samuel and Zachariah in the water if you like.' She picks up the two toys, which Sam immediately grabs from her. 'No, they don't want to go in the water,' he says.

'I'll go on, then, if it's all the same to you,' Daniel says to her. 'There's some work needs doing if I'm to get the grain to the miller at Woodley for you. You're nearly out of flour.'

'I'll call you for supper as soon as Sam's bathed and in bed.' She unfolds two blankets and hangs them to air over the back of the settle, and Daniel goes out. Alice turns to Sam. 'Off with those things, now,' and helps him to remove shoes, breeches and shirt. 'I don't suppose you even know what having a bath means, do you, Sam?'

He shakes his head. She leans over the tub to test the water. 'Just right,' she confirms. 'This'll be fun.' She sweeps him up and hugs him briefly before gradually lowering him. 'Down we go, into the lovely warm water.'

Suddenly Sam is kicking and rearing in her arms, struggling so hard in her hold that she is in danger of dropping him. 'No! No! No!' he shouts. His knee catches her chin and sends her backwards. Alice plumps onto the settle with Sam all kicking limbs on top of her. He fights free and slithers off her lap. 'No! No! I don't want to! I don't!' He hops from foot to foot, terror crumpling his face.

'Sam, what is it?'

I don't like it!' His hands clutch her sleeve as he tries to pull her with him, away from the tub.

'What's wrong, sweeting?'

'I don't want to go in there. It hurts!' A splash spatters

onto the floor, and a puddle forms and spreads on the flags between his feet. 'Don't make me, don't make me!'

He is sobbing, dancing from foot to foot and pulling, always pulling Alice away from the tub. Alice twitches one of the blankets from the back of the settle, abandoning on the instant all thoughts of the luxury she has prepared for him. She throws it round his shoulders and sweeps him up in her arms.

'It's all right, I won't make you,' she assures him. 'I promise I won't make you. It's all right Sam.'

She carries him out of the kitchen and through the dark hall, enfolding him within the softness of the blanket as she goes. In the winter parlour, she sits down on a cushion by the hearth, all the while soothing and talking to him and pulling the blanket close until he is covered and enclosed from neck to toe, sitting across her lap. She rocks him for a few minutes until his sobbing calms into uneven gulps and he becomes quieter.

In the flickering firelight the two of them talk softly for a long while.

40

Jonah Kettlewell, silversmith, curses roundly and looks towards the way ahead, then back the way he has come. Hillbury has a blacksmith, he knows, but it will waste time returning there. He was supposed to be in Longburton tonight, and should be well north of here by now, but the sleet has been deadly and he will not risk cantering his horse on the slippery road. Now it has thrown a shoe. He is close to Woodley, the horse could manage that distance with him walking alongside, but he cannot recall a blacksmith from his previous visits.

With a sigh of resignation, the silversmith turns round and leads his horse back the way he has come.

41

There's a deal of winnowing to be done, Daniel thinks to himself. He estimates that with the amount of bread Alice is baking for the three of them, plus the extra she is taking to the village for those in need, she will need a couple of sackfuls of grain. He did some threshing after midday meal, before Sam came and he took him on their long wander round the fields and woodland. The grain lies in a heap on the barn floor, the threshed-out straw stacked separately. He only threshes when grain is needed, he said in answer to another of Sam's seemingly endless questions. After threshing comes the winnowing, the separation of the grain from the chaff, then sieving it clean of the last dusty bits, before the resulting grain can be bagged up and taken to the miller in Woodley to be ground into flour.

There are several of the large round winnowing trays in the corner of the barn. Daniel crosses to the other side, propping open the double doors opposite those on the yard side. It is late afternoon now, clouds obscuring any sun that might have countered the chill, and he shivers in the icy gust. But it is the very wind he needs for the job of separating out the light husks from the grain. Collecting one of the shallow winnowing trays, he scoops some grain and experimentally casts it into the air. Much of it goes in his face and he shakes his head, ruffling his hair to free it of bits. A few more casts and he remembers the hang of it. He starts pitching great gouts of grain in the air to let the through-draught carry away the chaff. Toss and catch, toss and catch. It won't take long to get the rhythm of it, even though he is years out of practice.

The sleet starts up again, blowing in through the far doors and spreading shiny wet on the packed earth, and he knows he must work fast. The last thing they need is wet grain threatening mould. Gradually the pile takes on a more pebbly look as the chaff blows away. When he judges it pure enough he pulls a sack from the store and cleans the grain through a sieve into the sack. He rakes out some more grain from the heap. Drawing it as before to the centre aisle between the doors he starts the rhythmic scooping once again. The chickens have already discovered the chaff; a few, shrewdly noting further opportunity, draw near the door of the barn and peck at odd bits of grain that drift their way.

Minutes become a quarter-hour then a half-hour, and he is warm with the exercise, sweating even. Dust and husks stick to his damp forehead and neck as stray eddies of wind push it back in his face. He keeps going, hardly noticing time passing until he realises the light is rapidly going and he can no longer see clearly what he is doing. For the first time, he becomes aware the dust is sticking to him all over. He will douse his head and arms in the trough and change his shirt before he eats. Alice will probably finish putting Sam to bed soon, he guesses, and then—

The kitchen door is yanked open, the glow from the rush lights throwing soft shuddering shadows in the yard. Hunched over the sack, Daniel watches dumbfounded as Alice strides towards him.

'Daniel!' she hisses. 'Daniel!'

'Alice? What is it?' He straightens, comes to the doorway and leans on the jamb, frowning in puzzlement. She plants herself opposite him, glaring, hands on hips. Her fury crackles, but she has herself in hand, just.

'That man!' A choking gulp.

He stares at her. Jerrard?

'That man! I can't believe. Ooh!' and one hand goes to cover her mouth.

'What man? What are you talking about?' Lord, he thinks, what's Jerrard done to upset her so much?

She stops, facing him, hands on hips. 'His father!' Her voice wavers. 'Sam's father. You know what he did?'

Not Jerrard. 'What did he do?'

'He stood his own child in a bucket of hot water, held him there, until his feet were' – she chokes on the word. She looks away for a second, biting her lip, then – 'scalded ... and told him it was punishment ... for his wrongdoing!'

'He never!' He feels his sinews knot from shoulder to fingertip. *The bastard!*

'A child!' she cries. It is a repressed shouting now. 'He tortured his own child!' The fingers of her hand are curled into a hard ball. 'If he comes here, God forgive me but I shall take a knife to his black heart,' thumping her fist on the door, 'and stick it in again and again—'

'Hey. Hey! Alice!' Daniel reaches for her hammering arm.

'— until he screams and begs for mercy—'

'Alice!' He grips her, catches her other hand. 'You forget yourself! Are you out of your wits?'

As he intends, the strangeness of being held by him brings Alice to her senses. He continues to hold her while she quietens, still breathing hard.

'Where's Sam now?' he demands. 'He mustn't hear this.'

She blinks and looks afresh at him, her hand gripping his. Inclines her head back towards the house. 'He's in bed,

I got him off to sleep eventually. He won't hear from there, I wouldn't do that to him.' She takes a wavering breath and hunches her shoulders. He lets go of her. She sighs. 'I'm sorry, Daniel.'

Together they walk towards the kitchen. At the door she turns before going in and he catches the glitter in her eye. 'I would, you know,' she says quietly, 'I would kill him.'

'Then I hope for your sake he's never found.'

He follows her in. After the chill outside, the heat from the fireplace is stifling and he feels the sweat break anew. 'When did this happen? What did Sam do wrong?'

'I don't know.' Her voice cracks. 'What could a child barely out of swaddling bands possibly do to warrant such treatment?' And there in the middle of the kitchen, she puts her hands over her face and bursts into tears.

'Dearest Alice.' Daniel puts out his arm to encircle her. He catches sight of his hands, his forearms, covered in chaff, his shirt, his jerkin likewise, puts a hand up to his face, feels the covering layer of dust sticking to his sweat. Abruptly he changes direction to the ale barrel, quietly draws two mugs. His heart hammers. Did he only think it or did he actually say it?

By the time he has replaced the bung she is pushing the hair off her forehead, her face is streaked with tears but she is calmer. 'How could anyone do such a thing?' she asks.

He hands her a mug and takes a pull from the other. She rubs her face with the heel of her palm, and points to the tub. 'He wouldn't let me put him in the bath because he thought his feet would be scalded again. He was so frightened he wet the floor – oh, I must clean that.' She casts around for a cloth.

'Well, if it's any comfort Alice, when you've had a go at him, just in case you don't do it properly, I'll finish him off myself. How's that?'

'It's not funny Daniel!'

'And I'm not being funny neither,' Daniel says. 'Anybody who does that to a child deserves their neighbours' justice, and I'll be more than glad to do it for you.'

She has found a cloth, and bringing it to the tub soaks it and wrings it out. He takes it from her and mops the floor where the terrified four-year-old stood. 'Wouldn't have minded a bath myself,' he says as bits of chaff flake from his clothes.

'Then why don't you use it? It will only go to waste.' She sits down on the settle and takes up her drink again.

'What, here? Now?'

'It was effort enough to heat it, Daniel, and there's hot water to warm it again if it's cooled.' She points the toe of her shoe at several steaming pots and bowls on the hearth. 'You cannot wash from the trough in this weather.'

It's true, he saw it iced over when they came in.

'Look, here's the other blanket I had for Sam,' Alice is saying, 'you can dry on that.'

As she drapes it to face the fire, the thought of the comfort of water, the pleasure of a bath, keeps him from an outright refusal. 'Alice I'm not sure I should. If you know what I mean?'

'I'm going upstairs, so that I can be there if Sam wakes,' she says. 'There is a book my father brought me back from London that I've hardly looked at these past weeks. It has receipts for brewing and suchlike that I want to try. I'll be there until you call up to me. Then I'll get something for supper. You must be hungry.'

'A warm bath would surely be a rare treat, Alice.'

She gets up. 'Good, I'll put out fresh things for you. If you leave those on the floor, I'll collect them later and wash them tomorrow. We can brush the jerkin, the leather will take no harm.'

It looks like it's settled, then. 'I'd better go and close up first, or all the chickens will be in there.' He turns at the door. 'I like the sound of receipts for brewing. If you want some sampling done, I'll be happy to help out.'

His small jest draws a smile from her at last before he latches the kitchen door behind him.

As he stands in the darkness, he lets out a long shuddering breath.

42

John Patten, Nick's eldest, a lad of twelve summers or so, sulkily takes the lantern and starts the long climb to Hill House. Why they have to run around for a poxy silversmith, he cannot think. The man could just as well wait till morning and John could take one of the inn's horses to fetch Daniel for the re-shoeing. But oh, no, his mother says Daniel has to be fetched tonight, so that he is ready to fire up early in the morning for the silversmith. It will serve the old fool right if Hill House is all shut up and Daniel not available.

He arrives in the pitch dark. The barn and stables are closed and the only glow comes from the rush light in the kitchen. An inquisitive young man, John first shutters his lantern with his short cloak. It will be a good jest to boast to his younger brother that he knows what Mistress Edwards gets up to when she thinks nobody is looking. He wonders if he might catch her with her back to the fire, skirts raised to warm her bare buttocks. Once, he saw his mother doing that, before she grasped hold of him, catching him a great clout and calling him a poke-nose.

He feels his way creeping across the yard towards the dim square of light, and stands on tiptoe to peer in the unshuttered window. What he sees takes him by such surprise that he falls back and nearly upends into the water trough. Daniel has suddenly reared up from a bathtub and reached for the blanket in full view of the window. Water drips through the dark hairs of his chest and down the muscled whiteness of his body. Confused, the lad creeps away. For some minutes he hangs around irresolute, shaking with cold by the stable block. He cannot bring himself to knock on the door. His father might have done but in John's view his father and Daniel are both old. John hesitates to assume familiarity, apprehensive that Daniel might be affronted at being seen uncovered. What if he waits until Daniel comes out? His mother said Daniel sleeps in the barn. Then again, she said it with much eye-rolling and John knows what that means. Perhaps Daniel might not be leaving the house at all. A short shivering wait is enough to decide him. He will knock. But first he will check through the window that Daniel is dressed. He steals across the yard to the corner of the window and peers cautiously over the sill. The high settle back is blocking much of the view from here, but Daniel must be sitting on it, because John can see the back of his head sticking up over the top, his hair shiny wet. The murmur of voices draws John carefully creeping along the sill for a better view.

Standing by the hearth and facing the settle is a smiling Mistress Edwards, her unconfined russet hair fanning round her face, two ale mugs in one hand, and Daniel's shirt, hose and breeches in the other.

43

'I need money.' The words slur as Bart takes another swig of ale. He checks that Jem is keeping a lookout by the stable door. Across the yard, the firelight through the inn's kitchen window is criss-crossed frequently by the shadows of the landlord's wife and daughter passing to and fro with food for the taproom customers. The three in the stables have been there long enough to discern each other in the darkness, make out the ends of the stalls, the shifting rumps of horses. From where he stands, Jem can see if the back door of the inn opens. The last thing they want is Nick Patten, or worse, Margery, finding them here with the filched ale.

Lounging next to Bart on a heap of tied sheaves, Dick tries leaning back against a stack of loose straw but pulls away as it threatens to give. Dick turns to Bart. 'What d'you need money for?'

'What d'you think, what for?' Bart growls. 'I'm desperate, that's what for. No money in weeks.'

'Nor me neither.' Dick says. 'Haven't had work in months.'

'You haven't had work in years – you just scrounge off the rest of us.'

'I worked for Sir Thomas in his fields last harvest,' Dick reminds him. 'I'm as desperate as you, but with this bad leg of mine—'

'Nothing to do with that, Dick. You just don't want to work.'

'That Alice Edwards messed around with my leg and it's

234

never got better!' Dick declares.

'It's never got better 'cos you keep picking off the scab.'

'And why? Because it looks lumpy and no woman fancies me.'

'What's women got to do with it?'

'Women don't fancy a man with a lumpy leg—'

'Gawd-a-mercy, will you shut up about your blasted leg!'

From the door Jem says, 'I ain't never had any work, except when I repaired my auntie's mattress where the straw got unplaited. So I'm worst off, especially now my auntie's dead. She used to give me money. When you find work again, Dick, will you let me know?'

'Why should I find work for you Jem? Find your own.'

'I can't,' Jem admits. 'They laugh.'

'Who?'

'Sir Thomas, Master Cooper. I asked both of them.'

'What made them laugh?'

'They asked me what work I'd done and I told them I'd done my auntie a favour.'

Bart rolls his eyes. Dick sniggers.

'What sort of favour, Jem?' Bart nudges Dick.

'That's what Sir Thomas wanted to know.'

'And what did you say, Jem?'

'That I'd done her bedding.'

Bart gives a horselaugh and Dick lets out an explosion of mirth that tips him backwards, legs in the air, into the straw pile. Both of them howl afresh while Jem, perplexed, asks, 'What? What?'

Bart takes another pull of his drink and watches Dick right himself. As he clambers back onto the bale, Dick grabs at the leather bottle and manages a quick swig before Bart can wrestle it back.

'You should be asking a woman on her own.' Bart advises. 'That was Dick's mistake. No good going to one like Lady High-Nose Cazanove with all those lackeys around.'

'Scuse me!' Dick says. 'It was your idea to go there and you chickened out.'

Bart ignores him. 'A young woman, Jem. They can't do men's work so they're properly grateful when somebody offers to help.'

'How do *you* know, since you can't get work anyway?' says Jem, rallying.

'The idea's not to get work, numbskull.' Both Jem and Dick wait, expectant. 'The idea is to make them think you're willing and they give you some work to do. But really what they want is company and they'll pay for that. And even if they don't, well then, you stick around getting it all wrong until they pay you to go away.'

'Who's going to pay us, then, Bart?' Dick asks.

In the belief it makes him look wise, Bart strokes his greasy stubbled chin. 'I've been thinking. It's a matter of choosing your subject. Lonely is best. Helpless.'

'Yes?' the other two say together.

'I hear Alice Edwards might do the sort of favour we're looking for. Daniel's up there, she must be paying him. And spring's coming soon. Company or no, she'll need to pay more than one man to work there. Maybe I'll go up to Hill House and have a word.'

'I'll come with you,' Dick says, and Jem adds, 'And me.'

'No, I'll do this on my own. You made a mess of your visit to the mansion, Dick. Think of this as me doing you two a favour.'

'Doing yourself one, more like,' Dick mutters.

'Preparing the ground, Dick.'

'Somebody's coming!' Jem calls quietly. 'Oh, it's all right, it's only John coming back. He's gone inside.'

Dick turns back to Bart. 'If Daniel's already got himself nice and comfortable, he won't want you going in and messing around on his patch. Likely beat you to pulp.'

'Uh, uh.' Bart holds up a staying finger. 'Daniel spends the odd few hours at the smithy. He doesn't need to know until we're in there, feet under the table. If I pick my moment, I reckon I could persuade poor grateful Mistress Edwards to part with a nice lot of her Pa's cash in return for ...' He pauses, grinning.

'Easy work,' Dick says.

'More than that. we'd be doing *her* a favour,' Bart suggests, 'by keeping things respectable and by saying nothing.' He gives Dick a meaningful look.

'I get it,' Dick says. 'So her and Daniel don't get talked about.'

'Which means a bit more of this,' Bart's rough-skinned finger and thumb rasp together, 'on top of what she'll pay for our company.'

'But she'll just tell Daniel when he gets back there,' Jem points out, 'and he'll beat you to pulp like Dick says.'

'There's a particular reason she'll dole out the cash and not tell Daniel,' Bart says. 'She's due to marry that Gerald Cooper.'

'She's not, is she?'

'Word is. At least, Old Man Cooper's been making noises. And he's not happy about Daniel being up there.'

'So you mean Gerald won't want to marry her if he hears she's given away all her money,' Jem says.

'That too, Jem.' Bart turns to Dick and murmurs, 'Just think, Dick, there could be cash in the offing from the

Coopers too, paying us to keep Alice respectable.'

Dick is at sea. 'By keeping her company round the farm, you mean?'

'No, you lob – by telling them we won't talk about the Daniel rumour.'

'There isn't a Daniel rumour.'

Bart chuckles. 'But there could be.'

From his lookout, Jem hisses, 'Door's opening! It's John again. Oh no, it's Nick too …'

The other two start up, lurching behind the stacked straw, Jem scuttling after them. Nobody comes into the stables. Faintly, two voices drift towards them from the yard. Bart pokes Jem in the ribs, whispers, 'Get to the door and tell us what's happening.' He adds, 'Go on!' as Jem hesitates. Bart and Dick follow him out of the hiding place, ready to leap back in. They watch Jem's shadow creep towards the stable door and peer round the jamb. As one, they steal past the stalls to join him by the door. In the yard, Nick stands arms akimbo, frowning at his son. John shivers, lantern in hand, insistent. Their voices are loud whispers, John's excited, Nick's disbelieving.

'… saw it myself, I tell you, Pa!'

'No clothes on? And Alice in her kitchen? You sure?'

'She had them in her hands. And Dan was just sat there and she was looking at him. Smiling! I'm frozen, Pa. Can we go in now?'

Nick rouses from his astonishment. 'Yes, of course, son,' as he ushers him back inside. 'Lucky dog!'

The rushlight swells and fades as the door opens and closes. The inn yard is dark once more. Only the frosty starlight reaches into the stables, gleaming on the faces of the three listeners looking open-mouthed at each other.

44

Margery Patten looks up briefly as Alice walks into the kitchen at the inn carrying the basket of provisions she has made up for those in need. 'Mistress Edwards,' Margery acknowledges, and returns to showing a younger one of her brood how to make the rushlights used throughout the inn. Without Alaric Ford the tallow chandler, everyone now makes their own lights, and it is a slow business, so the children are roped in to help.

'That's right, Nell, draw it through the grease. No, keep it under,' pushing the child's fingers down into the shallow three-legged pan of warm mutton fat on the floor. 'Now, hold it up, that's it, until the grease has dripped off and lay it there on the bark.'

There the greased rush will dry hard, alongside its fellows on the strip of bark, ready to be clamped in the holder when needed.

In from the yard clatters young Nick, clearly running from pursuit, and cannons into Nell, knocking her off balance and upsetting the rushlights onto the floor. He is laughing and in high fettle.

'Clumsy oaf!' Margery shouts. Nell starts to cry. 'Look what you've done, hurting your sister!' Alice goes to help Nell to her feet but Margery intervenes. 'Leave her! I can pick up my own daughter.' The innkeeper's wife grasps young Nick's arm and pulls him close as he tries to wriggle away. 'You've been drinking again!'

'No, ma, course not!'

'Liar! I can smell it on your breath.' He wriggles in her hold. 'I told you after you finished off Cazanove's drink that day, if I ever caught you filching your father's ale again, you'd have a beating and bread-and-water for a week! Thought your father was too busy getting rid of Abel Nutley and his quarantine orders and nobody would notice! Like now you think I'm too busy in my kitchen to work out what you're up to, young thief. Now get out of here, I'll deal with you later.' She glares at young Nick, who scowls, but runs.

Nell has regained her feet and Margery sends her off too, collecting up the spilled tapers and continuing the job herself. Alice might not even be there.

'I see I disturb your work,' she says. Relations with Margery have been strained since their return after the quarantine but today is worse than usual. Alice tries again. 'Village is filling up slowly,' she says.

'Not a shadow of what it was,' Margery says.

'Anyone I've not seen yet?'

Margery sniffs. 'Deborah Wilkins and her family beyond the old 'pothecary's, they came back yestereve.'

'Ah, yes, Rob will be the head of the family now, with his father dead, poor lad.' So already Frederick is the 'old' apothecary, Alice thinks. She rests her basket on the table and looks through it. 'I think I have one or two things they might like.'

'They're comfortable enough. No need to call,' Margery says shortly.

'Oh, I shall call in anyway. It'll be good to see them again.'

'Take my advice, stay away.'

Alice is perplexed. 'Why? There is no illness is there?' She has heard it can happen like this, several weeks clear and then it hits again without warning.

'Nothing amiss,' Margery says, drawing another rush from the bunch. 'You just leave them be.'

It is like a slap in the face. The silence grinds on. Alice starts again. 'Is anyone else returned?'

'Old Tom Wemyss, on the Woodley road.'

'Old Tom?' Alice makes herself laugh. 'I'll wager he didn't announce his return with a drink in the taproom! More like he would proclaim up and down the street that we are all an ungodly lot! How did you hear that he's back?' When no answer is forthcoming, she adds, 'Still, he may be in want of things so I shall call by. It's but a short walk on from the Wilkins.'

'Not if you wish to avoid a dressing down,' Margery advises.

'A dressing down? Why, what has the village done now to upset him?'

'Not the village.' Margery appears to be engrossed in pouring more fat into the little three-legged pan.

Alice regards the woman so carefully avoiding her eye. 'What are you saying, Margery?'

Still the innkeeper's wife does not look at her. 'I'm saying you're a single woman, and decent single women don't live on their own.' She replaces the pot on the hearth and picks up another rush.

'Not usually, it's true. But Margery, you know it is the pestilence that has caused such havoc to all our lives. My being on my own was not my choice, but Hill House is my home and my parents are dead. Old Tom cannot hold me responsible for that.'

'You guard your tongue, Alice Edwards.' Now Margery

Patten sits up, resting her wrists on spread knees and glowering at Alice. 'It's not only old Tom can see that you keep Daniel Bunting up there to dance attendance on you. No respectable woman lives on her own, because she can't manage except by having a man with her.'

'He does not dance attendance on me! He was grieving for David as I was for my mother and father, and we were the only people left alive. How could I ignore him – particularly after all he did for this village?'

It stops Margery Patten's train of thought for a few seconds, which she fills by lightly pressing the greased rushes to see if they have set. 'That was then, this is now. A young man, spending the night in the company of a young woman, week in, week out. Folk draw their own conclusions.'

'Then their conclusions are at fault,' Alice retorts. When no response comes, she tries again. 'Margery, even if you believed such things of *me*, do you really think Daniel would be taken in?'

Margery turns her back on Alice and reaches for another bunch of rushes. 'A man may be taken in by a woman's witchery.'

Alice laughs at that. It is preposterous. 'Margery! You've known me all my life.'

'I knew you when your parents were there to control you, Alice Edwards. Now you seem to be getting up to all sorts of frolics, and that *is* witchery as far as a simple innkeeper's wife like me can see.'

'What do you mean, frolics? Daniel helps me with the work on the farm and gives me protection by being there, you know that. I should be lost without—'

'And prances around undressed in your kitchen as I hear. And you there watching! How else would he be doing that except he was bewitched?'

'That's not true!' Alice cries. 'Who tells you such lies?'

'Such lies, as you call them,' says Margery, looking up at Alice, her mouth curling, 'were told me by my own son, who went to your place to find Daniel and saw him babe-naked, standing in a tub of water, and you running around carousing with pots of ale for the two of you!'

Alice is speechless. A couple of weeks ago. Nick's boy John sent to fetch Daniel.

'Yes, I thought that would bring you up short,' the innkeeper's wife goes on. 'I don't want to know what arts you practise to snare him, Alice Edwards, but when he comes to his senses and sees your carnal lusts for what they are, I hope he will beat you as you deserve. And now, I shall be glad not to see you in my kitchen again.' She jerks her head towards the door in dismissal.

Alice stands her ground. 'Mistress Patten,' she says, 'I do not believe your John ever suggested I was in the room while Daniel took a bath in my kitchen. He had been winnowing. You know how that stuff sticks, it is like a mud all over the skin. He could not wash from the trough, it was iced over. He was dusty and the bath was there.'

'Just happened to be there, did it? A bath does not simply happen, you have to plan it, it takes time. Unless of course you waved your broomstick and produced it on the instant!' She pokes a finger at Alice. 'No, you planned it, Alice Edwards!'

'Of course I planned it!' Alice cries. 'I had filled it for Sam who had got himself very dirty. He did not use it in the end and I offered it to Daniel. I went—'

'How fortunate – so Sam was not that dirty after all.'

Alice breathes out hard. 'I went upstairs and I sat with Sam as he slept, and I did not go back to the kitchen until

Daniel was fully dressed again.'

'That's not what John said, and he should know, he was there.'

'Your son did not knock on my door until I was back downstairs and preparing supper.'

'So how did he see Daniel without a stitch? You can't have it both ways, Alice Edwards.' Before Alice can draw breath, the innkeeper's wife continues, 'And putting a child in water! That's abuse.'

'It was a treat for Sam to have a warm bath.'

Margery pounces. 'You cannot really have thought that, if you did not put him into it after all.'

'He did not want to—'

She cannot go on, cannot say what Sam suffered at the hands of his own father.

'I'm not surprised he didn't want to. It sounds as if he has more sense than you! Taking a bath for pleasure is a heathen rite. And if you paid attention in church, you'd know what happened when Bathsheba the Hittite took a bath. It got her husband killed!'

How is it always the woman's fault? she thinks. King David spied on Bathsheba and murdered her husband to get her for himself. Alice takes another deep breath to suppress the protest she wants to make, and says wearily, 'I am sorry you view it in that way, Mistress Patten, but I think you know in your heart that there has been no wrongdoing in my house and I shall be glad if you will make that clear to any who seek to say otherwise.' Even as she says it, she knows it for a vain hope. 'And now I shall go to see the Wilkins family, *and* old Tom, because I have nothing to be ashamed of. Good day to you, Mistress Patten.'

She picks up her basket, turns her back on the innkeeper's

wife and walks out. In the back of her mind a nagging thought persists. If young Nick finished up Cazanove's drink that day, then Grover Price did not poison it.

Have I simply imagined this whole issue of poisoning? Warped the evidence to fit the facts in order to absolve myself of causing the deaths of my parents and our two maidservants?

If Margery has me put in the ducking stool, they will say 'She was guilty' when I drown, and they will be right, though not of witchery but of breaking a promise, that amounted to murder itself.

45

'Susan, do you think I am setting my cap at Daniel?'

Susan Cushing stops dead in the act of unstoppering a bottle to stare at her young friend. 'Of course not. Who says you are?'

'Margery Patten says young John saw Daniel taking a bath in the kitchen, which is true, he had been winnowing. And she's made up a whole story around it that I am trying to snare Daniel.'

Alice sits in the parlour of Susan's cottage, her empty basket on the floor beside her. Susan pours mead into two glasses.

'No one thinks that, I feel sure, Alice. We know you too well to believe you capable of such arts.'

'Then why is she so full of bile against me?'

'You must not let these things upset you.' She hands a glass to Alice and sits down next to her. 'I expect you came upon her when she was distempered.'

'She looked as if she was enjoying herself. As though she had set out to get the better of me. What have I ever done to make her feel so?'

'Nothing at all, Alice. As if you would.' The two women sip from their glasses. 'Still,' Susan looks knowing, 'there is the old story, of course.'

'What old story?'

'Margery and Daniel.'

'What? You jest!'

Susan thinks. 'I suppose you would have been very young. Margery once had a very strong inclination for Daniel.'

'But she's a deal older than him.'

'The heart is no respecter of years, Alice. She was always up at the smithy for some reason or other, and she got herself talked about.'

'And how did Daniel feel about it?'

'As far as I recall, Daniel was embarrassed but not embroiled. He was too young or he'd have gone away. If he'd had anywhere to go, that is. Then Nick started courting her, she stopped going to the smithy and all was forgotten.'

'But not by Margery?'

'Heart-burning dies hard.'

Alice takes another sip of mead. 'She made me feel the whole village disapproves of me. Deborah Wilkins, Tom Wemyss.'

'I thought you had just called on them?'

'Yes, I did. I was not going to be frightened off by Margery's words.'

'Quite right. Did Deborah say anything?'

'Not at all. She was very glad to have the cheese and bread I took. I suppose she couldn't say anything under those circumstances, for fear of my not coming again.'

'I feel sure Deborah thinks no ill of you, Alice. Now Tom is a different case. Whatever his fondness, you know he would have told you in no uncertain terms if he had the smallest doubt of your virtue.'

'He said nothing either.'

'Then all is well. Margery is a little jealous and has loosed her dart at you. She will probably forget it by morning.'

'Of course, Tom only came back yesterday, so he may not

have heard the rumour yet.' Alice muses. 'There was worse, Susan. I could be in such trouble if Abel Nutley got to hear, he would so enjoy acting on it.'

'Acting on what?'

'Margery said I was practising witchery to snare Daniel.'

'Did she? Then it's high time I had words with Margery Patten.'

46

It is two days later that Daniel comes to the end of a desultory day at the forge and rakes apart the dying coals of his furnace until he is satisfied they will subside into ash. Collecting up tools and implements, he hangs them on the ceiling hooks ready for use the next time he comes to the smithy. The work is getting a little more regular now. Shoeing will always be needed of course and he has also been taking on general repairs like mending wheels, things that always need doing. These are things David would have done in the past, in the course of busy days when the smithy's furnace never completely cooled from one day to the next, even Sundays occasionally. But things are different now, there won't be the level of work to keep even one man going, and Daniel periodically considers the future without enthusiasm, finding no solutions to how he will make his living. Some would advise him to leave, but he has lived in Hillbury all his life and feels no inclination to uproot and go to foreign parts.

He takes a last look around, twitches off his leather apron to hang it on the door hook and dons a long-sleeved padded jerkin and wide brimmed hat for the walk back up to Hill House. As he closes the door behind him, the lights in Nick Patten's taproom up the road beckon. Perhaps a mug and a chat will lift this melancholy he seems unable to shake off.

He has to stoop slightly under the lintel. Within, a handful of local men and idlers sit on settle and stool around the fire, their faces flushed from heat or drink or both. Most of the pipes usually stored in the recesses of the brick chimney are in use and the smoke rises as they talk, thickening the haze clinging at ceiling height. In the corner by one window Ralph Cooper shares a table with a companion. Daniel notes that Ralph seems at last to have severed the tight rein his lady has always held against his visits to Nick Patten's. There is a pause in the murmured talk as Daniel turns to shut the door. Across the taproom by the barrels lying ready on their trestles, Nick raises a hand in greeting, 'Evening Dan.' Clay mugs hang from the rafter above him and Nick reaches up in readiness.

'Evening Nick, I'll take a pot, if you will.' Daniel crosses over to where the landlord is already closing his fingers round the stopper in the end of a barrel. 'The usual, Dan?' Daniel nods and puts down a coin. One of the seated men removes the pipe from his mouth and elbows a gangling youth next to him. 'Go on, Rob. Ask him. Go on.'

Rob Wilkins is the lone son amongst a host of sisters, and now lone man in the family. His father was one of the first to succumb to the plague. So Rob is the head of the household. What a responsibility, Daniel thinks, with some compassion for the awkward sixteen-year-old.

'Ask me what?'

There is a snort from two of the others in the circle. 'Go on Rob. You want to know about women, he'll tell you.'

Daniel takes a draught of his ale and waits.

Rob begins. 'Bart there, and Jem, they say ...'

Even in the shadowed gloom, Daniel can see the boy reddening. He thinks, so Rob's being teased about a girl is he, poor lad? 'Don't you let them get at you, Rob,' he says easily. 'They're just a bunch of knockheads.'

'He knows, cos he's had plenty,' Bart assures Rob. In a

high-pitched simpering voice, his hands gesturing obscenely, he goes on, 'Oh, Master Bunting, you're so *big*! I think I shall swoon. Please loosen my clothes. All of them!' The sniggers explode around the little circle, and the unfortunate Rob squirms the more.

'Take no notice, Rob. If you want to know about women,' says Daniel, 'ask one of the married men, Nat, Silas, or Nick here, they can tell you more'n I can.'

Dick Winter chips in. 'Oh, it's not *married* women Rob wants to know about,' he says, with a gargoyle's leer. 'It's the other sort isn't it, Rob?'

Ralph Cooper and the other man with him turn back to their talk, but one or two look expectantly at Daniel. Nick Patten intervenes. 'Go to, go to, all of you, the jest is over. Come now, who's for a top up?'

'No, I want to know too,' Jem persists. 'I want to know how you get Alice to take off her clothes for you.'

There is dead silence in the room as Daniel turns slowly to his questioner. Nick Patten steps in. 'Now Jem, I'll have no language like that in my taproom, as you well know.'

'But you said it,' Jem whines. 'It was your John saw it all, and you called him a lucky dog.' His neighbour by the hearth is shaking his elbow in a vain attempt to stop the cascade of indiscretion. 'Jem!' hisses Bart between gritted teeth. 'For fuck's sake, shut up!'

'No I won't!' Jem turns on his friend. 'You said we should go up there, offer to do a few odd jobs for her and see what favours she gives in return —'

He gets no further. In a couple of strides, Daniel kicks away two joint stools as though they don't exist, grasps Jem's tight-buttoned jerkin by the back of the neck and hauls him off the settle. Jem falls sideways, choking and grimacing and

251

clutching wildly at his throat. His legs kick convulsively, catching the shins of Dick who yelps in pain.

'Mistress Edwards to you.' Daniel's voice is cold and deliberate. Looking round the room, he booms, 'Back in your seat, man!' to Ralph Cooper, who has quietly got up and is standing frozen by the door, hand on the latch. He slinks back to his companion.

'So that's the jest is it?' says Daniel to the room in general. He hardly seems to notice Jem dangling from his hand, eyes bulging, gesticulating frantically and managing only a strangled cough. 'Well, you must have been enjoying yourselves, all you respectable men of Hillbury. Planning a little visit to Hill House, were you? Lots of merry japes, I'll be bound.' Daniel tosses Jem aside as a dog a gnawed meat bone and turns his eyes on Nick Patten. Nick backs away from the barrels and comes up against the sideboard. He holds out his hands defensively.

'Now, Daniel, he didn't mean it. You know he's just a loudmouth.'

Daniel calmly smashes his ale mug on the wooden surface, all the time looking in Nick's face. Bits of pottery fly. Ale splashes over the two men and runs across the surface of the sideboard, dripping down by stages to the lower shelf, the floor. He crushes the handle before tossing the fragments behind him. 'I thought better of you, Nick Patten. You were always a wily one, but I thought at bottom you were a fairly good sort. Should have known better maybe, when I saw a dead man's property in your taproom.' He indicates the six fine pewter ale mugs hanging from new hooks in the joist above their heads. 'Thought I'd seen these before,' he says, unhooking each and placing them one by one on the sideboard. 'They were 'pothecary's. Did you steal them yourself, or get one of your boys to do your dirty work?'

'Oh, come now, Dan,' Nick protests.

'I heard the linen had gone as well. I suppose if David and I hadn't used one of his sheets for his winding cloth, you'd have had that too?'

Daniel turns his back on a speechless Nick and faces the room. He has their full attention now, except for Jem clutching his throat and hoarsely coughing.

'Let me think now, Rob,' Daniel says. 'Who brought vittles to your family when you came back here?'

'Mistress Edwards.'

'And tell me, Nick,' Daniel says over his shoulder, 'who is it who shares the poor-visiting with your wife?'

Nick rolls his eyes. 'Mistress Edwards.'

'And who poulticed your leg ulcers, Dick Winter, when no one else would come near you for the smell?' He goes on, 'Part of the smell being because you never wash.' Heads nod around the room and Dick's cry of protest turns to a grunt as Silas elbows him hard in the ribs.

'And you sit around idle and make merry by dragging her name in the mud. For a jest. I'll show you a jest.'

In front of the thrall of onlookers and to Nick's aghast horror, Daniel lays each of the apothecary's pewter mugs on its side, and one by one with his great hand crushes each top flat.

Nobody speaks. Nobody moves. Nine pairs of eyes stare at the useless tankards while Daniel proceeds to the ale barrels. A log splitting apart in the fire is the only sound in the room.

'Bart Johnson, come here.'

Bart glances behind him, then back. 'Who? Me?'

'Don't know anyone else called Bart in this room.' Daniel says.

Bart laughs, but it is strained. 'I'll just stay here, if it's all the same.'

'Do I have to come and get you?' Daniel asks.

'Huh! I don't care.' Bart rises from his seat, stuffs his thumbs into the armholes of his jerkin and swaggers towards Daniel, stopping just out of arm's reach. He turns to grin at his friends. 'I was going to get a round anyway,' he says. 'Who's for a—?'

'So tell us about this little plan of yours to visit Hill House,' Daniel says.

'It's nothing.' Bart spreads his hands. 'Just talk. The way you do.'

'The way *you* do, mayhap,' says Daniel. 'Like you talked of going to Cazanove House?'

'I never went there.' Bart winks at Dick to share the point scored, but Dick's tense face is expressionless.

'That's right,' says Daniel. 'As Wat had it, you got cold feet halfway.'

'Tain't true!' Bart stuffs his thumbs deeper into his armholes, chin jutting. 'Anyway, that were different.'

'How was it different?'

'I thought she'd like to help the poor.'

'*She* being Mistress Cazanove. Neighbourly of you. Which poor were you thinking of?'

'Well … any of them,' Bart offers.

'Which poor?'

'Er … Mistress Ford. Her with all that brood.'

'Think again, Bart.'

'Mistress Ford is very poor and in need! And you should know that, you buried her old man!' Bart growls. It is likely he has convinced himself that he was indeed crusading for the poor.

'Mistress Ford is surely very poor and in need. But she hadn't returned to the village when you decided to go creeping to Cazanove House.'

'Well, I didn't know that.'

'I'm not surprised, when most of your life is spent tipping Nick's ale down your gullet.' Daniel is leaning back against the wall by the barrels, arms loosely folded across his chest.

Bart balls his fists and pokes his head towards Daniel. 'So why did you ask me, if you knew?'

'I asked you, to give you the chance to tell us the truth, but the truth is, you sent Oz Thatcher and your smelly crony Dick here, to plead poverty for yourselves. You thought you could touch the widow for direct outdoor relief. Money she would normally pay for the poor of the parish!'

'We *are* poor!' Bart shouts. 'We don't have any money! We can't get work. Life's hard! Dick's got a bad leg!' He is getting into his stride now but Daniel cuts him short.

'There are two sorts of poor, Bart. The deserving poor, like Widow Ford, is one sort. The other sort is the idle poor like you and Dick there, and Jem, who won't work for your living.'

'We fed the sulphur fires.'

'Jem fed the fires. And that was only when the children came in here and dragged his face out of his mug. You and Dick Winter cheated money out of old women and used it to get drunk in here.'

'Nobody else paid us!'

'Nobody paid Master Cooper here for the wood he brought,' says one of the men by the fire. Ralph Cooper chips in, 'Or Master Marchant for the sulphur.' And Daniel adds, 'Or the children who did your fire-watching for you. Why should anybody pay you, Bart?'

'One of the old ladies paid me with a chicken, and old man Edwards, he pinched it from me and made her take it back,' Bart whines to the room at large. 'He was a righteous bloody puritan, who's he to judge us? And his daughter the same! Round she goes with her basket of food for all her friends and never a bite for us, we weren't good enough for her!'

'Quite right. She was helping the *deserving* poor,' Daniel says.

But Bart's catalogue of woes is now unstoppable. 'Then last Summer, running around like the Virgin bloody Mary just because 'pothecary asked her to help him. Thinks she knows it all.'

'Have a care what you say, Bart,' Daniel warns.

'Do this, do that, bossing poor old Dick around when he's got a bad leg. Look at it, it's never healed, 'cos *she* botched it! And another thing—' Bart pokes his head in Daniel's face, eyeball to eyeball now. 'More'n one was asking what she was doing, all that while in 'pothecary's house.'

Old Silas counsels, 'You could do worse'n mind your mouth, Bart.'

But Bart is now beyond reasoning. All the imagined ills and wrongs of his life, the frustrations and failures and rejections are spilling over into the mostly sceptical ears of his audience. He flings the words at Daniel. 'Learning about herbal matters, my arse! Learning about "country matters" is what I say! Creeping out the side door after they've been at it! And now he's gone, look who she's chasing — is it any wonder we're all agreed she's free with her favours?'

The blacksmith's fist shoots out and smacks against Bart's face with a force that lifts him off his feet and slams him against one of the trestles. He slides down, huddling in a heap on the floor, blood oozing from nose and mouth, eyes wavering and unfocused.

Daniel steps across Bart, leans down to the barrel of ale Nick keeps for special and pulls out the bung. A jet of barley gold spurts out and down in a graceful curve, making further fountains as it lands squarely on Bart's scruffy breeches.

'Now that's too much, Daniel!' Nick Patten strides across the room in protest. Daniel reaches out to put the flat of his palm on the landlord's chest, bearing him relentlessly back against the sideboard. 'Stay,' Daniel recommends. Nick stays.

The wide puddle on the floor spreads slightly frothing under the trestle. Back at the spurting barrel, Daniel picks up Bart none too gently by the scruff, grabs his wrist and turns it up his back.

'Aagghhh!!' Bart screams, trying with his free arm to indicate his bloodied nostrils. 'You broke by doze!'

'I wish!' Daniel says.

Bart spits a tooth onto the floor.

'You want something for free, Bart. Have a drink on the house.' So saying, Daniel wrests Bart's arm further up his back and locks his other arm round the idler's neck. He ignores Bart's grunt of pain, and bears down, forcing him towards the barrel. The golden stream splashes against Bart's chest and down his hose. Daniel pushes his face under the flow and holds it there. Bart coughs and spits as the slow drowning commences. He squirms and struggles but is no match for the blacksmith. Red blood mixes with golden ale in a sunset-streaked flow. 'Did you mean what you said about a certain lady?' Daniel asks.

'I ... bub ...gurgh ...' is all Bart can get out.

'I didn't hear you,' Daniel says and pushes his head back under the spout.

'No! No!' Bart shouts as he is pulled clear.

Daniel leans close to the whimpering lout. 'If I hear of you going within shouting distance of Hill House Farm, I promise you I will personally tread your face into the nearest midden.'

Daniel straightens, discarding his hold, and Bart falls heavily against the trestle with a final agonized 'Aaghhh!' He lies in the flood with his hands cupped round his dribbling nose.

Daniel walks away to the door. Immediately, Nick strides across, thrusts Bart aside with his boot and crawls under the legs of the trestle desperately searching. His jerkin and shirt take an instant soaking from the escaping ale. Not finding the bung, he backs out, hitting his head on the barrel's edge. In desperation he rips the bung from the small-ale barrel and pushes it quickly into the first to stem the flow. But this bung is smaller than the hole and disappears inside. Now two fountains spurt and the froth spreads. On his knees and cursing, Nick stuffs a thumb at each bung-hole and screws round, his eyes pleading.

At the door, Daniel addresses the rest of the room. 'Know this, all of you. Next time I hear a whisper of this slander, I won't just take out the bung. I'll stave in every one of Nick's barrels.' Nobody moves a muscle. He lifts the latch. 'I have your bung here, Nick.' He places it gently on the windowsill. The innkeeper vainly reaches out with one hand, and the best ale flows afresh.

The latch clicks shut behind Daniel, and there is dead silence as the drinkers contemplate the horrors of Nick's taproom devoid of ale. Then seven men make a dash for the windowsill.

47

Alice pulls on the rope and to her aching arms the full bucket weighs heavier than ever. She peers down. The recent rain has heightened the level of water in the well but it is still a weary pull to the top. Her murmur of effort, the slop of water as she raises the bucket, are the only sounds in the empty courtyard. She pours the water into the bucket at her feet and takes it indoors.

The fire needs more wood, but her supply is running low and there never seems to be enough hours in the day to forage in the copse for dead-wood. She has stopped keeping a fire in the winter parlour.

She keeps the bar across the door most of the day now. A feeling of being under siege has set in since Daniel left so abruptly after spending one of his rare days at the smithy. He misses it, he said, and there is work building up now. She wonders where all this work is coming from, given that few of the people who returned own a horse. But who is she to call him a liar? It is still difficult to think that she just stood there in silence watching him shamble round the kitchen collecting up his mug, a couple of pieces of washing she had done for him, his whittling knife, his greatcoat, the leather bottle he uses for ale when he is out of doors.

His hands shook, she noticed. His knuckles were bloodied.

When she found her voice and asked, 'What is it, Daniel? What has happened?' he would only say, 'Nothing, nothing's happened.' But he would not look at her.

A strong smell of ale hung around him. She knew he could carry his drink, but he was acting as if under the influence of it, his face flushed and set in hard lines as he scanned the kitchen for anything else that was his. Was something said at the inn? Did Daniel see herself as another Margery, out to entrap him? The very thought made her shrivel with embarrassment. Surely not. But what other explanation was there? She flitted over to the door, standing with her back to it, and pleaded with him, 'I am your friend, you can tell me. Look at me, Daniel. Please, talk to me.'

And she thought for a minute he would. He stopped and faced her. But then he sighed and gently but irresistibly put her aside, opened the door and reminded her, as he always did, to put the bar across.

Ten minutes, that was all it took. Ten minutes. And now the life she was so confidently rebuilding has turned to rubble.

48

Ralph Cooper sits at the head of the table but that means nothing, as they both know. His appetite dwindles as he prepares to listen to another tirade on his shortcomings.

'Why on earth did you have to let that knockhead Jem into the general whisper?'

'I didn't, Emeline. Once people start to talk, anyone may listen.'

'I suppose you all drank too much and someone spoke out of turn. Typical men.'

'You women are no better. I hear Susan Cushing put the fear of God into Margery so she's not saying an ill word about it any more.'

'Just as well, mayhap. The Patten woman had her own reasons for taking a shot at Alice.'

'Well, the end of it is, Daniel is out of Hill House. That's what you wanted isn't it?'

'I don't wish it to get out of hand. Alice must retain some reputation, for our sake.'

'Oh, so now that it's going wrong, it's not *her* sake, its *ours,* is that it?'

'Well, now, let me think.' His wife puts an ostentatious fingertip to her chin. 'Who was it let Cazanove make such a fool of him that half our wool money was tied up in that clip you failed to sell to him? Oh yes, that scheme was for *our* sake too, wasn't it Ralph. And anyway, it's to Alice's advantage in the long run. The sooner it all comes to a head the sooner we can shorten the agony.'

'I see you've no objection to Alice going through some agony, Emeline.'

'Alice rejected my kindly advice and my offer of a home. Perhaps a little agony will bring her to her senses.'

'She can find other help to replace Daniel.'

'I think not. The women agree with me – it's a man's task to hire men. For Alice to do so is unmaidenly and forward. No, the wives will hold back from supporting her, as any decent woman would.' She pulls a dish towards her, selects a dainty star of marchpane and pops it in her mouth.

Ralph adds, 'And the men won't help her for fear of a brush with Daniel Bunting, is that it? When do you next turn the rack, Emeline?'

He wonders at his wife's ability to smile and purse her lips at the same time. Whenever she does, it fills him with dread.

49

Alice visits the village as little as possible now. When she does, she studiously avoids the smithy and is acutely aware of people finding matters of intense interest on the other side of the road as she approaches. Sam keeps asking to see Daniel and she has to take hold of his hand to force him to stay with her. He sulks by her side, stamping in the February mud as she stops to talk with Susan Cushing.

Susan is understanding. 'These things always blow over soon enough, Alice. Have faith, my dear, the tangle will sort itself out.'

'But why do they all avoid me? The women! See Jem Thorne's mother over there? If looks could kill I'd be dead where I stand.'

'Oh, my dear.' Susan's extends a gloved hand to take Alice's arm. 'If it is any comfort, it was not my talk with Margery that has turned the women against you. I gave her cause to think hard and we parted if not in great friendship, at least with understanding. I expect she is being a little more civil towards you?'

'I've not been to the inn since that day. But Susan, it's the men too. The men shun me as if I didn't exist.'

'You know something happened at Nick Patten's, that day Daniel left your house?'

'At the inn? About me, you mean?' Being talked about is bad enough. Having her name made common currency in the taproom is disaster.

Susan sighs. 'I don't know, Alice. You could say it is a blessing that the men are being tight-lipped about it. Silas's wife says she had to tend Bart Thornton's bruises, though he wouldn't say how he got them. But then, Bart is forever getting himself in a scrape. I hear Dick Winter and Jem have had a falling out with him, so perhaps …'.

'But what has that to do with—?'

Susan shrugs. 'That's all I've been able to glean.'

'It'll be March soon and I need help on the farm,' Alice says, 'but whenever I ask, none will help me. And yet I hear the Coopers have taken on several labourers in the last fortnight. I asked Deborah Wilkins, though I have to admit that with all those women in the house Rob is needed there. I've been to Norah Abbott to ask if Nat could give me a day, he only has their small strip to look after, but she insists he has a bad back. Everyone I ask makes excuses. But the sheep still have to be seen to and the sowing is upon us. At this rate, I shall have to sell the sheep, and they with lambs coming anytime soon.'

Susan is genuinely sympathetic but in no position to help. 'Sexton Whitehead, God rest his soul, used to do the odd bit of heavy work for us. He would surely have helped you out, but now we do not have even him.' She brightens. 'If it would help you, bring Sam down to us for a day or two, that you may give your attention to the farm. You would like to come and stay in the village for a bit, would you not, Sam?'

'Yes!' Sam hops from foot to foot, and Alice thinks, it's Daniel he really wants to see. She says to Susan, 'I am grateful at least that you and your sister will still acknowledge me in the street.'

'And shame on those who do not!' Susan says. 'I gave

Margery Patten a piece of my mind for what she said to you.'
She leans towards Alice and places a hand on her arm. 'For what it's worth, she was sore and repentant by the time I had finished rasping at her.'

'It's true she has never before been unkind for long.'

'And she will think twice before saying things about witchcraft or anything else concerning you.'

'I am grateful to you, Susan, but I am so mortified that Margery thinks I was keeping ' – she glances at Sam – 'D-a-n-i-e-l dancing in attendance.'

'Alice, people forget. Believe me, there will be a man soon enough who needs the money and he will break ranks and come and work for you.'

The support brings a brief smile to Alice's face, but the fact remains that more people than Margery have long since spread amongst the good folk of Hillbury the story of Alice Edwards' lust for Daniel Bunting.

50

She sits over another solitary breakfast, picking at food, her mind nagging at the problem. Sam has gone out into the yard. He has taken to kicking stones around. Alice will not allow him to throw them, but equally she never has any time nowadays to play with him. She stares unseeing at his desultory figure while her thoughts circle, trapped in her head for want of company.

Margery's information came from her son, she said. A growing boy, anxious to enter the world of men, he might pass round the story of what he has seen, exaggerate a bit to attract interest. Alice begins to grow hot at the idea of what might have been said. He wouldn't enhance Daniel's part, that would only take the attention away from himself. No, far more likely he would embellish hers. Is that what has happened? And has it been repeated in the inn in front of Daniel? Making Daniel feel a fool in front of all the men? The great strong blacksmith dancing attendance on a coarse woman. Falling for the lures she has put out. It explains his sudden departure, his refusal to talk to her.

The 'old story' about Margery haunts Alice. "... *got herself talked about ... embarrassed but not embroiled ... he'd have gone away if he'd had anywhere to go.*"

Well, this time Daniel has somewhere to go and has gone there. Alice puts her head in her arms and groans, and her face burns.

Sam comes in from his solitary play in the yard. 'That frog man is here again.' He plumps down on the settle, kicking his heels on the wooden panel.

'Gerald?' Alice sighs. Well, he and his mother will have to put up with a mug of ale in the kitchen and Alice in her rug-gown. She is wearing the seam-rent one that Henry Jerrard found so contemptible. So who cares? Alice reflects that she has no 'servants' of any sort now, so Gerald will have to deal with his and his mother's horses himself. She quickly presses one of the glazed mugs to her face to cool her flushed cheeks.

When the knock comes on the door, she takes a deep breath and pulls it open. Gerald stands there, no ruff, no embroidered doublet, no ribbon-ties crowning the folly of pluderhosen. Instead, a wool cap, thick linen shirt under a rough, padded jerkin, calf-length breeches, thick stockings, stout shoes. Here is a man dressed for work. Alice stares at him.

'Give you good morning, Alice,' Gerald greets her as though this is an everyday occurrence. 'My mother sends her compliments and I am here to help you.'

Alice looks over his shoulder into the yard, then back at him. Gerald suddenly grasps at his cap and snatches it off. 'Sorry,' he mumbles. Alice finds her voice.

'No, not your cap,' she says, 'where's your mother?'

'At home,' Gerald replies, as though to say, where else would she be.

'Oh, Gerald,' Alice breathes. She resists the impulse to put grateful arms round his neck. Instead she stands back for him to enter. This is worth a mug of the very best ale.

Gerald arrives each morning and leaves before dusk.

Alice is studiously circumspect. After that first tankard of ale, she never again shares a drink with him, nor takes a meal

267

in his company. If he eats in her kitchen she makes sure she stands the whiles, or waits shivering in the yard. She keeps her eyes down and her smiles guarded. And she keeps Sam with her at all times Gerald is around. She digs out her mother's old caps that hide more of her face, and wears them everywhere. Puritan Tom Wemyss approves, sly Dick Winter sniggers and Susan Cushing silently fumes.

It lasts two weeks to the day.

51

Alice has a handful of eggs which she is carrying to the kitchen when Gerald arrives. 'Give you good day, Alice.' He twists his hat in his hands.

'Give you good day, Gerald.' She stands, eyes down, and waits.

'Alice, I am truly sorry about this, but—' He takes a step forward, reaching out, but she backs away, dislodging a couple of eggs which smash on the ground.

'I cannot help you. There is work to do at home.'

'Can't help me?' Surprise raises her eyes to his face for the first time in days but he will not meet her look.

'I am truly sorry, Alice,' he says again. He is, she can see.

'What is it?' she asks.

'My mother says I must help my father at home.'

'That's all right for today, Gerald. You'll be back tomorrow, then?'

'Not tomorrow.' He has difficulty getting the words out. 'Not any more.'

'Can you not come and help for a while longer, so that we can get the sowing done at least?' she asks.

By now he has screwed his cap into a rope. 'I would, you know, but my mother insists.' He shrugs.

'You have not lost your labourers? The ones you have just taken on?'

'Oh, no, nothing like that. I am simply needed at home.'

'What about two days a week, a day, even? You can choose your own day, Gerald?' she begs him, while he shakes his head back and forth, back and forth. 'It is so difficult at present, with everything happening. How am I to cope?' She stops. Self-pity is not the way. She tries again. 'You cannot leave like this, Gerald, please.'

'I wish I ... I am very sorry, Alice, really I am. I tried to persuade her ...'

Yes, Alice thinks, I can see your mother's seal all over this. She sighs. 'Oh well, now you are here, can you help me this morning?'

'Well, to tell truth, no. I shall go straight back.'

'Oh, Gerald,' Alice groans.

'My parents have come also, they will be here directly. My mother wishes to explain how it is, Alice, and to offer her sympathies. She is truly sorry for you.'

Oh, Gerald, if you believe that, I am truly sorry for you.

Emeline Cooper's timing, for it is surely hers and not her husband's, is well planned. They round the barn moments later and Gerald goes to help his mother from her horse. They have a brief exchange in which she does the talking and he the nodding, while Ralph dismounts and stands to one side. Then Gerald leads the horses into the stable and his mother approaches, sympathetically smiling, head on one side. Here is a wolf that would like Alice to think it a sheep.

'My dear.' Emeline Cooper touches cold lips to Alice's cheek and closes her fingers round Alice's arm. She glances back, 'Come along, Ralph,' and steers her into the kitchen. Alice detaches her arm and stands watching Ralph Cooper, silent and subdued, trail in Emeline's wake towards the hall door.

'There is no fire in the winter parlour, Mistress Cooper,'

Alice says. She gestures to the settle before the hearth. Emeline Cooper's mouth turns down as she approaches the dying logs. 'Dear me, Alice, you really should try to keep this place a little more cheerful. The hearth is the heart of the home, you know.' She runs a gloved finger across the settle and flicks invisible specks from it before taking her seat at the end nearest the fading warmth. She pats the space next to her. 'Now, my dear, do you sit down here.'

Alice ignores her. She places a chair for herself and gestures Ralph Cooper to the settle.

Emeline starts, 'My dear, this is such an unfortunate turn. I know how much alone you have been, and how difficult that is in so many ways. We are all devastated of course. Gerald particularly, but I cannot see a way round it.'

'I have been very grateful for Gerald's help,' Alice says, 'It has meant a lot to be able to keep the farm together. Labour is not easy to find.'

'Indeed, you speak true,' Emeline Cooper's sympathy oozes. 'You do not know how we are struggling ourselves at Cowper with those we have. We've done our best by letting you have Gerald, but it is impossible for my husband to cope any longer without his help. I fear Ralph will kill himself else, truly I do.' She remembers to sigh.

'Perhaps Gerald can continue for one or two days in the week,' Alice says, 'so that we may complete the sowing.'

'Would that it were possible, my dear. But his father is adamant, I cannot shift him.' She gives her husband a look. 'Can I, Ralph?'

He glances up. 'I fear not, Alice.'

Alice bites her lip. The thought of Mistress Cooper being unable to browbeat her husband into whatever scheme she has in mind is inconceivable. 'I shall have to sell the remaining ewes then,' she says. 'There is nothing else for it. They should make a reasonable price, being about to lamb. If you know of anyone interested in buying, I shall be glad to hear. Otherwise I suppose I must take them to Sherborne and sell them at market.'

'It is a difficult case for you indeed, Alice. If you cannot get help, what can you do?'

'There is nothing else to do.' Alice struggles to keep her voice even. 'I cannot watch over the new lambs as well doing as the sowing, and I cannot leave them to starve or be taken as prey. I shall continue the sowing on my own.'

'You may always come to me, you know, Alice, if you need a shoulder to cry on.'

Alice eyes the older woman narrowly. 'You have just shown me how impossible it would be for me to burden you with a difficulty that you are not in a position to alleviate.'

'But you cannot do all that and run the house.'

'If I cannot get help, I must do as best I can on my own. I have considered selling the farm complete, house and all, and moving to Sherborne.'

'Oh, that would not do at all,' Emeline says immediately.

'Why not?'

'Well, you would not be happy with that.'

'You're right,' Alice agrees. 'I should hate it, but it would solve my current problems. The land will fetch a good price, and I could set up a shop making pies or preserves, something of that nature.'

'You would not be allowed to.'

'Now what's the problem?' Alice demands.

'You're a single woman. You cannot simply set up.'

'Why?'

'You must have a man stand surety for you.'

272

'Oohh! Everywhere I turn, some man is standing in my way!'

'I don't make the rules, Alice.'

No but you know how to use them. She says, 'Then, as Master Cooper is unable to let Gerald help any more, perhaps he will help me in another way?'

'Oh? And what is that, pray?' Emeline's words swift and clipped, the tone unwelcoming. Loopholes are not part of her plan.

Alice addresses Ralph Cooper. 'If you wish to help me, sir, I ask your surety, so that I may open a shop and earn my living.'

'Oh, Alice, as if that's likely,' Emeline Cooper interjects. 'And in any event, you know how my husband distrusts women.'

If he does, I can see why. 'But surely—,' she starts.

'My husband has a most correct antipathy towards women in trade,' Emeline says. 'He will not be prevailed upon, under any circumstances' – she looks hard at her husband – 'to support such an immodest measure. But let us ask him anyway, Alice, since you are so determined.' She sits back, the picture of even-handedness. 'Let us see what answer he gives.'

Ralph Cooper avoids the eye of both women. He murmurs, 'It would be a little difficult, Alice.'

'Why difficult, sir? You, a justice, a well-respected man in the community?'

He manages, 'Well … yes—' before Emeline interrupts.

'In this community of Hillbury and Westover, yes, Alice. But a shop would have to be in Sherborne or some such large town. My husband has no influence in such places.' She nudges her husband. 'Do you Ralph?'

'Er, I fear not.'

'But you know the justices there, sir,' Alice insists. 'It's March, you'll all be attending the winter assizes. Surely you can talk to one of them?'

He half smiles at Alice but says nothing and again Emeline picks up the thread. 'You see, Alice? I did warn you. But listen, there might be a way.' She pauses, adopting a thoughtful look. 'I need to think it through, for it is only now coming to me.'

Alice lets the lie pass and waits with foreboding.

'Ralph,' Emeline says. 'The fire is dying down. You'd better add those logs by the side there, or we shall all freeze to death.' Alice watches as Ralph drops the last of her small supply of rotting wood onto the fire.

'You may not like it at first,' the older woman says, 'but you should give this due thought. If we were to join your Hill House to our Cowper, we could share the work of it more easily. No, please listen,' as Alice sits back folding her arms. 'You have said yourself you see no other way, and this could help all of us. The two properties share a common boundary. By treating them as one demesne, we could rearrange the fields to make the work easier, keep all the wheat together for instance, move the sheep into one area. It could make very good sense, Alice.' She smiles at Alice as though she has just realised what a clever idea it is, this sudden, detailed plan of hers.

'When you say "join",' Alice asks carefully, 'what exactly do you mean?'

'Well,' the other chuckles, bridling, 'there is only one meaning, which I think we both understand.'

'I am to marry your son, to save my farm.'

'To increase your prosperity, and brighten your outlook, Alice. Think of it in that way. It will be a great step forward for you, especially as things are at present.'

'I cannot do that, Mistress Cooper.'

'Why not?'

'I do not have the regard for Gerald that is necessary to make him happy.' Alice is firm.

'You seem to have been marvellously successful at making Gerald happy these past weeks. He is always so keen to visit you, and I am simply dragging him away, he is so reluctant to leave here to help his own father.'

Alice says, 'Gerald has been a great help to me. But a husband is entirely different.'

'Not so different. You must lay aside your girlish notions of love. Your mother told you so, many times, to my knowledge. Gerald would be very content, I assure you.'

'And what of my contentment?' Alice demands, sitting forward.

'Yours? Attending your husband, of course. And on top of that, a most advantageous marriage for you, Alice. Attorney Handley is very much of the same mind. At least,' she adds hurriedly, 'he has always thought so in the past.'

'Attorney Handley?' Alice asks. 'What has he to do with all this?'

'Oh, I happened to bump into him the other day and we were discussing this and that, as you do. A young woman inheriting. Someone will need to check that it's all above board, you know.'

Handley, the attorney from Woodley who does as he's told "as long as someone makes it worth his while." So Mistress Cooper has already discussed this "sudden idea" with him, no doubt making it worth his while to take her view. Alice fervently wishes she had listened to her father when he talked of a good law man in London. Henry Jerrard might know who this is, but where to write to him? All she knows is that he lives in a place called Guildford.

'Indeed, you will be protected from all that by a union with the Coopers of Cowper. And your mother so wished it.' Emeline Cooper lays a gentle hand on Alice's as she finishes, and Alice feels the tears start in her eyes.

'Think on it Alice, it is a very good offer, particularly for a woman of your current standing.'

'What do you mean, my current standing?'

'Well, my dear, this talk, of course, that has circulated about you and poor Daniel. Completely and utterly untrue I feel sure, but stories are stories, and a good marriage would scotch them forever.'

Alice tries to evade. 'I beg you will give me a little time to think about this,' she says. 'We have not discussed provision for Sam's education, and Gerald has not been asked for his agreement to adopt the lad.'

'Oh, you don't need to keep Sam, Alice. He can go to the Abiding Place as I told you.'

'It would be a condition of my marriage that I adopt Sam, Mistress Cooper. I would accept nothing less.'

'So you haven't begged him?'

'I've been rather busy, as you know.'

'Oh dear, it looks to me as if you are guilty of abduction, Alice. And abduction of a child is a particularly serious matter.'

'I've not abducted him, you know I haven't. He'd have died of the cold if I hadn't looked after him.'

'But you withheld him from the Abiding Place once quarantine was over, Alice. The Justices will take a very dim view of that. Isn't that right, Ralph?'

'I fear so,' he agrees.

Alice can almost feel herself sinking. Whatever she says

will be countered. Still she fights on. 'I was trying to find his father. Vicar Rutland was enquiring too.'

Emeline Cooper's thin lips curl. 'Those enquiries came to a sudden halt, I hear.'

Alice bows her head. Pleading Sam's need for a secure, loving home will have no effect on this woman. Tell her the real reason the search stopped? Tell her of Sam's terror of having his feet scalded again? Alice wouldn't put it past Emeline Cooper to let the Poor House know that there is an effective way to ensure Sam's obedience. Such a woman!

Anger like a red-hot poker stabs through Alice's mind, and suddenly the way is clear. Her head comes up. 'And what of the talk about a certain undeclared wool clip?'

Emeline Cooper's smirk falters. 'Who told you—? What are you talking about?'

'How *were* you planning to hide your fraudulent activity?' Her voice changes as realisation dawns. 'You were going to wait until I had married your son, and then "discover" that my father had held back part of our wool yield … That's it, isn't it? Blame it on a dead man who can't defend himself.'

There is a short silence. Ralph Cooper's look is hunted, Emeline's is bland.

Alice leans forward. 'It wouldn't wash. Father declared his clip and it was the same weight as most years. Let us understand each other clearly, madam. If you make any move, any move at all against me or against Sam, I know of three witnesses who knew what went on between your husband and Rupert Cazanove last Autumn. The Guilds would take more than a passing interest in evidence of that sort.'

It is partly bluff because two of the witnesses are dead, but she is counting on her opponent's consciousness of guilt.

'Your mother always said you had a head full of fantastical

thoughts, Alice.' Emeline Cooper folds her hands on her lap and raises enquiring eyebrows. 'Tell us more of this fancy of yours.'

'You cannot deny it, madam. Believe me, I am quite prepared to petition the Guilds, or even the Justices at Sherborne or Dorchester.' She turns to Ralph but Ralph is looking at Emeline, whose lips slowly stretch into a smirk.

'I tell you, I have no idea what you are talking about, Alice.'

Not understanding why the ground is sliding, Alice turns to Ralph Cooper. 'Several people in this village know of it, sir, they saw you doing the deal with Rupert Cazanove at Nick Patten's.'

'Several people are mistaken, then,' Emeline interrupts. 'Let them come and look around Cowper. They will find no illegal clip.'

Alice watches the truth dawn on Ralph Cooper at the same moment she realises it herself. Emeline Cooper has long since found a buyer, apparently without Ralph's knowledge. Alice fights to keep the crushing disappointment from showing on her face. The sense of defeat brings it home to her how much she was pinning her hopes on this as an unassailable weapon.

Emeline Cooper inclines her head and smiles. 'Alice, my dear, let us mend some fences here. We did not come to argue.'

'Then what did you come for, madam?' *As if I didn't know.*

'I have thought much of your welfare these past weeks, Alice.'

'Welfare or ill-fare?' She hardly cares what she says to this woman now.

'This is no time for wit. The lack of assistance you are suffering from the village is a two-edged sword. It is damaging both the prosperity of Hill House Farm and your reputation as a woman of virtue. I am offering you a way out. Marriage with Gerald will restore your standing.'

She clamps her mouth shut. *A way that would push me into an alliance I abhor, serving no ends but yours, and condemning Sam to a life of drudgery.* She considers approaching the other local justice, Sir Thomas Harcourt. Considers and rejects. Sir Thomas did not rise to his senior position by helping discredited young women. He has a reputation for hard dealing. Twice as powerful as the Coopers, if he discovers Alice is losing control of Hill House Farm, not only will he find legal means by which he can smilingly dispossess her of her land, but he will likely use his justice's powers to remove Sam from her unfit care.

'Well?'

'I cannot see my way clear to do that, madam.' *And my body cringes at the thought of marriage to Gerald.*

'You will have to do better than that, Alice.'

'I am sorry, madam, I cannot.' *Live with his worship and his fumbling fingers for the rest of my life?*

'Then when are you going to decide?'

'My mother will long since have made you aware of my concerns on the subject.'

'You will fall in love when you are married, Alice.'

Oh, give me strength.

'No call to roll your eyes like that!' Emeline snaps. 'You need us. Go on refusing and my son may well look elsewhere.'

She cannot help it, she laughs. 'Madam, I have never known Gerald look anywhere you did not dictate.'

'This is no laughing matter, Alice. Your situation is untenable. You cannot continue to live here alone.' And Mistress Cooper adds, 'Unprotected.'

What's that supposed to mean?

'This offer will not be available for ever, you know.'

No, she thinks. And when I'm ruined, you'll scoop up the land on the cheap and take Sam away from me. 'Sam stays with me,' she says.

'Forget him. I want your answer, Alice.'

'Sam,' is all she can say. 'Sam …' Her eyes are welling.

She starts as Ralph Cooper suddenly leans forward. She has forgotten all about him. In a kindly voice, he says, 'You and Gerald will adopt Sam, Alice.' For a moment she stares unbelieving at him. 'I give you my word,' he adds.

'Does Gerald know of this?'

'I have talked to Gerald about it and he is quite happy. He likes Sam.' Almost, he seems to be conveying some sort of apology for her having to marry his son. Against her will, Alice feels her opposition weakening in response to Ralph's offer. He goes on, 'I will prepare the Begging papers myself.'

Even Emeline is quiet, watchful. A dangerous liking is stealing over Alice for this pathetic man who has struck at her weakest point.

'I can do it today,' Ralph Cooper says. 'You will have the paper to sign this evening.'

Well, what is it? What are my choices now? I'm failing with the farm, rejected by the village, unable to support myself. I've made a mess of this. And yet …

'I can't …' She shakes her head. 'I can't do this.'

Emeline abruptly stands up. 'Gerald will be getting cold waiting for us, and we are busy at Cowper. This is what will happen, Alice. I shall allow you seven days to consider your position. We shall return for your answer this day week. Save yourself and this house and demesne or watch it all crumble away into ruin.' Her icy fingers flash out to grip Alice's chin.

'Do not lightly throw it away. Come, Ralph.'

52

Alice looks at the pregnant sheep and realises she will never get them to market without doubling their numbers on the way. She wonders whether to bother to reply to the note in Ralph Cooper's hand but dictated no doubt by Emeline, to buy the dams at rock-bottom value *"as they might not make the journey whole to Cowper"*.

53

The sun slants in through the window of the chamber. Alice jerks her eyes open with sick realisation. Sam always wakes early and wants her awake too, it has become her way of getting up to each weary day. With Sam down at Susan's for a couple of days, there is no one to rouse her and she has slept half the day round. No bread made, no sheep checked, and whole acres of sowing still to do.

54

In the breath-cloud chill of pre-dawn, Alice shivers as she fights her way into her clothes. No more dressing by the warmth of the kitchen fire. The terror of unseen watchers has long since driven her to struggle into her clothes upstairs with neither fire nor candle. She curses as she wrestles with ties and lacing. Sam stirs. 'Is it time to get up, Alice?'

'No, Sam. I'm just going out to the sheep, I thought I heard something. I'll not be long.'

She isn't. By the time she has slithered and stumbled by the weak light of her lantern to the fold on the opposite hill, it is too late for the three newborn lambs lying still and forlorn, their curly baby wool blood-spattered from their slit throats. As the sun rises on a cold dawn, Alice makes a promise to herself. One day, Mistress Cooper, I will avenge these innocent, butchered creatures.

55

'For heaven's sake, Sam!' she bursts out one afternoon. 'I don't know why grain only grows in Spring. It just does, so I have to sow it now!' She staggers away with another load, the heavy wooden seed lip strapped across her shoulder and knocking painfully on her hip. She gets as far as the end of the yard, trips on a loose stone and falls flat on her face, scattering grain and scoring her hands.

'Oh, Christ in Heaven!' she shouts and bangs her fists on the ground as frustration and despair overwhelm her. She gets to her knees and sees that her sleeve has torn on a rough flint, her skirt is muddied and there is a hole in her stocking. Sitting back on the ground she rocks her head in her bloodied hands.

It is ten minutes later as she sits staring at the cold kitchen hearth that the door opens. Hastily she rubs her fingers under her eyes, but it is only Sam. He walks carefully in. Both arms are wrapped round one of the leather buckets and he stands by the door unsure of his welcome.

'I picked up the grain, Alice,' he says. 'The chickens were trying to eat it.'

56

It feels strange being dressed in lawn and wool as she used to. The coarse linen and lockram of the past weeks have become a part of her life now. The fine chemise feels almost silk-smooth against her skin, the embroidered doublet and blue worsted skirt are as strange as if they belong to someone else. Under the high-crowned, silk-worked hat her hair is washed, brushed and arranged for the first time in weeks. She has searched for her gloves but in vain, so she will simply have to hide her work-worn hands. Then she looks in the mirror and takes a deep breath.

This is the last resort, she tells her reflection, and it is only now in extremity that I go to beg help of the woman who abandoned her duty to my mother. Mistress Cazanove expressed a sense of obligation for that, let us now see if she meant it.

What if Mistress Cazanove gives me the same look she directed at Abel Nutley that day he sat down uninvited in her house? A look of well-bred distaste in the face of presumption. But it is to save the farm, and to save Sam, so I must be prepared to go on my knees to her if that is what it takes.

She turns from the mirror, takes up her cloak and leaves the house.

57

The sound of voices, wheels, hooves, shouts, grow in volume as she rides round the corner of the mansion. Through the entrance arch at the side, the courtyard is alive with padded and muffled figures, their breath vapouring in the raw grey air as they labour to and fro. Great-coated men harness horses, others load carts from a massive table dragged out into the yard, maidservants carry laden baskets two-handed from the kitchens, adding them to the collection arranged on and around the table, before scurrying back indoors with huddled arms. The smells of new-baked bread, of roasting meat, waft on the air. Two men roll barrels out of one of the storehouses and stack them with others waiting to be loaded. In the middle of the courtyard Ursula Cazanove directs the whole, her face alight, eyes looking all around, pointing here, asking there, calling to one or sharing a jest as another passes. In one hand is a list she constantly checks. Her feet stamp the ground now and then against the day's chill. With a sense of disbelief, Alice dismounts and watches the preparations for a hunting party.

For a few moments no one notices her standing at Cassie's head on the edge of the bustle before her, until a voice behind causes her to start and turn. Wat, the man who was Rupert Cazanove's body servant, is leading two horses, one of which, by the look of the saddle, is Ursula's mount.

'How do you do, Mistress Edwards? We have not seen you

in some weeks,' he says, 'Do you wish to see my mistress?'

'I came to call on her, yes,' Alice says. She steels herself to press on with her plan, dreading who might turn up here to join the party. Probably Sir Thomas and Lady Harcourt and their boys, they will see her and expect her to be joining the festivities. What excuse can she make? And worse, what if the Coopers arrive? She can just imagine Emeline with sham concern wondering aloud why Alice does not apply goose grease to her reddened hands. Her brief courage dissolves. 'This is not a good time. Do you give me a step up, please, Wat?'

'If you will wait, mistress, I shall tell her you are here.'

'Please, don't trouble her.'

'It is no trouble, mistress.' He still has the slightly wary courtesy as though expecting opposition. He walks under the archway drawing the horses with him and approaches his mistress. She looks round his shoulder, smiles at Alice. Anyone would think she hasn't a care in the world. She hands Wat her list, indicating something on it, and steps forward, beckoning to one of the outdoor men as she approaches. He is vaguely familiar but Alice cannot immediately place him.

'Mistress Edwards, this is a pleasure to see you again.' Mistress Cazanove's smile is warm. 'I hope I see you well?'

'Thank you, Mistress Cazanove, I am well. I hope you are long since recovered from Master Nutley's visit.'

'Indeed, I have not seen him from that day to this and I thank God in His mercy for it! Please excuse me a moment.' She turns to her outdoor man now waiting a pace or two off. 'Oswald, do you take Mistress Edwards' mount and see it fed and watered.'

'No, I'm not staying—'

'Also the two that Wat has, until I need them.' Alice gives

288

up the reins. Oz Thatcher, that's who it is. Wat mentioned him.

'But let us not be *Mistress* this and *Mistress* that. Please call me Ursula. And I know you are Alice. It is chilly to stand out here. Will you step into the house, let me offer you refreshment?'

'It is kind in you, but I see I have called at a bad time.'

One of the maids approaches and bobs a curtsey to Ursula. 'Mistress, Wat says to keep back this basket separate from the others, but I do not see why I should do as *he* says.'

'He is quite right, Margaret. Do you follow Wat's directions. I have a particular purpose for that basket.' The maid pouts, bobs again and turns for the kitchens, tossing her head as she passes Wat. Alice glances again round the courtyard. At the far end, several men pile up wood and planks, while others select and load what they need, along with various tools, into one of the larger carts. Not a hunting party after all, but what is it?

'I have found Alaric Ford's widow and family a good house, Alice,' Ursula is saying, 'the one at the far end of Bakery Row, do you know it?'

'The extra space will be welcome I'm sure, they are so cramped in their present place. But what about the leaky—?'

One of the men dealing with the wood approaches. 'Mistress, are we to take roof tiles or thatch?'

'It is on Wat's list that you are to take thatch. I wonder you did not ask him.' As he walks away, Ursula says to her, 'I am trying to get them to understand that although I make the decisions, there are others who carry out my wishes. They all became so used to taking their orders from my husband only, I suppose.' Her eyes scan the activities before her.

'You were speaking of Mistress Ford,' Alice prompts her.

'That is who the basket is for. Once we can get those cottages into better condition, we shall have a whole row right there in the village.' Alice stares in surprise, a look unseen by Ursula whose eye has been caught by Wat. He indicates a kitchen maid next to him carrying piled trays of pies, then his list, and shrugs his shoulders. 'Four of those,' she says, holding up her hand, fingers splayed. 'Four. You know, Alice, there is so much work to be done, repairing roofs, re-plastering, glazing windows. That was a sin, leaving them in their old state.'

'I suppose the rent will be increased to reflect the improvement?' Alice says carefully.

'Heavens, no! All credit to you that you caused me to look at my husband's properties. The rent was by far too high, even had the cottages been sound. No, I shall house those in most need and the rent shall reflect their station in life. It is the least I can do. I only hope I can get all this done before they find Bernard. That's my late husband's brother, the one who will inherit.' Ursula puts a hand on her arm. 'Do you excuse me one moment, Alice. I see Esther there, I must have a word with her.'

Alice's thoughts are in confusion, struggling to adjust to what Ursula has said. All this commotion that she assumed to be some expensive entertainment is nothing of the sort – on the contrary it is a mission to her most vulnerable tenants. What she took for wilful ignorance on the part of the widow, was probably exactly what Ursula Cazanove said previously, that her husband ordered her to refrain from involving herself in any way, even almsgiving. Now that the wife is a widow she chooses another way. Too late, it comes home to Alice how severely she has misjudged this woman. Too late, she sees how impossible it will be to ask for assistance. What right has she, mistress of a weathertight house, owner of a freehold, to be counted a higher cause than the homeless, the hopeless, the crushed who have suffered for years? Shame washes hot through her. She wishes she had kept Cassie beside her so that she could mount and leave this minute.

Ursula has had her word with Esther and returns to Alice. Her eyes sparkle, her face is eager. 'Really, Alice, it seems I have neither the hours in the day nor the people on hand to do all I need to do!' She spreads her arm, indicating the food baskets now being loaded into the carts. 'This is for the dyeworkers who live this side of the hill in Woodley. They are my most pressing responsibility, I feel. We do this once a week now and it helps them while I try to see to other matters like the grievances they have. In between times, we make preparations for the next week's visit. But Hillbury is my true parish and I need to do more for the poor there as well. I thank God that there is at least yourself and Margery Patten who are looking to their needs.'

'Well, to tell truth, I have not—' begins Alice.

'And then there is the Poor House at Westover. Abiding Place, I should say, though how anyone can abide that place is more than I can imagine. It's a disgrace!' She stops and gives an embarrassed laugh. 'Alice, forgive me. I talk on forever about my doings. Of course, you came to ask about the records my husband kept of his tenants. I confess it has gone completely from my mind these past few weeks—'

'No, please!' Alice has long since forgotten about Cazanove's untidy papers. How can she now say that the last thing she wants is to find Sam's father? She summons a laugh. 'I expect any notes he kept were torn up after those high words between your husband and the man. You would have found his records by now if they existed. Please, do not worry any more about it.'

With a shake of her head, Ursula says, 'No, he would not have destroyed even a scrap of paper, not my husband. It's kind in you to excuse me, Alice, but I confess I have hardly looked and I shall make a point of doing so. Now tell me, how are things at Hill House? What is happening with you? Do come and take a little refreshment, I beg you. They will be a while here yet and it is well that I should leave them to get on with it and learn to trust Wat.' She takes Alice's arm, gently urging her.

Alice forces a smile. 'I thank you, but no. You have so much to do, and as you say, not enough people to do it, so every pair of hands is precious. No doubt I shall call again one day when you have leisure. And please, I truly do not wish you to worry about that particular tenant.'

A reluctant Ursula finally summons Oz Thatcher to bring Alice's horse. As Alice rides away up the hill, she says to the mare, 'Oh, Cassie, how could I have been so self-righteous? So contemptible? I entirely misjudged her. I don't deserve her help.'

She rides on into the woods. Deep amongst the trees, Cassie slithers on packed wet leaves. All around, black trunks reach up black branches as though in despairing entreaty. The silence is broken only by the thawing frost, its slow tears dripping unseen from a million bare twigs onto a dead season's rot.

58

Nick Patten is a happy man. Today he can smell spring in the air, not that that is the cause of his happiness, but it seems to him appropriate that the turn in his fortunes should match the turn in the season. Business has been improving gradually after that slump caused by Daniel, when the men of the village for a while deemed it advisable to shift their loyalty from Nick's hearth to their own.

It wouldn't last, Margery told him, as the two sat staring at an empty taproom for yet another day. She was right, she knows his customers better than he does. One by one and then in twos and threes they have trickled back to enjoy the delights of his home-brew and to escape from the sight of females, Margery Patten excepted.

Along with the return of custom, he now has to bear frequent heavy-handed jests about tight-lipped tankards and the superiority of fine ale over water for washing floors. But although the loss of his best beer still rankles, he bears no grudge against Daniel. He now believes Daniel did the right thing in tackling Bart Johnson as the source of all the trouble. His own role in encouraging and embellishing the story young John returned with, Nick entirely discounts. It is his task as landlord to keep his customers amused and Nick did his best to maintain the tradition. Even the useless pewter tankards he has hung up for all to see. He is perversely proud of them, and right now has an opportunity to show off by telling their story to the stranger who stopped by last night for the third time in as many months. Not so much a stranger now, Henry Jerrard is a good friend as far as Nick is concerned. Little perquisites regularly find their way into the landlord's discreetly ready hand.

'This was the way of it, you see,' Nick says. He launches into his version of the story, in which Daniel expressed his admiration of Nick's promptness in saving the tankards from thieving hands. The flattened tops are the result of general agreement amongst the customers that a dead man's property should not be used by the unworthy. With Jerrard's nodding encouragement, the innkeeper warms to his theme, aided by some pots of old March beer imbibed while he waited for his visitor to come down to a late breakfast.

The next subject for Nick's scrutiny is the perfidy of certain lewd fellows in regard to a – possibly – innocent young woman, to remain unnamed of course, but she lives up the hill there beyond the church. Nick is very encouraged by the close interest shown in his story, and by the probing questions as to the degree of the lady's blamelessness or otherwise.

By way of reply, he shrugs meaningfully and relates the story about a bath for a small boy – cock-and-bull of course, sir – who'd waste hot water on a child? He then proceeds to point out the differences between that story and what his own son witnessed. Not wishing to do the lady any injustice by spreading rumours himself, but it's interesting how violently the blacksmith reacted to the lewd fellow Bart, isn't it, sir? And suddenly the young woman is getting betrothed to the local justice's son. Judge for yourself, he invites Jerrard.

Jerrard appears to think for a minute before replying absently, 'Yes indeed,' and drains his ale and rises. 'I must be on my way.' He reaches for his cloak. 'I need to be in

Salisbury by this evening.' It is disappointing, because Nick wants to discuss other possible versions of the story. It would while away a quiet midday period while the local men are out in the fields. He offers to call one of his boys to fetch the man's mount. He will tell young Nick to take his time over it, give his father the chance to prolong this enjoyable visit.

'No, don't worry,' Jerrard says, 'I'll fetch the grey myself.' He throws his cloak round his shoulders, loosely tying it, dons his hat and takes up his gloves. 'I'll leave by the kitchen and bid farewell to Margery on the way.' Almost as though she has been listening at the door, Margery emerges at that moment to meet them in the passage.

'We're always glad to see you here, sir, whenever you chose to come,' she says breathily, palm not quite extended, and Nick adds, 'Must be something marvellous to bring you so out of your way to stay with us.'

'What man would not veer aside from his route for good ale and an excellent table?' Jerrard says.

Nick watches Margery tweak a few locks that peep out from under her cap. She curtsies, something she rarely does. She's taken the compliment seriously, but proud as he is of his maltster's skills, Nick is not vain enough to believe it is either his home-brew or Margery's cooking that brings Jerrard.

'No other business to transact then, sir?' Nick asks, digging around to discover more about this generous-handed man from Surrey who visits the West Country at regular intervals. Why stay the night here in out-of-the-way Hillbury? Is it the cloth industry he is in? Something to do with Cazanove and the dye-works? It would explain that first visit in December. Jerrard could not have known Cazanove was already dead. On Jerrard's second visit in January, the attorneys were looking for Cazanove's brother. And of course, Nick reasons, no serious merchant would do business with a woman instead.

'We shall await your next visit with pleasure, sir,' Nick says, when Jerrard does not enlighten him. 'Always ready to be of service to a gentleman of your stamp.'

'I thank you for your kind attentions, Nick, and those of your good lady,' Jerrard says, nodding to Margery as he draws on his gauntlets. 'Sadly, however – and it is no reflection on your excellent house – I doubt I shall have cause to stay here again.'

He offers no further explanation and Nick, disappointed, but still as hopeful as Margery of another bonus to add to their collection, accompanies him across the yard to the stables.

In fact, Jerrard's humour seems to have darkened. It all fits with the scraps of news Nick has picked up that they still haven't found Cazanove's heir. Plainly, Jerrard is vexed over these wasted journeys and is going to take his business elsewhere. A pity, but Nick does not entirely give up hope that when the brother is found these visits might resume.

His palm sweetened with a final groat, Nick walks alongside the grey into the little village street to take public leave of his guest for the benefit of any watchers. Jerrard bids him a short farewell and turns the horse's head north for Woodley. Once he has crossed the bridge over the stream, he nudges the grey into a canter, then a gallop. Nick watches until Jerrard is a dot in the distance. At that rate, and with some decent changes of mount, he will be in Salisbury well before dusk.

59

Ralph Cooper hands his wife with an ill grace into the small coach.

'I know not why you have to come along too, Emeline. I could have ridden to Hill House on my own, without the need for all this state.'

'Because you always get it wrong!' his wife snaps. She squashes herself into one corner; it's what she always does to make her point about the smallness of the coach. 'I'm quite capable of asking her a simple question. Will she or won't she?' He slams the door and the coachman starts off.

'You've not done that well to date,' Emeline Cooper accuses. 'You should have controlled the loose talk at the Pattens' that day. Instead, with the rumours going around now, she's in a fair way to being completely unmarriageable!'

'You wanted me to encourage it!'

'Only slightly!'

'Have you ever heard of a slightly fallen woman, Emeline?'

She crosses her arms and looks out of the window. 'I should never have trusted you with anything to do with it.'

'I wish now I'd never encouraged the rumours.'

'As to that, a few minor inconveniences will be nothing when it proves to have been just what was needed to prod Alice into making up her mind. You wait.'

'I don't like this Emeline, it's all wrong. This poor girl is being pressed into—'

'This poor girl, as you call her, is flagrantly defying her dead mother's dearest wish!'

'And having her reputation destroyed in the process,' he protests.

'Of course she's not! I'm saving it for her! And saving us into the bargain!' Emeline jabs a finger at his chest. 'You're the one who bungled that stupid bargain with Cazanove. Sure enough, he left you dangling. You should be grateful I was able to get rid of the wool to Sir Thomas, albeit at rock bottom. He's the only other one around here who can hide that sort of quantity from Guild scrutiny. It'll tide us over for a while but we'll be hand-to-mouth after that.'

He turns away from her to stare out of the window.

'So you're going to sulk, are you?' she says. 'In that case, you'd better leave all the talking to me.' He does not reply. 'Just remember, unless we secure Alice, you might have to sell part of Cowper to tide us over.' He remains silent, hunching his shoulders. 'Yes, that would hurt, wouldn't it, Ralph? All that land passed down father to son and you go and lose it. Be grateful you're married to me. I'm not about to let that come to pass.'

She regards her husband's averted head, and silently congratulates herself once again that she has not told him all that is to happen at Hill House before they get there. Ralph has no stomach for the cut and thrust of real life, she reflects. To think the wastrel Bart Johnson dared to sidle up to her in the village with the suggestion she should pay him not to spread any Daniel rumour. The presumption! No, he will dance to her tune. She digs a bony elbow in her husband's ribs. 'It was right to take Gerald away from her. Nothing was progressing while he was there, so she had to be softened up.'

'Leaving her on her own all this time was cruel, Emeline.'

But his wife is having none of that. 'Being on her own simply means the corners are being knocked off. You'll see.'

60

Alice crosses the yard to the kitchen door and stops to wait for Sam plodding behind. She is carrying the heavy seed lip, now empty. The grain is late going into the ground, but it is nearly done. 'Sam, sweeting, do you go into the house. The winter parlour is warm with the sun in there. I'll shut this back in the barn and draw some water and then I'll be in.' Kneeling down to his level, she slips her arms round him and kisses his forehead.

He droops against her and kisses her neck as his head nestles on her shoulder. 'My legs want to go to sleep.'

She holds him close. 'We'll have midday meal in a few minutes. You shouldn't have to work in the fields, I'll do the rest of the sowing on my own this afternoon.' She straightens and opens the kitchen door to let him in.

The leather strap of the wooden seed lip has dug painfully into her shoulder whilst full of grain, and even empty it still drags heavily. In the gloom of the barn she heaves a sigh of relief as she slips it over her head. She puts it down next to the seed-grain sacks on the wooden platform raised on its staddle stones to keep the rats away. The sack she has been filling her seed lip from is half empty and she flaps the top over and weights it with a heavy stone against the greedy chickens.

She flexes her arm and feels the aching stiffness ease. The Coopers are due back today and still she cannot bring herself to accept Gerald. The village remains as hostile as ever and her thoughts revolve without cease, unwilling to accept that she cannot find labourers for the farm. She almost went back to the smithy yesterday, to beg Daniel to return, even if only for a day. She got less than a hundred paces from the house. In her mind squats the unwelcome awareness that the last thing Daniel wants is to see her again after the rumour of his "dancing attendance" on her drove him away. It would be a humiliating and fruitless encounter to go to him now. She turned back.

Outside the barn, she leans her back against the door to push it to. The yard is quiet, no bird sings, the water in the trough runs with dark ripples in the slight breeze. Water. She crosses to the well and unlooses the rope to let the bucket down. The simple winching device Gerald set up for her during that fortnight is something to be grateful for. It means that the rope pays out over a crossbar at head height, making it easier to raise the bucket than hauling on it as previously. It was his own idea, she reflects as she lets down the bucket hand over hand. There are things Gerald is competent to do if only his mother would leave him—

'Hello, Alice.'

'God-a-mercy!' Her heart bangs at her ribs as the figure suddenly rises up from behind the parapet. Irritation at the shock sharpens her voice. 'What do you want, Bart?' The inn being his usual haunt, it is long since Alice has seen him, longer since they have spoken. He snaps upright and makes an exaggerated arm-waving, body-bending show of bowing to her. She continues to let the bucket down.

'Well, I like that!' he says, affecting an offended tone. 'I bow, but I get no curtsey in return.' He slumps against the winch frame, arms folded.

'It wasn't a bow, Bart; it was your idea of a jest. What do

you want?' she repeats. She is uneasily aware of the emptiness of the yard, the silence all around.

'A curtsey, from A Great Ladie to A Poore Man.'

Don't let him unsettle you, she tells herself. She sketches him a quick bob, lightly mocking, still letting down the bucket. A faint splash as it meets water and the rope slackens. The sooner it fills up, the sooner she can retreat indoors, away from this oaf.

'If you've got work for me, Alice, I might draw water for you.'

'Don't trouble yourself, Bart, I can do this, thank you.' The bucket is ready to come up. Hand over hand she pulls on the rope to raise it. Bart swings himself round the strut, leans on the parapet and ducks his head along his shoulder to look at her slantways. He is nearly within arm's reach. If she increases the rate of pull, she can get hold of the bucket sooner and retreat.

'Maybe the horses need tending.'

She keeps pulling.

'I can work for my keep, Alice.' As he says it, his hand shoots out. She twists away. The rope slides burning through her fingers and they listen to the bucket smack into the water below. She backs a pace.

'What do you want, Bart?' she asks for the third time.

'Now, if you'd let me do that for you, you'd have a bucket of water by now. I'd even carry it into the house for you.'

'Thank you, but I don't need your help.'

'Of course you do.' He indicates the yard. 'Nobody here helping you.'

'Including you,' she says, starting the long pull again.

He laughs, a shade too long. 'That's very funny, Alice.'

'I'm busy, Bart, so if there's nothing else, I'd like to get on with my work.'

He picks up the pail to be filled from the well bucket and leans over the parapet, swinging it.

'Leave that alone, Bart!' she says. 'I can manage it.'

'I'm holding it for you.'

'Just put it down, please. I don't need help.'

'That's not true, Alice.' He keeps using her name. If her mother had been here, he wouldn't have dared. If her father had been here, Bart wouldn't even have come. She is acutely aware of her aloneness, begins to wonder when the Coopers will arrive. It's come to something when she wishes they would appear.

'Believe me, I don't need your help, Bart.'

'Yes you do, you asked.'

'I did not!'

'You've been down in the village half a dozen times, asking for men to help.'

'That's not – I'm getting help now,' she lies, 'so thank you, I don't need yours.'

'Daniel coming back is he? For a few favours? Ooh! That's a guilty blush!'

The bucket is nearly within reach. All she has to do is pour it into the pail – if Bart would put it down – and go indoors. Put the bar across and wait for the Coopers.

He goes on swinging the pail from hand to hand over the drop, grinning. She's busy, Sam needs his meal, there's sowing still to do, bread to make, wood to collect. She grips the handle of the well bucket and lifts it over, takes a deep breath. 'Put that down here, please, Bart.'

'All I'm asking is a bit of money from you for a bit of help from me,' he complains. 'You got me all the way up here to help you and then—'

'I never asked you to come here.'

'I've said I'll work for you,' he says, 'so pay me for work and I'll give you your pail.'

'How many times do I have to say it? I don't want your help, I didn't ask for it.'

He looks across at the kitchen door. 'Maybe I'll go into the house and get some money out of your old man's stash.'

'The pail, please, Bart.' Keep him out here. Keep his attention on her.

'Your pa pinched a chicken off me that old Sarah Coppen gave me. You owe me!'

'I heard about that,' she says. 'He told me you pestered Sarah Coppen beyond bearing. She only gave it to you so you would go away. That's why my father gave it back to her.'

'All I want's some money to live,' he grumbles. 'Your sort never gives away anything.'

She is losing patience with his persistence. 'Then do an honest day's work and earn it! The Coopers tell me they are finding it difficult to cope. Ask them.'

'Word is, they won't pay anyway, they're short of cash. That's why they want you to marry Gerald.'

Tell me something I don't know.

'They say you don't want to.' His face changes as a new thought occurs to him and he puts down the pail. Crafty. Calculating. 'Were you hoping Daniel might come back after all? Keep you company since the other one won't?'

'What?'

'Don't bother pretending, Alice. I saw you. Kissing.'

'That's a lie!'

'Came out the door, you did, and he grabbed you. Kissed you.'

'You little toad, making up stories.' She snatches the pail

304

and quickly backs away.

'And you kissed him back. What do you think the village would make of that?'

'Forget it, Bart. The village has had its sling at me, and from all I hear, Daniel is getting work, so you cannot harm him.'

'Not him. What went on in the stillroom, tell me that?'

She stares.

'That's made you think, hasn't it, Alice?'

This is not about Daniel.

'All those weeks last summer prancing around in the apothecary's shop, coming out with your holier-than-thou face. And then that kiss! I can keep quiet, Alice. On condition.'

Keeping a wary eye on him, she pours the water from the well bucket and releases it, picks up the pail. 'As far as I'm concerned, you may say whatever you wish to the whole world, Bart.' Her reputation is so low in the village, what's another story? But for all her defiant words, she must get rid of Bart soon, because even the Coopers won't want her if they see him here, if they hear of the kiss. It is a treasured memory, and she is determined never to explain it away as though she were ashamed.

With a jolt she realises that she is going to have to accept Gerald; and ensure she is not just betrothed to him, but handfasted – unbreakably pledged by law to marry – because this harassment will not stop here. With stories going round about Daniel, about Frederick, more will come visiting, pretending to ask for work, intending God knows what …

She is jerked back to the present as he takes a step closer. 'They say your Pa kept a stash. Your reputation in return for the stash.'

'I'm not giving you money, Bart,' she declares. 'Just leave

and we'll say no more.' This is no longer the feckless, whining Bart Johnson she has always known. He has switched in moments to something dangerous. Hostility stares from the hooded eyes. While she casts around for how to meet this fresh threat, his gaze flicks away from her. The house.

'Fine. I'll ask the littl'un where it is.'

Sam. Never.

As he turns and walks towards the house, she darts to block his path, 'Leave him alone!' But he grabs at her hair and twists, pulling her head painfully back. She gasps, the pail tumbles, water sloshes. 'Let go! How dare you?'

'Show me the brick it's hidden behind!'

'No! Let go of me!' There is such a brick. In her fury at his manhandling, she has a wild vision of taking it out of the wall and smashing it in his face. But no, not the house. Anywhere but the house. How on earth would she get him out again? 'Let me go, Bart!'

He shakes the ball of her hair in his hand. 'When you tell me where it is.'

'No!' How to get away? A fragment of thought skips, there and gone. 'It's not there, anyway,' she says. The thought skips back, beckons. 'Father moved it, years ago.'

'Liar! I'll find it myself, even if it means turning the place over.' He drags her towards the kitchen.

'All right, all right, I'll show you.' She is clutching at his hand, trying to ease the pain; the thought is blossoming into a plan. 'The barn.' A plan that will put a weapon in her hand. She points. 'I'll show you where, on condition you promise to leave after.'

He leans close. 'You'd better be telling the truth.'

Heart juddering, Alice stumbles before him across the yard. Can she do this? Despite his lazy, drunken ways, he

306

is no weakling. If she fumbles it … The flail is kept in the barn. She remembers Daniel storing it on the grain platform, saying, best kept out of Sam's reach. The flail, with its vicious hanging stake. Grab it and swing. Stun him and escape into the house where she can drop the bar across the door.

He hauls at one of the double barn doors, lets go of her hair and shoves her through. Alice is acutely aware that she should be showing her fear, which is real enough. She should be pleading with him, perhaps crying, no, she can't do that. Even the act of pretending to weep could undermine her fragile courage. The trembling is uncontrolled, her legs will barely carry her. After all the anxiety of the past weeks, she thought she could at least still be mistress of her own home. But now this shabby drunk is threatening even that.

'Please don't … please don't,' is all she can bring herself to implore. Please don't what? How dare he make her feel so powerless? He doesn't look much like Bart the witless oaf at this moment. This is a man she doesn't know. Violent, relentless.

'Show me!'

'The seed-grain. It's hidden in one of the sacks.' From here she can't see the flail but there are only three sacks, and the half-full one. It will be somewhere amongst them. Her eyes roam this way and that. Grasping her shoulder, he steers her towards the grain platform, waist high on its staddle stones. It will be easily seen, each section is as long as her forearm. She must catch sight of it first, divert his attention to something else.

'Which one?' he demands as they reach the platform.

Her glance darts to and fro across the rough wooden boards. 'I … I'm not sure.'

'You're lying. Aren't you, you're lying!'

'I'm trying to remember.' *Where is it?* 'It's one of these sacks.' Searching, searching.

'Come on, which one?'

The flail is not there.

61

I n the Cowper coach, husband and wife are still at odds.

'I don't see why you had to keep on whispering that silly rumour about Alice and Bunting,' Ralph says. 'You got him out of Hill House. What else was needed?'

She rolls her eyes. 'I had to make sure anyone else thinks twice before getting ideas about marrying her. Hasn't it occurred to you that Sir Thomas has two sons to marry off and her slice of land is almost on his doorstep? How long before he starts sniffing around for a wife for one of them? We've given her a week, Ralph. It's time for a decision.'

'At this rate, thanks to you insisting on the coach being turned out, we'll be lucky to be there before sunset,'

'Don't be ridiculous. It's no distance to Hill House.'

'It's a fair way via the smithy.'

Emeline lifts the coach-leaves to look out. 'This is the wrong way!'

'I told you, we're going via the smithy,' he reminds her.

'What!' The horror shows on Emeline's face. 'We have to go to Hill House!'

'After we've had the horse shod,' he says. 'As usual, you weren't listening.'

'It's vital we get to Hill House first!' She fumes silently. *If Bart Johnson realises we're not coming when I said, Heaven knows what that stupid lout might do.*

'For goodness' sake, Emeline,' Ralph says. 'The smithy

will be closed if we spend as long at Hill House as we did last time.'

'Turn round!' She bangs the side. 'Coachman!' Pokes her head out of the window. 'Turn round instantly!'

62

Alice looks down at Bart Johnson lying sprawled on his back in the spilled seed-grain, then at the stone still in her hand. She wonders whether she hit him too hard. It must be over a minute now and he has not moved. He was so intent upending the sack, sweeping his arms back and forth through the grain for imagined gold coins, that he hadn't seen her close her hand round the stone on the flap of the half-full sack.

The hens have drifted in, wise to the drama diverting her attention from their small thieving around the grain spread. In the dimness of the barn she steps warily round him at a distance. His chest rises and falls but his eyes are still closed. From here she cannot see the side of his face where she crashed the stone against his skull. Disbelief that she actually did it makes her breath come short and rapid. It was the only defence she could think of, but what if he dies? Putting her toe out, she cautiously nudges him and hops back. Not a flicker.

Please don't die. She bends over him to see the injury she inflicted.

'Bart? Bart, can you hear me?'

His arm sweeps up, hauls her down.

He crows in triumph as she falls, but he is too slow, still stunned, and she pulls back. She is scrambling away when she feels his hand grasp her ankle, then the other, and she crashes down again with a breathless cry. Something rips. He throws himself across her legs, pinning her face-down.

She still has the stone in her hand and curls round, hitting out with it to swipe him away but only grazing his chin. He grabs her wrist and launches himself, crushing her, and she cries out as her body painfully twists under his weight. Then he has hold of her other wrist and she cannot dislodge him and he is banging and scraping her knuckles on the hard-packed earth floor until she lets go of the stone. Now she is fighting, wriggling, twisting this way and that, but if he was stunned before, this time his grip is solid, and he is so close she can see each stubbly hair on his greasy chin. 'You lying bitch. You're coming with me into the house and you're going to get me the stash.'

She brings her head up fast. Forehead meets nose with a crunching crack. He cries out, jerking back, losing his hold of her wrists and she strikes blindly at him, but her reach is too short to do any damage. He swipes back, his rough nails scoring across her neck before he catches hold again, both wrists in one meaty hand. He slaps her and pushes her head sideways, rasping her cheek in grain and gritty dust.

Her ears are singing and through half-closed eyes she sees his features drawn into a tight knot of hate. Down one of those lines the welling blood from his nostril seeps. She knows a flare of malicious pride that she did that.

Pride.

He releases her wrists. 'Now get up!'

James Edwards' pride in "my wilful daughter".

The thought is the spur. As Bart makes to rise, she musters every ounce of vigour and punches her knee up as hard as she can. The crunching impact as bone mashes into target is pure empowering joy. The force drives him upwards and he seems to hover for an interminably long shaking gasp before he buckles alongside her, hands clutching his agony. The air reeks with stale sweat. She thrusts and kicks herself away, rolls onto her front, ears still ringing, but blessedly free of his touch. Perversely, she wants to laugh, but there is this greater temptation to rest. Just for a moment.

Sam. Alone in the house. Defenceless.

She looks hard at her arm inches from her face, concentrates through misted vision. She wills it to push her up, gives each muscle, each sinew, its separate command.

Bend the elbow, push on the forearm, lift your head, do it!

All so slow, and Bart close by, groaning. '"No resistance?" Christ's nails, I'll give her "No resistance"!'

Her? Who? Margery? Surely not! Concentrate. Who? Concentrate! Draw the hand back, now the other. Bend the wrists, push, straighten your elbows.

Scraping sounds in the dust behind her; he is working himself towards her, grunting with the effort.

Get up. Get to the house. Put the bar across. I'll kill him for sure if he so much as touches Sam. Get up!

Her legs come to her aid and she scrambles to her feet. Straight away, she trips on the torn hem of her skirt and falls to her knees. Before her the open door, behind her, a gritty scuffling, Bart spitting dust. She is up again when she feels her skirt yanked. The crash to the ground momentarily winds her. Already he has tightened his hold. She kicks convulsively but can feel herself being dragged back inch by inch. Digging desperate fingernails into the dust, she searches for a handhold, a crack in the ground, a protruding stone, anything to pull herself away. His grip transfers to her knee. Frantic, she looks round. His face is warped in vengeful fury but he is hindered, lying there clutching himself with his other hand. She rolls round and drives her work-muddied

313

boot straight at his hated face. He jerks away. She kicks again, he howls, and in bleak triumph she kicks and kicks and her heel scores across his face and at last she is free.

All anyhow, she scrambles to her feet and lurches for the barn door, rounds it, slams it shut behind her. Even a few seconds while he blunders in the dark will help. She picks up her skirts, runs headlong across the yard, past the water trough, the kitchen window. Behind her, the barn door scrapes. Grab at the latch, stumble into the kitchen.

She reaches instinctively for the bar and meets only the wall. Not there? It must be! The bar is always by the door. Where? Desperately she looks around – on the floor – in the corner – outside the door. Where did she put it? Through the window she sees Bart let go of the barn door and break into a shambling run.

Again her eyes scan the kitchen. Where? Where? The other side of the door? On the table? By the window? Think!

She can see him already halfway across the yard, can hear his scuffling footsteps. By an effort of will she drags her eyes away, searching, searching. She hears her despairing voice gasp, 'Oh, God! Oh, God!' over and over. It distracts her, she can't concentrate. What is it she's looking for? Her wits have flown. Now she can hear his animal grunting. There's no time, no time at all …

She kicks the door shut and puts her back to it, her body taking the juddering jolt as Bart's swinging fist hammers on the outside, once, twice. She hears his footsteps back off and leans hard on the door, clutching at the latch to hold it in its rest. The shock of his running assault jolts it out and the door opens a crack but her own might pushes it shut. Again she hears his run, feels the slam of his battering shoulder. One end of the latch bursts from the wood, her feet slide on the stone floor. He will have heard the wood splinter. The latch dangles useless. She braces her back against the door, but she knows she cannot hold him off now. She hears him back away again.

In the far corner of the kitchen, the long-handled loaf peel rests by the bread oven. She leaps and skids across the flags, seizes hold. Behind her, Bart's shoulder punches again and the door flies open, slamming back against the bracket that should have held the bar. To the sound of splintering timber, he falls into the kitchen. The door bounces back, shards of wood falling. As she races to take a stand, he gets to his feet and punches away the door without a glance. He advances on her, sending a chair flying. The blood from his nose runs like a jagged tear over his lip and through the stubble. The bruise shows livid where she butted him. Muddy grazes score his cheek. Bull-like, his head pokes forward, his eyes are black with intent.

She lowers the peel and lunges as hard as she can straight at his chest. He cannons backwards out of the door, loses his footing on the step and thumps on his back. She springs after him. There he lies helpless, whooping for breath, and she rejoices at it as she raises the bread peel high. She brings it scything down, and wood meets steel with a jarring shock. The bread peel bounces from her hands, cartwheels in the air and lands harmlessly several feet away. Stupidly, she stares at it, at her empty hands.

'What the devil's going on?'

As though jolted from a trance, Alice whips round. Henry Jerrard stands pointing twenty-seven inches of gleaming sword blade straight at Bart Johnson's throat.

63

'Alice, what was that noise?' Sam tries to see into the kitchen but she is already in the hall and closing the door, leaning momentarily against it for support.

'It's nothing,' she tells Sam. 'A chair fell over. Let us go into the winter parlour, Sam, it's sunny in there.' Her hands have gone numb from the jarring they received as Henry Jerrard brought up his blade to break her swing.

'What the hell do you think you're doing?' she thundered at Jerrard.

'She's trying to kill me!' Bart gasped, still winded.

'Yes,' she told him, going after the peel, 'and I don't need his help!'

The iron taste of blood is in her mouth. Her tongue is swollen, she must have bitten through it while they were fighting.

'For God's sake,' she snapped at Jerrard, 'point that thing somewhere else.' She raised the peel but he deftly stepped over Bart's prone form, putting himself between the two of them.

Sam races ahead of her and turns at the parlour door. He stands, legs apart, arms outstretched, barring her progress.

'You can't come in!'

'Stand aside, Master Jerrard,' she ordered him. 'This is none of your business.'

'It is my business,' he said, still holding the sword to Bart's throat, 'if you're going to batter him to bloody pulp.'

'Why? What's wrong?' she asks Sam, feeling her mouth wobble dangerously. Her bodice feels as if it is crushing her, her breath coming short and shallow.

'Help me, help me,' Bart sobbed.

'So you're on his side, are you?' she demanded.

'I'm on no one's side except Sam's,' Jerrard countered. 'How are you going to explain blood and brains all over the yard to a child?'

Oh dear God, dear God. All her panic-fuelled rage flown, the sense of a gaping void under her ribs. Confusion, quickly filled by irritation with the author of her transformation. She threw down the peel. 'Then don't just stand there,' she snapped, 'kill him yourself if you like, and get out of here, for Heaven's sake.'

Then flew for the door to the hall that Sam was already jumping to open from the other side.

First the men of the village, then Ralph Cooper, then Bart, now another man making her life difficult. If either Bart or Jerrard is discovered here it won't just be the final ruin of her reputation. It will be the end of everything she has left. She will be rejected, reviled, hounded out. It will be the end of Hill House, the end of her darling Sam.

'I've built a castle and it isn't finished yet,' Sam says. 'You came back too early.'

She takes a deep breath and drags a smile from somewhere. 'I'm sorry, Sam, I didn't mean to.' Too early? She must have been out there a half-hour at least. Surely twenty minutes, anyway. It feels like forever since she sent him to the winter parlour. 'But indeed, I'd like to see your castle.' It's a lie, all she really wants to do is sink down and curl into a ball on the floor. She might have killed. It is hardly conceivable to her that she has been in that place, in that humour where killing was her intention. The moisture gathers in her eyes.

'Oh, all right then,' Sam concedes. 'It's nearly finished.'

On legs that feel like quaking-custards, she follows him from the gloom of the hall into the bright parlour. He has dragged two backstools to face each other a short distance apart, and draped the rug from the sideboard across their seats, hanging down to the floor on one side, thus creating a sort of open-sided tunnel. At the back of one chair, he has stacked the foraged pieces of wood from the pile at the hearth, and at the other, the log basket closes off that end. The whittled figures Zachariah and Samuel, along with the faggot-horse, are grouped at a distance, overseeing the construction of their new stronghold.

At any other time she would commend his building skills. Pleasurable anticipation glows in his face and he dances from foot to foot, fingers splayed in excitement as he confidently awaits her praise. And after all, it is a good fortress. It even has a roof. And all she can think is, If I let myself laugh now, not only will he never forgive me, but I shall be unable to stop.

Spanning the gap between the chairs and holding the rug in place is the bar from the kitchen door.

64

Inside she is numb, drained of feeling. All she wants is to wash every part of herself Bart Johnson laid his foul hands on. But there is Sam, looking up at her and asking her, when are they going to eat. The best she can do is rub her hands on her working skirt. She cannot even splash her face with cold water, the house bucket lies in a puddle in the yard. She shepherds him back to the kitchen and at that moment Henry Jerrard walks in, the bread peel in his hand. Alice gapes as he calmly props it in the corner. He closes the door. His eyes rove over the splintered damage but he says nothing, looks across at her.

'You can't stay here,' she snaps. 'I've told you. Just go.'

Jerrard's brows draw together. 'If you wish. But I'd like the chance to talk things through.'

Courteously as he has phrased it, there is something decided in his tone, in the grimness of his expression. She is almost frightened of him. She wants to tell him, Get out! Get out before I'm ruined for ever! but she cannot summon the energy. At any minute, she is thinking, the Coopers will return, Emeline – yes, Emeline of course, not Margery Patten – confident of finding a compliant Alice reduced to a state of "no resistance". But it will be impossible to explain away a strange man standing in her kitchen. The whole sordid betrothal to Gerald hangs on Jerrard leaving. Now. All she wants from him is to know what has happened with Bart, to be assured he will not come back, and then be left alone to ready herself for the graveyard that is her future.

Jerrard picks up the chair still lying where Bart kicked it, and places it by the table. 'At least let me see for myself that all is well.'

Sam is big-eyed, looking at the door, at the latch lying on the floor. On his face is the frantic urge to tell Alice that somebody has broken it, but on his face also is the doubt due to Jerrard's presence.

'Did you …?' she asks Jerrard, and stops.

'Yes, it's dealt with.'

'You didn't—'

'No, his worthless hide is still relatively intact.'

'Thank you,' she says, then again, 'Thank you with all my heart. But you should not be here.'

'I wouldn't worry about that.' He smiles at her. It wipes away the grimness in a moment. It is such a warm, uncomplicated smile that she is shaken with gratitude to see a friendly face. How long it has been.

She pulls herself together. 'I was doing the sowing,' she says.

If he thinks the comment absurd, he doesn't show it. He regards her dishevelled state. 'It looks as if you will have sewing of a different sort to do now.' She looks down at the cheap lockram of her working skirt, torn and frayed from the struggle in the barn. Gives a reluctant laugh, remembering a different visit from Jerrard. 'Truly a seam-rent gown.'

He draws a quick breath through his teeth. 'I stand corrected,' he says.

'But why are you here now?'

'I had the desire to call on you again.' He makes it sound so simple. He was passing, thought he'd spend a pleasant half hour on his way through. 'It seems I chose my day well.'

Jerrard steps past her, unhooks three pewter mugs and proceeds to fill them from the little barrel.

Alice stands drained of thought in the middle of the kitchen. He gestures her to the settle but she says, 'Please, you have to go. I'm expecting … visitors.'

He looks at her dishevelled state, her face where Bart scraped her cheek on the ground. 'If they are friends, they will be glad I'm here to help. If they are not friends, I need to be here to help. Come, sit down.' He hands her a mug. 'You look as if you need this, and more.' Sam takes up station by her side, says nothing and looks.

'Good morrow, young master.' Jerrard passes him the second mug.

Sam does a bobbing nod which passes for his bow. 'Did you do that to the door?' he asks.

Before he can answer, Alice breaks in, 'No, Sam, I had … an accident with it.'

'Why has the bread thing got a big gouge in it?' Sam asks. 'Were you playing a game, Alice?'

'In a way, yes.'

'Tis not a plaything,' he says severely.

She gives an unsteady laugh. The ale stings her bitten tongue as she takes a mouthful and she swallows painfully, putting up her hand to cover her grimace. When she looks up, Jerrard does not seem to have noticed, he is taking a seat beside her and diverting Sam.

'So what have you been doing today, young man?'

'I was helping Alice.'

'Well, I'm glad you are making yourself useful. You will soon be so grown up that you will need to be apprenticed.'

'No, he will not be apprenticed!' Alice tightens her arm

321

round Sam. 'He won't be apprenticed and he won't be going to the Poor House!' Immediately she relents. 'Forgive me. You did not come here to be treated to my shrewish temper.'

'It's all right, it's all right,' he says and puts his hand momentarily over hers. Once again he gives that brief, warm smile.

'Sam,' she says. 'There's a pudding for our meal. It will be warmed through soon but why don't you go to the still room and find one of those apples to eat until it's ready?' Sam does not need a second bidding.

'Now tell me,' Jerrard says, 'why are you doing the sowing? I thought you had Daniel here.'

This is not the question she was expecting. Somehow this one is harder. She pushes herself to her feet and throws the latest foraged deadwood onto the smouldering ashes. 'Daniel was here until a while ago. Then he left to go back to the forge.' She pushes the chimney hook across so that the pudding pot hangs above the fire.

'I see. He simply left? Some friend he was.'

'It was … complicated.' Right at this moment she is too weary to explain, so she just sits down again and takes a sip from her mug.

'And you've been coping on your own?'

She leans against the back of the settle and shakes her head. 'A neighbour came in to help but his mother … he could not come and help any more.'

'His mother is ill?'

'Not she!' Alice sighs. 'No, she tells him what to do and he obeys. He was a help while he was here. We were managing. Just.'

Sam has found an apple and stands by the still room door, biting into it.

'What about help from the village?' Jerrard asks. 'Plenty of lummocks I saw idling around as I came through. Surely one of them—?'

'You just met one of them,' she says shortly.

Quietly, he says, 'But that's the one they call Bart!'

'How did you know that?'

'He was at the inn last night. Fellow called Silas was telling me about him. Surely he didn't come up to help you?'

'No, he came up to help himself.'

'Ah!'

While she sits with eyes closed, sinking through waves of relieved despair, there is a short silence. Then he asks, 'Why did your helpful neighbour leave you? He must have known you would be vulnerable.'

'Gerald Cooper? Oh yes,' she says. It is almost too much effort to speak. Absently, she traces a finger round the ragged tear in her skirt. 'He knew; at least, his parents knew. They've been watching while I squirm and struggle like a fly in a web. They knew it was only a matter of time.'

'Time until what?'

'Until I agreed to marry their son so they can get their hands on my land.'

Jerrard is silent.

'They sent Bart to help make up my mind. It worked. I can't do this alone.'

'My God!' he breathes. Then again, 'My God! But you're not going to—?'

Suddenly, she realises time is passing. She sits up. 'When I tell you that you shouldn't be here, I mean it. Please. For my sake, if not your own. You have no idea what people will say. The Coopers could be here any minute. If they see you here …'

Jerrard doesn't seem to be listening. 'He's hurt you.' Indicating her face, her grazed knuckles.

'That will mend in time. He didn't get what he came for, which was to steal money.'

He says simply, 'If I'd known all this, I'd have helped you kill the reptile.'

I almost wish you had. 'When the Coopers come, I shall ask to go and live with them straight away. Even before I marry Gerald. That's exactly what they want, of course.'

'You've clearly no wish to marry the son of the house,' he says. 'Is there no other choice?'

She gives him a tight-lipped smile. 'I suggested his father might stand surety for me to take a lease on a shop but Mother Cooper ruled that out. She blocked off all escape for me. She knows even if I go to Daniel, he can't help me.'

'His station is blacksmith, is that right?'

'Yes.'

'No land?'

'Not enough. Below the threshold for standing surety.'

'Ah. And he left you here.' After a moment, 'Is there no one else?'

'Not even our local Attorney. Mistress Cooper got there first and money talks with Master Handley.'

'You're caught in a coil,' he says.

She takes a deep breath and straightens her shoulders. 'Oh, I don't know. Let us look at it in a favourable light.' She puts down her mug and counts off her fingers. 'I shall marry into a respected family, and since their criminality cannot be proven, surely it matters not? The farm is saved, albeit for them, not for me. I shall have my husband's parents to make all my decisions for me and for Sam. Oh, and let us not forget, I shall be safeguarded from Bart Johnson's thievery, how fortunate is that?' She sags. 'Yes, coil is the sum of it. I am as good as betrothed to Gerald and he will believe it is what he wishes so all they await is my word. What felicity to look forward to. My condition will be that they may have what they wish so long as I adopt Sam.'

'When you say *betrothed*—'

'Oh!' With clenched fists she bangs the seat on either side of her. 'A pity I'm not a man.'

'It seems to me you've been taking the man's part, and more.'

'If I were, there are so many things I could do.'

'You seem to be doing them anyway. Anyone would think you'd fought in the lists. You just about finished the reptile off with that—'

He breaks off as she makes warning signs to him. Leaning against the still room door and biting shapes into his apple, Sam is all ears.

'If I were a man, I could face down the townsfolk—'

'Yes.'

'Run the farm, open a shop—'

'Both of those. What if—'

'Escape from the Coopers, anything—'

'Now you're talking. Though I don't suppose Gerald would relish the thought. But that would be nothing if—'

'Well, at least Sam is safe.' She stops. 'What did you say?' She can feel her heart starting to beat fast.

'I said I don't think Gerald would fancy it if you were a man, and I wanted to ask you—'

'No, before that.' There is a strange taste in her mouth that has nothing to do with her bitten tongue. 'You said you thought I was taking—'

'— taking a man's part. Well, you are. Now, don't take it

amiss, I only meant—'

'Marry me.'

'What?'

'Marry me.'

It is out now, she cannot withdraw, she has to go on. Her mouth has gone dry. Eyes locked with his, she sips her ale before the next words will come.

'Henry Jerrard, I'm asking you to marry me. Do I have to go down on one knee to do the man's job properly?'

It is done. No turning back. She stares into his face as, open-mouthed, he stares back at her.

'But—'

'I do not expect you to love me,' she assures him, 'and in truth I cannot offer you a whole heart.'

'What are you saying?' he whispers.

'You are tired of life without companionship, you said. I can give you that, I can run a household, and I bring as my dowry the income from Hill House.'

'But, Mistress Edwards, are you sure you want to do this? You've said you're getting married.'

'I'm not promised. I am still free. For a little while.'

'But how—?'

'The Coopers are coming here because they know that they have forced my hand. Once I have declared myself, before the vicar, betrothed to Gerald Cooper, I shall be handfasted. Nothing then can prevent the marriage.'

He is silent for a space, searching her face. 'And you?'

'Me?'

'What do you get from this barter you're proposing to me?'

'I shall keep Hill House, people will come and work here again. And Sam will truly be safe.' The room has started to mist.

'And you are prepared to marry me for that?'

She cannot trust her voice, she nods. From the other side of the room comes the sound of Sam rummaging afresh in the still room. Why doesn't Jerrard say something? His face is unreadable, withdrawn. The smile of a few moments ago has vanished and he is no longer looking at her, but down, slightly shaking his head. He doesn't want her. She has offered herself like any wanton and has deeply embarrassed a decent man. He is going to be angry, disgusted, he will rebuke her. She turns her head away and her dusty kinked curls drop around her face. Her hand flies to her hair. And no cap, she must have lost it in the struggle. Well, now he can even report her for unwomanly behaviour. Appearing with hair unconfined, brawling, proposing to a man. Is it the neck pillory or the stocks for lewd conduct? Oh Lord, Abel Nutley will take such pleasure in it. It will be the crowning humiliation of the last few weeks. The hands clenched on her skirt have started to shake. Pray God Jerrard will just be angry and go because the wait is unbearable.

A tear runs down her face.

A chuckle escapes him, followed by another, and now he is laughing in earnest. He is still shaking his head to and fro. Laughing.

To her shrinking ears his amusement seems to fill the room. It bounces off the walls, it goes on and on. Sam comes to the door of the still room, looks across at Alice, seeking reassurance. She shrinks within herself at the hilarity, feeling her face, her neck, even her hands reddening. She wants to put her arms up over her head, hide from the ridicule she has brought on herself. She sits rigid, dumb with shame.

Jerrard gasps and gradually his laughter subsides. 'Oh,

Alice, you don't know how——' His laughter breaks out again even as he fights his mirth. 'What a tale I could tell! No one would believe——'

She throws the contents of her mug in his face.

'Be sure to add that to the tale you tell!' She jerks to her feet and glares down at him. 'If a man asks a woman to marry him, does he expect her to laugh in his face, make a jest of it to her friends?'

He is pushing his wet hair off his face, looking up at her, the laugh obliterated. She can feel how tight and angry her face must look, all glowering eyes amidst a mess of unkempt curls.

'It was an honest question, sir. Your manner of refusal was dishonourable and unworthy.'

'I know. But it wasn't——'

'You should leave now. And you need not visit again.'

'Let me explain——'

'Just go!'

'You have to listen to me, Alice!'

He tries to take her hand but she thrusts him away. 'I don't have to do what you say! Get out of my house!'

'Then I shall come back and come back until you *do* listen!' He is shouting now.

'I shan't be here!' So is she.

'No, that's true——'

'I shall be at Cowper! You may laugh at me from a distance.' She gulps out the words, struggling to choke back her tears.

'You'll be with me! No, don't frown at me like that. Listen to me, Alice!'

'Just go! Go! Please, go!' she begs him. Her arms go up to clutch at her bowed head and she sobs her humiliation.

'For God's sake – I came to ask you to marry me!'

In a small voice she wails, 'Don't do this, please.'

'Alice Edwards! Do you think I travelled for three days all the way here on the most God-awful roads in freezing winds to talk about sowing the bloody spring crop?'

Through the stockade of her forearms she can see one of the logs on the fire take flame, wavering and flickering up and down its length. She lowers her arms and gapes at him.

'Do you?' he demands.

'You laughed when I said—'

'Alice, listen to me! I laughed because you were the second person today to tell me you're as good as betrothed and I had almost given up any hope of asking you. This is all going to come out back-to-front but I was kicking myself for not coming straight here last night. When I heard this morning at the inn that Daniel had abandoned you too, I knew I should come over here as soon as I could. And I'm very glad I did. I laughed because you took the words right out of my mouth, you came out with what I was trying to get round to saying. I was laughing at myself!'

Alice sinks onto the settle, shaking her head in disbelief. 'Now I feel an even bigger fool.'

'What if I go down on one knee, like this?' He looks up at her and gently slips his hand under her fingers. 'And beg you to be kind to a complete and unmannerly lobcock by asking him once more to marry you, and this time he'll say Yes? Will you?'

'Why?'

'Why?' He casts around for words. 'Because I think, despite what you have said, you like me; because time is pressing; because I can offer you a way out. Oh, and I'd very much like to marry you. Have I missed anything?'

She says, 'No, I mean, why did you come? What's the real reason? I know I have said what I should not, but you don't have to rescue me from my own folly by pretending that you came to propose. You will regret it in the morning; you will pay your shot at the inn and ride off, thanking your luck that there were no witnesses.'

'That would really put the cat amongst the pigeons,' he says gravely, 'since I've already paid my shot and Nick believes I'm halfway to Salisbury. No, I'll have to have a good solid reason for coming back. So, what if I say you and I are betrothed?'

Still on one knee, he takes her mug and puts it on the hearth, reaches up and possesses himself of both her hands. Ignoring her protest, he places a kiss on each wrist. 'Bring on as many witnesses as you like. This will be before the vicar, in church, with a licence, a Special Licence, however far I have to go to get it.'

'Bristol,' she says.

'Bristol or the Bay of Biscay, I'll get it. Alice Edwards, this is Henry Jerrard asking you to marry him, and Sam there is my witness. I came all the way from Guildford to ask you this question, and then by an extremely roundabout way via Woodley to ensure Nick Patten didn't know I was coming here. Now do you believe me? Sam? We're all going to live in Guildford, what about that?'

'Can I ride your horse, then?' says Sam, and adds, 'It'll be better than the frog man.'

'Frog man?'

'Gerald wears green and yellow to go courting,' Alice explains.

'It's decided then. Sam recommends me over the frog man. And for that kind compliment, Sam, yes, I will take you up on the grey. Oh, I nearly forgot.' He reaches between the buttons of his doublet and draws out a miniature posy of limp, purple flowers. He looks ruefully at it and holds it out to her. 'Another bunch of squashed vegetation, I fear, but I have kept my word to bring violets.' He lays the little bunch on her lap. 'What do you say, Alice? Will you marry me and come to my rather draughty home? And Sam must come too, or I refuse to marry you.' She can't help smiling at the absurdity. Warmed from his body, the sweet perfume of the flowers wafts up. 'Say you like me a little?' he pleads, looking up into her eyes. 'A little?'

She is so moved by what she sees there, she can only say formally, 'I am so grateful to you, so much in your debt. If it had not been for you—'

'Well, in truth I didn't do that much but we'll pass over such irrelevancies. Just think, it will put paid to Gerald.' His smile shines out again. 'And to the dame. So you will marry me?'

'Oh!' A hand goes up to her mouth. 'We can't.'

'We can't what?'

'Get married.'

'But you just asked me!' Jerrard frowns in confusion.

'I know, but I was forgetting.'

'You haven't married someone else in the meantime?'

'Not yet.'

'Not yet? How many men are you planning to marry?'

'No, I mean, we can't get married yet.'

'Why not?'

'Think of the date. What's the date?'

Jerrard flounders. 'March the . . . March . . .'

'Exactly. We're in Lent. We can't get married during Lent.'

Jerrard climbs to his feet. He looks as if he would like to consign Lent to the lower regions of the next life, but he says

331

only, 'Very well. The Tuesday after Easter – no questions, no objections. So you'll say Yes?'

She grips his hands, warm against her own. 'Yes.'

Of course it's too good to be true. It occurs to her that she has done what her mother urged and she always resisted, agreed to marry a man she does not love. Except that in this case, she could add the word *yet*.

Don't hope, she tells herself, this is not real, but even as the thought stays her, he sweeps her into his arms and kisses her mouth, neck, eyes and once again her mouth. She knows she ought to resist, but it is so sweet to feel his arms round her and to tighten her arms in return.

She tries not to lean, not to weaken, but something keeps telling her this is not the last time. Eventually, he raises his chin and props it on top of her head.

Muffled, she quietly asks, 'I still don't understand *why*.'

'I love you, Alice Edwards,' he breathes, 'Your treatment by the Coopers makes you wary but it's true.' And this time there is no amusement in his tone.

Nestling within his embrace, Alice knows the first moment of peace since her ruinous visit to the Cazanove mansion. That moment in the barn, she realises, that gave her the strength to break free of Bart, that was a turning point. She felt her father's presence so strongly, his voice declaring his pride in her. From that moment, she started to cast off the slough of guilt she has carried these past months. She defeated Bart Johnson, defeated the Coopers, and Sam and she are safe. It is as though she is forgiven at last. The tears that threatened earlier now loom very close, but these are tears of relief.

Jerrard rouses. He is suddenly very serious as he says, 'You know, I think we should go to the vicar this very hour and make it handfast. Or I fear the Coopers will have discovered another way to snare you the moment my back is turned.'

Sam frowns and shrugs. He returns to his search through the still room shelves. Alice loosens her hold and looks up at Jerrard. 'One day perhaps,' she says, 'when small ears are not listening, you will tell me the fate of the reptile.'

'Oh, him.' He props his chin on her head again, thinks for a moment, and chuckles. 'I fear my Latin truly is every bit as rusty as my manners but here goes anyway. *Una salus victis nullam sperare salutem.* You are rid of that trouble, Alice.'

She smiles. *The vanquished may expect no safety.* 'Not rusty at all. Gramercy, sir.'

'Henry.'

'Thank you, Henry. Most truly. And now tell me, what did you say to him, that he will not feel safe?'

'I threatened him with all sorts of laws, some of which may actually be laws … and I may also have asked him how he would feel if a story got out that a young woman had given him a worse thrashing than the blacksmith.'

'Daniel?'

She can hear the broad smile in his voice as he recalls, 'Some uproar it must have been. A whole row of pewter tankards that used to belong to the apothecary destroyed. Nick gave me his version this morning, but I had the truth from Silas last night. After a fight like that, the last thing Bart wanted was a—'

'What fight?'

65

The sound of hooves draws Daniel to the doorway of the smithy where he comes up all standing.

'Daniel! Daniel! We came to see you! Look at my sheep Gerald made for me!'

Daniel drags his eyes away from the woman to the boy now running towards him, the little wooden toy clutched in his hand. He smiles. 'That's nice.' It's true, he has to admit it. Gerald is a finer craftsman than he with his whittling. Daniel's eyes return to Alice sliding off Cassie's back.

'Daniel, give you good day. You are well?'

He extends his arm, indicating the empty yard. 'As you see. A thriving business and queues of customers.' He doesn't mean to talk to her in this way, it's not her fault. But she is the one apologising.

'I am sorry,' she says. 'It has not been easy for you. But I wanted to talk with you, to ask you something.' She stops.

'Alice, just say whatever—'

'I know what happened at the inn.'

'Oh, Lord.' He runs a hand over his face.

Whatever she feared before of rumours that she was following in Margery's footsteps, all that has been mercifully obliterated by Henry's story from old Silas. It has freed her to come here and talk once again with Daniel as friend to friend. 'I must talk with you,' she says. 'Please, Daniel.'

'Yes,' he says. Of course it's yes, for her it will always be yes. He casts around. 'Sam, if you go into the wood yard over there, you'll find some interesting bits of wood to play with.'

'Will you come and play too, Daniel?'

'Maybe later. Do you go now.' Sam trots off, none too convinced.

'I'm sorry about the inn,' Daniel says.

'You're sorry?'

'It should never have happened, but you don't mention a lady's name in that sort of company. I don't know Alice, I accused you of losing your wits that day I was winnowing, but I surely lost mine that night at the inn. And did no good by it.'

'You defended my name, Daniel. You did it when you could have stayed silent. When some were even admiring you for what they chose to think was going on between us.'

'I don't value men of that stamp, Alice. They are wastrels and midden-rats. Do you think I would smile and smile and do nothing while they peddle their filth?'

'No, I know you would not.'

His voice changes. 'How are you managing, Alice?'

'I am well, Daniel. I—'

'How are you really? I should not have left.' None have dared mention Alice's name in his presence since that night at the inn, and he has been careful not to ask after her. This is the result.

She puts out her hand in a calming gesture on his sleeve. 'Don't punish yourself, Daniel.'

He takes hold of her wrist, looks hard at her. 'What happened to your face? Your wrist? Why are your knuckles bruised?'

'I fell.' She pulls back her hand, drags at the sleeve. 'Scraped them.'

'On the back?'

She smoothes the cuff over the back of her hand. 'Daniel, I came to speak with you about something. As my friend, I want you to hear this from me and not through another. Taking the sum of all the things that have happened recently, I think you will not be surprised to know that I am shortly to be married.'

His head feels like a silent explosion has gone off. 'Married.'

'Yes.'

He blazes inside. So the Coopers have won. Gerald. Witless, gorbellied, mother's boy Gerald. 'No! Alice! You're doing it to save the farm.'

'I cannot keep it going when village opinion has seen to it that no one will come and work for me.'

What a dullard he has been. Why didn't he ask her himself, that night, instead of slinking away like a coward? Well, no, of course he couldn't, not with that other so recently dead. But he should have had the wit to let her know the offer was open if she needed it. Now she's had to accept Gerald.

The sound of approaching wheels draws their attention and they watch as the Cooper coach draws to a halt outside. Into the yard scurries Mistress Cooper, calling over her shoulder, 'Here she is, Ralph!'

Oh Lord, already she shadows Alice like a costly possession.

'Alice dear, we missed you at the house. You did know we were coming.' Her tone speaks her irritation. 'We were worried about you.' She draws herself up. 'But I see you are well.'

'Good day, Mistress Cooper,' Alice says, and Daniel is glad that she does not put on a false air of affection. 'I have called in to see Daniel.'

'I can see that, but he will excuse us.'

336

'I came to see Daniel on business,' Alice insists, 'and I need to talk with him. I prefer not to keep him waiting. Then you and I should talk.'

'That's all right, Alice,' Daniel says. 'You've private things to discuss with Mistress Cooper. I'll be at the fire.' He walks away, he has no place here.

'You see, it is quite easily done,' he hears the older woman say.

'I came to tell Daniel I am to be married, Mistress Cooper.'

With murder in his heart, Daniel turns to see Emeline sail towards Alice and envelop her in bony arms. 'Dearest Alice, I love to hear you say it, it makes me so very happy. You have decided at last?'

Alice extricates herself. 'I have, my word on it.'

'Of course, Alice, you know it is my dearest wish for you.' Patting Alice's cheek.

'Yes, but—'

'And your mother's dying wish—'

'Mistress Cooper, please do not—'

'Silly girl, and what a long time you kept us all waiting,' she teases. 'I have been telling all the world of our hopes.'

'I should tell you—'

'So there was no need for you to announce it here at the smithy of all places! Such low tastes as you have, Alice. He would have found out in time.' Indicating Daniel with a flick of the hand. Daniel knows he should walk out of earshot but something is not right here; Alice's manner has changed.

'There is the matter of Hill House to settle,' Alice says.

'Attorney Handley will do all that.'

'There is the matter of who is to live there when I leave.'

Emeline Cooper gives a playful laugh. 'I see you wish to move straightway into your husband's home.' She pats Alice's

337

cheek again.

'Of course, where else should I be?'

'Yes, yes, but there is no need for you to move out of Hill House.'

'But he will wish me to live in his home, and I am happy to.'

'Alice, listen to me, he will move in with you.' As Emeline Cooper prattles happily on, Daniel notices that Alice's face has changed from mild annoyance to the wide-eyed expression she wore that day when she was teasing Gerald about the perilous connection between spotted fish and the pestilence. Emeline Cooper is still talking. '— And you and he can have the chamber over the front door. You still have your parents' great bed do you not?'

'Not the feather mattress.'

'Well, what does the feather mattress matter! You can use the one from your own bed.'

'Sam sleeps in my bed.'

'What!'

'Sam sleeps in—'

'I heard you! Where do you sleep then?'

'In my bed.'

'With … him?' Emeline Cooper indicates Sam who has returned from the wood yard and is leaning against the smithy wall, arms crossed. 'With that—'

'I warn you, madam, my husband will be his father.' Alice says. 'When I am married, Sam will have his own chamber.'

'We'll not argue about that. Given his station,' she concedes, 'Sam can sleep in one of the servants' rooms.'

'No, those are separated from the main chambers.'

'What are you talking about? They are all part of—'

'Sam's room will be next to mine.'

'Next to yours? But that's the great room; that's where you'll be!'

'No, you misunderstand, madam.'

'I understand a great deal more than you realise, Alice. Now, listen to me. No, don't say another word. You will be married by Vicar Rutland as soon as I have … as soon as my husband has agreed the marriage articles. There will be the traditional bedding of the two of you—'

'Madam!'

'Don't be shy, Alice. I am your mother now, am I not?'

'No!'

'Let us not split hairs. In all but deed, I am.'

'No!'

'No?' says Mistress Cooper.

'No?' repeats Daniel.

'You think I am to marry Gerald,' Alice says, 'but I am trying to tell you—'

Sam has had enough. 'She's going to marry Henry, and Henry says it will put paid to Gerald,' he says simply. 'And to the dame.'

There is a stunned silence as the two women absorb the effects of this blunt declaration, and Daniel, struggling with his own shock, rejoices in a four-year-old's plain speaking.

Emeline Cooper is the first to speak. 'What are you talking about? Henry? Who is Henry?'

'Henry Jerrard, who was known to my father, and to whom I handfasted myself before Vicar Rutland not half an hour ago. Henry is at the inn at this moment, reclaiming his room for the night.'

'Is this true? You have betrothed yourself to this unknown when you were promised to my son?'

'I have never said yes to your son, Mistress Cooper.'

'Your mother wished it, miss!'

'My mother wished me to be happy, and by that token, as she told me herself, would never have forced me into a marriage with your son, whatever her own partiality.'

'She must be turning in her grave now, Alice Edwards!'

'If she is turning, it is in disgust at the way you and your husband have used me since her death in your attempts to secure for yourself all the land that now belongs to me!'

'I have no idea what you mean.'

Alice's hands clench by her side. 'You can pretend that, if you like.'

'You can't do this!'

'I can, and I have.'

Emeline Cooper's eyes are like glinting jags of seacoal. 'You scheming hussy! You wicked temptress! You led my son on with your smiles and your invitations—'

She gets no further. Daniel strides between the two of them, grasps Emeline Cooper bodily above her elbows and carries her, vainly kicking and protesting, beyond the palings of his yard. He sets her down, gently enough, outside. His tone is very calm. 'I guess your man will have told you, Mistress Cooper, what happens to those who make foul slanders against an innocent woman. If I hear of you saying such things about Alice again, I will carry you further, down to the river, and we should collect quite a crowd by the time we get to that end of the village. And I will duck you off the bridge in the middle of the river in front of everyone. Do you believe me, Mistress Cooper?'

Emeline Cooper vouchsafes no reply but shakes out rustling skirts.

'And remember that the dyeworks is upstream and the water takes on interesting hues at times.'

There is a brief silence, and then with sharp clacking steps she retreats to the coach and slams the door. Of the valiant Ralph Cooper, her lord, protector and fellow traveller, there is no sign, unless the closing door of the inn down the road is any indication. Daniel walks back into the yard.

'You'd better come over to the fire, Alice, and tell me. I took the same notion as Mistress Cooper so you'll have to explain how it is.' He has himself in hand now. So, it's Henry Jerrard, the elegant traveller who comes and goes so fast, gossip never even started in the village. Too old for Alice. Still, he thinks, that would make me too old as well, wouldn't it?

He lets Alice tell him a version of the story up to the point of her betrothal, and knows there are whole sections left out that he might never fill in. The way she tells it, Gerald was helping almost all the time, they managed the farm between them with hardly a setback, the weeks on her own counted for nothing, and then Henry Jerrard arrives on the scene and suddenly everything is as fine as a summer's day. Ah well, perhaps in time the truth will come out. And not only about those scraped knuckles.

'There is still the other thing I wanted to talk to you about,' she says, and offers him a lease on Hill House Farm.

66

He looks at her seated on Cassie's back where he has just tossed Sam up behind her. 'Wish you happy, Alice,' he says, 'and you just tell that fine husband of yours to look after you.'

'Wish you happy too, Daniel. Come up to the house whenever you're ready and we can discuss what's to be done. And I should so much like you to visit us in Guildford some day, when you can spare the time.'

'Goodbye, young Sam,' he says. 'Mind you be good and do as Alice says.'

He lifts the rein to her and as she goes to take it, lightly holds her hand. This time she does not pull away. He pushes back the fabric of her sleeve and kisses the bruise that she tried to conceal from him.

67

In the bright spring sunshine, Alice walks with Susan Cushing outside the winter parlour at Hill House. Susan is speaking with great relish, her eyes sprinkling her words with capital letters.

'... And apparently, your Betrothed is a Mightie Fine fellow from London, who owns a Clutch of Properties, knew your father for years and has the Ear of His Majestie himself!'

'They are not saying that!' Alice is amused and aghast in equal measure.

'More, Alice. The women will have it that you and Henry have had a Long and Hopeless Passion for years because your father demanded that he do Great Deedes before he could win you—'

'Great deeds? What great deeds did he do?' Actually she can answer that herself – he saved her from committing murder.

'Better not to ask. The more modest tales have, shall we say, a classical bent, concerning monsters and treasure and suchlike. There are some less savoury ones involving deliverance from Deceit and Lust and suchlike evils, but I should not heed them if I were you, they came from Silas's wife. Oh, you need not look so worried, Alice! She is spending her days patching up Bart Johnson, and it's giving her fancies a somewhat livid hue.' Susan chuckles heartily. Alice swallows hard. As unobtrusively as she can, she checks that the ties of her chemise come high enough to conceal those recent scratches. Her hands she has studiously kept hidden in over-long sleeves since Daniel's comment on her raw knuckles. As to her face, she repeated the lie about falling.

'And what else do they say?'

'Ah, the best of the bunch is the account of The Proposal. Apparently it culminated in an ecstatic and rapturous declaration from Henry and – you never told me this, Alice – a shy and panting acceptance from yourself!'

The two women dissolve in immodest laughter. When Alice is finally able to enlighten her friend on the true nature of the proposal, they dissolve once more, at the vision of Alice all outraged virtue and Henry dripping small-ale. Thus Charles Rutland comes upon them. Alice moves to welcome him. 'Vicar, take a seat here, and some refreshment. I shall open a bottle of wine for us all.'

Susan interrupts her. 'No, Alice, let me.' She addresses Rutland. 'I am not allowing her to do any work today. She has been wearing herself out with this and that, but I am trying to persuade her to unbutton a little. And look, I have had some success already. She has actually dispensed with those ghastly old caps. I loved her mother dearly but her taste in caps was abominable.' Fondly she strokes Alice's cheek. 'Life's bruises are banished and today is your holiday.'

As she disappears round the stable block, Alice stands staring after her, a hand up to her neck.

Charles Rutland lets himself down gratefully onto the stone bench under the window. 'Ooh! I believe it's a steeper climb every time I come up that hill.' He raises his eyes to her. 'Something you've forgotten, Alice?'

She is not really listening. 'Unbutton,' she murmurs. A picture is taking shape, though parts are still hidden from her.

They are like air bubbles in a jar of preserves, waiting to be teased to the surface.

'I fear you've lost me, Alice.'

Alice rouses. 'Forgive me, I was thinking of something Susan said.' She sits down next to him. 'You will have noticed changes as you came here?'

'Plenty of fellows helping around the place, I see.'

'Indeed. They seem to be falling over themselves to do the heavy work. Henry has been directing everything from his room at the inn when he has not been up here.'

The vicar's smile creases his face and he reaches out a blue-veined hand to cover hers. 'I did not think that first day of Christmas that you and I would be sitting here today seeing your prospects so changed, Alice. I am very happy for you.'

'Thank you, Vicar. I shall miss you when we go. I have learned from you all my life, and you gave me your advice and your help when I most needed it.'

'Sam?'

'Sam. I hope his father never returns, and I am glad I shall be away from here if he does.'

'Nothing ever came of my enquiries and I ceased looking when Daniel told me how Sam's father had used him so ill. I leave it in God's hands to direct the business as He sees fit.'

'Henry is happy that Sam will be with us, and in time we shall adopt him as our son.' She feels warm sitting here in the Spring sunshine, warm in body, warm in mind, warm towards all, even towards the men who have suddenly appeared looking for work, having previously been too busy, too sick or otherwise prevented.

'I imagine adoption will not be a difficulty if a decent period elapses with no trace of further family,' Charles Rutland says. There is a short silence, in which Alice detects a slight frown dawn on his forehead. 'We shall miss you and Sam, and I don't mean merely the reduction in numbers.'

'I am sensible that by leaving here, I reduce the village even further, and we can scarce afford it. There cannot be more than a few dozen here now, where there were so many. I often think to myself, if only we had known earlier, we could have acted, and might have avoided so many deaths.'

'So we might have.'

She would like to tell him that Ralph Cooper suppressed the Orders in Council in order to close his murky deal with Cazanove, so giving the plague time to get a hold, but she cannot prove it. 'We did what seemed right at the time. I did, you did. I felt for a long while that by walking into Mistress Cazanove's house that day, I brought the miasma back with me. But my father or Ian, or even my mother, might have done so days before. We were all in the village at some time or other, doing what we could. Were we to stand back? Pass by on the other side? Leave others in need while we made ourselves safe?'

'Alice.' He encloses her hand in both of his. They both know these are unanswerable questions.

'If we had left, we might have carried the pestilence with us. And Sam would never have been found, and would have starved to death or died of the cold. But, you know, I still wake in the night, and think to myself, what if?'

'Alice, my dear, we all have those thoughts, but what's past is past. We can only learn for the future. When this comes again, and it will, we must try to be better prepared. Do what our apothecary was trying to do and set up a proper pest-house for a start. That is the way we shall defeat it, by looking forward.'

He smiles at her and she thinks with gratitude, at last, one who understands what Frederick tried to do.

He goes on, 'If you want to know, I have often asked myself whether it was wise to go to Bristol for help. Whether it would not have been better to stay and do what I could. But without our apothecary, I thought ...' He spreads his hands wide.

'He was already dead when you left, then?' Alice wonders.

'Sadly, yes,' he says. 'With Sexton Whitehead gone as well, that was what decided me to leave for Bristol.'

'I learned much from Master Marchant last Summer,' Alice says. 'It was he who gave the receipt of the snatchers' vinegar to David and Daniel to help protect them.'

'A pity no one could protect against David's seizure.'

She nods. 'David's death hit Daniel very hard, but speaking selfishly, I was so glad to have him here those weeks. He is going to take a lease on the farm, you know. His business cannot prosper at present.'

'Daniel supped with me last night,' Rutland says. 'We had chamerchande. He tells me it's his favourite.'

She sits staring at the ground. '"All so dainty with parsley sprinkled over",' she murmurs. More bubbles are beginning to rise.

'Indeed,' Rutland answers, 'though I think he misses your cooking.' And Alice thinks, I have missed him being here, not only for all the work he did.

Rutland adds, 'An interesting man, that. His business will recover, Alice.'

'I hope so, for his sake,' she says, and at that moment Susan appears with a tray.

'I found this in your still room, Alice,' she announces. "This" is a dumpy bottle. The wax seal on the top is cracked and jagged where she has broken it away to get the stopper out. And three Venetian goblets. 'These glasses were in the cupboard in the winter parlour. I hope you approve? I couldn't use pewter mugs for wine, could I?'

Alice, staring unseeing, says, 'Pewter mugs.'

'Alice?' When no answer comes, she peers at her young friend. 'Alice, you are unwell. Come, sit down, you have overtaxed yourself.'

Startled, Alice rouses. 'No, I am well, Susan, I was thinking of something. You are right. Not the pewter.' The dusty bottle she remembers. 'I had forgotten about this but it is very apt, we have just been speaking of the giver. This bottle came from Frederick Marchant after I helped him with his work last Summer. He brought it to my father. I think it right we drink it now in his honour.'

'I'll join you in that,' Susan says, pouring the straw-coloured wine into the glasses. 'He was a dear man.'

'To Frederick Marchant,' says Charles Rutland, holding up his glass. 'A man who gave more than he received.'

'And to all such,' says Alice, and thinks of another, one who is unaware of the impending danger which possibly only she can avert.

68

Alice has waited until the working men have left Hill House for the day and Sam is in bed. It is with difficulty she has persuaded a sceptical Susan to agree to her going out unescorted. She has taken Cassie on a wide circuit of the village and over the hill to fetch up here at the Cazanove mansion in the low radiance of the sinking sun.

The maidservant Esther closes the great front door and leads the way down the marble-floored screens passage, calling an instruction as they pass the kitchens for one of the menservants to stable Mistress Edwards' mount. Alice follows Esther down the dim passage lit with sconces casting small pools of radiance along the way.

Ursula Cazanove is in the same room as when Abel Nutley called that memorable day. She sits writing at the table which has been moved over to the window. She wears a deep maroon open-necked loose-gown of cut velvet trimmed with a wide braid of dull gold bobbin lace over an ivory-hued kirtle. Her smooth features gleam in long curves and oblique shadows, and her dark, braided hair takes a fiery sheen from the glowing sky. Looking at her, Alice reflects that though her face is too long and her lips too thin to describe her as beautiful, there is no physical defect by which the baron's daughter could ever have been deemed "unmarriageable".

'I am glad you have come, Alice,' she says, setting down her quill. There is the rustle of silk as she rises and moves to greet her visitor. 'Indeed, when you came over that day in the courtyard, I was so wrapped up in my own concerns, I was less than courteous. I ask your pardon.' She takes Alice's hands as she speaks.

'There is nothing to forgive,' Alice says. 'You were busy looking after your people's needs.'

'And I hope I may be able to continue that work.'

'Have the attorneys found your husband's heir?'

'After a fashion, yes. I believe I told you it was his younger brother Bernard?' Alice nods. 'It turns out that Bernard the seafarer was in fact Bernard the pirate. He and his fellows were drinking the New Year in, and rashly decided to attack a merchantman. Fortunately for the merchantman the captain was alert and the pirates were repelled with heavy losses, Bernard amongst them. The attorneys tell me they can discover no issue and that under the terms of my husband's will, the estate reverts to me. I need to discuss this with you Alice, it is a happy chance you are come. Let me offer you a glass of wine.'

'Please excuse me, I have most urgent matters to speak of with you.'

Apart from a slight rise of enquiring eyebrows, Ursula says only, 'Why, certainly. Please sit down by the fire here. Thank you, Esther.' She indicates a cushioned backstool for Alice, and as the door closes takes her own seat, folds her hands in her lap and waits. Alice faces her across the wide-arched hearth. She takes a deep breath.

'Ursula, I have come here this evening to tell you that I am aware your husband did not die of the plague.' She gathers herself to continue, 'It was hemlock that killed him.'

There is a long silence in which the two women hold each other's gaze. At last, Ursula speaks. 'Are you saying he

350

destroyed himself?'

'No, Ursula. Esther served him hemlock with the meal that day.'

'Esther? Never! Alice, he drank nothing with the meal. He refused the small ale and we had no other.'

'Hemlock doesn't have to be in a drink, Ursula.'

'Sauces, then. There was only the mutton stew and—'

'And he did not touch it. I know; he had an accident, spilled it in his lap.' And as Ursula looks her surprise, 'Wat saw it on him.'

The widow sighs. 'Alice, there is something I have to tell you. Something I am not proud to admit.'

Alice waits.

'My husband, before he left for the inn, upended just about every dish from the table. Swept them onto the floor.'

'Wat told me that too.'

'Do you remember you spoke of "wild behaviour", that a person suffering early symptoms of plague might act in this way? This was the same, was it not?'

'Esther knew where she had put the hemlock.'

A note of desperation is creeping into Ursula's voice. 'There was nowhere to pour hemlock. He only touched the roast meats.'

'There was no call to pour anything, Ursula. There was parsley sprinkled on many of the dishes was there not?'

Ursula shrugs. 'My husband was partial to a well-flavoured dish.'

'Leaves of hemlock will look very much like parsley when dried.'

'This is ludicrous! He and I ate the same food. By his instruction. How is it that I was not also poisoned?'

'One who knows what parts are poison can avoid serving

351

them. A particular dish, perhaps? The partridges? The spinach tart? Or one where the parsley is sprinkled around but not over it?'

'Esther and I prepared the food together, Alice. I crumbled the dried parsley myself. Esther would never do anything against me.'

'She has been with you long enough for you to know that, has she?'

'Since shortly after I was married. She was already working in the house and my husband recommended she become my waiting woman. And I have never had cause to complain of her.'

'So you think someone at the inn poisoned your husband?'

'I think no such thing. They weren't expecting him at the inn. He went there on a whim because we had nothing here he cared to drink.'

'That's not why he went to the inn. You yourself told me that he complained of the food, called it "revolting". He had a headache, which he blamed on your talking, but it was the first effects of the hemlock served him in his food.'

'You have no proof; this is all fancy.'

'You are right. I have no proof, Ursula. But you are very loyal to Esther, are you not?'

'The loyalty is rather the other way round. You have to understand, Alice, Esther had very little contact with my husband. She had no cause to wish him ill.'

'On the contrary, I think she had cause. Because she knows, Ursula, that your husband abused you, such that for years you wore gowns that buttoned to the chin, and sleeves reaching to your knuckles, to hide your injuries.'

At last, Ursula looks straight at Alice, her eyes pleading. Alice wonders how long she can keep this up. Deliberately wearing down the persecuted is not a role she relishes.

Then, suddenly, it comes.

'I did it. Not Esther. I killed my husband.'

Alice waits.

'No one wanted the daughter of a baron with gambling debts. I was nearing thirty. Then Rupert offered, rich, coarse, keen to buy the power and influence of an alliance with lineage. My father was desperate for Rupert's cash. He gave me an ultimatum. Marry or take the veil. That meant exile overseas, of course, with no hope of return. I had no wish to incarcerate myself in the English Benedictine house at Brussels.'

'So you married.'

'I believed the lesser evil was a loveless marriage. Lesser!' She gives a short, mirthless laugh. 'From the outset Rupert sought to control. He found small faults, then large. He frequently ... punished me. I came to realise that he enjoyed doing it.' Her hands appear to rest in her lap, except that the white knuckles betray how hard she clings as though to hold herself together.

'But didn't your father do anything?' My father, Alice thinks, would have brought down the whole weight of the justices, the church, local opinion and in the last resort, brute force.

Ursula regards her almost pityingly. 'I wrote telling my father, asking him to take me back. He replied that a husband only corrects his wife when she errs and I should mend my ways. That's what he called it, "correction".'

'And no one knew? No one said anything?'

'Alice, the entire household knew. They came in for their own share of his fists, his riding whip. I wrote to Sir Thomas Harcourt saying I wished to lay an information for assault.

Rupert intercepted the letter, confined me to the house and let it be known that I periodically lost my wits. Some believed it; I could tell by the way they treated me with exaggerated understanding. I became convinced that I was surrounded by those who would betray me. So I tried harder and harder to show that I was not a witless fool. When that didn't work, I tried to make myself quiet and unnoticed, so that he would pass me by.' She sighs. 'That was what I became.'

'But that's no life.' Now she has heard this admission, Alice is finding the reality hard to stomach. 'That's a cage!'

'My life was always going to be a cage!' A brief flash of anger. 'A nunnery, marriage ... Let me tell you what happens in a cage, Alice. How you lose the person you thought you were. One day last year, he accused me of – I forget what – something trivial. I assured him I had not intended it. Wat overheard from the next room. He had only been with us a short while, but he knew what was happening. He came in and admitted to my husband that the error was his. I knew it wasn't, it was my lapse, but in my fear I said nothing. My husband appeared to accept Wat's guilt. The next day ...' she catches several short breaths and a tear spots the cream silk. 'The next day he gathered the whole household together to witness Wat being "corrected".' The last words come in a whisper. 'And I stood with the rest, watching, too afraid to stand up to him.' She cries quietly into her hands.

What would she, Alice, have done? So this is why Wat said Ursula did not hate her husband. It was true. Her fear of him had blotted out any possibility of hate. Hate, albeit perverted, is a life-force, and Cazanove had beaten her life force down to a mere spark. And yet, what a spark! Sufficient in the end to fire Retribution's torch.

Alice rises, stands in front of Ursula. 'I believe you. I'm

354

sorry.' Sorry for what she has forced her to admit, sorry for what she is about to do. 'I'm going to find Esther.' Alice quietly leaves the room. She walks back along the passage past the sconces. Light and dark, light and dark.

Esther is counting linen in a small room nearby. The maidservant looks up and smiles. 'I did not hear my mistress call,' she says. 'Are you leaving?'

'Not as yet, Esther,' Alice says. She closes the door and leans against it. 'I have to tell you that Mistress Cazanove has just admitted to me that she poisoned her husband.'

Esther does not stare or look open-mouthed at Alice. Does not turn Alice's statement into an incredulous question. Apart from a short, rapid blinking, she merely slides her hand under the sheet she has counted down to. Carefully and deliberately, she turns that section of the pile crosswise as though she will resume her counting later. She smoothes the surface of the top sheet. Several times. Finally, she turns to Alice. 'Impossible. You don't know her. Such a gentle creature could never do murder.'

'You don't ask me how she killed him?'

'I don't need to,' Esther states. 'He died of the plague.'

'No, Esther. And I'm not the only one who doesn't believe it. Wat might believe it. But he will never say anything, will he? After taking a beating on her behalf.'

Esther fixes her eye on Alice. 'There was nothing going on between them! Not on her side, not on his. I'd have known.'

'I believe you, Esther. But a wife made to watch her husband punish a servant as a way of punishing her, might well feel there was just cause to wish that husband out of the world.'

'You've worn her down.' Esther points an accusing finger. 'You saw her the day that man Nutley came here. He did the same. You're as bad as him!'

'He came here to shock. I came here to help.'

'Some help you are!'

'Grover Price didn't believe it was plague, either.'

'Let me go to her.' Esther reaches for the latch but Alice stands her ground.

'Do you want to know why Grover didn't believe it, Esther?'

'I don't care what he did or didn't believe. Stand aside, Mistress Edwards.' Years of servitude are holding Esther back from laying hands on a guest, but her fists are balled.

'With his memories of Harman's Copse, Grover was keeping quiet about any suspicions he had.'

Esther pushes her face into Alice's. 'I don't know what you're talking about. Nobody goes to Harman's Copse. The place is accursed.'

'Then let us go to your mistress and ask her about Harman's Copse.' Alice stands aside.

'God a' mercy, can't you see? She didn't kill him. I did!' Esther tugs open the door, breaks into a run.

Alice enters the sunset-lit parlour and both women glance up. Ursula's face shows signs of tears but she has had time to collect herself since Alice left the room. Esther, leaning close at her mistress' ear, straightens. 'My mistress knows nothing of Harman's Copse.'

Alice closes the door. 'If you say so, Esther. But my guess is, your mistress knows Master Cazanove murdered the woodsman John Kelsey and his young son there in 1618. And very nearly murdered the woodsman's wife too.'

'No good can come of this, Alice,' Ursula warns. 'Everyone knows that the family was lost.'

'Everyone thinks they know,' Alice tells her. 'But Grover

Price knew the truth. One night he talked.'

'What did he say?' This from Esther, clipped, wary.

'Apparently he had drunk more than usual. They said he was talking with someone who wasn't there. A spirit, he called it.'

'A man will talk much nonsense in his cups,' Ursula says.

'There were three in the Kelsey family,' Alice says. 'There was a father, and there was a son, and Grover was talking to the spirit. He said, "For earth thou art, till thou return to earth."'

'You mean,' Ursula says. '"For dust thou art".'

'No, I believe he meant what he said. Grover was too terrified of your husband to say anything directly, but my guess is he knew the truth, because Master Cazanove had him fill Mistress Kelsey's coffin with earth as a make-weight.' Alice turns to the maidservant. 'She was virtually unknown in the village, so it must have been simple to conceal her, possibly nearby, while time passed. But one other person knew, and that was Mistress Kelsey herself. Am I right, Esther?'

'How would I know?'

'Your mention of decoction of elm bark as a treatment for burns suggests you know.'

'What's this?' Ursula is all at sea.

'Most people use sengreen,' Alice explains, 'but Esther's treatment is favoured by charcoal burners. If you are who I think you are, Esther, please believe me when I say I've no wish to distress you nor accuse you, only to understand. Will you tell me what Grover knew?'

Esther's mistress puts up a staying hand. 'Esther, you do not have to say anything.'

'Yes, I do. I have been buried long enough.'

'But I have already confessed to Mistress Edwards. Leave

it be, I beg you.'

'I cannot!' Esther's voice wavers with the distress of revived memories. 'All those years I felt that what happened to us was my fault, because of what I did. Unless I speak now, I shall never be free of it.' She draws herself up, addresses Alice. 'My name is Esther Kelsey. In the autumn of 'eighteen, my husband took work with Master Cazanove and we moved into the old collyer's hut with our son. The hut leaked badly. John would come home rain-soaked and I was unable to dry his clothes before he went out next morning. Within a short while, he grew ill. The sickness lingered so I removed our young son because he was not robust. I settled him in the hayloft at the end of the kitchen court while I made John's deliveries. I thought ...' She shakes her head in disbelief. 'I actually thought that if I could just keep up with John's work while he recovered, no one would mind. Even now, I can hardly believe what a monster we worked for.

'Grover Price discovered my son and told Aled the steward. Master Cazanove summoned me and said that John was being punished for my deceit. He said it was to teach us to know our place. I took my son and ran. By the time we arrived at Harman's Copse, Grover and Aled were there nailing boards across the windows with John inside. Aled pushed us in with him and they imprisoned us all three in the hut as though we had the plague, though he knew we did not. I shouted and kicked and beat but I couldn't get us out. They had taken all the food and water out of the hut. Nobody came. John died after two days ...' Esther stops and a hand goes to her mouth. She takes a deep breath. '... Our little boy kept asking for a drink. I had nothing. His tongue swelled, it choked him to ...'

In the silence that follows Alice thinks, he murdered them

on our very doorstep, and we all believed his story of plague.'

Ursula takes Esther's hand in both of hers. 'She was barely alive when Grover Price was sent to unboard the hut after several days.'

'Did your husband mean murder?'

'As I said, he liked to control,' Ursula says. 'He may not have thought beyond that impulse.'

'He'd have been happier if we'd all died,' Esther says in bitter tones. 'It would have been simpler for him.'

'Rupert put her in the Poor House in Westover,' Ursula continues, 'and told them she was a madwoman. More control, you see? No one would believe her if she declared who she was. Her hair went the grey it is now. After things died down he fetched her back to the house as a scullion. By then, servants had moved on and no one else would have recognised her. Shortly afterwards, I married him and Esther became my waiting woman.' She turns to smile at her servant. 'I never told him what a great favour he had unwittingly conferred upon me. Even so, I knew her only as Esther. For years I believed his story that John Kelsey and his family died of the plague. So you see, Alice, she had reason to wish him dead,' Ursula says, 'but Esther did not kill him. I did. I am responsible.'

'No, I prepared his last meal!' Esther insists. 'And I am glad I did. Glad!'

Alice shakes her head. 'It was the two of you together. Why else did you both stand at the front door and tell me a lie?' She pauses, but they are both silent, waiting. 'You told me, Ursula, that the apothecary had attended your husband. Then you, Esther, said he had diagnosed plague.'

'You weren't here. How would you know what he said?' Esther demands.

'Because I know he was never here. That afternoon, Master Cazanove had been at the inn drinking autumn ale from a pewter tankard that was looted from Frederick Marchant's home directly after his death the day before.' Henry telling her the story of those pewter mugs she saw in the taproom cupboard. 'That same morning my father saw Vicar Rutland leaving for Bristol; the vicar tells me he went to seek the bishop's help, because Frederick Marchant was dead.'

Esther glares. 'Why did you come, Mistress Edwards? To accuse us? To gloat over what he did to her? To show us how clever you were to work it all out?' Esther's face is set in hard lines, her eyes narrowed, accusing.

'You inspire such loyalty, Ursula,' Alice says, admiring. 'Esther here, and Wat as I have seen for myself. Others too, no doubt. They close ranks around you, when one of them at least should look to his own protection.'

'To his own?' Gently, Ursula puts a staying hand on Esther's arm and turns her attention to Alice. 'Wat, you mean?'

At last Alice moves from the door, approaches. 'Ursula, I came here tonight to persuade you that even though there is currently no talk, rumours can start from the smallest thing.' As I know to my own cost. 'You need to be prepared. If I can come to certain conclusions, so can others.'

'You had better sit down, Alice. What conclusions?'

'When I was last here, I saw an army of indoor and outdoor servants. Some of them clearly did not want to take their orders from Wat. It only takes one of them to be disaffected and a rumour could start from things that must surely have been said.'

'What can they accuse him of now, though?'

'You sent Wat that day to follow his master to the inn, to

see that he came to no hurt.'

'Indeed.' Ursula frowns in puzzlement at this new turn.

'Later, your husband was brought back unconscious, and then he died. Wat followed him when he was apparently well and brought him back dying.'

'Grover Price helped bring him back too,' Ursula reminds her.

'And Grover is also dead,' Esther says, big-eyed, and mistress and maidservant regard each other, aghast at the implication. 'Oh, mistress, they'll think Wat killed both. It never occurred to me.'

'The more reason you should be prepared, both of you,' Alice says. 'And Wat, too.'

'Ay, that might be—' Esther starts to say.

'No!' Ursula's voice cuts across her. 'He has suffered enough. We must ensure he is protected without loading him with our guilt.' She turns to Alice. 'Are there others you think might make accusations?'

'You say the steward Aled was with Grover Price boarding up the hut,' Alice says to Esther. 'Aled left, did he not? Might he hear of Master Cazanove's death and voice doubts at some time?'

'He might have,' Esther answers. 'He and my master were two of a kind, taking pleasure in cruelty. But one day last year Aled went too far at an inn over Yeovil way. There was a fight and he was stabbed in the stomach. It was not a quick death.' Where Ursula might have expressed genuine regret at an untimely death, there is only a bleak frankness in Esther's tones.

Alice gathers her thoughts. 'I am thinking your husband's symptoms could be questioned. His headache could have been the result of lacking ale to drink. Then the quantity of blood in the head, a sign of hemlock poisoning but also of being carried, head down, across his saddle. His 'wild behaviour' we have already discussed as a known symptom of plague. As regards Grover, from what I recall, the vicar's records show he died of plague some time after Wat was gone to Wells with your household. I know not who else might ask questions, but if you will consider these instances, you can guard against unexpected enquiry.'

'I shall,' Ursula confirms. 'I greatly value Wat, he is an excellent servant. How he bore with my husband's abuse I do not know. He deserves better. But Alice, we have committed a terrible crime, Esther and I, yet you have clearly decided to help the two of us, by not handing us over to justice. Why?'

'Why? Perhaps because I can imagine circumstances when I too would feel just cause to kill.' Bart Johnson's murderous eyes and the hot flare of her own intentions as she stood poised with the bread peel. How much more just a cause did each of these two women have, from the slow burn of years? 'What of you, Ursula, how could you endure it? Why did you stay?'

The widow gives a desolate smile, 'All the years of my marriage, I tried to use what precious little courage I had to protect our people where I could.'

'My mistress protected the household better than she admits,' Esther says. 'Many's the time she took blame upon herself that was none of hers. And he would surely have continued until he killed her. There would be no reprisals on him, a husband killing his wife.' She shrugs. 'To the law, it is of little moment. The law upholds his right while it denies hers.'

Ursula continues, 'Esther was silent when I first knew her. But later, when she tended to me after an incident and told me her story, it showed me I was simply the current object in his power to treat as he pleased. If – when – I died, he would find another and another, as long as he lived. We finally resolved that he had to be stopped, and that we were the only two who had the power to do it.'

There is a long silence as she finishes speaking. Alice says, 'I knew his reputation as a cruel oppressor – in truth, I was not sorry to hear he had died. But I am sorry I did not understand when you failed to visit your tenants and my mother went instead.'

'I was so grateful to hear of her visits, but he would not allow any communication. I am glad that now, at least, you know the truth.'

Alice reflects a moment. 'Hemlock,' she says. 'It's an uncertain killer. You took a great risk.'

'We laced every possible dish with it,' Ursula explains. 'No matter which he chose, he could not avoid eating it.'

There is grim satisfaction in Esther's tone as she says, 'While he sat down to enjoy his hour of triumph, we watched him swallow the fruits of his labours.'

'And had him buried at Harman's Copse.'

'On the site of his murderous crime' Esther finishes. 'There was surely justice in that. What a man! He carries a huge debt where he has gone.'

And Alice thinks, perhaps Rupert Cazanove is starting to repay that debt already. The secrets locked within the dead to be used for the benefit of the living. How that would have galled him!

Ursula sighs. 'But Alice, what do you intend to do with all you have learned this evening?'

'It seems to me that this business is not for me to judge,' Alice tells her. 'I came here with an idea of the truth and a wish to warn you about the risk to Wat. And I hope I have done that.'

''We both have much to thank you for,' Ursula says. 'And now I have something that I hope will help you.'

'Me?'

For answer, Ursula rises and crosses to the table near the window. The sun is sinking behind the horizon, throwing the last long shadows of the day across the room. 'I said when you arrived it was a fortunate chance. I was writing to tell you of my find. You shall have it now.' She picks up a slim, long leather pouch. 'In some ways it will not be welcome news for you, Alice.'

With a dread of its contents, Alice thinks, no news of Sam's father is welcome, but how does Ursula know that? She takes the pouch and loosens the draw cords at the neck. Within is a single sheet of paper. She draws it out and its stiff folds crackle as she opens it up. What immediately catches her eye is not the black, clerkish writing covering most of the sheet, but down at the bottom a brown-red scrawl. Not a crude mark on a pauper's tenancy. A signature on a formal lease. A literate man, then, Sam's father. Her glance slides into a stare, and she knows why Ursula said it would be unwelcome news. Without looking up, she says, 'Margery Patten thought she knew him, but it was the family likeness she was seeing.'

'I suppose so,' is all Ursula says.

69

Alice lets Cassie stroll along at her own pace in the darkening evening. The mare knows her way homewards, the weather continues mild and there is no breeze to excite and make her skittish. The earth scents of spring are sweet on the air. A sliver of moon hangs in the blue-purple sky. As they come up the track that leads to the front door, the shape of Hill House stands out black and featureless but for the slight star-glow reflecting on the window of her chamber where Sam sleeps, and below, candlelight in the winter parlour where Susan awaits Alice's return. Susan, the friend who has accepted that she will never know where Alice went this evening or what she did, and who has agreed at Alice's behest to say nothing, even to her own sister. A true friend.

Alice draws Cassie to a halt and looks at the house that has been her home all her life, the home she is soon to leave, probably never to be her home again. She feels a pang at the thought, but also a deep content. The farm has been saved and Daniel will have a future for as long as he needs it. She still has a sense of shock at the way events have shaped her actions; at the way her actions have shaped events. And now, here she is, facing a future not shackled to a Thi lumpen pawn driven by a ruthless and domineering mother, but with a sense of hope that she has lately believed could never be hers. Yes, there is good reason to be hopeful.

Most importantly, Sam is safe, Sam has a bright future.

One day she will tell him about it.

Alice draws out the leather pouch and feels inside for the paper. Although it is almost too dark to read, she unfolds it anyway. She can just make out the clerkish hand, and at the bottom the two slightly lighter brown-red words penned in the blood of a man outraged at the price demanded of his slender purse. A price that should not have been extorted, for a dwelling that should never have been offered. Perhaps after all, as Vicar Rutland confidently predicted, God has directed the business in fit manner. The lease on the little hovel in Bakery Row is signed in the blood of Bernard Cazanove, heir to the Cazanove fortune and father of Sam.

70

In the moonlight, the new burial ground seems peaceful. The grave is at this end, near the track, where they put the early victims, before the burials multiplied and demanded more and yet more rows beyond.

She does not need light to know the one amongst all the mounds of earth, for she has been here many a time, always on her own, always at twilight or at dawn while the world is within doors. She kneels down, placing her hands on the banked soil, and remains there long minutes while the last clouds clear from the horizon and a star brighter than the rest beckons low down in the deep purple heavens.

The sound of a stone dislodged at the other end of the burial ground causes her to straighten quickly and walk back towards her horse, as though regarding all the graves before leaving.

She hears him make his way back to the track, and at the familiar sound of his step she lets go the rein and turns. He comes to stand by her, head and shoulders taller. She extends her hand to indicate the rows of little wooden crosses.

'A village lost,' she says.

He nods but does not speak.

'I came to say my goodbyes,' she says.

'I did not mean to disturb you, Alice.'

'You did not—'

'I came to see my Davy, as you came to see your Frederick,'

he says gently.

'Oh …'

'Sam told me.'

'Sam? But I didn't—' She glances up at him but he is looking away at the mounds.

'I hope you are happier now, Alice,' he says, 'and no longer talk in your sleep.'

'Oh!'

Together they retrace their steps and stand by the mound.

'My father knew Frederick was dead, didn't he?' she says.

'Davy and I told him, that last day he came down with the logs.'

'When Abel Nutley came up to our house, Father stopped him from letting it slip – I remember there was some strangeness about the way Father cut him off. He would never have allowed me to hear it from such a one. He meant to tell me, I feel sure.'

'I thought it were strange when you asked me to get the physic for your father.'

'He would have told me the next morning, my father never gave bad news at night. I had only that day told him of our hopes. Then my mother was taken sick that evening and all else was driven from our minds.'

'Frederick Marchant was a good man. I am truly sorry he was taken, Alice. You would have been happy with him.'

She nods. 'He is what might have been,' she says. She takes a deep breath. 'But I came here to tell him that I am still of this world and …' she pauses for seconds, then makes up her mind. 'And I can say this both to him and to you, that I believe one day I shall love again.'

'I hope that for you, with all my heart.' He points to the sprouting clump of long, oval leaves, just discernible against the mound of earth. 'He sends a message to those who would read it, I see.'

'Forget-me-not,' she says, and smiles in the dark. 'Yes, that is indeed Frederick's message. I shall not forget him, but I have made my farewell and I believe he would understand that.'

She looks up and can barely discern his face. 'Daniel, there will be other farewells in the next few days.'

'Yes.'

'We shall leave direct from the church and I shall make my goodbyes there.'

'Yes.' She hears the sigh in his voice.

'It will likely be very public. At the church. The whole village sees this as a great event.' She finds she is having difficulty keeping her voice light-humoured.

'As it is.'

'There will be much waving of kerchiefs.'

'Much tossing of caps,' he adds.

'Kissing of hands.'

He gives a short laugh, or it could be something else. In the starlight she tries to make out his expression. 'Daniel, I cannot say goodbye to you like that, before all the world.' When he does not reply, she puts a hand on his arm. 'Not you.'

He shakes his head, whispers, 'No.'

'You have been so good to me, more than I can ever repay.'

His hand moves to take hers. After a minute he manages to say, 'You have been so to me also.' He draws her hand up and presses his lips against her knuckles; she cups her palm to his cheek.

'Daniel, best of friends,' she breathes and rests her head against him.

His chest heaves. 'Oh, dearest Alice.' His arms go about her, and each for a different reason clings to the other.

LOOK OUT FOR THE THRILLING NEW
STORY FROM GEORGIA PIGGOTT

COMING SOON

THE ALICE CHRONICLES

BOOK 2

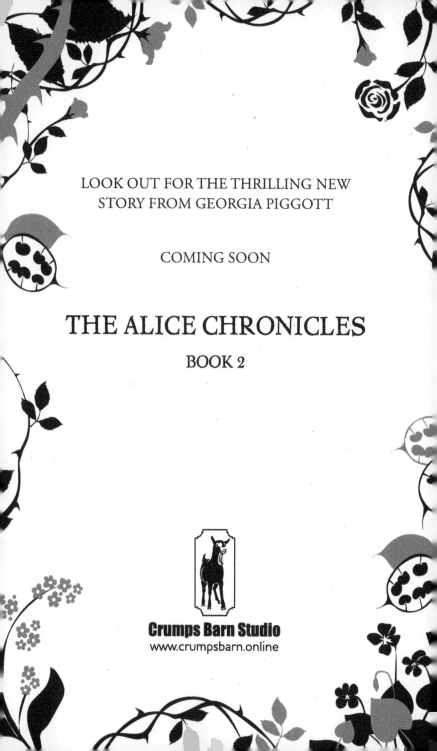

Crumps Barn Studio
www.crumpsbarn.online